The Paradise
Project

The Paradise Project

Suzie Andres

Hillside Education

Cover image:
Lisbeth Reading (w/c with tempera on paper), Larsson, Carl (1853-1919)/
© Nationalmuseum, Stockholm, Sweden / Bridgeman Images

Cover design and interior book design by Mary Jo Loboda

ISBN 978-0-9906720-6-7

Printed in the United States of America

Hillside Education
475 Bidwell Hill Road
Lake Ariel, PA 18436
www.hillsideeducation.com

FOR TONY

Serious she was, very serious in her thankfulness,
and in her resolutions;
And yet there was no preventing a laugh,
sometimes in the very midst of them.
—Jane Austen

CHAPTER 1

The Deal

Elizabeth Benning, unmarried, unemployed, and temporarily living in the guest cottage behind her parent's house,
was happy. She had no regrets about her past, at least none
that disturbed her sleep or her digestion, both of which were
excellent. She had no fears for her future, which she trusted
would work itself out when the time came. The present she
found particularly pleasing: she felt like a child on the first
day of summer vacation. In short, according to her honest
self-appraisal, she was happy. But she had begun to think she
could be happier, if only she knew how to begin.

She had grown up amid avocado orchards and citrus
groves in idyllic southern California, her plentiful joys and
rare sorrows shared with an older sister, Jane, and her best
friend Emily. Her father, an insurance salesman with a pre-
dilection for Jane Austen and a wife who indulged him, had

named his daughters after the eldest sisters in *Pride and Prejudice* and counted it one of the most amusing graces of his life that Elizabeth had formed a fast friendship in childhood with a neighbor surnamed Lucas, for such was Emily's last name. Had her first name been Charlotte, there is no telling whether Mr. Benning could have resisted the temptation to change his own family name to Bennet.

Higher education had separated the two sisters and Miss Lucas, their intimacy never to be perfectly restored; Jane left college with a husband as well as a degree. The Saturday after graduation she and Patrick Moore married, and when, some years and some children later, they returned to Jane's hometown so Pat could teach at St. Albert's College, Jane's life was necessarily taken up with her young family.

Elizabeth and Emily, neither of whom found her vocation at college, came home well educated and ready to meet Prince Charming. Or rather two Princes Charming. Meanwhile they rented a Victorian in which they shared one room and left eighteen empty but for castles in the air, and supported themselves by working at Emily's parents' bookstore.

Ten years later Elizabeth didn't blame herself for the recent closure of the formerly popular store. She'd sold books with all her might, but the face of bookselling had changed and the local megastore, after stealing their customers, had put Emily's parents out on the street. Easy Street, in fact.

The Lucases didn't complain. They were financially secure and pleased to take an early retirement. They ended their career profitably when Books-a-Trillion bought out their remaining stock, and more importantly they now had time to help their only child prepare for her wedding, which would take place in August.

For Emily's waiting had paid off and her recent engagement to Dr. Joe Collins, following their meeting in the bookstore and half a year's courtship, helped reconcile every-one to their changes in fortune. The shop had served its purpose in the grand scheme, supplying children with books, the Lucas family with a livelihood, the two friends with gainful employment, and now at the last, Emily with a husband. For a small family's small business in a small town, Adventures in Reading had practically worked miracles.

Miss Lucas' engagement to a man named Collins was kept from Mr. Benning while his wife and younger daughter consulted the actuary tables he habitually left about the house. To their relief, the statistical likelihood of a fifty-nine year old insurance salesman in full health with no pre-existing conditions dying of apoplexy was negligible. Apoplexy was no longer considered enough of a risk to be included in the extensive list of possible causes of death, and Mr. Benning was duly informed of the impending nuptials. His only disappointment was that Collins was neither a cousin, a clergyman, nor a rejected would-be lover of Lizzy.

Elizabeth herself did not regret the dissimilarities. Joe was a perfect match for Emily, and she rejoiced over her friend's luck in love. That Joe had a brother whom Emily insisted would be an equally perfect match for her, she dismissed.

No longer employed, the friends broke up housekeeping in the Victorian, returned to their parents' homes, and looked forward to renewing their childhood pastime of traipsing across the street and planning a wedding. That this time one of them would get married for real merely sweetened the anticipated pleasure.

Tonight, however, Elizabeth didn't traipse or plan or anticipate pleasure but sat alone at her sister's scarred dining table, her five nephews tucked securely into their beds. She was paying out the first installment of her Christmas gift to Jane, a year of Friday night babysitting that would allow a busy mother one evening each week free from the ten hands always reaching for her and the five voices repeatedly calling to her.

After three hours with those five loud voices and ten busy hands, Elizabeth reflected on the perfection of her gift. She'd given her sister respite and herself the satisfaction of a good deed done. She rested her head on her arms, exhausted but content.

She heard the crunch of van tires on gravel and shot up, fully alert. They were back. She had two minutes and life as she knew it would be over.

Noiselessly she crept to the door. She'd locked the dead bolt when Jane and Pat left but she checked to make sure, then darted into the boys' room as if they could save her. Anthony was lying on his back, one arm thrown over his forehead. Had it gotten this bad, that she expected a sleeping eleven-year-old to protect her? On the bunk below him Dominic coughed and rolled over to continue with the dreams of an eight-year-old. Luke and Jude were equally out, not that a six and four-year-old could do much for her at this late date. Matthew was in fact her last hope. She could pinch him when they came in and trust his cries to drive them out into the night. Pat maybe, but Jane would rush to console her usually placid one-year-old. She needed a Plan B.

Why weren't they opening the door?

She zipped to the dining room and peeked out the window from behind the drape she'd forgotten to close. They were still in the van talking. Probably about her idiotic happiness project. She should have resolved to exercise daily, like every other healthy American, but no, she had to be clever. She blamed Pat entirely.

They'd developed a rivalry, and while no one remembered precisely when it began, her brother-in-law's competitive spirit kept it going. Okay, so she was slightly competitive herself, but nothing compared to Pat.

Goaded on by tradition and her brother-in-law, each New Year's she made a resolution. She never got far into the year before she broke it, and he stood by to congratulate himself and give her a sympathetic smile. Sympathetic like a shark.

She customarily spent the week after Christmas coming up with a life changing resolution, but this year she'd defied custom and spent her time poring over *Bride* magazine with Emily. She was tired of failing, so instead of exposing some annoying imperfection she'd learned to live with anyway, she enjoyed herself and waited for inspiration.

By New Year's morning, none had come. By midday, still nothing. She'd have to appease the gods of tradition with a resolution that night at the family party, but she had no answers, no insights, no ideas whatsoever. She did have two books she'd received for Christmas—from her mother, *The Happiness Project* by Gretchen Rubin; from Jane, *Never Too Late* by John Holt. She hadn't read them, but they were pretty books and she spent the afternoon fiddling with them, mooning about, repeating the titles over and over: *The Happiness Project Never Too Late, The Happiness Project Never Too Late.* And then she'd reversed the order. *Never Too Late The Happiness Project. Never Too Late The Happiness Project.* Afterward she wondered if she'd hypnotized herself; never had two hours passed more quickly or more idly.

Next thing she knew, sitting in her parents' family room she raised a flute of champagne and resolved to begin her own "Never Too Late for Happiness Project." Whatever that meant. In the excitement of the moment—she had a resolution and everyone thought it wonderfully clever—no one asked her.

Any second now Pat would walk through the door and *he'd* ask her, and he wouldn't be satisfied with a half-baked answer. If only she could think of how to make her happy life happier. Or figure out what a happiness project even was.

A less creative person might have read the books, particularly the one offering a solution in bold type on the bottom of the front cover. "Start Your Own Happiness Project—Guide Inside." She refused to resort to a canned solution. Besides, she'd left the book at home.

A van door slammed.

She had a minute at most to think of something. Perhaps a quick note saying the boys had been angels but she needed to run, love, Lizzy. She'd sneak out the back and call Jane later.

The front door opened.

"How was the movie?" she asked with a bright smile. "Where'd you eat?"

"The movie was great." Jane yawned.

"She fell asleep during the best part," Pat said.

"Honey, I was resting my eyes. I've seen *Braveheart* before."

"You made her watch *Braveheart* again? Where was it even playing?"

"The Vintage billed it as a modern classic, and my dear wife was thrilled to accompany me."

"Let's get a cup of tea and I'll tell you what happened," Jane said. "How were the boys? Was Matthew fussy?"

"We had a good time, but the night was wasted if you spent it watching that dumb movie for the hundredth time. You better have a good excuse for giving in to him."

Jane filled the kettle.

"Pat was craving Italian food, and—"

"*Pat* was craving? Isn't that your job in the first trimester?" She turned to glare at Pat, but he was gone.

"I've been so tired lately I'm not sure what I want to eat. I didn't think Italian would agree with me, but then I remembered my plan, so I said yes."

"Guileless Jane had a plan? Tell me."

"Over dinner we chose the movie. I wanted a romantic comedy, but you know how Pat feels about *Braveheart*."

"I know how you feel about it too. If he picked the restaurant, you should have chosen the movie. Wasn't that your plan?"

"You underestimate me."

Elizabeth reached for the tea. She never could understand why they kept it so high. She caught Jane smiling at her and gave up.

"Okay, so I'm short. You don't have to laugh at me."

"I'm not laughing, you're adorable."

Jane gave her a hug and reached effortlessly for the box.

"So you know how Pat was going to ask you for details about your resolution?"

"I've been dreading it all week. Did you get him to put it off?"

"Better. He'd give half his kingdom for Italian food and the other half for *Braveheart* so I made him promise—"

"To drop it altogether?"

Pat reappeared, master of the inopportune moment.

"You girls better take those teabags out or it'll be stronger than you like."

"Would you do it, honey, and bring them to us?"

With a few steps Jane was on the couch in the family room adjoining the dining area. Elizabeth sat next to her. After the massive Victorian, these little places were a relief. Of course there were downsides. Jane's front room only had space for the couch and an old upright piano on the wall across from it. No comfortable place for Pat to sit.

She accepted a mug from him. He pulled out a dining chair and grinned at her. She ignored him and turned to Jane.

"You haven't told me what happened."

"Okay if I tell her?" Pat asked.

Jane nodded as she blew on her tea.

"Liz, you're one lucky girl. Jane pitched a deal for you and she may be sweet, but she drives a hard bargain."

"She's great. It's you I don't trust."

"They've made me head of the new Fra Angelico Arts and Events program at school. The benefactor who endowed it wants us to include visitors from outside the college. I barely have time to plan the events, let alone figure out how to attract outsiders."

"How is this related to Jane's bargain?"

"She wants me to go easy on your Never Too Late for Happiness resolution. Since we gave you Holt's book about learning to play the cello at forty or fifty, I thought I'd insist you do the same. Or if you'd rather, you could learn violin."

"I'm not forty or fifty, thank you. Jane had Italian food and suffered through *Braveheart* so you could insult me and then put me in the string section?"

"I'm saying I wanted to make you stick to the premise of both books, but I wanted Italian food and my movie more."

"You're letting me off?"

"Not entirely, no sport in that, but I'll be more relaxed this year. Jane thought up a way we could all be happier. Isn't she something?"

Jane smiled modestly and sipped her tea.

"She's the best," Elizabeth said, "but what does this have to do with your new position?"

"You know all kinds of people from working in the bookstore, and now you have connections through Emily's engagement to Joe. A neurologist's contact list must be extensive."

He rubbed his hands together. Did he look like the Grinch or Scrooge? A toss up.

"My proposal is that you help me out. Spread the word, bring some of your cronies to my Fra Angelico events and I'll go easy on you in my judgment of your happiness project."

She set her mug on the floor. Better to have both hands free in case he needed a smack.

"You've got to be kidding. You want me to steal Emily's fiancé's list of patients, take advantage of my friends by talking up your events, go to these events myself, and all you give me is the vague promise you'll go easy on me? I don't think so."

"Let me explain."

Pat spread his hands before him, palms up. As if a negotiating gesture would make him look honest and open. Like an honest and open rat, maybe.

"I don't know what you've planned for your happiness project, but here's my final offer."

The rat had her in a corner. She had nothing planned. If his suggestion was even barely acceptable, she'd have to take it. On the bright side, he'd never know she didn't have a clue what she was doing.

"I'm listening."

"You choose one new attempt at happiness each month. You can spend longer than a month if you want to, but not less than a month for anything you pick."

"And the Fra Angelico series?"

"Come to my events, maybe even help out, and in my excess of gratitude I'll go easy on your resolution. Keep Jane posted and I'll check in with you on Friday nights. A mere formality."

"I'll come to your events but I won't promise to bring outsiders."

"Fair enough. Do we have a deal?"

She looked from Pat to Jane.

"One question first. Did Mom and Dad put you up to this?"

Jane touched her arm. "Of course not, Lizzy. Why would they?"

"Dad's worried I'll bury myself in his library and cut off contact with the human race. He thinks between losing my job and losing Emily, I'm destined for a lonely spinsterhood and moving into the cottage hasn't helped. I see them all the time, and lately I've felt Mom watching me when I'm reading, and I don't dare ask what she's thinking."

"Poor Lizzy," Jane said. "I wish you'd let Emily set you up with Joe's brother, but I'm not plotting with Mom and Dad."

She relaxed into the couch. "Okay then. I'll go to the Fra Angelico events and pursue something each month to make myself happier."

"Deal," Pat said. "What's first?"

"Not cello or violin." She gazed at the upright. "I'd like to learn piano."

"But you play beautifully," Jane said.

"When I'm alone, or with you, but ever since that horrible recital I can't play in front of other people, and I'd really like to perform before an audience someday."

"Why haven't you?" Pat asked.

She couldn't tell him; too humiliating.

"Mom always said it was the four sandwiches she ate before the recital. She hasn't eaten peanut butter since."

"I get that. You never want to eat something again after you—"

"Pat!" Jane interrupted.

Elizabeth put her hand over her mouth.

"But I don't get the rest," Pat said. "What does overeating have to do with playing for other people?"

"I don't know—I didn't even play that day. It's silly and I want to get past it."

"I admire your courage, Liz, and I'd like to reward your efforts."

A slow grin spread over his face. There was something wrong with that grin; he looked like a crocodile.

"Why don't you play at our Fra Angelico concert for your first happiness project? Holt proved it's never too late for music, and you can too."

"For the whole school? That kind of courage would take a while. If you have a concert at the end of the year I'll try."

"Isn't the concert at the end of January?" Jane asked.

"No way." Just the thought of playing in a month made her mouth go dry. She clasped her hands in her lap to stop their trembling.

"It'll be fine, Liz." Pat's voice was full of oily wheedling. The reptile had morphed into a used car salesman. "Concert's in the library on a Sunday—the students will be studying in their dorms, faculty at home with their families. Any audience we can drum up will be tiny and you can choose whatever piece you like. Something short would be charming, and you'll have the whole month to get ready."

She closed her eyes and pictured her parent's baby grand. The image faded and a movie began to play behind her eyelids. There was the exquisite piano in the college library, and there she was in a long black gown, seated on the bench with perfect posture. The intimate setting felt comfortable, the audience embraced her with their affection. She lifted her hands in preparation for the first movement of Mozart's *Sonata in A Major*.

She opened her eyes and saw an audience of two staring at her uplifted hands.

"I'll do it!" she said, dropping her hands into her lap. "I'll play the piano at your concert, and I bet that's just the beginning. Too bad I'm Em's maid of honor—it would be cool to play at her wedding. And you're right Pat. Why switch off every month when I've found my bliss?"

Gone was the terror-stricken ten-year-old, gone forever. In her place sat a thirty-two-year-old woman ready to take happiness by the scruff of the neck and shake it. Jane and Pat were still staring, but they'd soon get used to her newer, more confident self.

"Right," Pat said skeptically. "Why don't we agree you'll play for a few other people this month and leave it at that?"

He underestimated her, but she'd show him. Her resolution was working already and soon she'd be the poster girl for happiness. She'd contact Gretchen Rubin and they could go on the talk show circuit. Maybe she'd even read the book.

CHAPTER 2

Recital

Elizabeth pulled open the library door and scanned the interior. Not good. No students off studying, no faculty spending the day with their families. They were all here, occupying the folding chairs Pat's minions had set in rows on the main floor. What had she been thinking? She'd visualized herself performing, last weekend she'd even played her Mozart here after regular library hours. But the place had been empty.

Jane sat in a row about half way up. Walk across the tile floor, don't look at the people, pretend they're off studying, like they're supposed to be. Better yet, think about something else altogether.

Taking a seat, she leaned across two spit-shined nephews and whispered to Jane.

"How do you like my haircut?"

"It's adorable. I've wanted you to bob it under your chin forever. Your dark hair framing your face really sets off your complexion. Did Em go with you?"

"She was supposed to, but she canceled to finalize the wedding date with Joe. They won't be coming here either, which is good, I don't think there's space for two more bodies. Where are Mom and Dad?"

"They've got Matthew in a little alcove so he won't disturb anyone if he fusses."

"Looks like there's plenty of people to disturb. Clever of Pat to change the concert to a Saturday."

"Sorry about that. You feeling okay?"

"A bit nervous and I'm starving. Mom made me eat a ham sandwich but it's wearing off."

Jane patted her hand.

"Don't be nervous. She said you played for her bridge group and they loved it."

"There's only one problem. I've been reading a book Emily gave me on overcoming performance anxiety, and it says positive physical energy is key. I need a candy bar."

Anthony started to speak from his chair between them but his mother shushed him.

"Wouldn't an apple be better?" she said to Elizabeth. "You have time to get something in the cafeteria. Pat said you're playing last before intermission and they're not ready to start yet." She handed Elizabeth a program.

"You sure you don't have a candy bar?"

Someone tugged on her black dress. It was Anthony.

"What is it buddy?"

He looked at his mother. Jane was leaning over, picking up the crayons Luke had spilled.

"Here, Auntie Beth." He handed her a red bag. "If you need more food than apples."

"What about you?"

"It was for Daddy," he whispered, "but you can have 'em."

Chocolate and a chance to even the score with the man who'd crammed the library full of people. She'd never seen a red bag of M & M's; they were probably left from Christmas. A little peppermint in her chocolate would be ideal. The book said mint was calming.

"Thanks. I'll have them with milk." She gave him a kiss. "Jane, I'm going now, save my seat."

"You won't need it. Pat wants you in the front row with the other performers." Jane gave her hand a squeeze. "Get some food and hurry back."

Elizabeth made it to the door and took a last look at the rows and rows of chairs, most of them occupied. Overcoming performance anxiety had made more sense at home in the cottage.

The campus wasn't large and neither was the cafeteria. She found the huge metal fruit bowl they left out for hungry students, and chose a banana instead of an apple. Way too many negative associations with the apple, from Adam and Eve to Snow White, and she couldn't risk dragging her mental energy down. Plus bananas were an excellent source of potassium which the book said prevented cramps. That was in the chapter on competitive swimming, but still, she could only imagine how debilitating finger cramps would be at this point in her career.

She helped herself to a glass of milk; the book highly recommended milk as a source of protein which sustained physical energy. Glass at her lips she smelled something awful. She held the glass at eye level. It looked fine. She brought it to her nose and sniffed warily. No smell at all. She turned to the counter behind her. It couldn't be the bread, neatly twist tied. It couldn't be the crocks of jelly or honey.

It could be and was an earthenware vat of peanut butter for hungry students with bad taste. She stepped away and concentrated on the cold frothy milk, drinking it in one long series of swallows. There, that covered the protein angle. Now for dessert.

The first handful of M & M's was on its way to her mouth when three men in tuxes approached. She popped the candy in and smiled, lips firmly closed.

"Scuza. We come for the music but the libary we can't find her."

Their spokesman had asked a question she normally could have answered, but his request came at a bad moment. She now knew the flavor which distinguished red packaged M & M's from the traditional chocolate ones. There was no mistaking the repulsive taste she'd avoided for twenty-two years and which threatened to bring back the banana. Only the presence of strangers kept her from spewing half-masticated candy bits in every direction.

Directions. They wanted directions. She tried to ignore the rising nausea.

"Scuza, pretty lady. You show us music? The libary, we need her."

Time was running out. She pointed to the glass exit doors, through which a mission style building was visible. She hoped they understood, but she had an urgent need to be alone. She fled for the restroom, their "Grazie, grazie!" ringing in her ears.

Jane looked at her watch. Pat looked at Jane, at his watch, at Jane again. He tapped his foot, but it wasn't in time to the music. He craned his neck and looked behind him toward the library entrance.

"An apple and a glass of milk." He kept his voice low. "How much milk can your sister drink?"

"Pat, she'll be back." Jane said. A whisper of anxiety broke through. "Nothing could have happened to her, could it?"

"Of course nothing happened to her! But something will happen to her if she doesn't show up in the next three minutes. Who's going to play the Mozart? I put her before intermission so we'd end on a bright note. No one will come back for the second half if we leave them with the *Miserere*. The Ghirardelli brothers made it from Italy. She can't make it back from the cafeteria?"

"Honey, shhh."

Pat sighed heavily. "The turnout is fabulous, our boys are good as gold, the students are doing a tremendous job, and your sister disappears. The second half of the program is loaded with my guest performers, and no one will return to hear them."

"Excuse me." The man sitting behind them leaned forward. Jane blushed and Pat crossed his arms.

"Excuse me but I wanted to assure you the concert is going splendidly. We'll all be back for the second half."

"Thanks," Pat said.

"I couldn't help but overhear. Is it the Sonata in A Major you need?"

"That's the piece. My sister-in-law," Pat glanced at Jane to indicate that his sister-in-law was her fault, "disappeared."

"Elizabeth Benning," the man read from the program. "What a pretty name. I hope she's not in any trouble, but if she doesn't return, I'd be glad to take her spot. The A Major is a favorite of mine, and it's only the first movement."

Applause filled the room, interrupting their conversation. Pat strode to the microphone and turned to the packed house with a smile at its highest wattage, as if his only feeling were delight at the performance.

"Wasn't that lovely? Thank you Katrina. And now, please join me in welcoming members of the sophomore class who will sing Faure's *Miserere*."

More applause and Pat settled into his chair at the front. He looked back to Jane and the man behind her; they both watched him expectantly. He shrugged and motioned to the empty chair beside him. The man slid out of his seat and made his way silently forward.

CHAPTER 3

Dinner for Eight

The student lounge was empty but for a crumpled black lump on the leather sofa in the corner. The door creaked open, and Dominic Moore shot past his mother.

"I found her, Mommy! Auntie Beth is here!"

"Lizzy? Are you okay?"

The heap moaned.

"We were worried about you. Are you all right?"

"Is it over?" she asked, her words muffled by the pillow resting on her face.

"It was really boring Auntie Beth, but a nice man behind us played piano and there was intramission and we got cookies and Daddy said we can eat dinner with the students. Can I go Mommy? I know where dinner is."

Jane sat on the edge of the sofa next to her, a serene presence. How had she produced such bouncy children? Too much Pat in them.

"Go straight to the cafeteria line. Grandma's waiting for you by the blue trays. Can you carry your own tray without spilling?"

Dominic didn't answer but Elizabeth heard a whoosh of running boy and the door creaked shut.

"Is it safe now?"

"It's safe, darling."

"Just the two of us?"

"Just the two of us, just like old times." Jane removed the pillow. "Want to talk about it?"

Elizabeth groaned. Would she never grow up? She was like a female Peter Pan, only he had fun.

"It's been twenty-two years since my last recital. But I did it again, the exact same thing."

"Peanut butter sandwiches? I don't believe you."

"Okay, not exactly the same, but close enough. Anthony gave me a red bag of M & M's to have with my snack, and—"

"Lizzy, you can't eat those. Pat loves them but they're filled with peanut butter."

"I know. Now." She smiled a tight unhappy smile. "I put a bunch in my mouth and three men in tuxes walked up looking for the library. The peanut butter broke through the shells, these overdressed men were waiting, and what could I do?"

Jane's eyes were laughing.

"It's not funny. There I was, ready to retch with these three men waiting for me to point to the library. So I did."

"Which?"

"I pointed to the library."

"And then?"

"I made it to the restroom so fast they must have thought I was an Olympic sprinter."

"I guess we've learned something," Jane said, sounding like a mom. "Recitals and peanut butter remain a very uncomfortable combination for you."

"Uncomfortable my foot. I threw the ball, as Jude would say." She smiled at her nephew's euphemism. "I made it to the restroom in time, and some sweet college girls helped me clean up afterward and brought me here where I had the most wonderful nap. I was feeling better before you came in, but when I think about Pat I feel sick again." She sat up. "Is he furious?"

"Not in the least. A man overheard us talking about you and said he could fill in if you weren't back in time."

"You're making this up."

"It's true."

"Pat always gets lucky and I always lose." She had a hopeful thought. "Did the man play terribly?"

"He was perfect. When it was time for your performance, Pat announced Ralph and he played beautifully."

"Ralph? And you're not making this up?"

Jane cocked an eyebrow.

Elizabeth fell back on the sofa.

"So that's the end of me."

She couldn't let him off that easily. She sat up again.

"Do you think my playing for Mom's bridge group counts for my happiness project? Pat only said I had to play for a group, he didn't say it had to be his group."

"Of course it counts. Now stand up and let's face him. You can't miss the dinner or he'll nail you for skipping the whole event. Can you eat?"

"I can always eat, as long as they're not serving peanut butter and crackers."

Jane smiled and tugged Elizabeth's dress straight.

"The dinner should be delicious, Pat arranged it for the guest performers."

"Couldn't I sit with the boys?"

"They're with Mom and Dad and the college kids who think they're cute. You get to sit with the grown-ups, and I for one think you're adorable."

Jane took her hand and led her out of the lounge. "Our dinner's in the coffee shop."

They were in the room before she could escape, Pat kissing Jane and leading them further in, to a group seated at a round table. Jane whispered something in his ear and he smiled.

"Everyone, this is my sister-in-law, Elizabeth. She missed the concert because she was throwing the ball with some students. She's such a people person, she must have lost track of time."

He touched Elizabeth's arm and motioned to the other side of the table. There was only one empty chair, between a pale lanky man and a tall blonde wearing a black sheath dress identical to her own. The woman stood to greet her, and she waited for Pat to make a crack, but the effect of the two dresses was so remarkably different, he must not have noticed.

The blonde towered above her, gracefully, like a willow tree. She took the woman's extended hand, and shook. No dead fish here, no clammy palm. The hand gripping hers was smooth, cool, and toned. Could a hand be toned?

"I'm Gretchen," the woman said in a low velvety voice.

Pat completed the introduction.

"Gretchen lives and works nearby and played a Chopin mazurka for us at the concert."

He sat down, and Jane sat in the chair next to him. Leaving her no choice but to sit between the two blondes.

"These three men to the right of Gretchen are the Ghirardelli brothers, Alfredo, Romano, and Giuseppe. They've been touring the States and were kind enough to play for us today because they know one of our chaplains, Father Serkin."

The man closest to Gretchen opened his wide mouth. He was the one who'd asked for directions, he must be their spokesman.

"I am first violin of Italian National Orchestra, my brother Romano is playing the cello. 'Seppe, he is a master of the wind instrument, but most of his music she is his voice. Today he sings Verdi like an angel."

"It was lovely," Jane said. "I wish you could have heard them, Lizzy."

"Your other neighbor is Ralph. You ought to thank him Liz, he played piano in your spot," Pat said. "Which I guess means your gig is up."

Ralph gave a little half bow from his chair. He had a pleasant smile, but more distinctive was his fine straight blonde hair.

She felt a surge of repulsion for the very blonde Ralph. She'd been practicing for weeks and this guy got up and played just like that? She'd deal with him later, but she couldn't let Pat get away with sweeping her resolution under the rug.

"Not at all, dear brother-in-law. Did you forget my playing at bridge? A marvelous time was had by all."

"I love bridge," Gretchen said. "Contract?"

"You might say that. And I'm still in the game, eh Pat?"

He shook out his napkin and placed it in his lap. Silence was consent.

23

She turned to Ralph. "What did you play?" she asked sweetly.

"The Variations from the A Major, of course. I was only sorry you didn't plan to offer the Menuetto, Trio, and Alla Turca."

He'd played her piece. Of course. He only wished she was more proficient. Without thinking, she blurted out the truth.

"I apologize for limiting your performance but I could never master the Alla Turca."

Gretchen made a noise that in someone shorter or less blonde would have been a snort. From the Swedish princess it sounded like the distant echo of an elegant horn.

Elizabeth stayed seated, but drew herself up to her full if unimpressive height.

"And as for the the Menuetto," she continued, ignoring Gretchen, "I think it's a lapse from Mozart's usual genius. No emotion at all."

"Ralph," Gretchen said, speaking across Elizabeth, "don't you agree the Menuetto is more playable precisely because it breaks up the humor of the Variations and the forcefulness of the Alla Turca with a pleasant absence of emotion? Like sorbet between the courses of a fine meal."

As if on cue, the first course arrived. Scallops. There was a God, and He loved her. And there was justice, for who but Gretchen turned up her exquisite little nose and pushed the plate away?

"You don't like scallops?" Elizabeth asked.

"I never eat seafood after a performance."

The Italian next to her grabbed her plate. "Shame. Seafood is best for brain advance." He slid the round buttery pieces onto his own plate and sniffed appreciatively. His brothers nodded while they chewed.

Pat was listening to something Jane said quietly, the Italians were digging in with gusto, and Elizabeth was stuck with Gretchen and Ralph. The she-blonde sat with her impeccably manicured hands resting in the lap of the dress that fit her like a dream. The he-blonde began a conversation directed to both the rumpled and the sheathed.

"Elizabeth—what a beautiful name. Not that Gretchen isn't a wonderful name too, but unusual in our day."

And this from a Ralph, no less.

"I wonder if it's making a comeback. I came across the name recently when my mom gave me a book for Christmas. Have you heard of *The Happiness Project*?" he asked them.

Ralph's remarks fell into the momentary silence of the company like a handful of rocks onto the glassy surface of a still pond.

Everyone began talking at once. Pat and Jane explained to Ralph that Elizabeth had received the same book, and the Italians got so excited their trio exploded into what sounded like an octet.

Amidst the noise Elizabeth stared vaguely at her remaining scallop. She and this Ralph person both had mothers who'd given them Gretchen Rubin's book for Christmas. Scary.

Through the many voices, Gretchen's reached her.

"If one more person mentions that book, I'm going to change my name."

She kept her eyes down and Gretchen continued.

"It's been a month since Christmas. Obviously you've read the book, in compliment to your mother. Tell us the truth."

Mortifying. She'd have to confess she'd barely read the title page.

"Don't you find it absurd that a grown woman living with her family in the richest sector of the richest country of the world should waste an entire year on the self-absorbed pursuit of an unreasonable degree of happiness?"

It sounded bad when Gretchen put it that way. Was her resolution self-absorbed? She tore her gaze away from the scallop. Gretchen was leaning forward and looking earnestly at Ralph. Naturally. Gretchen wasn't interested in her opinion.

"The happiness project is a misnomer. More like a paradise project, isn't it Ralph? Surely she can make peace with her God, live quietly with her family, and be done with it."

Gretchen had finished her diatribe, and Alfredo, waving his fork, began his. It was too much to absorb—his brothers hanging on his every word, Pat enjoying the conflict, Jane smiling at her across the table, and Ralph, sitting next to her like some Mozart playing surfer, an amused expression on his face.

The Italian seemed to be nearing the end of his impassioned speech.

"Americas they coddle their childs! 'Okay honey. You can quit piano, honey. Go play football, honey. Watch MTV, honey. Live at home till you thirty, honey. Anythings you want, honey.' Never was this in Italia! The Americas she think only from Asia is hard work, but I tell you in Italia we know also the labor."

Gretchen dabbed at her lips with a napkin. Had she even eaten anything?

"I agree with you, but not one hundred percent, Mr. Ghirardelli. Although I'm American, I'm of Swedish descent and my parents held the ideals of the old country. I'm a successful businesswoman and a proficient musician for one and the same reason."

Extremely long fingers? An octave would be nothing to that reach.

"My parents never let up on their discipline. But one must give credit where credit is due and I ask you to consider the Asians as well. You will agree, since we are speaking of books, that the Tiger Mother is a creditable spokeswoman for our position?"

College students were serving the main course, grilled fish on a bed of wild rice. Gretchen would have to change her principles or go hungry. Elizabeth smiled at her sister.

Jane didn't look so good; she was leaning back as far as her chair allowed. Was it the fish, or Gretchen's remark about the Tiger Mother? The book had disgusted Jane when it topped the charts with its admonitions to, as she put it, torture children.

"Excuse me, Mrs. Moore, can I get you anything?"

Jane really did look pale. "Thank you, Ralph. I'm suddenly feeling under the weather."

"Jane, why don't I take you home?" This was her chance. She couldn't change the cold hard opinions of the Nordic goddess or the intense vivacity of the Italians, but she didn't have to stay. "The boys are fine with Mom and Dad. Pat can ask the servers to box our meals. I'm sure the party will go on splendidly without us."

She went to her sister. Pat was promising he'd be home before long and Jane was, in usual Jane fashion, insisting he not rush and apologizing to the company.

Ralph stood and smiled and gave his little bow to Jane, then sat again as Gretchen moved into the seat beside his. She placed her hand on his sleeve and began again about the Tiger Mother book. Those two deserved each other.

The Italians tucking into their food paused to nod at the two sisters. Elizabeth nodded back, took Jane's arm, and led her outside.

"I'd like to check on the boys before we go," Jane said.

"I'm sure they're fine, but if you need to."

Elizabeth looked up at the cold distant moon and thought of Gretchen. Was the Swede right? Was she a spoiled American squandering a year in pursuit of paradise? She had eleven months, more or less, to find out. Less, if tonight was any indication of how the year would go.

CHAPTER 4

The Statue

Elizabeth picked a piece of white fluff off the red dress she wore. The fluff didn't float down softly when she let go but stuck to her finger. She examined it closely. A piece of sugary coconut left from the Almond Joy she'd eaten on her way here. No one was watching. It was the work of a moment to lick the candy from her finger.

"I saw that," a voice said from behind her.

She pivoted.

"Pat! Don't scare me like that!"

"Milky Way or Three Musketeers?"

"I've branched out into the coconut food group." She picked a real piece of lint from the lapel of his navy blue sport coat. "Where's Jane?"

"Bad news on that score. She doesn't feel great—touch of all day morning sickness."

"But I was counting on her for moral support." She looked at him suspiciously. "Why are you here if Jane's sick?"

"She'll be fine and I can't skip my own events. Where's Emily?"

"She bailed to look at reception sites so I really need Jane."

"No can do."

She looked around at the crowd. "If she's that bad I'd better go help with the boys."

"And miss our February event?" The crocodile smile appeared. "If you must, I'll understand."

"And my happiness project ends today, is that it? I don't think so. I'll stay, but what about Jane?"

"Jane wants you here too. This is your first exhibit and she resolved you wouldn't miss it."

"She resolved? She's making a habit of that."

"You have to admit her idea for February was a winner." He surveyed the room, full of art and people, and beamed with pride. "Have you found your sketch?"

"I just arrived when you waylaid me, but honestly are you sure? February second, Jane drags me to the fish hatchery for nature study. I sketch the worst imitation of a fish ever—Luke thought I drew a banana—and now my work is here?"

Pat put a hand to his mouth and gasped.

"You slipped your banana fish into my exhibit?"

The room was getting smaller. Too many people and Pat stood between her and the exit.

"You'll have to choose," he said.

"Choose what?"

"I see you eyeing the exit. You can go to Jane if you must."

"And say good-bye to happiness?"

"I never said the project was about you being happy, Liz."

"Of course not, it's about me doing your bidding. But making me a featured artist was a stretch, don't you think?"

"So you saw the program. The students did a terrific job."

"I only glanced at it," she said, "but it looks professional."

If she could get rid of him, she could go hide in the bathroom at least.

"Don't you need to welcome people or pour champagne or something?" She made a shooing motion. "Go be important."

"I do have to make a few remarks at the podium and announce the winners. Did you see our grand prize?"

The table next to the podium was dominated by an exquisite statue.

"You can't be giving Fra Angelico away. He's the patron of your series."

"Hand carved with gold leaf applied in some time-honored Italian way. Worth a small fortune and we'll award it to the winner."

"Can you award it to me? I think it would bring me more happiness. In fact, I know it would."

"Dream on, kid." He walked toward the podium, then turned back. "And no hiding in the bathroom, I'll be watching you."

Of course he would, and he was such an insect his eyes probably had weird fly features that could see her even when he wasn't looking. He was fast, too, already at the front of the room. He went to the table and picked up the statue that was easily the most beautiful work of art she'd ever seen.

Winning it was about as likely as winning a life-time supply of chocolate. Don't think about it; better not to even look at it.

Everywhere she did look, she saw people. Most of them stood before folding panels which held framed artwork. They glanced from the pictures to the identifying labels affixed to their right, and then to their programs. At the side of the room a well-dressed elderly woman was inserting money into the "Support the Catholic Arts!" box. Pat would like that. Others were writing on the slips of paper she'd seen near the door. If only they'd write the number of her sketch on the slips that would be counted to award her statue.

Her statue. It would fit perfectly above her dresser on the shelf that used to hold a plaster St. Anthony. He had gone to her nephew Anthony, a gift from Mrs. Benning for his First Holy Communion, but his life in the Moore household had been short. Two weeks of Jane's moving St. Anthony and baby Jesus from one safe spot to another had preserved them, but only temporarily. A late night grocery run on her part and an exuberant father and son wrestling match in her absence had reduced that statue to rubble.

Her nephews weren't always so heedless. At the fish hatchery, for instance, Anthony had laughed at her banana-fish but then had become so absorbed in his drawing that she couldn't resist drawing him. Half an hour later she showed Jane a very creditable sketch. She'd gotten kind of vague around his hands, but his face silhouetted against the trunk of an oak tree was, even Pat admitted, well done.

Jane's reaction was intense, a combination of sisterly and maternal pride. She'd begged Elizabeth to draw the other boys too, and now their portraits were framed and hung in the Moore's dining room. Her first had been her best, and the sketch of Anthony was on loan to the Fra Angelico February event, and if only it was good enough to win the statue, she'd be ready to retire from the pursuit of more happiness. What could be happier than having Fra watch over her from his special shelf?

She'd been unconsciously moving toward the artwork and now stood before a group of small icons. Were they saints staring back at her? She'd never been much of an icon fan. She didn't understand them.

A priest brushed past her. Father Serkin. He must be on his way to the podium to offer the opening prayer.

A student took the box of votes from its stand. She watched as he sat on the floor, pulled out a slip of paper, and checked the program. He must be finding the name that matched the number. Maybe the mark he'd made on the clipboard was next to her name. Stranger things had happened, like Jane marrying Pat. Another slip, the program, marking the clipboard. *Please*, she prayed, *let him be marking my name and I won't need anything else. Let me bring Fra home and that'll be enough happiness for at least a year.*

Father's prayer was over. She'd missed it, good thing she'd said her own. Her gaze lingered on the statue. No doubt it would go to one of the artists who'd lent a sculpture or oil painting. She pulled on a hang nail nervously.

Pat was thanking all those who had made this possible. One by one. He was as painstaking as the student counting votes. She glanced at the icons next to her. Still nothing. Strange how people could be moved by this sort of thing.

Pat was still blathering. She walked around the screen. Another icon, but not miniature at all, more like what Plato talked about. What had he called this sort of thing? The Form, that was it, this must be the Form of Icon.

Pat's voice droned on—the O'Callaghans who had so generously sponsored the Fra Angelico arts and events series, sent their regrets, they would have liked to be here for today's closing reception—but Elizabeth no longer cared. She gazed at the larger than life face of Christ and He gazed back at her. His eyes were incredible. She was alone with the Alone. She heard her name.

"Elizabeth Benning, my sister-in-law. I have special gratitude for her participation in today's event because my wife was behind her efforts. Jane, who couldn't be here today, asked me to thank Elizabeth for taking her suggestion and devoting this month of February to art in the spirit of Blessed Fra Angelico. And so, Liz, if you would please come forward . . ."

Elizabeth stared in wonder as Pat reached for the statue. She'd won! Her heart in her throat, she almost ran to him.

Pat picked up a blue ribbon. Her pace slackened, but she forced herself to keep walking till she reached him.

"In thanks for your creative efforts and in recognition that it is never too late to use your gifts to glorify God, we present you with this ribbon, a small token of our gratitude."

She took the ribbon, gave Pat a quick hug, and retreated to her former place. She was ridiculous and absurd. Her sketches were sweet but they weren't grand prize winners except in her sister's eyes. She looked again at the Christ-icon. At least He wasn't laughing at her. She sighed.

Pat was awarding the other ribbons now, reading from a clipboard. She glanced at Fra Angelico standing on the table next to him, then at the face of Christ beside her, then at Pat. Would he never finish? The guests looked like they were hanging on his every word. How many of them were also featured artists waiting for him to award the statue?

It would be a shame to die of ennui before she could grab one of the chocolate cookies she'd seen on the refreshment table. She began to glide, unobtrusively she hoped, toward the corner of the room. She was almost there; she could smell the chocolate.

"And now," Pat said as she reached a hand toward the table, "it is my pleasure to announce the grand prize winner. This Italian statue of Fra Angelico is from the O'Callaghans' personal collection, and will go to the artist whose work our patrons have selected as contributing most to the glory of God."

She was touching chocolate. She brought it to her mouth, inhaled deeply for maximum effect, and tasted sour saliva at the back of her throat. Someone was trying to poison her, but she couldn't be duped. A ficus tree flanked the table, a fitting burial plot. She dropped the peanut butter cookie into its welcoming soil and spied the chocolate. Four should be enough to expunge the memory of the dearly departed.

She had them, the first one en route to her mouth when she heard her name.

"Elizabeth Benning! Elizabeth, where are you?" Pat called, his voice full of surprise. "Come forward Elizabeth! You've won the Fra Angelico statue. Your work, number thirty-seven in our program, has earned nearly every vote. Don't be shy, Elizabeth. Come on down!"

He sounded like a game show host. Couldn't he have waited until she'd eaten at least one of the cookies?

From her left came a whisper. "Hand them to me. I'll hold them till you get back."

Ralph, in a suit. Beside him stood Gretchen, gorgeous as ever, wearing a red dress so vivid it made hers look slightly orange.

Pat was waiting. She deposited the stolen cookies in Ralph's hand.

"Charming," Gretchen whispered softly to Ralph, though not softly enough. "She shared her cookies with you."

Elizabeth focused on her statue and began the long march to the front of the room.

She strode forward without looking back. What did she care that the Mozart-and-mazurka duo were here and in possession of her cookies? She was about to get something better. She was the grand prize winner and if the statue's rim of hair was golden, she could always repaint it.

CHAPTER 5

The Winner

Pat's eyes shone with amusement as he held the statue out to her. She took it gingerly and looked into the delicately crafted face. No ridicule there. Like the eyes of the Christ-icon, Fra's eyes were gentle. She smiled at him, smiled at Pat, smiled at the crowd and curtsied.

"Would you like to say something, Elizabeth?"

She moved closer to the microphone.

"I just want to say thank you. Thank you to my sister Jane, who encouraged me in my art, thank you to Pat, who insisted I display it here at the exhibit, and thank you to the patrons who awarded me this prize."

She stepped back and Pat concluded with a final thanks. If only he'd be quick about it; she couldn't stand here in front of all these people for long, holding her statue. Her statue.

Pat turned from the podium.

"Jane's gonna be thrilled."

"You think so?" She gave him her biggest smile. "I can't wait to show her. I think I'll go now."

"Not so fast, the patrons want to congratulate you. Why don't I take the statue?"

She handed it back with a sigh. She needed chocolate to get through this, and Ralph had probably eaten her cookies. It didn't matter. Gretchen could mock her food choices like she'd mocked her happiness project, but she, Elizabeth Benning, had won the grand prize.

Pat knew his business. A line was forming, and a portly gentleman reached out and took both her hands in his.

"My dear," he said, "I'm Dr. O'Reilly. I came to your exhibit because we don't see Catholic art celebrated in these dark days. But my wife and I—"

He let go of her and brought forward a tiny woman from behind his ample girth.

"—my wife Mabel and I haven't been this moved in I don't know how many years. Mabel, tell her, I don't think I can say any more." Dr. O'Reilly pulled a massive handkerchief from his trouser pocket and blew his nose.

Mabel's eyes were wet with tears. How had it come to this? Paradise project indeed. Her pursuit of happiness, her competition with Pat over the New Year's resolution had brought such emotion to people. The line stretched behind the O'Reillys to the other side of the room. Were all these people waiting to congratulate her?

Mabel cleared her throat, stuck her neck out and opened her mouth.

"My dear child," she said in a tiny voice that matched her body.

Elizabeth leaned in to hear.

"My husband and I have grown old together, but we were something in our day. We traveled the world collecting art, and the treasures that fill our home today are priceless. Yet never have we seen a piece like your number thirty-seven. If it were for sale, we'd snatch it up for any amount you might name, but we won't even ask because we understand how much it means to your family. Only promise you'll never set aside this talent. It's a rare and precious gift from God."

Dr. O'Reilly caught up Elizabeth's hands once more, Mabel's dry lips brushed her cheek, and the couple moved away.

It was a full hour before she'd completed her duties. The last hand-shaking patron satisfied, Elizabeth sank with relief onto a plastic chair. She lifted a heel out of one pump and massaged it. Sore feet and an aching back, but they were a small price to pay for her statue.

She stood up so quickly the chair fell onto its side. Pat was at the refreshment table talking with two student workers as they gathered crumpled napkins and Styrofoam cups.

"Did you see where I put the statue?" she called.

"I took it from you when the line formed, it's on the table by the podium."

Saved. She righted the chair and set off to retrieve her statue, pausing at the mini-icons. They were still unidentifiable, but voices from the other side kept her motionless.

"I don't understand why you didn't say anything. That was wrong of you, Ralph."

Gretchen's low voice was edged with anger.

"It's ridiculous. A sketch of a feminine looking boy's head? Sweet for the mother, I'm sure, but certainly not the caliber of your work."

Feminine looking? Gretchen obviously didn't have nephews or a sister who loved her and probably couldn't even draw a fish. Not that she could either, come to think of it, but all those people she'd just met had certainly liked her sketch better than anything else on display.

She didn't wait to hear more but hurried to the front of the room and, statue in her arms, returned to her chair. She took a deep breath, exhaling slowly. The students were gone, the room empty but for Pat.

"Tell me you have chocolate for me."

"Tough break," he said. "Everything was scarfed up. The kids found a cookie in the ficus—"

"No thanks, I'm good."

"You look shot. Why don't we get you and Fra home?"

He really was a dear man, and he had a fine sense of where to go when, unlike some people, people who came to events where they weren't welcome.

"Pat, what were Ralph and Gretchen doing here?"

"Excellent to see them, wasn't it? Ralph and I hit it off at the concert dinner after you and Jane left. Turns out he plays basketball, so we've been shooting around on Saturdays. Last weekend I found out he wrote icons when he lived with some monks."

"Well rounded surfer."

"I don't know if he surfs, but I asked him to let us display an icon, and he said yes. You wouldn't be responsible for my locals, so I told him to bring someone and he brought Gretchen. I think they're seeing each other."

"Mozart, basketball, monks, icons. He even socializes with Nordic ice queens. Quite a friend you've picked up."

Bitterness wasn't becoming, but there it was. She didn't know much about Ralph, but he had a terrible effect on her. He'd played her piece, despised Gretchen Rubin's book, taken her cookies, and had awful taste in women. Actually, she knew far too much about him.

Pat raised an eyebrow. "Hated his icon, or holding a grudge about the concert? He didn't steal your thunder today, you know. You're the winner, you can afford to be generous. Unless, of course, you're jealous."

"Jealous of what?" She cradled the statue. "I don't know which little icon he painted, but you're right, I won."

"I wasn't thinking of the icon. You're a single girl. Doesn't that make every unattached male a prospect? Must be annoying that Gretchen nabbed Ralph before you had a chance."

This was the Pat she knew. What a jerk. She raised her arm to huck her lovely prize at the prize-giver's head when she realized what she was doing. She lowered her arm and looked into Fra's gentle face. So what if Pat teased her about Ralph's girlfriend? She'd won, and she'd be taking the statue home.

"I wish them all the happiness in the world, and now I'm ready to go."

"Have you seen much of the art?" He crooked his arm. "We've got the place to ourselves."

She could accept the olive branch and go on a private tour with the curator, or she could refuse and he'd revert to form, concluding she was sensitive about Ralph and Gretchen being an item.

"I've been here for hours, but I haven't seen a thing." She slipped her arm through his. "Show me the highlights."

He led her to the icons, passing by the little ones and stepping with her around the panel. Speak of the devils. Their twosome was now a foursome.

"Congratulations!" Ralph said. "The statue is a perfect prize for your sketch."

"Thanks. Pat told me you have an icon here. I didn't know you painted."

"Wrote," Gretchen corrected her.

"Excuse me?"

"One doesn't paint an icon. Ralph wrote it."

The writer looked uncomfortable. Were his ears turning red?

"Elizabeth," he said, "did you see the icons from Russia? I don't know how Pat got them, but if you're interested in icons you have to see these."

He made a move around the screen to the miniatures. Elizabeth followed but stopped dead when Gretchen laid a hand on her arm.

"Wouldn't you prefer to see Ralph's icon first? It's right here."

She could be gracious, and she'd rather walk of her own volition than be dragged by Gretchen. She gripped the statue and reminded herself she was having a great day.

There were several icons on this side, starting with the enormous one she'd admired earlier. Ralph came back around. His ears were definitely pink.

"Which one is yours?" she asked.

Gretchen, whose hand was now on Ralph's sleeve, answered for him.

"It's this one, of course."

She didn't see the "of course," but she certainly saw the icon. Again. She stepped back to take in the whole face. It was more amazing than before, if possible. And Ralph had done this?

"Isn't it something?" Pat said quietly. "When Ralph brought it up for the exhibit I didn't want to leave it unguarded so I kept it in my office for a few days. I've never seen a Christ so compassionate and yet so strong. I felt like I was on retreat just grading papers under His gaze."

Ralph was silent. Elizabeth looked from him to the icon and back.

"I know what you're thinking," he said. "How did I write that, huh? But I didn't really. When I lived with the monks we all contributed to the common work."

"Oh, so several of you made it?"

She knew not to say 'paint,' but she wasn't about to gratify Gretchen by saying 'wrote.' 'Made' worked, no need to be pretentious.

"I guess it would be misleading to say several of us wrote it. In one sense I wrote it myself, I mean the other monks didn't physically work on it, but I never could have translated that vision of Christ without them."

"In other words," Gretchen said, "he wrote it himself."

"I'd rather say the charity of the monks wrote it. Their prayers spoke His likeness, even while my hand held the instruments. I hope this won't sound conceited, but I love His eyes too, and I know I couldn't have invented them."

He was right, the eyes were incredible. They were almost too much for her. She looked away from the icon . . .

. . . and saw for the first time a white card affixed to the edge of the panel. Printed on it in clear black ink was a large 37. The number had a familiar ring. She closed her eyes, trying to remember, and it came to her. Tentatively, unhappily, she opened her eyes.

A folded program stuck out of Ralph's sport coat pocket. She shoved the statue into Pat's hands, grabbed the program, and skimmed down to #37. There it was, plain and wrong, horrible and clear:

"#37, Elizabeth Benning, The Christ of Mercy, Icon."

She kept her eyes lowered. She couldn't breathe very well. She'd felt this way when Luke jumped onto her stomach last week, but Luke wasn't here.

"Um, Pat? Have you read the program carefully?"

"The students showed it to me before they printed it up. I thought they did a fine job."

"But did you read it carefully?" She held the program close to his face, her finger pointing at #37.

Pat held the statue in one hand, and with the other he moved the program slightly away. He read aloud and lost his grip. Ralph shot out a long arm and caught the statue just before it hit the tile floor.

"I told Ralph he ought to draw your attention to the mistake," Gretchen said. "But now he has the statue, and all's well that ends well."

All wasn't well. She'd been the winner, and now she was simply the woman dressed in orange who didn't know her place. Though on the other hand, she knew her place quite well. Or was it her lack of place? Ralph's icon had won. Her sketch of Anthony was a nice little family drawing, that was all.

Ralph was trying to hand the statue back to Pat, Gretchen was clutching Ralph's arm, and Pat was backing into a sculpture of St. Francis. Elizabeth moved around him and saved St. Francis.

"I think Elizabeth won it fair and square," Ralph said.

"I didn't," she responded. "The students goofed up the program. They wrote my name next to your icon, but the patrons voted for the icon, which means you won."

Ralph shook his head and Gretchen nodded vehemently.

The she-blonde stated her case.

"You're quite the gentleman, Ralph, but Elizabeth is now fully aware that her art didn't gain a single vote. You earned the votes, you earned the statue, and justice is done."

"You have no evidence," Ralph said. "You can't prove that."

This was beyond mortifying. What was he talking about?

"It's impossible to say with certainty that Elizabeth got no votes. We'll have to investigate further. Did the students save the voting slips, Pat?"

"Great question," Pat said. "I don't know, but we could find out."

"Please!" the two women said at once.

The men looked at them.

"Ralph won," Elizabeth said, "and I'd like to go home."

"Well said," Gretchen agreed. "I'd like to go home also." She looked at Ralph.

"I'm ready to go," he said, "but I won't take the statue. I didn't win it."

Fra Angelico stood on the floor between them.

Pat sighed. Unusual for him, but apparently the students' mistake, the confusion over the statue, and Ralph's refusal to take it were putting a damper on his sanguinity.

"Listen, Pat," Ralph tried again, "Elizabeth won it, she deserved it, her artwork's terrific." He waved toward the icon as if it were nothing. "I didn't even do this recently. Shouldn't that disqualify it?"

Must he be so humble and generous? He was only putting her in an awkward position. Meanwhile Gretchen looked down on her as if she were a bug ready to be squashed and Pat wore an unfamiliar pleading expression. She'd waited years for him to look at her in that pathetic way, but now she couldn't enjoy it.

"I won't take it, Pat."

He would believe her; they'd known each other long enough.

"Okay," he said, picking up the statue, "Fra comes home with me then. We'll figure out his rightful owner later."

He looked at her expectantly.

"You can't take him home," she said, knowing she was walking right into his trap. "He's too valuable."

"I'm only taking him because no one else will. Ralph?"

Ralph stepped back. "He belongs to Elizabeth."

"Gretchen?"

Pat was now the victim of the Swede's evil eye.

"I'll take that as a no. And Elizabeth, you said you won't take him, so that leaves me. Happy to oblige, wanted to show him off to Jane anyhow."

She couldn't have this on her conscience. Sending Fra to Pat's house wherein dwelt the wrestling nephews was sending him to sure destruction.

"Pat, the boys are too rough."

"The boys'll be fine, we'll put this up on top of the piano."

"But I spent all last Friday night trying to keep Luke off there."

"Have a better plan?"

"Oh, all right." She took the statue. "But only for now."

Gretchen glared at her, Ralph smiled hugely, and Pat motioned them to the exit.

Ralph held open the door, still smiling approval, and she followed Gretchen out. Were those smoke tendrils rising from the long flaxen hair? The sun was setting. Gretchen wasn't literally fuming, just creating an optical illusion against the glorious colors of the sky.

Pat locked the door behind them.

"Nice to see you again Gretchen," he said, walking to his car.

The happy couple was ahead of her.

"Good night Elizabeth," Ralph called over his shoulder, "and congratulations."

She ignored him and rubbed the statue's tonsured head as if it was a lamp and she could summon Fra's genial spirit. Would she even know what to do with three wishes?

Her first had been to win the statue. Wish granted, and she was no happier.

Her second was to make Ralph take what he'd rightfully won. Wish denied thus far, and as to giving it to him in the future, a stronger wish overpowered her—never to see either blonde again.

"Ever!" she told the statue.

One wish left. She stood on the verge of March and was not inclined to heed Mabel's advice to continue drawing. She looked into Fra's kind painted eyes, wishing with all her heart he'd tell her what happiness to pursue next.

He didn't say a word.

CHAPTER 6

Vocations' Day

On the first Friday of March, inspiration came over dessert. The boys were debating the pros and cons of possible Lenten sacrifices while Elizabeth savored her third brownie, smiling at a lifetime of failed attempts to give up chocolate. Mid-bite a vision of renewed happiness burst upon her. Why not a month of holiness?

An hour later she presented a long list to Pat, proof that asceticism was the new happiness.

"I'm weakening, but okay," he said. "As long as you keep at least one of them till the end of the month."

"Piece of cake," she said.

"If it's chocolate you've violated number one." He handed the list back. "And I expect your help at Vocations' Day."

"Expect or request?"

"Part of the deal, but you can quit anytime." Did his face actually grow longer when he smiled, or was it the crocodile in his soul peering out? "The Fra Angelico Arts and Events Series will be more event than art this month."

She agreed. He could hardly force her to join a convent.

Ash Wednesday marked the onset of her penances and the following days passed quickly away, though not as quickly as her good intentions. No cause for guilt, her motto would be live and learn. Recently she'd learned that eleven Lenten resolutions are more than anyone needs. Besides, letting go of the impractical ones increased her happiness immensely, and wasn't that the point?

Three weeks into March, Vocations' Day arrived. A single resolution cheerfully defied the odds, and so did Elizabeth. She and Emily sat in the college cafeteria lunching amidst sensory overload. Displays crowded the outer edges of the room while priests in their black clerics, Sisters in full habits, and dozens of children of the faculty and staff circulated among the college students.

Pat wanted Elizabeth to save places for Jane and the boys, so she and Emily had leaned six chairs against the table and set before them six plates loaded with food.

"No sign of Jane yet," Emily said.

"She and the boys could be in the library."

"If they talk with everyone there, we won't see them for another hour. How many religious orders did Pat invite?"

Elizabeth shook her head, her mouth full of hot dog.

"All of them. I got here for early Mass and I've been dodging Sisters ever since."

"But they're so sweet! Why are you avoiding them?"

"Hand over your engagement ring and you'll see." Elizabeth ate a barbeque chip. "I started out asking if they needed anything, but they need more Sisters, and when they find out

I'm not married and not a student . . ." She picked up a carrot stick. "It's like Pat taped a sign on my back saying 'No vocation, no job, will work for food.'"

"So which are they offering?" Emily adjusted her ring, and they watched the diamond sparkle under the fluorescent lights.

"For the most part no food, but vocation, job, it's all the same to them."

A pair of Sisters in brown habits materialized.

"Excuse me, girls, may we sit with you?" asked the shorter one.

"I'm sorry," Elizabeth said. "We're saving these spots for my sister and her family."

The second nun took over. "How thoughtful. And your other sister is getting married soon?" She smiled at Emily's ring, then at Emily.

"We're Carmelite Sisters of St. Anne," the first nun explained, her hand on Elizabeth's shoulder. "We work with children, and every woman has maternal love that shouldn't be wasted. Come see us after lunch, dear."

With a parting squeeze to Elizabeth's shoulder, the Sisters walked away.

"See?" She took a brownie from the plate in the center of the table.

Emily's green eyes danced with laughter. "Don't tell me you've been hearing that all day?"

"That's exactly what I'm telling you."

She felt the hand on her shoulder again and held her breath.

"Exactly what are you telling her? Something happy, I dare say."

Just Pat. She exhaled.

"Not exactly happy, but it could fulfill my happiness project. What if I join the nuns?"

He pulled down a chair and grabbed a hot dog. "Join them for what?"

"For my vocation."

Pat took an enormous bite of hot dog and spoke with his mouth full.

"Doesn't make sense. Your resolution's for happiness and you'd be miserable, plus you'd make the other nuns miserable."

"But they're all worried about my being single and vocation-less."

Emily smiled. "You know that's by your own choice, Lizzy."

"Not entirely. I know I shouldn't be a Sister, but how am I supposed to get married if the right guy doesn't come along and ask?"

Pat shoved the rest of the hot dog in his mouth and leaned forward to say something, but Emily spoke first.

"If you're waiting for the right guy, you can't object to meeting Joe's brother."

Elizabeth put down her milk. "Don't start this again."

"Watch out, Emily," Pat said. "Last time Jane suggested a blind date, Liz gave her the cold shoulder for a week."

"You can tell Jane I'm giving Emily the cold shoulder for two weeks. Honestly, Em, I thought you promised to stop talking about Joe's stupid brother."

"How can I stop when you never let me start? You say you want happiness, and he'd be a perfect match. You'll meet him when he's best man at the wedding, why not meet him sooner?"

"Because you've got some fairy tale fantasy I'll fall in love with him and we can have the double wedding we always said we would, but then who would be your maid of honor?" She broke off half a brownie as Pat reached for another hot dog.

"Those are for the boys," she chided.

"Right," he said. "Jane mixed up the dates. Dentist today so they can't make it." He bit into the hot dog. "Don't give me that martyr look, you know you love helping out and the food won't go to waste." He drank from a glass of lemonade she'd meant for the boys. "So tell me about the double wedding."

She took the other half of the brownie.

"I see you gave up giving up chocolate," he said. "I'll need proof you're keeping at least one of your Lenten resolutions, then."

"If you and Em don't stop, I'll sign up with the Sisters and their misery will be on your conscience."

She dug into her skirt pocket and set her list before Pat, items one through ten scratched out in various shades of pen and crayon, number eleven shining in pristine glory.

"'Be nice to Gretchen if you ever see her again,'" he read aloud. "So have you seen her?"

"No, and if I'm lucky I won't, but it's a fine resolution and I'm sticking with it come hell or high water."

Pat had an odd look on his face.

"So you'll be nice to Gretchen for the rest of the month." He stirred a glass of lemonade with a carrot stick. "Admirable. What can I say?"

"Nothing, for once."

"Sure you don't want to expand it to include us?"

"No way. I'll be nice to Gretchen, but not to either of you unless you drop Joe's brother. I've told you for years I won't be set up."

"I was only suggesting—"

"No, Em. No suggestions, no blind dates, no semi-blind dates, no accidental meetings you cleverly arrange, none of that." She turned to Pat. "And that applies to you too."

"Me thinks thou dost protest," he said.

"When the right man comes along I'll know it, I don't need you talking me into anything. Father Barkley used to say when God wants us in a particular vocation, He makes it attractive to us. It's a Jesuit principle of discernment, so there."

"So there?" Pat said. "I'm crushed."

"Enough already." Emily nabbed his carrot stick stirrer. "I'm not sure I agree with you, Lizzy, but I'll let it go for now."

"You're disagreeing with a much higher authority than me."

"I know. I can't believe after all these years hearing about your Father Barkley, I'm missing his talk."

"You don't have to miss it," Pat said. "Stick around. I moved heaven and earth to get him here, the least you can do is stay."

"I can't. I'm going with my mom to Lisa's Bridal Castle."
He snickered.

"Don't laugh. We have an appointment with Lisa herself."

"Thanks for fitting us in. I'm surprised Joe let you come."

"I had to promise I wouldn't talk to any Sister for more than thirty seconds."

"And you've managed it?" Elizabeth asked. "Tell me your secret."

"I say hello, grab the freebies, and flash my ring." From under the table she hauled out a yellow bag imprinted with garish green letters.

"'You have not chosen me; I have chosen you. Go and bear fruit that will last.'" Pat laughed.

"You sure know how to find the kitsch." Elizabeth took another brownie.

"I'm glad I came," Emily said. "Beats a publisher's trade show by a mile."

"With our compliments, but you'll miss a terrific talk, Father Barkley's one of a kind." Pat picked up the last brownie. "Am I allowed to eat this, Liz, or do you need it?"

"I'm covered. Is Father here yet?"

"His plane landed at ten, so we could see him anytime." He wiped his hands on a paper napkin and stood, smiling down at Emily. "Good luck at Patty's Palace."

They watched as he left them for a flock of nearby nuns.

"You know he did that on purpose."

"The name of the store? I know. He's a tease, but an excellent organizer." Emily looked into her bag and pulled out a pen. "Before I forget, this is for you."

"'We are not called to be successful.' Thanks, that's encouraging."

"Click the pen."

She clicked it and the phrase disappeared, replaced by another.

"'. . . but only faithful.—Mother Teresa.'" She laughed.

"Keep clicking it, and remember, stay true to the dreams of your youth."

"I'll be true to Father Barkley's principle of attraction."

"Touché. I get the hint, no more about unattached Collins brothers today."

"How many are there?"

"Just the one you won't let me tell you about." Emily slung the bag over her shoulder. "Stay out of trouble. And call me tonight, I want to hear about the talk."

"You will. Good luck finding a dress."

"Good luck dodging the nuns."

"That's about it."

She looked over her shoulder. She was safe, no hovering nuns. She turned back and Emily was gone.

Their table was a mess. She put the two uneaten hot dogs together on one plate. A few carrot sticks, some untouched potato chips—good as new. If Father Barkley arrived hungry, she'd offer him lunch.

How long had it been? He was a visiting priest her sophomore year. She clicked her pen and calculated on a napkin. Twelve years. She drew a heart around the number.

She remembered like yesterday the things he'd said in confession and in his sermons, and most of all his kindness in arranging the D.C. trip to meet Mother Teresa. It wasn't his fault he'd gotten sick and sent their entourage with a priest who didn't know them.

She put her hands over her face but couldn't block out the image of meeting Mother Teresa. The strange priest had introduced her as a girl thinking of joining the Missionaries of Charity, which she absolutely wasn't even then. She'd stood there, a living lie looking into the eyes of a saint. It didn't matter. Thanks to Father Barkley she'd met the saint and they'd held hands for a moment. Not everyone could say that.

And soon she'd be with him again, the priest to whom she owed so much. January and February had been more purgatory than paradise, but today her cup of happiness would overflow. She put a chip in her mouth, savoring the salt.

"All alone? You don't need to be, I'm sure one of these orders would take you."

She cringed and swallowed the soggy potato chip. Could she pretend she hadn't heard? Doubtful. She'd have to be deaf to have missed the dripping sarcasm. And blind not to see, looming over her like a Valkyrie, the woman she'd counted on not seeing.

CHAPTER 7

Renewed Resolve

Behind Gretchen stood Ralph. She was tall but he was taller, and they made a handsome, if extremely fair, couple.

"Hope you didn't give up chocolate for Lent," Ralph said, tossing a small blue package onto the table. "I got them at the gas station to replace the cookies you loaned me at the art show."

She reached for the package and Pat walked up. Great, a witness. Gretchen was looking down on her as if she held a dead fish rather than a couple of Oreos, and her only recourse was niceness.

"Good to see you Ralph, Gretchen. Where's Father?" Pat lowered himself into a chair. "Grab a hot dog if you're hungry."

"Thanks, we're good, we ate on the drive back from the airport," Ralph said. "Got here ten minutes ago and Father wanted to see the chapel."

"You picked Father Barkley up from the airport?" What were they doing with her priest?

"Pat's big man on campus today so we offered limo service," Ralph said.

"You got to meet him, then." She directed her annoyance toward Pat. "I would have been glad to do an airport run."

"Gretchen met Father when she was at Princeton," Ralph said. "Her spiritual director knew him and she accompanied the two priests to Calcutta. Now tell me, how's Fra?"

Ralph sat next to Pat; Gretchen remained standing. The woman certainly lacked flexible features. Right now, for instance, was her expression a mask of self satisfaction or unattractive peevishness?

She was on the wrong path, mentally criticizing the one person who could sustain her Lenten resolution and keep her happiness project alive. She eked out a smile and motioned to a chair.

"Please join me. Can I get you some coffee or tea or soda? They have diet and regular or I could get you a glass of water, with or without ice. You must be tired after the drive to the airport and back, I know I always am. That's so neat you went to Calcutta, did you meet Mother Teresa? I met her once in college too, but I sure never made it to India. What was that like?"

Her chattering was inane, but it was something. She didn't have to be clever, just nice.

Gretchen folded her long body smoothly into a chair. No doubt when she got up her linen dress wouldn't show creases. It wouldn't dare.

"I worked in the Home for Dying Destitutes over the last months of Mother's life. We spent every evening together, a great privilege since she would soon be going home."

"I thought Calcutta was Mother Teresa's home."

Gretchen arched a perfect blonde eyebrow. "Home to heaven."

Elizabeth nodded dumbly, fake smile in place. Her cheeks were starting to ache.

"Ralph, you gotta help me out." Pat was eating again. "This hot dog's my third and Jane'll kill me if I have four."

He shoved Father Barkley's plate toward Ralph.

"I'm full, but Elizabeth can have it." Ralph pushed the plate across the table.

Why her? She looked at Gretchen. Clearly not a hot dog consumer.

"Thanks, I've eaten."

Keeping up the friendly veneer would require chocolate. She opened her Oreos.

"Dessert anyone?"

"Thanks." Ralph reached over and like a Philistine took two. "So you didn't give up chocolate for Lent. Or you did, and you need help with these, is that it?" He took a third.

A clean fork rested on the table in front of her. One more and she'd stab him.

"Liz avoids peanut butter every Lent," Pat said. "Offers it up like a saint."

She eyed the fork. No, she couldn't stab them both.

"Isn't Father speaking soon?" Gretchen asked.

"He's slated for two." Pat checked his watch. "Only one-fifteen, but I should make the rounds again. Can you get Father to the hall, Ralph?"

Her chance to be nice. She lunged at it.

"Gretchen, would you like to escort Father?" She smiled so widely her facial muscles cramped. "Then you could have more time with him."

Gretchen stood, her linen dress smooth as silk.

"I intended to stop by the chapel, but I'm not the one who knows Father best. Ralph?"

He knew the priest better than Gretchen? Gretchen who'd accompanied Father Barkley to Calcutta so she could minister to Mother Teresa in her last days?

She gazed at the fork as if it held the secrets of the universe. Amazing. In ten minutes they had reduced her spiritual friendship with Father Barkley to the merest acquaintance. Why not face facts, he wouldn't even recognize her. The Oreo package beckoned but only one cookie remained. Soon as the interlopers left she'd sneak home, change out of her wrinkled cotton skirt, and break into the Godiva.

"You go ahead, Gretchen, I haven't seen the displays. Take Father to the hall and I'll meet you there."

Pat had left. Gretchen nodded curtly and walked off. If Ralph would go she'd be free. He didn't go.

"You never answered my question," he said.

"Which was?"

"How's Fra? I was mighty relieved you took him from Pat, he couldn't have survived a week with your nephews."

She smiled, genuinely this time. "Fra's an artist, not a missionary, and you're right, life among the savages wouldn't be healthy for him." Her smile faded. "But he doesn't belong with me. It was a mistake."

"Let's not start that again. Your sketches are excellent. He's at your place and I'm glad."

"Thanks, but that doesn't make me the winner."

Ralph rocked his chair back, balancing it on two legs, looking like a college kid. She'd never get anywhere with him.

"Do you mind if I ask about something else?" she said.

"Shoot."

"How do you know Father Barkley?"

"How do I know thee, let me count the ways. You've heard of Xavier Institute?"

"The school in San Francisco where Father taught?"

"One and the same. I went there for college and graduated in two thousand two."

"That's the year I graduated from Christ the King!"

"Born in nineteen eighty?"

She nodded. "You too?"

"Yes ma'am." He let the chair fall forward and put his elbows on the table. "Went to college at the Institute and took Father's Biblical Studies class first semester. Ended up majoring in theology and when he needed an assistant, I applied. Summer after junior year I went to the Holy Land with him."

"That must have been incredible."

"Three months in Jerusalem with the holiest man on the planet. It was awesome."

Gretchen had gone with Father to India, Ralph had gone with him to Israel, she hadn't even gone to the airport to pick him up. She sighed.

"Sounds like you could use another Oreo," he said, pushing the package toward her.

She smiled despite herself. He wasn't such a bad guy; no wonder the Moores loved him. Jane said he and Pat played basketball every Saturday now and he always stayed for supper, buying pizza for them half the time, not wanting to impose. They must be dying to set her up with him, but he was taken. Which was good, right? Anyone who could stand to spend time with an Ice Princess couldn't be the man for her.

"I bet I know what's on your mind," Ralph said.

She took out the last Oreo, acting unconcerned. Was it that obvious she'd been thinking of him?

"Your happiness project, right? Or should I call it your paradise project?"

She sat up straighter. Of course he and Pat got along, they were two of an obnoxious kind. Now he was making fun of her.

"I think it's cute you're doing what the book said. Pat told me about your resolution and why you signed up for the concert and started sketching. I only hope the mix-up over the statue didn't put a damper on things. I'd hate to be the one who put the last nail in the coffin."

His words stung like salt in a thousand pinpricks. She hadn't played in the concert and he had. She hadn't truly won the statue—he had. She hadn't read the book, of course he had. And he thought her happiness project was *cute*? His affinity with Gretchen at least made sense: he was as patronizing as she was.

"It's been interesting, Ralph, but we'd better go to the talk. I want a front row seat."

Or did she? Would she even say hello to Father? Ralph and Gretchen were his friends, she was merely one of thousands who'd gone to confession to him. And that was, after all, anonymous.

Emily's pen swam before her eyes. She wouldn't let Ralph see her cry, she was being too childish. She clicked the pen. Faithful, not successful.

He rose and stretched.

"Ready when you are."

"I guess I'll see you over there," she said.

"Sure, see you there."

He walked away and she crumpled up the Oreo package. A familiar piece of binder paper caught her eye, lying on the table at Ralph's place. She moved to his chair to see what he'd seen.

Her Lenten resolutions were a mess, thank heaven, slashed by pen and crayon, impossible to make out.

Except for the item at the bottom. Mostly unslashed and completely legible, it fairly jumped off the page and slapped her.

Be nice to Gretchen (if you ever see her again). (which hopefully you won't).

She leaned down until her forehead touched the table. Had he read it? She didn't know and she didn't want to care, but one thing was certain. The blondes had done it again, stolen her happiness without even trying.

CHAPTER 8

April Fools

Elizabeth was sitting on a throw rug in her father's library, surrounded by books. Cheek by jowl they lined the built in bookcases. They rose in unwieldy towers like stalagmites from the floor. They nearly spilled off her father's desk. She'd unshelved every poet, and if Elizabeth amidst books was happy, amidst books of poetry she was even happier. It was about time.

She'd chosen poetry as her April project, explaining to Pat this was National Poetry Month, and instantly he'd turned her passion into profit. His duties on the hiring committee competed with his need to head up an April event for the Fra Angelico series and Elizabeth's poetry saved him, though he made a show of indulging her.

His plan was simple. She could supply him with poems and he would enlist students to print them out and post them in cheap matte frames on the cafeteria walls. Just like that, the Arts and Events' series was hosting "National Catholic Poetry Month—celebrating the Culture of Life!"

Yesterday Pat had informed her they'd wall-papered not only the cafeteria, but Fra Angelico Hall and the classrooms as well, and he threatened to print up toilet paper with the next poems she offered. The month wasn't finished but he was, and her current revelry in words was purely for her sake, sheer joy.

"Penny for your thoughts, my dearest bookworm?"

Elizabeth dropped the book she held.

"Dad. Hi. I didn't see you."

"Only just arrived." Her father looked down on her, smiling, from the doorway. "But you've been here for some time, by the looks of it, wreaking your lovely havoc on my collection."

She followed his gaze around the room and took in the extent of the damage.

"I'm sorry I've made a mess. I'll put everything back, I promise."

"You'll have to move quickly if you don't want to be late."

"What time is it?"

He took out his pocket watch and flipped open the cover.

"Four-thirty on the nose. Your mother sent me to tell you dinner will be at five sharp. She and Jane are planning some sort of party."

"But it's Friday. I'm babysitting the boys, they can't mean tonight."

"I only repeat what I was told." He returned the watch to his pocket and clearing his throat, spoke with mock formality. "Your presence is requested in the dining room at five o'clock for a casual Lenten repast. The Moores will bring champagne and two guests. Jane has found another sitter for the boys, and there is to be an announcement."

She stared uncomprehendingly at *The Collected Poems of Alice Meynell* resting near her left foot.

"Emily and Joe are invited, but you need not dress for dinner. Your mother insists our meal will be casual."

"Should I go help her in the kitchen?" Elizabeth rose to her feet, careful not to step on the books.

"I'd say your work is cut out for you in the library, young lady." He attempted a serious expression, but the corner of his mouth tugged upward. "I expect my room returned to its customary order by five o'clock."

"Or you'll suspend my library privileges like you did when I was a girl?"

"Precisely." He smiled. "But of course, by now you're an old hand at shelving books."

She reached for the Alice Meynell, and when she looked up he was gone. Mechanically returning the book to its proper place, she considered the question of Pat and Jane's announcement.

Gradually she cleared the floor and desk, but she was no closer to discovering the secret of tonight's party. They were bringing two guests . . . Her arm stopped midway to a shelf, and Coventry Patmore's *Angel in the House* waited patiently to rejoin the rest of his works.

"Twins," she said to the book. "They're having twins!"

A shiver of joy tingled down her spine and she set the book on the shelf. She brushed her hands on her sweatpants and checked the brass clock on her father's desk. She was seven minutes late.

CHAPTER 9

The Announcement

When Elizabeth entered the dining room at eight minutes after five, the table featured a beautiful centerpiece of roses. Tea lights alternated with gold tapers to cast a romantic glow over the china and crystal, and Pat in his suit was pouring champagne for—Gretchen and Ralph?

Her father had said her mother said casual, no mention of even business casual, simply casual, like sweatpants. The dynamic blonde duo, he in a suit and she in a dress bordering on a gown, were not following protocol, and no one else was wearing sweats either. Maybe they hadn't received the casual memo.

"Lizzy, sit here." Emily beckoned to the chair beside her. "You're just in time for grace."

Elizabeth touched Joe's shoulder and kissed the top of Emily's head. At least the damask tablecloth would hide the bottom half of her outfit.

"I'm so glad you're here." Jane beamed at her from across the table. "We have the most wonderful news!"

"Grace?" Mr. Benning solicited their attention and bowed his head for the blessing.

Martini glass of shrimp cocktail, gold rimmed salad plate of greens and mandarin oranges, steaming bowl of clam chowder. She should have changed her clothes.

"Amen," her father said.

"I'm sorry for the plain fare," her mother said from the other end of the table, "but it is a Friday in Lent. French rolls are in the baskets, and you'll find butter in the silver shells."

"You certainly don't need to apologize," Pat said. "You've outdone yourself, especially at the last minute like this."

"We couldn't wait to share our news," Jane said.

"Pay close attention, Liz. This could change your life."

Pat sure knew how to milk an audience. Would they ask her to be godmother of one of the twins?

"I took the liberty of filling your glasses before dinner." Pat lifted his champagne flute and she smiled at him encouragingly. Twins. She'd be godmother for both if they asked.

"We've finally done it. We've rented an RV for a week in June, and Jane has agreed to let me take her to the Grand Canyon." He paused and looked at Elizabeth. "On the condition that you accompany us."

"But what about the twins?" she asked.

Jane, cheeks flushed, spoke quickly. "You're the only one I'd trust to help us keep the boys safe. I've wanted to see the Grand Canyon for so long, and at this rate," she put her hand on her stomach, "I don't know when we'll get there without little ones."

So much for the twins. Pat was entirely capable of asking his mother-in-law to throw a dinner party so he could announce an RV trip. Especially if it provided him the opportunity to ask her, in front of her closest family and friends and two of her least favorite people, to accompany them to the Grand Canyon. An obvious destination for someone afraid of heights.

Pat was waiting. Everyone was waiting.

Gretchen broke the silence.

"The Grand Canyon is one of the most exquisite spots on earth. Honestly, Elizabeth, if you haven't gone there by now, surely you ought to avail yourself of the opportunity while you can."

Was she looking aged as well as underdressed? The unwelcome words from the unwelcome guest goaded her to an immediate response.

"I don't know how it is that in all my travels I haven't made it to the Canyon, but I'm nothing if not adventurous. Pat, Jane, I'd be honored to go with you."

"Marvelous. Knew you'd come through," Pat said. "Think of it as your June happiness project. If you survive May, that is."

"Thanks for the vote of confidence."

Pat refilled his and Ralph's flutes, then raised his for the second time.

"Now that's settled, we have a much more important announcement."

That sly dog. He'd tricked her, diverting them with the Grand Canyon, pretending not to hear her ask about the twins. What a master of suspense.

He was looking at Ralph meaningfully, probably intending to ask him to be godfather, hopefully of the twin she wasn't godmother of.

"As you all know, we've been interviewing at the college for a new hire. Tonight I have news I'm confident will bring happiness to many of you."

Pat winked at Joe, the other godfather no doubt. Dang. That meant Emily as the godmother for twin number two and she'd be paired with Ralph for twin number one.

"I'm pleased to announce that this afternoon at four o'clock, the committee unanimously agreed to offer the position to Dr. Collins."

Gretchen turned to Ralph and hugged him. Emily squealed and hugged Joe. Jane calmly took a sip of water. Her parents exchanged a glance.

"But what about the twins?" she asked.

"You sound like a broken record," Pat said. "I ignored you the first time assuming you wanted to change the subject, but if you're stuck on twins, why don't you tell us what twins, because I, for one, am mystified."

"I mean what about Jane's twins?"

"My twins?" Jane set her glass of water on the table. "*My* twins, Lizzy?" Her eyes widened. "Oh darling, you thought we were going to announce twins? Honey, no, that's sweet, but let's not ask God for two at once. My hands will be full as it is."

Pat grinned. "That's cute, kid. I was thinking Moses or Elijah, but if Jane has twins, we can use both names."

She gulped her ice water and held the glass to her warm cheek. Rule one, never act nonplussed before strangers or Pat.

"But what if they're girls, these twins Jane won't have for us?"

"Petrina and Jamesina, for the Apostles who witnessed the Transfiguration," Pat said without missing a beat. "And if we have triplets, a Joan too."

Emily pointed her soup spoon across the table.

"Jane, you know Joe and I are getting married on August sixth, so you can't have your babies on the Transfiguration."

"Baby." Jane smiled. "Singular. And she won't come till at least mid-August. My due date's a week after your wedding, and I always go late."

Pat put his arm along the back of Jane's chair. "You'll be early this time. We'll name our triplets for the Apostles and always remember Emily and Joe's anniversary. The day our three girls were born."

"No chance, buddy." Emily put her arm around Elizabeth. "I need her on the sixth of August and she's all mine, all day. I called her first, and since Jane needs her too, you'll have to wait."

Gretchen placed an unbuttered half roll onto the edge of her salad plate.

"Elizabeth, Ralph told me Emily has chosen you for her maid of honor. Are you Jane's mid-wife as well? That's quite unusual."

"Elizabeth will help me care for the other children when Jane goes into labor," her mother said. "We all depend on Lizzy for so many things, but I'm sure we can spare her on Emily's wedding day."

"Mrs. Benning," Emily said, "if the baby comes early you need to be at my wedding too, you've been a second mother to me. And we wanted Dominic to be our ring bearer."

"Of course we'll be at the wedding, and Dominic too. Don't worry about any of it, dear. Let tomorrow's troubles take care of themselves."

"Emily," Ralph said, "you and Joe will be married on the Feast of the Transfiguration, and I have a suggestion. Whatever else happens that day, the two of you will enter into the Sacrament of Holy Matrimony. The Great Sacrament, the

Apostle calls it. Don't let anything distract you from your joy. Christ's grace makes all things possible."

So now he was Solomon, dispensing wisdom as if someone had asked his opinion.

"Thank you, Ralph. You're right."

Emily was too kind, but that was like her.

He wasn't finished.

"And now, although I'm not surprised by Pat's announcement since he told me the news shortly after four, would the rest of you join me in raising a glass to Dr. Collins and his new job?"

She'd been so obsessed by Jane's twins, she'd forgotten Pat's actual announcement. She leaned forward and spoke across Emily.

"Joe, what's going on? St. Albert's is a liberal arts college, not a medical school. Why would they hire a doctor to teach?"

"The students call me Mr. Moore," Pat said, "but I hope you haven't forgotten I'm a doctor of philosophy. Of course doctors teach."

"But Joe's a neurologist."

Joe laughed. "What makes you think I'm the only Dr. Collins? Maybe there's another in the area with a theology degree instead of a medical degree. Would that help?"

Another Dr. Collins. She smoothed her napkin. An idea formed. An idea she didn't like.

"Emily, you wouldn't tell me about Joe's brother—the one you wanted to set me up with—because I wouldn't let you." She appealed to Joe. "Please tell me your brother, your best man, the one you said from the beginning was perfect for me—please tell me he's not a doctor of theology." She looked at Pat. "Please tell me you didn't hire him today."

"I didn't hire him. The committee did."

Elizabeth turned back to Joe and waited for his answer.

Emily giggled. "Don't tell her, honey. She'll never forgive you, but she has to forgive me. She promised in fourth grade to forgive me forever no matter what if I shared my Ho-Ho's with her at lunch all year. I did, Lizzy. You remember, don't you?"

"How can I forget when you bring it up once a month?"

Gretchen made her would-be-snorting-but-sounds-lovely-from-me noise and looked appalled that Hostess snack cakes had made fourth grade bearable. Let her eat unbuttered rolls and scoff at America's finest baked goods, there were bigger fish on the table yet to be fried.

"Emily. Please don't tell me you're going to tell me what I haven't let you tell me."

"I can't change the facts. My Dr. Collins' brother is Dr. Collins too, and he's the new hire. But I promise I won't try to set you up with him. You can decide for yourself what you think of him, and I promise to stay out of it."

"And you?" Elizabeth asked Jane. "Will you promise that when he gets here and works with your husband, you won't try to set me up with the other Dr. Collins?"

Jane nodded meekly.

"And you." She glared at Pat. "Tell me you didn't talk that committee into hiring him so you could play Emma. Not that I'll believe you."

"I wish I had that kind of power."

"I've told you all I'm happy as I am. I'll play maid of honor opposite his best man at the wedding, but I won't have any of you trying to get us together."

She surveyed each face in turn, from Pat to Jane to her mother avoiding her glance, to Joe to Emily to her father who smiled kindly. She even paused at Gretchen and Ralph, who looked embarrassed. Well, Ralph looked embarrassed. Gretchen looked as disdainfully remote as ever.

"Anyway, I'm thirty-two and my best friend is getting married and I'm happy for her and the real Dr. Collins and I even wish the other Dr. Collins happiness as he begins his new life, as long as he stays away from me. In fact, now that you've all agreed not to set me up with him, and to show there's no hard feelings, here's to the new professor, the other Dr. Collins, wherever he is."

She grabbed her champagne glass and drained it in two gulps. With no chocolate in reach, it would have to do.

The grandfather clock ticked loudly in the corner, otherwise the room was still. She stared at her uneaten soup, and feeling slightly ill she looked up, right into Ralph's eyes. He smiled at her, scraped back his chair, and stood to full height.

"I'd like to thank you for your good wishes, Elizabeth. I'm not sure we've been formally introduced. I'm Ralph Collins, doctor of theology, Joe's brother, and as of four o'clock today, the new professor at the college."

CHAPTER 10

The Truth

If she were a character in one of her beloved Jane Austen novels, Elizabeth would have waited for the floor to swallow her up, but obviously that wasn't going to happen. Stuck in the twenty-first century she couldn't even swoon to get past the awkwardness of Ralph's announcement which had handily trumped Pat's. Calling for smelling salts wasn't an option either; Pat would bring her the cleaning ammonia.

Congratulations flew from every mouth but hers. The truth was out, the many truths they all must have known and kept from her. Ralph was Joe's brother, Pat's friend, and to universal acclaim, the newest employee of St. Albert's College. Whether she liked it or not, and she inclined like the leaning tower of Pisa toward not, he belonged here as much as she did.

Emily, her expression contrite, turned from Joe to Elizabeth.

"No." Preferring not to be overheard, Elizabeth dropped her voice to a whisper, "I don't forgive you. I can't believe you didn't tell me. I feel like an idiot, especially after that stuff I said about not setting me up with him. Gretchen must think I'm after her man."

"You're totally wrong," Emily whispered back. "Ever since you met Ralph and Gretchen I've wanted to explain. They've known each other forever, but they're not romantically involved."

"Right. If you wanted to tell me so bad, why didn't you?"

"If I told you he was Joe's brother and single, you'd have thought we were pushing him on you."

"I know he's got a girlfriend, and I still think you're pushing him on me."

"I rest my case. I've been dying to reveal his secret identity ever since you met him, but Jane and I thought we'd better not. You've always been so suspicious of any guy we introduced."

"Because you're a couple of yentas who won't mind your own business," Elizabeth hissed.

The others were asking Ralph questions about the interview process. Good, she wasn't finished with Emily.

"You should have told me. This is worse than anything you could have done. I feel like a total idiot now."

Emily put a hand on her arm. "It's not like you've never felt like an idiot before."

"Thanks."

"The new Dr. Collins brought dessert," Mrs. Benning said, rising. "Why don't you each take a dish or two into the kitchen. We'll have dessert in the living room and you can help yourself to chocolate cake while I get the coffee."

Near the living room, he accosted her.

"Elizabeth, I'm sorry. It was wrong of me to go along with Pat."

She stared at his hand touching her arm, and he removed it.

"I would've told you I was Joe's brother the first night we met, but I didn't have a chance. You came to the dinner late and left early and the Italians made conversation impossible. The next time I saw you, well, you won my award." He smiled mischievously. "You didn't seem in the mood for meeting someone new that day."

Emily was on the sofa eating cake. The man didn't know when to speak and when to be silent. If he'd finish the history of their non-relationship she could sit with her best friend and stuff her face with chocolate. He couldn't spin it out much longer; they'd only known each other a few months.

"What about Vocations' Day? You could have told me then who you were."

"Didn't seem the right time either. Pat said you might be annoyed when you found out and that was our first chance to talk alone. I didn't want to spoil it, I guess. I am sorry."

He was winding down. If she forgave him quickly, there'd still be cake.

"Whatever."

It came out rude, but whatever. He couldn't even apologize without irritating her. She tried again.

"It wasn't entirely your fault. I'm sure Pat and Jane and Emily and Joe swore you to secrecy."

That was better. Forgiveness-like without committing herself.

From the doorway to the living room they could see the whole party. Pat and Jane sat in the recliners near the piano, talking to Joe and Emily, who sat on the long white sofa. Mrs. Benning poured coffee at the buffet while Mr. Benning took a cup to Pat.

Gretchen sat alone on the piano bench, her back ramrod straight, hands clasped in her lap, close enough to the others to partake in their conversation but holding herself aloof. She had no cake and no coffee cup, and she was staring at Ralph and Elizabeth.

"I think Gretchen's waiting for you."

"Shoot. I forgot she doesn't do cake or coffee, and the poor girl doesn't really know anyone here but me," Ralph said.

The poor girl could get to know people. As to her not "doing" cake or coffee, did he mean never? Poor girl indeed.

"Excuse me."

He crossed the room. Elizabeth put her hand to her mouth to hide her smile as he stood before the narrow piano bench, apparently gauging its capacities, and settled for the floor at his lady's feet. Clearly they were a couple, and not just a couple of friends.

She joined Emily on the couch.

"Forgive me for having a brother?" Joe said.

"Get me chocolate and I'll think about it."

He went to the buffet and sliced an enormous piece of cake. Good man. She'd forgive Ralph too if his dessert tasted as good as it looked.

Joe handed her the plate with a flourish. Lifting a forkful of moist chocolate to her mouth, she inhaled to get the full effect.

A wave of nausea swept over her and she recoiled. Careful to breathe only through her mouth, she examined the thing on her plate. It looked like chocolate cake.

"Oh, Lizzy! I was hoping you wouldn't notice."

Jane's voice, louder than usual and sharp with anxiety, cut through every conversation. Six curious faces and an indifferent one turned toward Elizabeth. She addressed Ralph alone.

"What kind of cake is this?"

It came out more an accusation than a question.

"Chocolate peanut butter," he answered brightly. "Pat said you always give up peanut butter for Lent, so technically I shouldn't have brought it, but I thought if you took a bite before you noticed, it wouldn't count."

Retorts crowded her mind, none of them fit for mixed company.

"Peanut butter's my favorite flavor too," he went on. "I can't imagine giving it up."

Her father chortled, trying to cover it with a cough.

"Dr. Collins, I don't know what Pat told you but he's not wholly trustworthy when it comes to Elizabeth. I'm afraid he has no scruples about lying in the service of a joke."

She focused on the cake. She could practically hear the chocolate crying for her but how could she get to it? There was nothing to scrape off or eat around, it was the most thoroughly peanut buttered chocolate ever.

Emily gently pried the plate from her fingers. "Forget it, Liz. Follow me and we'll raid your mom's baking chocolate."

She abandoned Ralph to his regrets. Like he had any. The men were discussing the morality of the jocose lie, as if trying to poison her was a joke.

Once in the kitchen, she looked furtively behind her.

"What are you doing?" Emily asked.

A last glance down the hallway and she dropped into a chair at the kitchen table.

"I'm not taking any chances. What I have to say is for your ears only."

Emily pulled a yellow box from the cupboard over the stove. "Should I be scared?"

"Hand over the chocolate and no one will get hurt."

Emily handed it over and walked around the table.

"I'll sit on this side if you don't mind. A little distance goes a long way when you're in this mood."

Elizabeth paused with a chunk of semi-sweet near her open mouth.

"What mood?"

"Put the chocolate in."

They were silent while Elizabeth savored.

"Better, huh?"

"Mmm-hmm." She broke off another square, popped it in her mouth and closed her eyes. Her body melted into the chair.

"You were saying? For my ears only?"

She opened her eyes with an effort.

"Thanks for chocolate. Something important to say. Can't remember."

"Something about Joe's brother, possibly? You wanted me to be the first to know. You think he's cute, huh?"

Elizabeth sat up and pushed the box away.

"That was it!"

"I'll never consent to his being cuter than Joe, but Ralph's handsome in his own way."

"No, that's not it. I mean Ralph is it, but I don't think he's cute. I mean he's okay, but that's not the point."

Emily laughed.

"It's not funny. I might forgive you someday, but that stupid peanut butter cake was the last straw. You had some, you knew it could kill me, and you didn't warn me. Exactly like with Ralph. You should have warned me he was Joe's brother."

"You're such a drama queen. That cake wouldn't kill you. You don't have a peanut allergy, you just don't care for peanut butter."

She tried to interrupt, but Emily kept talking.

"I knew you'd figure it out and I didn't have the heart to say anything. Poor Ralph was hoping to please you with that cake."

"Poor Ralph my foot. The man is a pest, a nuisance, a pain in the neck—"

"Stop it, Lizzy. He's going to be my brother-in-law."

"Fine, but that's all he's going to be. I'm not blind, I see the set-up. You and Joe, Pat and Jane, even my mom and dad are scheming. You're happy couples and you want me to be a happy couple. I get that, it's natural. But to be a couple I need a man and that man will never be Ralph." She snapped off another piece of chocolate. "And what about Gretchen? She's half of Ralph's couple already, and I'm not feeling the love."

"I told you, they don't love each other like that."

"Have I told you I don't believe you?"

"Right." Emily looked at her suspiciously and shook her head.

"What?"

"You're not worried about Gretchen. You're mad because Ralph is the other half of your happy couple and we all saw it before you did."

Elizabeth fell back in her chair. "I don't know what to say."

"Say I'm right."

"Em, I don't know what to say because you're insane. I don't even know where to start."

"Start with another piece of chocolate."

"No. I'm not giving in that easily. Which part don't you get? I can't stand Ralph. I can't stand being set-up, I hate being the butt of jokes, and I can't believe you didn't tell me. You should've told me who he was."

"How? You never let me talk to you about Joe's brother."

"But that's because I didn't want you to set me up."

"And now you blame me for setting you up even though I never told you about him. You can't have it both ways, Lizzy."

"Why not?"

Emily gestured impatiently.

"It's been four months since Joe and I got engaged at Christmas, and nearly a year since I met him in the bookstore. Not once did you let me tell you about his brother Ralph, not when I first found out he had a brother, not when I first met his brother, not when I knew you'd met his brother without knowing he was his brother. I can give you all the reasons in the world why I didn't tell you Joe's brother and Ralph are the same person, but I only need to give you one. You wouldn't let me."

Elizabeth reached for the box. More chocolate would ease the pain of concession.

"I guess you're right."

"Thank you."

"But just because you're right that I didn't let you tell me about him, doesn't mean you're right about anything else."

"Such as?"

"You still think Ralph's the man for me, I can tell, and you're wrong. He wasn't before I knew his last name, and he isn't now."

"But can't you give him a chance?"

"I won't, and puppy dog eyes won't help your cause."

"But he could be your new passion and you wouldn't have to keep switching every month. You could declutter your happiness project."

They said clenching was bad for the jaw, but how could she help it?

"Emily MaryAnne Lucas. Can't you hear a word I'm saying? I don't like Ralph and he's not a way to be happier. He's like my unhappiness project."

Emily sucked on her thumbnail.

"Can you tell me again why you don't like him? Because I think he's a nice guy."

"First, he ruined my recital." She ticked off her complaints on her left hand. "Second, he ruined my art show. Third, he ruined Vocations' Day. Fourth, I was perfectly happy with my poetry and now he's ruined April. Isn't that enough?"

"You're not being logical." Emily held up her left hand to counter count. "First, he wasn't the one who gave you peanut butter the night of the concert."

"But he played my piece. Who does that?"

"Second, it wasn't his fault the students messed up the program at the art show."

"But he should have taken the statue home!"

"Okay, I'll grant you that. He was so generous he let you keep the statue. Third, he wasn't behind all those nuns trying to get you to join up in March."

"But he and Gretchen ruined my anticipation of seeing Father Barkley."

Emily stopped counting.

"How?"

"You know how much Father meant to me. I always thought of him as my friend, and then they got him from the airport and talked about him like he belonged to them."

"You blame them for knowing Father Barkley better than you?"

It didn't sound so good when Emily put it like that but she couldn't back down.

"You're holding that against Ralph?"

"I am," she said. "So what?"

"So you're the one who's insane. Ralph got you out of a tight spot by playing your piece, he made a beautiful icon and let you keep the prize he won, and he's such a good man he's friends with a holy priest, and that bothers you. Am I missing anything?"

She broke off another bit of chocolate, but her heart wasn't in it.

"Maybe you're one of those women drawn to jerks, and I never knew it. Ralph's too perfect, is that it?" Emily asked.

She nodded. "Yeah, that's it."

"He's too perfect? That's your objection?"

"I hadn't thought of it until you said it, but that's why he and Gretchen make such a grossly ideal couple. They're both perfect."

Emily stared at the box of chocolate.

"Lizzy, you've stumped me. I don't know what to say."

"You can say I'm right."

"No, I can't. You're nuts. And you're wrong about Ralph and Gretchen."

"Don't you dare tell me they're just friends. We're not in high school anymore, Em."

"You're not in high school anymore?" Joe asked from the doorway. "Have you been lying to me about your age?"

"You're barely in time to rescue me." Emily hugged him. "She's not in an agreeable mood. Will you please tell her about Ralph and Gretchen?"

"What do you want me to tell her?"

Elizabeth rested her chin in her hands, elbows on the table.

"Tell him to tell me they're just friends, and I'll believe him. Ha. I don't think so."

"You girls can sort this out later. Party's breaking up and I'd like to walk Emily home before I go." He looked at Elizabeth without a trace of a smile on his face. "For what it's worth, Ralph and Gretchen are just friends, so he's totally free if you're on the hunt."

Emily poked him in the ribs with her elbow.

"What?" he said, putting his arm around her shoulder. "Now she knows he's my brother, can't we speed things up? I thought you wanted a double wedding?"

Emily slid out from under his arm to hug Elizabeth.

"He's right," she whispered. "It's still my dream, but I'm not apologizing anymore."

"I'll talk to you tomorrow," Elizabeth said, hugging back. "You better let Joe take you home."

She followed them to the front door and stepped into the cool night air. She could hear Jane and Pat saying their good-byes in the living room, and then they were beside her.

"I hope you enjoyed your night off," Pat said. "I've got to go home and pay the student who babysat for you."

Jane kissed her cheek. "We're lucky to have you, and it's good for him to realize it."

Elizabeth kissed Jane and punched Pat in the shoulder. Back inside she locked the door and leaned against it. This must have been how Greta Garbo felt.

So Ralph was Joe's brother, and Emily was crazy. Let them try to set her up. Elizabeth Bennet had refused a Collins, and she could as well. Not that she'd need to. Aside from Emily's wedding she'd avoid him, and he wouldn't come looking for her: he already had everything. A brother, a job, a blonde girlfriend. What more could a man want?

"Why don't you come in here and join us for a drink?"

She pushed away from the door, the solid, locked door, the door she'd closed to shut out the night's guests, and stepped to the living room. Immediately she wished she hadn't.

Ralph looked comfortable on the sofa, his shoes off, long legs stretched out before him. He held a snifter full of amber liquid. There was no one else in the room.

CHAPTER 11

The Icing on the Cake

Only Ralph was visible, but on second thought that didn't necessarily mean everyone else was gone. Any moment now someone might pop up from behind a chair and yell, "Surprise!"

"Where is everyone?" Elizabeth asked.

"You said good-bye to my brother and Emily and Pat and Jane."

"But where's Gretchen? Is she waiting for you in the car?" She could not be stuck here absolutely alone with him. The night could not get that bad.

"She brought her own car and left half an hour ago. Has to work early tomorrow."

"My parents, then." Unlikely, but she couldn't help herself. "Mom? Dad?" she called toward the recliners.

"Your parents went to bed when Pat and Jane left."

"Then why are you still here?" Rude again. He brought out the worst in her, no question.

"Your father had just poured my cognac when he saw your mother nodding in her chair." He gestured to the straight-backed chair beside the buffet. "She couldn't keep her eyes open and looked ready to slip off onto the floor so he took her to bed."

"My mom always does that." Elizabeth smiled faintly. "It's incredible, but coffee puts her to sleep."

"I know where your dad hides the good stuff. Can I get you some cognac?"

The only thing she wanted to do with cognac was pour his down the sink, but what was the use? He'd follow her and raid the fridge; there was no escaping him.

She perched on the edge of her mother's chair.

"What do you say, will you have some cognac with me?"

"Water is all I want."

The glass pitcher on the buffet was half empty, no ice, but it would do. She poured water into her mother's empty cup.

"If you're sure that's strong enough." Ralph held up the snifter. "Cheers!"

Elizabeth lifted the coffee cup. "Cheers." She didn't sound cheerful, she didn't feel cheerful, but she could be polite. "I never congratulated you on your new job. You must be really happy about that."

He smiled. He did have a great smile.

"I can't tell you how happy. I get to stay near Joe, teach at the college, be part of this amazing community." He took a sip of cognac. "Who knows what else may work out."

A reference to Gretchen.

"You said you met Father Barkley at Xavier. Where'd you go for your doctorate?"

"Took me awhile to even start on it. I thought God was calling me to be a monk, so after college I went to a monastery in New York but it wasn't for me."

"Was that where you made the icon?"

"Yep. Then I went to work in New York City and met Gretchen in a Catholic singles group, then eventually I went to the Angelicum in Rome. Italy was fantastic, but I missed California."

"Not New York?"

"Not a bit. A few months ago I came here and moved in with Joe, and with Gretchen in the area, it was an easy transition."

Had it been California he missed?

"Then Pat and Jane took me under their wing. They're really terrific."

"Yeah, Jane is wonderful. And now you'll be teaching with Pat at St. Albert's."

"Tell you the truth, it feels like after all this time God finally has a plan for me."

"He always had a plan, He's just now showing you what it is." She took a sip of water. It tasted like coffee dregs.

"Only a few more things I'm hoping will fall into place."

"Like what?" she asked absently, looking for a clean glass. The unused tumblers were at the other end of the buffet. She retrieved one, and returning to her chair was surprised to see Ralph standing.

"I wasn't sure I should say anything tonight. You seemed kind of put out about not knowing I was Joe's brother. And I guess the cake wasn't a big hit." He laughed.

The faux chocolate cake. A sour taste rose in the back of her mouth.

"But since we're here alone, maybe this is the right time."

It wasn't. Whatever it was, it wasn't the right time.

"I heard you tell everyone at dinner not to set you up with Joe's brother, but you never made me promise. Elizabeth, would you go out with me?"

"But what about Gretchen?"

"I thought you might have the wrong idea about me and Gretchen."

"No, I don't. I have the right idea. You two are perfect for each other and I'd hate to come between you. Really, you have my blessing."

Ralph smiled. "Gretchen and I are just friends. We've known each other for years, and we understand each other."

She nodded like a bobble head. "Excellent, that's extremely important in a relationship, gives you the foundation you need. You understand each other, and I bet you have a lot of the same interests, and you're both blonde."

Ralph was laughing. He sat on the couch and put his cognac on the floor beside his feet.

"Elizabeth, you're the girl I'm interested in. We have plenty in common too. We both like music and art and books. You've got a great family and we'll be practically related when my brother marries your best friend." He looked at her earnestly, no longer laughing. "And let's face it, neither of us is getting any younger. We're old enough to know what we like. I like you. You're approaching forty—don't you think it's time to find the right guy and settle down?"

It was her turn to stand.

"We're exactly the same age, remember? And I for one don't consider thirty-two going on thirty-three as approaching forty. But even if I did, I wouldn't be desperate to settle down. I love my life, and I don't see any reason to change it."

"I didn't mean it that way. Of course you have a good life, but I think it could be better if you let me take you out.

Kind of like your paradise project. What's that mantra Jane quotes? You're happy, but you could be happier. Isn't that it?"

"Yes."

"So why couldn't I make you happier?"

A trick question. He was the quintessence of her recent unhappiness but she could hardly tell him so. She didn't want to insult him, but it was all wrong. He belonged with Gretchen. She belonged with . . . someone she hadn't met yet.

"If you want to think it over, I understand," Ralph said, stretching his arms along the back of the couch as if he'd wait. "Tonight you found out who I am, and you need to get used to the idea."

"No, I don't."

She sat down abruptly. She didn't like knowing who he was, but she could accept the facts.

"I don't need more time."

"Great. Are you busy tomorrow night? Or maybe we could go to Mass together on Sunday and then out to brunch."

"Ralph," she said, looking at her feet, "I mean I don't need more time because I'm sure I don't want to go out with you."

There. She'd said it. She stole a glance in his direction. He was looking at his feet too, putting his shoes on in fact. He stood. She'd forgotten how tall he was. He wasn't smiling and he seemed as tall as the sky.

"I'm sorry to bother you," he said. "If you change your mind, let me know."

He was past her, letting himself out the front door.

It was over. He was gone.

He'd been a perfect gentleman. Not that she'd expected him to snap at her or break down in tears, but he'd been so normal. More than normal, he'd been extraordinarily self-possessed. Which was a good thing, wasn't it? Except she could've done without that "If you change your mind."

She wouldn't change her mind; he wasn't the right man for her. The right man wouldn't make her feel like an idiot every time they met. The right man wouldn't make her unhappier. And the right man definitely wasn't blonde and a foot taller than she was.

So he saw God's plan except for that one missing piece, and he, along with everyone else, expected her to fall right into place. Well she wasn't a puzzle piece, and she wasn't the last one left on the table, either.

She leaned back into the uncomfortable chair; she'd let something of the wood's unforgiving strength enter her soul.

Approaching forty, indeed. Watching the clock and waiting for a man to save her from spinsterhood, was that it?

"If you want to think it over," he'd said, and "If you change your mind." He was Mr. Collins to the life, unable to accept a refusal. Fine, she'd be Lizzy Bennet, repeating her no as many times as it took and resisting pressure from whatever corner it came. Her mother was nothing like Lizzy Bennet's, she was safe from that quarter.

Emily and Jane, on the other hand, wouldn't give up so easily.

She knew them: they'd pester her, and Pat would tease her to death unless she convinced them Ralph wasn't the one. But if they didn't see the self-evident, how could she prove it? Jane would be sweet, Emily would be stubborn, Pat would be obnoxious, but they wouldn't let up till she was married to someone.

That was it.

Her next month's happiness project would not only make her happier forever after, it would solve all kinds of problems in the meanwhile. Ralph would be free to realize Gretchen was his soul mate, Jane and Emily would see her as part of a couple at last, and Pat would know he didn't know what was best for her. Happiness galore.

She turned off the lights and locked the front door. All she had to do now was find the one perfect person she could love and cherish till death did them part. How hard could that be?

CHAPTER 12

A Surprise

"You're going to do what?" Jane stared at her, horrified.

"I think it's a great idea," Pat said.

His wife swatted him with the dish towel. "You think it's great because it's ridiculous. Don't do it, Lizzy. We'll leave you alone, I promise."

"Speak for yourself, my love." Pat kissed Jane and turned to Elizabeth. "I won't leave you alone, no matter what she promises. We've hit May. No more Fra Angelico events till September. You need something big and you need it now. I say go for it, I'm on board."

Of course he was. He wanted to see her fall on her face.

"Your instincts are spot on. I will harass you into marrying Ralph unless you do something drastic." He pulled a sheet off the memo pad on the fridge. "I'll draw up a contract to prevent your sidestepping the action."

Jane's brow puckered, the way it did when she was about to say no to the boys.

"Let's not argue. Why don't you get ready?" Elizabeth suggested. "I can finish the mac and cheese."

"You sure? I don't trust Pat."

"Of course you trust me." He gave her another kiss and steered her out of the kitchen.

"Now then," he said to Elizabeth from the dining room, "I'll just review the facts before I make your to-do list."

Jane was right, he was entirely untrustworthy. "I won't do anything illegal," Elizabeth warned.

"Facts first," he said. "You're set on forcing a victim to marry you, but like a character in a Greek tragedy you're running from your destiny, namely the tall fair demi-god the fates have chosen, seeking instead an innocent bystander. That about it?"

She leaned away from the stove.

"I've had it up to here with your Ralph jokes. He asked me out, I said no, that's the end of it."

"More like the end of him. Poor guy's been languishing, dying of a broken heart. He may never get over this."

"It's been a week. I doubt he's even thought of me."

"You do him an injustice. We men aren't nearly as cold and calculating as you women."

The spoon in her hand slipped from her grasp and hit the linoleum with a dull thud.

"The facts are I'm perfectly capable of finding my own man." Into the sink went the spoon and she took another from the drawer. "I've already started looking."

"Good for you. Step over Ralph's body and go to it. Hordes of single Catholic men your age must be out there waiting anxiously for you to find them. What progress have you made?"

"Darling," Jane called from the bedroom, "our house is small and I'm listening to every word. Be nice or you go out alone tonight."

"Dearest," he called back, "I don't like keeping such close tabs on her but somebody's got to."

"Play fair, Mr. Moore."

"Of course, my love." He lowered his voice. "She's all for this. Tell me what you've done so far."

"I borrowed *The Tools* from the library, and I found a speed dating event."

"I've heard about that book." Jane appeared, hairbrush in hand. "You don't need advice on catching a man."

"Obviously she does, or she wouldn't have said no to Ralph and be stuck babysitting for us every Friday night."

Jane rapped him on the shoulder with the back of her brush and left them.

"You're doing the right thing," Pat said. "If you think Ralph's not the one, we've got to get you out there circulating. When's the speed dating?"

"A week from tonight," she said, plating the mac 'n cheese. A couple orange segments around the rim and she'd surpass the serving suggestion. "You and Jane okay with me skipping a night of babysitting?"

"Couldn't you take the boys with you?"

"Pat!" Jane called.

"Honey, it's ideal. The boys can protect her and report back if any of her speed dates act fresh."

"Speed dating's at the church hall," Elizabeth said. "I think I'll be safe without the boys' protection."

"I'm just watchin' your back. If you don't want the boys, we can get Ralph to babysit. Unless he's speed dating too. We need to encourage him to get back on the horse."

She spilled the milk she was pouring.

"Honey," Jane called, "Ralph promised the boys a night of Star Wars Monopoly. Why don't we make it next Friday?"

Through the open window came the voices of her nephews at play. She had no problem with Ralph babysitting. As long as he stayed away from her, everyone would be happy.

She brought the milk to the table.

"Finished yet?"

"Almost there," Pat said, hiding the paper with his left hand, green crayon in his right.

The boys tumbled in through the back door.

"Wash your hands," she told them. "Pat, you've got about a minute before we take over the table."

He was still writing, and she sat down beside him. Had his arm always been that hairy?

The boys raced back from the bathroom, Jane following, her purse slung over her shoulder.

"You look smashing." Pat set the crayon on the page. "Ready?"

"Ready as I'll ever be," she said, walking to the front door. "How about you?"

"Contract's on the table and if Liz does her part she'll find a husband before the end of the month."

"Lizzy, don't let Pat railroad you. This is your happiness project, not his."

"I know and I take full responsibility. This is my idea, and I'm sure it's a good one." She left the table to shake hands with Pat. "We're all set then. Have fun tonight."

The door closed behind them, the deadbolt shooting home before she touched it. Pat, locking it from the other side, keeping them all safe. He wasn't so bad.

She led the boys in grace and sank into Pat's vacated chair with a contented sigh. The mac and cheese looked delicious, the list lay on the table before her. She moved the crayon and read as she ate.

Sufficient Conditions for the Possibility of Elizabeth finding Mr. Right

#1. Read *The Tools* to glean helpful hints.
#2. Speed dating at church.
#3. Three real dates (or two dates and an engagement).

She sipped her milk and smiled at number three. Only two items left.

#4. Boyfriend at the end of the month or I set you up on blonde (if not blind) date.
#5. Include Gretchen in #1 - 3. Ralph says she's lonely & he'll send you her email address.

She gagged on a mouthful of macaroni.
"Are you okay, Auntie Beth?" Jude asked.
She chewed slowly and swallowed. What a weasel.
"I'm fine. Your dad surprised me, that's all."
Anthony grinned. "He's good at surprises."
"Sometimes he hides behind the door and jumps out when we come in!" Dominic said.
Luke's eyes were wide. "Did he do that to you?"
"Not exactly, but close."
A blonde date? He and Ralph could dream on. She'd find herself a man, and she'd find one for Gretchen too if Pat required it. Apparently she and the Ice Princess had something important in common. They were both willing to pass on Ralph.

CHAPTER 13

A New Friend

Elizabeth woke the next morning and found, thanks to Ralph's prompt cooperation with Pat's absurd plan, Gretchen's email address waiting in her inbox. No need to over think it then; she'd simply invite the she-blonde along for the ride.

Four drafts later, she pressed "send."

> Dear Gretchen,
> I'm not in a book group at the moment, but I'm wondering if you'd like to get together over lunch sometime this week and talk about *The Tools*. I'm not implying you need the advice it offers; just found it intriguing myself and hoped to talk with a friend about it. If you can't come, no problem. You're probably swamped with work, and I'd hate to take you away from your duties.
> Sincerely,
> Elizabeth Benning

She shot off the email at 9:03 and rewarded herself with a Hershey's Special Dark for breakfast. At 9:07 she read Gretchen's response.

> Elizabeth,
> I would very much like to meet over lunch to discuss *The Tools*. Today would be convenient. The Rose and Thistle at noon.
> Gretchen

Would a true Ice Princess be this eager to talk about *The Tools*? Maybe Gretchen *was* lonely, and by implication, human. Elizabeth replied she'd be there and hustled to get ready for the day.

By the time she sat down to read *The Tools*, she'd not only showered and dressed and tidied her room, she'd also called Emily, Jane, and her mother, finished a crossword puzzle cut from her parent's newspaper two weeks before when she'd solved 1-across (flightless bird: emu), painted her toenails, and washed a load of laundry at the big house.

From the alarm clock on the nightstand Minnie Mouse frowned at her, white gloved hands at the end of stiff black arms pointing to the wrong numbers. It would take her twenty minutes to get to the restaurant, which left seventeen minutes max to read the book they were meeting to discuss. Minnie was a reliable rodent, but discouraging.

Pencil in hand, she flipped to the Table of Contents and lightly check marked two promising chapter titles, then looked up at Fra looking down on her from his shelf. His mild expression reassured her. Inspired, she set aside the book and googled "The Tools."

Her decision not to actually read the book made her punctual for the first time in her life. Unfortunately Gretchen waited like impatience on a monument in the foyer, as if she'd been there since shortly after their email exchange. Elizabeth let it slide. She wasn't late, they were about to eat, and she took pride in her opalescent toenails.

The hostess led them to a booth.

"We prefer a table," Gretchen said.

The royal "we," apparently, since she never preferred a table, but it was all good. Tables with uncushioned chairs, for instance: weren't they good for posture? Besides, today was about reaching out to the other.

She followed Gretchen and the hostess away from the well padded booth to a table. Not quite Feng Shui, but then how likely was it that someone would creep up on her? She suppressed the unsafe feeling she got when sitting in the center of a room, and deposited herself in a chair at the center of the room.

"Perfect," Gretchen said.

Elizabeth picked up the menu, but Gretchen wasn't opening hers. Instead she looked almost apologetic. This might not be so bad.

"I'm sorry to say I haven't re-read *The Tools* this morning, but I trust my notes will refresh me." Gretchen pulled a thin binder out of her sleek black bag and opening it, revealed neatly written pages separated by colored tabs.

Elizabeth pushed her overstuffed backpack under the table with her painted toes.

"Do you always take notes when you read?"

Gretchen did a thing like smiling. Her mouth didn't curve into something as robust as a typical smile, but her expression indicated amusement.

"Not always. When *The Tools* hit the bestseller list, I led workshops as part of my job at Books-a-Trillion."

"My job at Books-a-Trillion." The words echoed around the room. Gretchen used to work at the store that put

Adventures in Reading out of business? That couldn't be right. She must have been a traveling workshop leader for smarmy self-help books. Unlikely, but more palatable than the alternative.

"How interesting. So you worked for Random House?"

Gretchen looked up from the binder. "Excuse me?"

"The publisher of *The Tools.* They sent you to Books-a-Trillion to lead workshops on it?"

If grasping at straws were an Olympic sport, she could earn a silver medal.

Gretchen's blonde eyebrows arched perfectly.

"No, I work at Books-a-Trillion and led workshops there when the book first became a bestseller."

"I see. You used to work at Books-a-Trillion when this book came out. And where do you work now?" Grasp, grasp. Going for the gold.

"I used to work at Books-a-Trillion in New York. I requested a transfer to southern California last autumn, and I continue to work at Books-a-Trillion currently."

The waitress arrived. Elizabeth wanted to ask Gretchen what she did at the megastore besides lead workshops on silly books and shut down independent bookstores, but the blonde was occupied with the waitress, dictating her intricate order.

Gretchen worked for The Enemy. Why hadn't anyone told her? Ralph must know. What would Em say? If Gretchen had come to California before Christmas, she must have worked at Books-a-Trillion around the time the slimy corporation bought out the Lucases remaining stock.

Someone was watching her, she could feel it. Why hadn't she insisted on the booth? Here in the middle of the room, unprotected, she was a sitting duck. She looked up warily.

The waitress and Gretchen were staring at her. Waiting for her. Of course. The waitress cleared her throat.

"My turn already?"

She hated when this happened, she couldn't make sense of the menu under pressure. The waitress tapped her foot. Gretchen paged through her binder with the assurance of a woman who never makes anyone wait, her quasi-smile replaced by a tight line.

"I'll have the same."

There, done. When her food came she always wanted what the other person had anyhow.

"And so," the other person said, "excuse my jumping ahead in the book."

The book. Right. Had she missed something?

Gretchen's eyebrows, now perfectly straight rather than perfectly arched, were exquisite. Did she shape them herself? Today's lipstick was a burnt orange. At the April dinner party her mouth had been mauve. Incredible how many colors suited Gretchen's lips. Which were moving.

"So I'd like your opinion. You've lived here as a single Catholic female. Granted you're not exactly a success at relationships, but I don't know who else to ask for advice."

She loved being asked for advice, though she'd never been asked quite so snarkily.

"Getting back to the book, then, and given your knowledge of this area, what ideas do you have on Tool Three. 'Go places and see people; don't hide out at work and at home'?"

This she could handle. She'd googled that tool.

"I'm glad you asked. Incidentally, I've been very satisfied with my relationships to date." Okay, not as in dating, but up until now in the more general sense. "But I have got ideas for going somewhere and seeing lots of people. Have you ever heard of speed dating?"

Gretchen smiled, this time for real. Her mouth did what other people's smiling mouths did, and her eyes did something too. Were they twinkling? Not quite, but humor lurked in their icy blue depths.

"I don't live in a vacuum. I even read the church bulletin. St. Paschal's pro-life singles' group is holding a speed dating event on Friday. But surely you don't plan to go?"

Before Elizabeth could respond, the waitress presented their food.

"Two grilled unsalted chicken Caesars, hold the dressing, hold the croutons, hold the parmesan, extra pepper. And two Perriers. Let me know if you need anything else."

She didn't know quite where to begin, she needed so many things. But the waitress hadn't waited this time. Elizabeth stared after her helplessly.

"Shall we say grace?" Gretchen asked.

They prayed, and Gretchen forked a lettuce leaf. Time to dig in. Elizabeth liberally salted her chicken. At least she could remedy that. Gretchen's fork pierced another bite of romaine, and she pointed the laden weapon at Elizabeth.

"What exactly did you have in mind with regard to the speed dating? Since you haven't said more, I assume you're embarrassed."

Her mouth full of dry chicken, now over-salted as well as over-peppered, Elizabeth couldn't speak.

Gretchen neatly chewed and swallowed a morsel of her own chicken.

"Ralph told me about your loneliness," she said. "And your unemployment. How mortifying."

Elizabeth began to cough and couldn't stop. Her unemployment was nothing compared to the humiliation she'd feel if she died from pepper inhalation. She guzzled the Perrier, but the bubbles made her cough more. She concentrated on breathing and, wiping her eyes, refused to entertain the image of Ralph telling Gretchen she was lonely. What kind of game was he playing?

"Are you all right? I didn't mean to offend."

"Too much pepper," Elizabeth wheezed.

"I'm not against accompanying you to St. Paschal's if you're afraid to go alone. One does need outlets beyond one's home and job, especially in a case like yours where one has neither a home nor a job."

Inner debate raged as she twisted the napkin in her lap. Assent to Gretchen's caricature of her as a lonely fearful vagrant in need of outlets? Or abandon her May project? Vengeance on Pat required her assent.

"Speed dating does provide a wonderful opportunity to apply Tool Three," she managed, "and I'd very much appreciate your coming with me."

The waitress passed by and Elizabeth grabbed her arm. Meekness only took a girl so far.

"Do you have chocolate cake?" she asked.

"Death by Chocolate and it's homemade." She eyed Elizabeth's salad. "Can I bring you a piece when you finish?"

"Why don't you bring it now, with a glass of milk."

"I have all I need," Gretchen said, dismissing the waitress with a flick of her wrist.

The waitress, purveyor of chocolate, had distracted her. Was Gretchen in? She wouldn't grab the blonde's arm, but she needed a commitment from her almost as much as she needed the cake.

"Shall we meet at St. Paschal's?" Elizabeth asked. "Speed dating starts at seven."

"Make it ten to seven. I always find it advantageous to arrive ten minutes before an appointment or event."

The waitress spared her commenting on Gretchen's unusual philosophy of time. A tall glass of milk and a healthy slice of cake replaced the inedible salad. Elizabeth dove at the chocolate and her fork barely missed the server's hand.

Gretchen was in, her May project survived. Now all she needed was three dates and a boyfriend.

CHAPTER 14

The Hunt

Gretchen's suggestion of ten to seven mobilized Elizabeth to arrive in plenty of time, only ten minutes past the hour. She immediately located the tallest, fairest woman in the room: like Scarlett O'Hara in the picnic scene, Gretchen was surrounded by men. Unlike Scarlett, she refused to flirt but stood with arms folded across her chest, vexation creasing her flawless brow.

Half a dozen men formed the closest ring around Gretchen while another dozen hovered nearby, waiting their turn. The rest of the men hadn't seen her yet and mingled with the dozens of short brunette women who littered the place. Apparently her type grew on trees.

The belle of the ball approached, shedding men like last year's shoes.

"Y'all look lovely, sugah," Elizabeth teased.

"Pardon me?"

"I see you met a few people already."

"I thought this started at seven."

"More or less." Did Gretchen get out much? "These events never start exactly on time."

A raucous clanging burst from the front of the room where a red-head in a purple dress energetically shook a bell with one hand and clutched a microphone in the other.

The clanging ceased as suddenly as it had begun, replaced by a strident voice. Microphone touching her lips, the emcee introduced herself as Andrea and rattled off instructions with the air of a drill sergeant.

Attentive and obedient, the singles powered off cell phones and moved away from tables and chairs toward the walls.

"Women, you'll travel from table to table while the men stay seated. You'll face a series of prospective dates one-on-one throughout the evening, but when the bell rings, it's time to move on. Use the pencils and scrap paper to trade contact info if you want to meet again."

Elizabeth felt fingernails dig into her elbow.

"Ouch!"

"Excuse me." Gretchen let go. "Are you ready to leave?"

"But we haven't started speed dating." Elizabeth rubbed her arm. "Is something wrong?"

"I've had a long week and I don't see anyone I want to date."

Gretchen did look paler than usual. Her burgundy lipstick set off her creamy skin, but was possibly a shade too dark. Or perhaps unintentionally fascinating a roomful of men tired a girl out.

"Why don't you give this a chance? We won't really be dating, just talking to each guy for a few minutes."

Gretchen inclined her head slightly.

"Okay, then," Elizabeth said. "We'll meet outside when it's over."

The red-head shrilled on.

"The gentlemen in sport coats with red boutonnieres will help you. Any of you girls get lost, they'll guide you to the next table and your next man. Let's give a big hand to our St. Paschal's ushers!"

Elizabeth clapped heartily. She hadn't been looking forward to her tete-a-tetes with the older men. Ushers she could use.

"I think that's everything, so good luck and have fun!"

She raised the bell high, and Elizabeth covered her ears. By the time the clanging stopped, the miracle of speed dating had begun.

Elizabeth found herself seated, the back of Gretchen's blonde head in sight. Opposite Gretchen a boy who looked about eighteen tapped a nervous rhythm on the table. Poor kid, facing the Ice Princess first thing.

"My name's Alex."

Right. She had her own date to attend to.

"I'm Elizabeth," she said to the large man before her.

"Do you go by Elizabeth, or a nickname? I once knew a girl named Beth. Or should I call you Liza? Like Liza Minnelli? You don't look like her, though. She has that really short black hair, and yours is more brown. Some people call me Al but that drives me crazy, so maybe I'll call you Elizabeth. Unless you'd rather go by Queen Elizabeth." He grinned, his wide mouth reaching almost to his ears. "Nah, I'm joking. I have a great sense of humor. You'll have to watch out for that. Maybe you'll tell me what your nickname is if you hear my middle name. It's Shane. I know that's unusual and believe it or not there's no connection to the John Wayne movie, it's not a cowboy name at all, it's a family name. My father's mother's maiden name was Shane and that's how I got it. My older brother's name is David but everyone calls him Dave, except I call him David Steven. Not that Steven's his middle name, it's his confirmation name. That's the thing. We all have middle names that are really family names, so his middle name is Bart, not short for Bartholomew, but after the Wisconsin Barts. I come after David and then comes Grace whose middle name is . . ."

She'd spend the rest of her life on a metal folding chair, kind of like St. Simon Stylites, only closer to the ground. Alex would keep talking, the ushers would bring warm milk and a pillow, and in the morning she'd wake to the sound of his familiar voice.

A mellow ringing broke through the fog of words. She said good-bye to Alex Shane and an usher whisked her to a new chair.

"Ted. Nice to meet you. And you are?"

It took her a moment to remember.

"Elizabeth?" And of course her middle name, he'd want to know that. "Elizabeth Therese Benning."

Proving how different two men could be, Ted didn't tell her his middle name. Or anything else.

Her turn to break the ice.

"I've never been to one of these, have you?" she asked.

"No, pro-life singles isn't my usual thing, but it sounded like fun. Saw it in the paper."

"The bulletin?"

"Not a bulletin board, the Santa Susanna Weekly. Funny thing is I'm not really pro-life, not that I ever thought about it much. And I'm not technically single, but it sounded like fun."

She had to ask.

"What do you mean not 'technically' single?"

"Well my girlfriend saw it in the paper first, and she's always sayin' I never take her anywhere, so when she told me it was free I said yeah that sounds like fun, and here we are."

He pointed to a table behind Elizabeth. "She's the one in the pink sweater." He waved, but Elizabeth didn't turn around. What would she and pink-sweater's boyfriend talk about for the rest of their lives?

Eventually the bell released her, but as the evening inched along she wondered exactly how long she was spending with each speed date—the name itself had to be hyperbolic. With Alex and Ted, she'd guessed about an hour each. Later with Robert, a forty-something IT guy, and John, a student at the community college, she realized her time at each table was an eternity, though the puzzle of an eternity following hard on the heels of an eternity mystified her. With Bill, a strong silent type, and his brother Ed in whom still waters possibly ran deep, time became fluid and inestimable.

Finally she sat opposite a huge wall clock. Exhausted by her fruitless attempts to engage and be engaged, she ignored the man seated across from her and watched the second hand tick around and around and around the clock. The bell's clanging startled her.

Three minutes? That couldn't be right.

At the next table she invited José to watch the clock with her. He was facing it, and she had to turn her chair away from him to see the second hand make its way around, but sure enough, again it circled only three times and the bell rang.

The folding metal chairs became more uncomfortable with each new seating, the hall was stuffy, and her head ached. She longed to meet a man who didn't talk endlessly yet wasn't silent as a stone, and it would be nice if he were actually, not merely technically, single. Were her standards too high?

The red-head announced the last round of the evening.

"So make it happen, now or never folks!"

As if she could make Mr. Wonderful appear. She smiled wearily at the usher who escorted her. She eased into the folding chair across from her final non-date, a handsome dark haired man who looked like a movie star.

"I'm Mark O'Reilly, and forgive me if I yawn." His smile revealed teeth like the ones on those whitening strips commercials. "I promise it's not you. This has been a long night."

She laughed for the first time in what felt like years.

"At least I'm not alone, then," she said.

"If only!"

She laughed again. "I'm Elizabeth Benning, and I love Jane Austen. That's all I remember about myself."

His gorgeous smile widened enough to bring out dimples.

"I've been told I look like Colin Firth. Will that help my cause with Elizabeth Bennet?"

"Benning," she said, and blushed. He did look like Colin's Darcy.

"So what brings you here? On a man hunt?"

"I could ask you the same." She wasn't about to admit the whole truth, though he'd summed it up neatly. "What brings you here?"

"Believe it or not, my grandfather."

"Is he one of the ushers?"

"Way older, but he says it's time I meet a girl and settle down, so he suggested I come tonight."

"You're a very good and obedient grandson."

"He's a very generous grandfather, and I like to make people happy." He pushed the small box of paper toward her. "So have you given out a lot of slips, Miss Benning? Tell me what kind of competition I'm up against."

She giggled. "None here."

"Excellent." He held out a pencil. "May I have this dance?"

She wrote down her name, number, and email. Nothing ventured, nothing gained.

The bell rang. So now she knew. Three minutes was a charming length of time, a little short perhaps, but otherwise delightful.

They stood, and he was just a few inches taller than she was. A shortish Darcy; perfect.

"Call you tomorrow then," he said.

She gave him her sweetest smile and left to find Gretchen. A sorry trade, but he could hardly call until she walked away.

CHAPTER 15

Paradise Lost

Elizabeth hadn't seen Gretchen since their first seating; they must have been in different sets. Hopefully the belle of the ball had met someone like Mark, and the four of them could double date.

Outside, one look at Gretchen's face told her all was not well. The burgundy lips were set in an unfriendly line, the shapely eyebrows lowered into a scowl.

"Do you know where I can find a garbage can?"

"Over there by the bike rack."

Gretchen threw a handful of something into the trash, her face a study in distaste. A moment for tact.

"Did you meet anyone?" Elizabeth asked. Not as subtle as she'd intended, but the direct approach had its advantages too.

"I met twenty men. I think we all did. Three minute intervals beginning at seven-twenty, ending at eight-twenty. Sixty minutes divided by three is twenty."

"Can't argue with that. Twenty men, then. Any of them hand you their info?"

"Twenty."

"Yes, I got that, we all met twenty men. I'll tell you right off, nineteen of mine were nothing to write home about. But I did meet one nice guy." One really, really nice guy. "So did you meet anyone who wanted your contact info?"

"If you're not listening, Elizabeth, I don't know why I'm talking to you. Twenty men asked me for my phone number and gave me theirs."

"Wow! Twenty for twenty, that's amazing." Apparently three minutes wasn't long enough for a man to notice he was sitting across from a human ice sculpture. "I guess you had a good night then."

"Not particularly."

A flash of insight and her headache was back.

"Gretchen, what did you throw away?"

"Those ridiculous papers. I'm not going to call a man."

"But they'll call you, right? You said they asked for your number too."

"I certainly didn't give my number to total strangers."

"Didn't three whole minutes make any of them into friends? Acquaintances at least?"

"There was one man who seemed different than the others."

"Terrific. Is he still here?"

She'd chase him down; he'd be thrilled to date a goddess. All she had to do then was kidnap Gretchen and explain away the duct tape over her lovely mouth.

"He told me about his possible vocation to the priesthood and I told him about my time with Mother Teresa."

"Oh."

"He's over there."

Gretchen nodded toward a white convertible in the parking lot. Someone was sitting in the passenger seat, and Mark was getting in. Her Mark. He saw them and waved.

"His name is O'Reilly and I wish him well. I'm going home now." Gretchen turned on her skinny black heels and strode off into the parking lot. At least she wasn't heading toward Mark, the good looking future priest.

So that was that. Her Mark was equally Gretchen's Mark, none of them had a date, one of them might be a priest, and if Pat ever found out he'd never stop laughing. He wouldn't find out; it was none of his business, and there were plenty of options.

She could fish Gretchen's slips out of the garbage can and cold call for the two of them. Better yet, she could climb into the garbage can and stay there for the rest of the month.

She turned on her cell phone. Three missed calls. She went to voicemail.

"Hey, this is Em. Just wondering how speed dating went, but maybe you're still there. Call me when you're done."

A beep and the next message.

"Liz, we're out but we should be home by nine. Jane wants you to stop by after the dating game and tell us how it went. Ralph's watching the kids, and if you haven't found Prince Charming yet, he might still be available."

She eyed the trash can. If she tossed Pat's voicemail in, she'd have to get a new phone. Not worth it.

A beep and his voice again.

"Hey, I forgot to congratulate you. Ralph says Gretchen went tonight. Don't forget, three more dates for both of you or your paradise project is over."

She stood near the empty parking lot, empty but for her car. Time to go home. She'd survived speed dating, and as for the three dates, if nothing else turned up, Mark "almost-a-seminarian" O'Reilly could alternate taking her and Gretchen to Mass. It was the least he could do after mimicking Darcy to her Elizabeth.

CHAPTER 16

Paradise Regained

"I still don't get it. Did he decide not to be a priest? And then how'd you steal him from Gretchen?"

Elizabeth, feet curled under her on Jane's sofa, took a sip of hot chocolate. From the boys' room she could hear the Oompa Loompas, their deep voices singing to the remaining children that they could have expected such an end for Augustus Gloop.

Bringing her portable DVD player had been an inspiration. Her nephews were glued to the small screen and she and Emily could finally catch up.

"You gotta love those little orange men," she said.

Emily sat Indian style at the other end of the couch, holding a cup of tea.

"That's another thing. I've been blabbing on about wedding plans, and I forgot to ask how you got away with *Charlie and the Chocolate Factory.* I thought Pat insisted they read the classics before watching them."

"Mark read it aloud to the boys when we were here last Saturday."

"The whole book?"

She smiled. "The whole book."

"And he alternated chapters with Gretchen and you called it a date? C'mon, the suspense is killing me."

"I think I'll let you die. You've been a terrible friend, and I don't want to tell you."

"Of course you do! It's not my fault we've been playing phone tag. It's the wedding, and I'm here now, so spill."

Elizabeth's smile became a grin.

"Where should I start?"

"Last I heard, Gretchen stole your seminarian and your paradise project bit the dust. Obviously I missed some-thing—you've been smiling like the Cheshire Cat all night. I want details."

"It's not that complicated, I just misunderstood Gretchen."

"She's actually a warm loving person and that's why I'm expendable?"

Elizabeth snorted. "Not quite. That night when she pointed at Mark's car and I thought she was pointing at Mark, she wasn't. Mark's cousin Mike was riding shotgun, and he's the future priest."

"What the heck was he doing speed dating?"

"Mark called the next morning and cleared it all up. Mike went with him to make a donation to the pro-life group and planned to spend the evening in the chapel, but they were short one guy and snagged him. They told him it would be an act of charity to speed date so they'd have an even number of men and women."

"And he sacrificed his night of prayer to flirt?"

"Not at all. Apparently he told each woman straight off he wanted to be a priest. Gretchen was the only one who didn't look like she wanted to slap him. Since she didn't want to be there either, her reaction was to warm up."

"And now she's your warm fuzzy new best friend."

"More like Mike's new best friend. He wanted to talk to her again because she told him the Missionaries of Charity have a branch for priests."

"So they've kept in touch?"

"Better. The four of us have gone out together three times now."

"So they're dating." Emily set her mug on the floor. "That's gotta be wrong, taking a man away from the priesthood so you can beat Pat. How do you sleep at night?"

Elizabeth laughed. "They talk about spiritual stuff. It's nothing like dating, really, but it doesn't matter. It looks like dating and that's all Pat needs to know." She pulled a package of cookies out from behind a cushion. "I brought these to celebrate. I've finally beaten the weasel at his own game."

"But you've only won May. You have the rest of the year left."

"Yeah, but that's in the bag. When you meet Mark, you'll understand."

She held out a cookie and Emily took it reluctantly.

"Just because I'm eating your cookie doesn't mean I'm giving up on you and Ralph."

"Sorry but Mark's definitely the one. He's handsome, charming, great with the boys. He's perfect."

"That shouldn't be a compliment."

"You have a problem with perfect?"

"I distinctly remember you complaining Ralph was too perfect. Now Mark's perfect, but in his case you don't mind."

"No one ever said love had to be logical. I guess Mark's a different kind of perfect. Perfect for me."

"Oh brother."

"Anyway, Ralph's not part of the picture anymore. I mean he's part of your picture, and I'm fine standing up with him at the wedding, but I hope you don't mind if Mark's my real date."

"I'll try to tolerate him if he makes you happy. But when things don't work out, Ralph can fill in. That's all I'm saying."

The door opened, and Pat and Jane walked in. A troop of boys stormed in from the bedroom and the family circle was complete.

"It was better than the book!" yelled Dominic.

"No way, the book was awesome," Anthony said.

"I like Mark," Jude said. "He gave us candy."

Luke tugged on Jane's maternity blouse.

"Matthew fell asleep, Mommy, can we watch it again tomorrow?"

Pat spoke over the boys. "What's new, Emily?"

"Lizzy's been telling me about Mark, but I'm not giving up on Ralph."

"Good girl. We've gotta protect her from interlopers." He scooped up Luke. "Jane says the new guy has dark hair. I'm thinking I'll ask Ralph to color his if that's the problem."

Elizabeth hugged Jude and Dominic close, like human shields.

"His name is Mark, and he isn't new. We've been dating almost a month. Jane and the boys met him last Saturday when you were at graduation and everyone likes him. And not just because he's good looking."

"Of course not. I've heard he gives out candy too."

"You hate losing."

"Who said I'm losing? Jane told me you've been on a date or two, but I haven't heard any particulars."

"Then you weren't listening," Jane said.

"Don't worry Jane, I've got it covered." She smiled smugly at Pat. "Happy to oblige." And she was. Just thinking of Mark made her happy.

"We went to dinner and a movie the night after speed dating, and Gretchen came with Mark's cousin Mike. The four of us went on a picnic last Friday, and Sunday we drove to L.A. to hear a chamber group play Mozart. That covers the three dates you specified, and if you want more I can tell you Mike is going running with Gretchen in the morning, and Mark has invited me to meet his family for dinner tomorrow night."

She held her chin high like Gretchen always did. Pat whistled through his teeth.

"Impressive. I didn't think you could pull it off, but you've hunted down an innocent man and even provided a victim for Gretchen."

"Don't listen to him. Mark's a lucky guy." Jane gave her a kiss on the cheek and rounded up the boys. She smiled at Emily. "You two stay as long as you like, but I'm going to bed."

Elizabeth leaned down to kiss Jude and Dominic, then did the chin thing at Pat.

The room seemed suddenly quiet, bereft of Jane and the boys. Emily sat on the couch, not exactly moral support with her delusions of Ralph.

"Aren't you going to congratulate me, Pat?"

"I'll admit I'm impressed, but it's only May and you've got to keep this dream alive until January. Many moons to go and you've never made it yet."

"Things are different this year. I'm different, now that I've met Mark." She joined Emily on the couch and helped herself to a cookie.

"We'll see," Pat said. "Dinner with his folks tomorrow night. I can't help but wonder—what if he still lives at home, all of them crammed in a two bedroom apartment on the other side of the tracks and he plans to install his bride right there with Ma and Pa and Grandma and Grandpa? What if you can't stand his family? What if they can't stand you?"

"How could they not like Lizzy?" Emily put a protective arm around her.

"I hate to say it, but one false move and they might find out what she's really like."

Jude was back.

"Daddy, Anthony's reading in bed and me and Luke want a story."

"I'll be right there, scout." Pat tousled his hair and moved him to the door.

"You girls are welcome to stay and finish your cookies." He followed Jude into the hallway, then turned back. "I almost forgot to ask. Does Mark know he's a guinea pig in your happiness project, Liz?"

"He's my Prince Charming, and that's entirely different."

"Well if he turns out to be a frog before the end of the month, I'll choose the next prince, and I've been thinking."

"Yes?"

"Ralph seems kind of lonely these days."

She restrained herself from throwing the bag of cookies at the back of his disappearing head. Proof right there Mark was transforming her into a princess.

CHAPTER 17

At Home with Prince Charming

The evening started perfectly.

At the sound of his knock, Elizabeth opened the cottage door to find Mark holding three dozen lavender roses. They came from the family gardens, he explained, and smelled like heaven on a stem.

He drove with the Sebring's top down, the wind caressing her face, and on the scenic route to his parents' house Mark told her his family couldn't wait to meet her. She was beaming; she couldn't help it, he was so sweet.

His grandparents would be at dinner, he said, and they looked forward to seeing her again.

Again?

They'd met at the art exhibit in February, Mark explained. Perhaps she remembered them—his Grandfather O'Reilly, rather a portly gentleman, and Grandma Mabel like a tiny bird.

She clapped in delight.

Once they'd realized his girl was the girl who'd won the statue, his grandparents couldn't stop talking about her spectacular icon, he said.

She thrilled at his calling her "his girl" but mention of the icon calmed her down. She clasped her hands in her lap, no longer in a clapping mood. The statue fiasco was months behind her, but Ralph's legacy haunted her. Would she never be free of him?

Silence was a woman's glory, they said, and she'd neglected it far too long. Mark kept talking. He was a good talker; maybe he wouldn't notice for a year or two that she was mute, and by then no one would remember the icon.

They entered the upscale development surrounding the country club and Mark pulled into what appeared to be Hearst Castle.

A butler opened the door, led them to the library and announced them like in a Jane Austen novel. Dr. O'Reilly and Mabel stood near the fireplace, while a couple she guessed to be Mark's parents sat in Queen Anne chairs facing each other.

"My dear," piped Mabel, "we couldn't be happier. We've prayed I don't know how many novenas for Mark to find the right girl, and it's you!" She hopped with excitement, like Grandpa Joe when he jumped out of bed to dance about the room after Charlie found the golden ticket. "To think it's you, the very girl who wrote the icon and won the statue!"

Mabel looked to her husband as if for corroboration.

Dr. O'Reilly rested one enormous hand on Mark's shoulder. "Can't tell you how it makes me feel after all this time. Our congratulations, son. I plan to call Hayes first thing

Monday morning regarding the transfer of funds. I've been waiting a long time for this."

He slapped his grandson on the back and burst into a fit of coughing. Mark's parents rose from their chairs.

"Father, breathe deeply," Mr. O'Reilly said, and then, "Hello, Elizabeth, welcome to our humble home." He shook her hand.

"Yes, welcome." Mrs. O'Reilly patted her cheek. "Now that we're all up, why don't we make our way to the dining room."

She loved Mrs. O'Reilly already. She'd forgotten lunch, and her stomach's rumblings would soon be audible. Mark took her hand and, with the grace of Colin's Darcy, placed it in the crook of his arm, leading her last in the procession of O'Reillys. Gallant, that's what he was.

Or determined to keep her from taking a breather on one of the inviting benches that lined the extensive hallways they traversed. She clung to his arm; the endless stairs almost did her in. No wonder his parents had stayed in their chairs when she entered; they'd been storing up strength for the journey.

Her new strappy sandals chafed painfully. Should she carry them, or would taking them off leave her stranded in a strange land?

Just when she couldn't take another blistering step, the party came to a standstill on the threshold of a dining room the size of her parents'. Not the size of their dining room, the size of their house.

Mark guided her to a Chippendale chair and deposited himself in the chair beside her. Dr. O'Reilly and Mabel sat across from them, while Mr. and Mrs. O'Reilly sat at the head and foot of the table, about a half mile away in either direction.

Given the grand scale of life here at the castle, she waited for liveried servants to bring the first of seventeen courses.

She would do justice to them all, if only she could keep from spilling on the exquisite carpet covering the marble floor beneath the table and chairs. How much did a Persian rug the size of a football field cost?

"Priceless," Mark whispered as if reading her mind. "Like your icon, from what I hear. I can't wait to see it."

She did her best to smile, but her lips trembled. Tremulous, that's what she was, a mix of humbled and murderous. She'd kill Ralph when she saw him. He was ruining her dinner and it hadn't even been served.

"Father, would you lead us in prayer?" Mrs. O'Reilly called down the length of the table.

"Certainly, Mother," Father called back.

He belted out grace, concluding, "God bless the cook. We're in for a treat tonight."

At the fifty yard line, Elizabeth squinted in her effort to see more clearly. He wasn't actually sitting in a goal post, those were pillars on either side of him.

"Mother gave Gaston the evening off because his sister Rochelle is visiting from France, and I, for one, am looking forward to the special meal my own dear bride has prepared for us. Mark, would you accompany your mother to the buffet and serve our first course?"

"Back soon," Mark whispered.

He receded into the distance, reappearing at the massive buffet that dominated the wall behind Dr. O'Reilly and Mabel. He was in time to stop his mother from picking up a large soup tureen that probably came from the Ming dynasty.

"Mother, let me. Why don't you hand around the bowls and spoons?"

The table was empty of china, crystal, silver, and linen. Just cherry wood as far as the eye could see, polished until it shone. Mrs. O'Reilly set bowls and spoons before Dr. O'Reilly and

Mabel, in front of Mr. O'Reilly in the back forty, and finally approached Elizabeth with—paper napkins, Chinette, and plasticware?

Across from her, Mabel dipped a plastic spoon into her cardboard bowl, raised it to her lips, and sipped delicately. The dish washers must have the night off too.

Mark set the Ming tureen directly on the table between their disposable bowls. She cringed for the wood; her family always used trivets, but families did things differently. Maybe the O'Reillys replaced the table between meals.

Mark ladled green liquid into her bowl and her stomach stopped grumbling to turn its face to the wall. She'd have to make the best of it; she could hardly blame him for the menu.

He whipped the paper napkin to his lap and raised his plastic spoon.

"Bon appétit! Split pea's my favorite, so I asked Mother to make it tonight. Dig in, you'll love it."

She picked up her spoon and smiled weakly at Mark.

"I never told you about our family business, did I?" he said, smiling back.

"I don't think so."

"Father took over from Grandfather, and my oldest brother Mick will take over from Father. Can you guess what we make?"

He looked meaningfully at her soup bowl.

She blew on her spoon and took a hesitant sip. Tepid.

"Are you pea farmers?" she asked with a sinking feeling. He was everything she wanted in a man, but a lifetime of peas?

He laughed quietly as if she'd been joking. "That's cute, but not even close." He scooped up a spoonful of soup. "We're in the picnic supply industry. You know: paper products, plastic products, they're not just for picnics anymore. That's

Father's slogan, though Grandfather did in fact start making them just for picnic supplies."

She adjusted her image of their life together. No peas, but the two of them eating every meal with plastic utensils. She'd never known how very attached she was to unbreakable forks.

Mark lifted spoon to mouth, his profile losing none of its manliness as he sipped and swallowed. She could deal with paper and plastic; she'd go out to lunch with Emily every day to places that used real forks. Still, she might as well know the worst.

"Do you use them at every meal?"

"Grandfather always said what's good enough for the common people is good enough for the O'Reillys, though Mick plans to reverse that in our next ad campaign. You know, what's good enough for the O'Reillys is good enough for the common people. We'll use photos of the family at dinner, maybe film a commercial in here."

She glanced up to the baroque molding. No cameras visible and she hadn't spilled anything so far. Her gaze fell on Dr. O'Reilly, souping it up across from her.

"But isn't your grandfather a doctor?"

"Ph.D in chemistry, specialized in plastics at Notre Dame, class of '41. Gave them a lot of money back in the day, once he'd struck gold, so to speak, but Grandma won't let him give any more. Says they're not Catholic, so he's put his overflow into a grandkid's fund."

"What a generous thing to do. Is that how you got your convertible?"

"Oh, no, I bought that with my own money. Grandfather has fifty-one grandchildren. Mike's in the running too."

"He and Gretchen went running this morning. Do you run?"

Mark covered her hand with his. "Not that kind of running, though it is a race of sorts. A race for the overflow."

"So what's an overflow? You've said it twice but you'll have to say more before I get it."

"No, you'll have to say something before you get it." His eyes crinkled up when he grinned. "But only one word."

"Mark," Mr. O'Reilly called, "please help your mother with the next course if you'd be so kind."

"Certainly, Father."

Mark winked at her as he picked up the soup tureen. Down the acreage of the dining room he went and back to the buffet.

Mrs. O'Reilly distributed the paper plates and plastic forks and knives. Mark made the rounds after her with a large platter.

As he served his grandfather, Dr. O'Reilly boomed out, "Knew you could do it, boy. Tremendous girl. Have her tell you about the icon."

She racked her memory for undetectable poisons. There had to be one. Not arsenic, the old ladies in the movie got caught by Cary Grant, though burying Pat and Ralph in the backyard—or was it in the cellar?—had its own charming appeal.

Mark returned to her. Time to talk about anything but icons.

"I'd love to hear about your Grandfather's race. He and Mabel are darling. Is she in on this too?"

"No question. They're inseparable, and she's as excited as he is. Would you like two pieces, or one?"

With a pair of plastic tongs he lifted from the platter a dripping piece of—it looked like a chicken leg, but it had an odor. She recoiled.

"Mother's own recipe, chicken with peanut butter sauce. You'll love it, especially over the sweet potato fries." He gestured at a pile of orange sticks poking out from the lumpy brown sauce.

Was Pat behind this? Or had Ralph told Gretchen to tell Mike to tell Mark she loved peanut butter? It had to be one of them. Mrs. O'Reilly couldn't possibly have come up with this unprovoked.

Mark waited, chicken aloft. Well she could wait too. She could wait for dessert. Better yet she could feign illness, excuse herself, and if the castle had cell phone reception she'd order a pizza.

He placed the chicken leg on her paper plate and lifted another from the platter.

"Feel free to take two. I like a girl with a full figure."

She waved it away. "Would you excuse me for a moment? I have to use the powder room."

"I'll take you there, we can use the elevator."

The elevator. Of course. Nothing more annoying than walking to the powder room.

From the back of her chair she retrieved her sequined black purse. Inside, a chocolate protein bar and sugarless gum nestled among the tissues and lipstick. If only she could make it to the bathroom, she could eat her emergency supplies in private.

"We'll be right back," Mark shouted to the others. "Elizabeth has to use the powder room."

He offered his hand and she accepted gratefully, light-headed now that they were moving.

Out in the hall, Mark squeezed her hand. "I knew my family would love you. Grandfather wants me to ask about your icon."

They stopped before an upholstered door.

"The Bayeux Tapestry," Mark said.

He couldn't mean the original. Could he?

"Hold on a sec. Gabriel downstairs has to release the elevator on his end." Mark let go of her hand and punched a number into the keypad on the wall.

"Yes?"

"Gabe, release the elevator, we're on the fourth floor and need to come down. Elizabeth wants to use the powder room."

"Yes, sir."

Wooden doors, all closed, dotted the hallway. "Isn't there a powder room up here?"

"Ladies' lounge around the corner, but you specifically asked for the powder room. That's on the second floor, near the nursery." He recaptured her hand. "Gives us a few minutes alone."

She inclined her head closer to the tapestry, listening. "Is that music?"

"The Mozart Divertimento we heard last weekend. I had Gabe change the CD for you."

She laughed. "I suppose Gabe needs something to keep him busy."

The door opened and they stepped in.

"Now tell me about the famous icon," he said.

She wasn't inviting Ralph and his icon into the elevator with them. "You haven't explained what kind of race your Grandfather's hosting."

The door closed. No tapestry on this side, but its shiny steel surface reflected color from the ceiling. She tilted her head back and gazed at God's hand touching Adam's.

"Wow."

"You can see why Grandma wants Grandfather to get rid of the overflow. She says Mother might like to do some decorating herself. The four of them live here, and Grandma Mabel's very sensitive to my mother's position as the daughter-in-law. As I'm sure she and mother will be to my bride."

So Pat was right about them all living together. Sort of right. The castle was plenty big, but the elevator seemed too small.

"I'm awfully hungry." She freed her hand and retrieved the protein bar from her purse. "Do you mind if I have a snack?"

"I'd love it. I love your hearty appetite."

He was surrounded by birdlike women who lived on pea soup and inedible chicken. She'd let it slide.

"So about your Grandfather and the race?" She popped a third of the bar into her mouth.

"He's a hoot." Mark leaned against the elevator wall. "Decided to give the money to his grandkids but then realized if he divided his overflow between us, we'd each get less than ten. Said that made him feel cheap."

Ten thousand to each grandchild would have been more than generous, but a man living in this kind of opulence wouldn't think so. What a sweetheart Dr. O'Reilly was to worry about it.

"So Grandfather decided to leave the entire overflow, the money he doesn't need, to just one grandchild, but how to choose between us? That's where the race comes in. He got the idea from a P.G. Wodehouse novel."

"I love P.G. Wodehouse."

"He and his accountant worked it out so he'd leave the overflow to the grandchild—male or female, Grandma insisted the girls have a chance—who married first."

"That is like something out of Wodehouse." Mark was a couple of years older than she was, he must have a whole slew of married cousins by now. "So who got the money?"

"We've had a few engagements, but they broke off before any weddings took place." He pushed himself away from the wall. "That's what makes tonight so special, Elizabeth. My dove won't fly the coop before the big day arrives and then I'll be able to offer her more than my heart. I'll be able to offer her a hundred and seventy million dollars."

CHAPTER 18

Proposal

The human mind is a marvelous thing, capable, unlike the human body, of being in more than one place at one time. Elizabeth had experienced this wonder on previous occasions and now, fortified by a dose of chocolate protein, her mind was up to its old tricks, simultaneously operating on four distinct levels.

On the most superficial level she was painfully aware of being in a frescoed elevator with the man she'd so recently fancied herself in love with and who was about to propose. One level down she was curious why they were still in the elevator, which didn't seem to be moving. Deeper still, the mathematical part of her brain announced that one hundred and seventy million dollars was an exorbitant amount of money. And finally, in the depths of her imagination she was picturing your average dove, which has the shape of a bowling pin, and concluding that if Mark made one more crack about her weight, she'd deck him.

Yet while the mind can encompass many thoughts at once—especially the female mind, always at its sharpest when the male animal has indicated an inclination for monogamous lifelong commitment—the mouth can utter only one word at a time. No matter the exigencies of the situation, no matter how quickly even the female mouth pours forth its words, they still only and always proceed singly into the surrounding atmosphere. In view of this fact, Elizabeth chose her words carefully. Marshalling her not inestimable forces of intellect, she spoke in a calm clear voice.

"Excuse me, Mark, but is the elevator moving? I could really use to get to the powder room. Or the ladies' lounge. Or just back into a hallway."

"Ah, yes, right. I haven't pushed the button."

He pushed the button and as the elevator began its descent he dropped to one knee. She wanted to blame the lurch of the elevator, but obviously the elevator in the Kingdom of Picnic Suppliers did not lurch. Which meant that unless Mark was searching for a stray contact lens, he was about to propose.

Two hours ago this image would have thrilled her. Fifteen minutes ago her heart would have raced. But now another race was on, and her knowledge of it had deadened the romance of an O'Reilly proposal.

"Elizabeth, you can hardly be surprised at my desire to obtain you for my wife."

Mark reached for her hand, and she stepped back to avoid his grasping touch. The elevator didn't leave much room to maneuver, but she could step out of his reach and she did.

"We haven't known each other long, but I'm sure you could make me happy, and we haven't much time left. We're both getting older, and your biological clock is ticking down. . ."

Mark paused, having talked himself into a corner. He'd said they didn't have much time left, but he really meant she didn't.

What had happened to the man she'd spent the last month dreaming about? There was his chiseled jaw, his cleft chin, his aquiline nose, his dark wavy hair. Had she been so enamored of his good looks that she hadn't noticed what a flake he was? Or did her newfound awareness of his motives change everything? It certainly did.

She had all the time in the world; he was the one whose time was running out, at least in regard to his infelicitous proposal.

A shame to lose any sequins over him, but she couldn't help that. The cad deserved a good thwacking and she wouldn't fail him now. She gripped her purse firmly and aimed for his head and shoulders..

"That's it!" (Thwack.) "I've heard enough!" (Thwack.) "I won't let you say" (thwack) "another word to me." (Thwack.) "You don't want me." (Thwack.) "You want that stupid money." (Thwack.)

She stopped to catch her breath and massage her wrist, which was getting tired. Her arm and tongue at rest, her mind began working furiously. She ought to resume thwacking instead of thinking, but she couldn't help it. She wondered.

What was she doing in the sight of God and Adam beating on a man in an elevator to the strains of Mozart's Divertimento in D? Was Mark really at fault, or was he the victim? Hadn't she been the one determined to find a man, ready to accept his proposal within two weeks of meeting him?

She stared vaguely at her purse, behind which Mark knelt. He switched knees. He ought to ask his Grandfather to carpet the elevator; no telling how often he proposed to women in here.

He looked determined, as if the O'Reillys were a race of men who completed their proposals regardless of their reception. He held a black velvet box toward her and opened it. The track lighting glanced off the solitaire's facets and shot out innumerable pinpoints of glittery light. It was a diamond as big as a Ritz, the size of a large cracker.

The O'Reillys of the past may not have encountered the Bennings of their day, but if Mark insisted on pushing his luck, she'd push back. The ring interested her less than a cracker would have. She reached forward and snapped the box shut. As Mark opened his mouth to speak, she raised her handbag in warning. Like the box, his mouth snapped shut.

"Thank you," she said. "I'm not finished speaking."

"Could you be finished thwacking?"

"If you'll get up. And isn't it time to open the elevator door? I imagine we've reached our destination."

Mark stood and brushed off his pants at the knees. "Elizabeth, you're so clever. Which is why I must ask you the one question—"

She raised her purse and his proposal died on his lips.

"Mr. O'Reilly, either you press the black button that says 'Open door' or I press the red one that says 'Emergency.'"

She couldn't actually read the tiny letters on the red button, but what else could they say? Unless that button sent the elevator rocketing up and out through the roof, like in the Chocolate Factory.

The image transported her, not through the roof but to the night before, when she'd sat on the couch with Emily while her nephews in the next room watched Charlie's adventures. How sure she'd been, how boldly she'd told Pat that Mark was her Prince Charming. Only twenty-four hours later and she was standing under Michaelangelo's masterpiece with a man who only wanted to marry her for his money.

She was furious at him, disappointed, sad, worn out, and yet there was still room in her capacious soul for a healthy dose of curiosity. She'd shut up the box and Mark, she'd ordered him to open the door, but he stood there, his shifty eyes glancing from her to the door and back. What would he do?

She wasn't ready to forgive him, but he ought to apologize for treating her like a meal ticket. Or was that too much to ask of a man who'd just lost a hundred and seventy million dollars? He wouldn't be trading his Sebring in for a Porsche anytime soon and he probably blamed her. Fine, she didn't want him to apologize. She couldn't trust him even if he did.

He raised a finger as if he would say something more, but it was a ruse. He pressed the button to open the door.

They exited the elevator as if nothing had happened. And really, had anything happened? He'd shown his true colors. She'd thwacked him and lost a few sequins. That was about it.

They walked along without a word. She should speak, tell him, "No, Mark, I will not marry you," if only for the sake of resolution. *The Tools* said ending a relationship with a quick clean blow was key, but had he literally proposed, or merely hinted? Anyway, the thwacks qualified as quick clean blows and she had other things to worry about. Like how to get home.

Delighted though she'd be to escape his company, she appreciated his expert guidance through the labyrinth. Silently he led her through the hallways and down a long curved staircase to the front door where the butler waited. Mark told him to call the chauffeur and offered her a seat on a wooden bench beside a suit of armor.

Had the butler been standing at attention since he'd escorted them to the library eons ago? Did he sit on the bench when no one was looking? Didn't he find it anachronistic to text the chauffeur on a cell phone he'd pulled from his trouser pocket?

If she agreed to marry Mark, all her questions would be answered. She could live in the castle forever after and befriend the butler. She could be like Carole Lombard in *My Man Godfrey* or Katherine Hepburn in *Holiday* and ask him silly questions to her heart's content.

When the chauffeur appeared at the door and Mark stowed her safely in the back seat of the Rolls, she had the only answer she needed. She couldn't marry a man, no matter how handsome, who proposed only to get rich quick, and she certainly didn't want to live here for ever after. There was no happily in the case, and that was the end of the story, even if it meant Pat would have the last word.

CHAPTER 19

Out of the Elevator into the Canyon

Stereo blaring the Chieftains, Pat drove at the top of the speed limit. Jane navigated from the co-pilot's seat while Elizabeth rode in the back, captive, switching between the dinette and the couch, trading seats and playing cards with restless nephews. She ignored Pat's suggestion of Old Maid. Slap Jack was her game. The evil one-eyed Jack represented Pat; the blonde, Ralph; the deceptively handsome rogue (a frog disguised as a prince) was Mark. Slapping had never been quite so satisfying.

Indoor plumbing meant no stops for potty breaks; she simply escorted little boys one after another to the motorhome bathroom, Pat yelling over his shoulder, "Isn't this the life?"

The Stockholm Syndrome, that's what it was. Loathe as she'd been to accompany them to the Grand Canyon, annoyed as she tried to remain at Pat's resolution for her June happiness, she found herself relaxed and amused for the first time since the ill-fated excursion to the powder room.

Her three weeks post elevator trauma had been the unhappiest yet: anger at Mark keeping her barely afloat, anger at herself threatening to sink her. Granted he was charming, good-looking, and good-natured about wooing her in style, but he had the depth of Saran Wrap. She should have seen through him from the beginning, passed him by for the talkative speed date with the fixation on middle names, but wishful thinking had blinded her. He looked like a short Darcy and that was all the encouragement the madman in the house, her overactive imagination, had needed.

In the limo on the way home from Hearst Castle she'd resolved to spend the rest of her days in seclusion, hiding from fortune hunters and blondes. The O'Reilly millions having pulverized her hopes for Prince Charming, she now lived in dread of Pat fulfilling his threat. His contract for May rested safely in her dresser's bottom drawer, but only a frontal lobotomy would erase the blonde date from his memory.

Jane's well-stocked RV pantry and slapping at faux princes did much to restore her mood to pre-elevator levels, but all too soon the nine hour drive ended. Pat navigated the beast into Grand Canyon Camper Village.

"Look over there," he said turning in. "Imax theatre's right across the street. If the boys can't be managed at the Canyon, someone can take them to the movies."

Can't be managed? *Someone* can take them?

"I'm sure they'll be fine," Jane said. "We have Elizabeth to help."

Sweet Jane, affirmation personified.

"If she overcomes her fear of heights."

Dear Pat, vitiation of his wife's goodness.

"Nice try, but I'll make it. No problem."

She was practically half way through her paradise project, and she wasn't about to let it die over something as small as the Grand Canyon.

"Why don't you start by taking the kids to the playground while Jane and I register? You're free, boys."

In two seconds they were unbuckled and out the side door.

"Thanks for your help, Lizzy," Jane said. "I'll take Matthew."

"Good luck, Liz," Pat said. "We're counting on you not to lose the others before we get to the rim."

By the time she reached them, breathless, Anthony and Dominic had joined a game of tag. Luke was barreling down a huge yellow slide, Jude right behind him.

Parents and grandparents drifted around the periphery of the playground, chatting, sipping beers, checking cell phones. The couple next to her argued about the shuttle schedule to the Canyon, he asserting the earliest bus left at nine, she insisting service started well before sunrise. If only he were right. Who could face that drop in the dark?

Her stomach heaved at the thought. She couldn't fail now, she was as determined to stymie Pat as the woman next to her was determined to drag her husband out before dawn, but with the mile deep hole so close to her, vertigo disturbed her equilibrium.

She sank onto an unoccupied bouncy snail and put her head down. Deep breath, let it out slowly. Careful to keep her feet on the ground and the snail stationary, she raised her head and looked for the boys. Jane was as clever as she was good, dressing them in highly visible primary colors—there they were, Anthony and Dominic laughing as they chased their newfound friends. Luke and Jude remained at the slide, but now they came down together, and with another small boy wedged between them.

She smiled. That couple pushing the little girl in a baby swing must be the new boy's parents; the dad faced the slide, recording the scene with his smart phone.

Beyond the proud papa, Jane approached with a lanky blonde man. Elizabeth almost fell off the snail, but caught a large antenna in time to save herself. What was Ralph doing here?

Jane held Matthew by the hand. He stumbled and she leaned over to help him to his feet, giving a better view of the man behind them.

Elizabeth laughed in semi-hysterical relief. Of course it wasn't Ralph, just a random tall fair-haired man visiting the Grand Canyon. She needed to get a grip; the place was over-run with campers, any number bound to be blonde.

Jane and Matthew joined her, and Elizabeth got off her slug.

"You won't believe this, but I thought I saw Ralph with you and I nearly had a heart attack."

Jane helped Matthew board the snail. He looked adorable clinging to its neck; they were exactly the right size for each other. Which meant she must have looked . . . she'd rather not think about how she'd looked.

"Too bad it wasn't Ralph," Jane said. "Pat invited him, you know."

The vertigo returned and Elizabeth clutched a nearby giraffe. The girl on it looked at her reproachfully and she let go.

"Unfortunately," Jane said, "Ralph said he was going on retreat this week."

"Did you go along with him?"

"With Ralph? Of course not."

"With Pat. You couldn't have encouraged him. Tell me exactly what happened."

She needed to occupy her hands. Of course it wasn't Jane's fault and it would be wrong to shake her just because Pat wasn't here to strangle. She picked up a handful of bark.

"Nothing happened. Pat invited Ralph after basketball one Saturday—I think the week after you and Mark broke up. I heard him tell Ralph you were going through a rough patch but our trip here would change that. Ralph said he loved the Grand Canyon and Pat invited him to join us."

"And you were there. And you didn't interrupt and say I was fine but I wouldn't be if he showed up? Was that Pat's idea of a blonde date? A week in a place I don't want to be with the one person besides Mark I least want to be with?"

"Lizzy, relax. I told you he couldn't come. He said he always spends the third week in June with his monks in New York."

"And then what?"

"And then nothing, except Pat teased him he couldn't get Nellie all the way here anyhow."

She dropped the birch bark.

"Why didn't you tell me Ralph has a girlfriend? That's great! That changes everything. We could be friends, and everyone would act normal."

"You're not acting normal. You showered Matthew with dirt, and you're yelling."

"I'm sorry, but this is the best news I've had since the terrible night I found out Ralph was Joe's brother." She crouched beside Matthew to clear off the debris.

"Do you know how much it costs to hire a plane to skywrite? I bet that's common here with such a big wide sky. I guess 'Praise God Ralph's out of my hair and happiness is right around the corner,' might get pricey. Could I borrow some money?" She laughed, a glorious feeling of freedom caressing her like the pine-scented breeze.

"I think I'd better explain something," Jane said.

"If you think Ralph will come after all, I'm fine with that. I'd love to meet Nellie, and they could help with the boys when we're at the Canyon."

Jane laughed.

"I'm serious." Elizabeth stood, smiling. "The only thing I've been sure of since January is that Ralph and I are a bad combination, but I want everyone to be happy. I'm overjoyed he's found someone. Have you met her?"

Pat's voice carried across the playground.

"Hey, Beautiful! I need your help!"

He stood beyond the swings, beckoning.

"I think he means you," Elizabeth said.

"He wants me as co-pilot when he drives to our spot. We'll come get you and the boys once we've found it and parked."

"We'll be here." Elizabeth swung Matthew to the ground. "Now that I know about Ralph and Nellie I could use a bottle of champagne, but otherwise I'm good."

Jane took Matthew's hand and walked toward Pat.

"Lizzy," she flung over her shoulder, "Nellie is Ralph's Vanagon."

"His what?"

"His Volkswagen camper van."

Elizabeth stared after her. Nellie was his car?

She sat down hard in the birch bark and rested against the snail. She put her arm around its neck and the metal felt cool against her cheek. At least she had one friend.

CHAPTER 20

God's Grandeur

Elizabeth spent the afternoon looking. When she needed a break from looking she gazed, and when her eyes grew tired from gazing she opened the journal she held in her lap. Then she closed it without having written anything. She couldn't bear to miss a moment of this beauty.

Yesterday she'd turned thirty-three, and Jane baked a chocolate cake for her in the RV oven. Her birthday had always been her favorite day of the year, but looking out over the Canyon, orange and tan and gold in the late afternoon sun, yesterday faded. Miraculous how each new day here was more wonderful than the last.

Two red squirrels chased each other around a ponderosa pine a few feet away, like her thoughts and emotions had raced until her first sight of the Canyon. Her fears, like the squirrels, had been harmless, and from this distance they were even funny. The view from the top of a two story escalator made her ill, but to everyone's surprise, sauntering near the edge of a mile deep hole in the ground hadn't fazed her. She'd felt only awe and a desire never to leave.

Jane's lifelong ambition had been satisfied at one-thirty Tuesday afternoon when she looked into the chasm while gripping two of her boys' hands. Pat carried Matthew in a backpack, Elizabeth firmly grasped another two hands, they came, they saw, they conquered. Elizabeth especially had conquered—her presence at the Canyon meant another month's happiness ticked off her list. That this month's success inspired actual happiness to go with her resolution both startled and gratified her.

The Moores settled into campground life, the boys' sights set on the playground and the theatre. Jane's dream fulfilled, her remaining wish was to relax with a good book in a lounge chair. Pat pulled out the RV awning, set up the grill he'd brought, and greeted passers-by as if he were a professional camper. Auntie Beth, having completed her assignment, they left to her own devices and back to the Canyon she went. She had discovered paradise at last.

They'd come upon this secluded bench Tuesday, and she'd returned to it yesterday and today. As long as Jane could spare her, she'd spend the rest of the week here, alone. Six months of unwelcome blondes and the double-crossing Darcy look-alike had sated her taste for companionship.

From her jeans' pocket she pulled a bag of trail mix, her own private blend of chocolate chips, marshmallows, craisins, and a fistful of pecans for protein. She opened the Ziploc bag and poured its contents directly into her mouth. A male voice accosted her from behind.

"Gorgeous."

She jumped and her journal fell to the dirt. Ralph. Her happiness poofed like a mushroom cloud.

She shoved the baggie into her pocket and stared ahead, blind to all beauty. It wasn't Ralph. Ralph was in New York, but whoever had called her gorgeous was still there, breathing, she could hear him. She'd been so relaxed she'd forgotten her Feng Shui, but what was a girl to do? She couldn't sit with her back to the Canyon, yet the alternative was worse, her back to a heavy breathing stranger hitting on her in the middle of nowhere.

"It's incredibly gorgeous, isn't it?"

The blood that had rushed to her heart rushed up to her face. The stranger was complimenting the view, not her. She nodded. Did a slight nod mean anything when glimpsed from behind? She nodded harder. Yes, the view was certainly gorgeous. If he wasn't a moron he'd read her opinion of the scenery in the motion of her neck and her dismissal of him in her refusal to speak. Even from behind, her body language shouted, "Go away." She could hear it, and if he wasn't a complete idiot, he'd notice.

He was a complete idiot, not to mention a terrible Indian, crackling twigs as he stepped around the bench. She bent to pick up her journal, refusing to look at him, willing him to go away, whoever he was.

"You're a hard woman to find," he said. "Pat told me exactly where to look, but I had to park Nellie down the road and then I almost didn't see you hidden among the pines."

The voice sat beside her. She could no longer deny it was Ralph's voice, and it brought the rest of Ralph with it. Here. Into the heart of her peace like an atom bomb. Or rather—no need to be dramatic—like a water balloon. Filled with gravel.

She slid as far away from him as possible. It wasn't the end of the world, just the end of her exquisite happiness. She could feel her face set into a frown with the inevitability of drying concrete. She stared straight ahead at the vista he'd robbed of its charm.

"Ralph, I thought you were in New York. Jane said you were on retreat. You shouldn't be here, you should be with your monks."

"They'll keep. Ever since Pat invited me, I couldn't shake the image of the beauty I'd find waiting here."

Was he talking about her this time? She peeked at him from the corner of her eye. He was soaking in the view. Good. The beauty of the Canyon had been waiting for him.

"My retreat always begins the third Monday of June, but I decided to go on the fourth Monday this year. They're flexible monks."

She pictured monks doing yoga.

"Problem is the Canyon's booked solid through August. Nellie's a breeze to park, I pop the top and I'm set, but security here can wake you up in the middle of the night if they don't want you. I've had it happen before."

"So you came for the day. Well, it's been nice chatting with you." She gripped her journal and stood to go.

Ralph laughed. "I'll give you a ride back whenever. I'm staying five days. Pat's awesome—he called the day before yesterday and said I could stay at your site."

Pat couldn't have invited him to stay in the RV with them. Could he?

No, it was unseemly, but a happy thought made her smile.

"What a card, he didn't tell me we're leaving early. So you're taking our spot, that's good. I'll miss the Canyon, but I'll return someday."

"That wasn't it. Pat said there's a space at the site for the toad, but he didn't bring one."

That would be Mark, the frog prince, and Ralph was right, Pat didn't bring him. Unless he'd be another late arrival.

"Most RVers tow a small car and drive it once they've parked the rig," he said. "Since Pat didn't, he's got extra room at the site. He noticed it Tuesday and called to re-invite me."

He pointed to her ponderosa pine.

"See the squirrels? I think the bigger one's the boy and he's chasing the girl."

What a shame nature was the same everywhere, even here. Ten minutes ago she'd found the scene fresh and original, but she'd been naïve; it was merely another instance of nature's plot to reproduce itself. She wished the female squirrel luck escaping from the male squirrel, and she hoped to set it a good example.

She couldn't be sure why Ralph had come. He loved the Grand Canyon—who that had seen it could help wanting to return? He enjoyed Pat and his family and Pat had invited him, several times it sounded like. His being here could easily have nothing to do with her. At least on his part. Pat had set her up before, and she'd rather think Ralph was a victim too. He liked the Canyon; he couldn't be all bad.

He pulled a sandwich from the pack at his waist.

"PB and J, made it yesterday, pomegranate jelly. Want one?"

He held out the sandwich and she sprung off the bench, alarming the squirrels. They scampered away and she considered following them, but held her ground. This was her scenic view. So what if the man beside her was an imbecile? He seemed relatively harmless. She retrieved her journal and returned to her seat.

"No thank you, Ralph." Better aim for the gentle firmness effective with her youngest nephews. "I thought we'd cleared up this confusion. You like peanut butter and I don't."

"Like giving up homework when we were kids, huh? You ever try that one?"

"Excuse me?"

"Now I get why you gave it up for Lent."

Either he was a clone of Pat, or they'd been hanging around so long he'd caught Pat's sick sense of humor like an infectious disease. She couldn't take another Pat. She'd have to find a way to get rid of Ralph.

"Your van-thing—"

"Vanagon," he corrected.

"Your Volkswagen," she said, refusing to be corrected, "brought you here and thanks to Pat you have a place to park it. But let's go back to the retreat. If you always visit the monks at the same time, they must be expecting you."

She'd seen ads for helipads near the Canyon. She'd pay for his ticket east and she could have her bench back.

He inserted the rest of the sandwich and wiped his mouth with his hand. "Things change. I was getting into a rut anyway."

"Ruts are good. The monks are probably waiting for you, looking in your rut right now, wondering why it's empty."

"You're cute." He smiled at her. "I emailed and they're expecting me next week. Besides, it's kind of goofy to spend my birthday with them every year."

"Your birthday? You should definitely go, I bet they baked a cake. I mean, before they got your email. When's your birthday?"

His smile broadened. "Today."

She shifted uncomfortably. Today. That made them practically twins. He didn't need to know about her birthday, but if today was his she ought to be civil. She held out her right hand.

Too late she remembered Tool Seven, "Avoid all physical contact, even the most platonic, with a man you've crossed off your list. The wrong impression can be fatal." The wisdom of *The Tools* was uncanny, possibly prophetic. If Ralph took her hand and kissed it, she'd have to jump. At least the Canyon would provide a spectacular view on the way down.

He gave her hand a firm shake and let go.

"Happy Birthday," she said.

"Thanks." He started on a second sandwich.

She rose and stepped toward the blessedly peanut-butter-free Canyon, but it was no use, she couldn't recapture her earlier peace. Not with him chewing audibly behind her. She glared at him but he didn't notice, just took another bite.

She snatched up her pack and shoved her journal inside. The shuttles ran on a continuous loop. As soon as she reached the bus stop and civilization, she could grab one and put distance between them.

"I'll see you later at the campground, I guess."

Ralph got up. "Jane's baking me a chocolate cake and Pat said he'd toss a couple steaks on the grill. He said make sure and grab you so you won't be late." He squinted at the sun as if gauging the time, then looked at his watch. "We should be going."

So Pat was throwing steaks on the grill and didn't want her to be late, though he knew she'd returned last night in plenty of time to help Jane prepare her birthday dinner. For which he'd thrown hot dogs on the grill. When Jane had asked about the steaks in the RV freezer, he'd said they were for a special occasion.

"Ready?"

Ralph waited for her, casual and self-assured as ever. She made a noise in the back of her throat, but nodded. She didn't want him to drive her; she didn't want him here at all.

159

She hated almost sharing a birthday, but there was solace in Jane's chocolate cake. Let him smear peanut butter on his piece if he must; she needn't sit near him when he did.

He led the way to Nellie, and she reached into her pocket for the trail mix baggie. She wouldn't ruin her appetite, but she had to reward herself. He'd spoiled her afternoon and she'd handled the disappointment like a grown-up. She hadn't run away, she hadn't jumped, and much as Ralph deserved it, she hadn't pushed him in.

CHAPTER 21

Over the Edge

When they returned to camp, Pat's grill was ready for the steaks and the boys were ready for Uncle Ralph to tell stories.

Elizabeth hadn't realized the second Dr. Collins now ranked as Uncle. She rolled her eyes and left the men to kibitz, all seven of them, including Matthew who'd tugged on Ralph's cargo shorts until the new uncle scooped him up.

Jane was in the RV frosting the cake. With one look at Elizabeth, she put a final dollop of icing on her masterpiece and handed over the bowl.

"He gets homemade frosting?"

"I only brought one can of Betty Crocker Ready to Spread. I didn't expect another birthday this week." Jane kept her eyes on the cake.

Elizabeth slid into the dinette.

"It's chocolate cream cheese frosting, isn't it?" He wasn't worth it, but she had the bowl. The first fingerful tasted heavenly. "Jane, look at me and tell me why Ralph is here."

Her sister pushed the cake to the back of the counter and sat on the couch across from her. "Sorry I can't sit with you, but I don't fit." She handed Elizabeth the spatula covered in frosting.

"I don't mind, you can tell me the truth from there. How long have you known Ralph was coming?"

Jane moved a seatbelt out from under her. "I knew he was coming when he showed up."

"No one told you? That's so rude."

"Don't be annoyed on my account. I was delighted to see him."

"So Pat didn't tell you when he called Ralph the other day?"

"He told me this morning he had a surprise but it wouldn't get here till this afternoon. I thought he'd ordered pizza. Ralph drove up in Nellie and you could've knocked me over with a feather. Of course the boys were thrilled and I couldn't be happier."

"I could. I don't get it. Why does everyone love Ralph?"

"You mean everyone but you? Because he's a great guy, Lizzy, and sooner or later you'll see that."

"Fine, he's great. That doesn't explain why he had to bring his greatness here when he's supposed to be in New York."

"He came because he loves the Grand Canyon and he loves our family, and if he decides he loves you too, that's fine with me."

The screen door opened.

"Daddy says it's time to eat!" Jude yelled from the step.

"And I get to sit next to Uncle Ralph!" Luke shouted.

"Mom," Anthony said, pushing past them into the RV, "Dad wants to know if I can help you."

"Thanks, buddy, but everything's out there already."

Elizabeth put the mixing bowl in the sink. "I'm sorry Jane. I'm giving you a hard time and none of this is your fault. You're slaving away and I'm blaming you for something Pat did."

"What'd Daddy do?" Anthony asked, following them out.

She didn't trust herself to explain Pat's sins to his eldest son. Especially in front of Ralph, who sat at the picnic table, Luke on one side of him, Jude on the other. A tinfoil crown rested on his head and Matthew snuggled on his lap.

"Let's pray and eat while the steaks are hot. Sit down, Liz." Pat indicated the place directly across from Ralph. She had no choice; it was the last empty spot.

"Thanks." She could only trust he heard the sarcasm in her voice.

Ralph smiled at her and helped Matthew fold his chubby hands. She closed her eyes and prayed to make it through dinner without using her steak knife for any purpose but cutting her meat.

Pat was eloquent, thanking God for His beautiful creation, their trip, their guest, Jane's hospitality . . . She had time for a second silent prayer and begged God to take Ralph away. She didn't wish him ill, exactly, just absent.

"So Liz, did Ralph tell you his plans?"

Pat had blessed himself and launched the conversation in one breath. She was afraid to ask about Ralph's plans. Adopting her nephews? Moving into her parents' house? It could hardly get worse.

Ralph was cutting up the boys' steaks. "You tell her, Pat."

"He's got two passes to camp at the bottom of the Canyon. He's leaving in the morning to hike down, and he has equipment for taking one of us."

The boys erupted in varying forms of petition. Even Matthew rapped his fork on the table.

"Quiet down, hooligans," Pat said. "You're too young, but if you're good, maybe you can help Uncle Ralph pack tonight."

"Of course they can," Ralph said.

He was cutting his own steak now, and she lowered her eyes to her plate, feeling her smile almost cracking her face. God had answered her prayer. Still, it was Ralph's birthday. She ought to hide some of this overwhelming joy at his impending absence.

"Obviously Jane and I can't go," Pat said. "Ralph has the two passes but we've got our hands full with the boys. We've talked it over, and the good news is we can spare you, Liz."

She looked up, a deer in the headlights. Ralph was watching her, but she couldn't make out his expression. He was chewing, maybe smiling too, but she couldn't be sure. Jane's face she could read. Hope, a trace of anxiety, big sisterly encouragement. Pat was an open book. Malice aforethought.

She kept her hand away from her steak knife. "Thank you for the offer Pat, but I don't think the boys could do without their Auntie Beth."

"Uncle Ralph's been telling us about going down," Anthony said. "It's awesome. You have to be really brave and you can't get tired. You have to watch your step and move over when donkeys pass and you need to carry a big pack with enough water and—should I tell her the rest?"

Ralph nodded as he chewed.

"Well you have to be really tough and calm and—is it okay to tell her everything?"

Ralph shrugged and took a swig of beer.

"And you have to bring your poop back with you," Anthony finished in a stage whisper.

Ralph burst out laughing, spraying Guinness at Elizabeth. He wiped his face with a paper napkin. "I'm sorry. I hope you're not wet."

She ignored him, choosing to focus on her meal. She cut a piece of steak.

"You can't eat steak because Uncle Ralph is bringing light things that don't rot, like peanut butter sandwiches and beef jerky."

"We had jerky for appetizers," Dominic said. "You got to chew really hard."

"But Auntie Beth," Anthony said, "I don't think you'd make it. Uncle Ralph said people could die if they don't do it right."

Now that was awful. Was he turning her nephews against her? What had he been telling them? That only someone as heroic as he was could make it into the Canyon and out alive? Absurd. She was more likely to survive than he was. She'd bring chocolate and raisins and pecans and when he begged her to share, she'd turn up her nose at his peanut butter and toss him a raisin or two, but she'd be the one to lead them out. He'd run out of water, and she'd have to share that too.

Glancing up she caught Pat's eye. Reality came crashing down. What was she thinking? Of course she wasn't going into the Canyon with Ralph. They'd inveigled Anthony into their scheming ways; he was part of the plot to get her alone with Ralph, but she was too smart for them all.

"I bet it is really hard to go down into the Canyon and come out safely," she said to Anthony. "I think I'd better not try it. I'd be too scared." She eased her conscience by imagining herself alone with Ralph and his peanut butter. A tremor went through her at the thought.

"Did Uncle Ralph tell you his book stories? Is that why you're scared?" Jude asked.

The other boys were nodding, eyes wide, and Pat smiled.

"Did you write a book about the Grand Canyon?" she asked Ralph.

"No, I didn't write it. The boys saw a book I brought with me, that's all." He looked sheepishly at Jane. "I wouldn't have told them about it, but when I let them climb aboard Nellie, Anthony read the title and wanted to know what it meant."

"What's the title?" Elizabeth asked.

Ralph's expression was half guilty, half proud. "*Over the Edge.*"

He and Pat started laughing, Jane put her hand to her mouth, and the boys all spoke at once.

"There's these stories about people falling in!" Dominic shouted.

"A woman who wasn't looking, tripped and fell about a mile," Anthony said.

Elizabeth couldn't make out Jude and Luke's contributions, but they seemed equally eager to convey the horror stories Ralph had told them.

Jane had been sitting in a folding chair at one end of the table, and she rose, queenlike.

"That's enough boys," she commanded. They fell silent.

"Dr. Collins. I'm letting you off this time because it's your birthday. I have a cake, and I'll get it now, though you don't deserve it."

Elizabeth basked in the warm glow of Jane's wrath. She only wished some of it were directed at Pat.

"As for you," Jane said, turning to Pat and granting her wish, "Dr. Moore, if your children have nightmares, we both know which of us will be up with them. I'm planning on a good night's sleep and you can pay for your mistake."

"What was Daddy's mistake?"

"Never you mind, Jude. Why don't you help me with the candles?"

Jane had said her piece, and Elizabeth marveled at her sister's ability to speak her mind without losing her temper. She had the sweetness of a saint, but when she needed to administer correction, she never faltered. Best of all, she could let things go. Elizabeth watched her climbing the steps into the motorhome, one hand firmly grasping the rail to pull herself up, the other tenderly holding Jude's hand as he clambered up behind her.

"So, I guess it's a no on the trip down, huh?" Ralph said.

She was gathering plates but stopped to glare at him.

A caustic remark was on the tip of her tongue but she bit it back. This was her chance to be more like Jane. She took a deep breath, and spoke plainly and sincerely.

"Yes."

"You'll go?" Ralph looked at her quizzically, eyebrows raised, beer bottle halfway to his mouth.

"No. I meant yes, it's a no go."

"Don't sweat it Ralph, you'll get her eventually." Pat tossed a beer cap in the air and caught it. "Her yes means no, but then, conversely, her no often means yes." He winked at her.

She ran up the RV steps, tripping, but catching herself before she fell. Now Pat would make some awful joke that Ralph was better off going down without her. He'd always teased her about her clumsiness; no doubt he expected she'd be the next victim over the edge.

To her surprise, it wasn't Pat's voice that called out after her.

"No problem, Elizabeth," Ralph said. "Maybe some other time."

CHAPTER 22

A Change of Plans

"They're gone, Lizzy. You can open your eyes."

Elizabeth groaned and kept her eyes shut. "I hear voices in the cab-over."

"Jude and Luke are up there with Matthew watching a DVD, but the big boys and Pat won't be back for hours."

She smelled coffee and opened one eye. Jane held out a steaming mug.

She sat up on the couch and took the mug. "I told you I wouldn't open my eyes till they were gone."

Jane lowered herself onto the end of the couch and rubbed Elizabeth's foot through the blanket. "I never doubted it. You're stubborn as a mule."

"Our movie has a mule." Luke's head popped out between the overhead curtains. "His name's Brighty. Will Uncle Ralph ride a mule today?"

"No, honey, he's walking into the Canyon."

"Doesn't he want a mule to carry his pack?"

"He might let Anthony carry it a few minutes, but when Daddy brings Anthony and Dominic back, he'll carry it the rest of the way by himself."

"I want to carry his pack. It's not fair!"

"Your brothers are only going a little way down the trail, then Daddy's taking them to the nature center. Don't you like the movie?"

"I like it," Jude said. His head disappeared.

"How about you? Wish you were there on the trail with Ralph?" Jane squeezed Elizabeth's foot.

"Hardly. I don't know what it is about him but he annoys the heck out of me."

"He's sure patient with you, considering how rude you've been. Any other guy would have lost interest ages ago."

"I wish he would. My only hope is to keep avoiding him. It worked last month, and it was working this month till Pat foisted him on me. You're sure we won't see him before we leave?"

"I don't see how we could. He'll spend two nights at the bottom and return Sunday, but Pat says we're going to early Mass in town and leaving from there. We'll be gone hours before Ralph hikes out."

"So when did they start?"

"About an hour ago. They grabbed granola bars and off they went. Are you hungry?"

"If you have any chocolate cake left. Or did Ralph finish it last night?"

Jane got up. "I managed to save one piece. I hid it for you." She reached into a cupboard.

"You're a gem. I don't know how—"

The door shook as someone outside pounded on it.

"Mom! Hurry up! Open up!"

Elizabeth shot up from the couch and unlocked the door. Anthony was standing on the top step.

"What's wrong?" she asked. "What happened?"

"Uncle Ralph fell over the edge!"

She had some feelings she was ashamed to investigate. They were too much like joy, senseless joy.

A crash resounded behind her, and there was Jane holding a bit of cellophane, a mess of chocolate at her feet. The plate had hit the ground cake side down, of course. Even from the bottom of the Canyon, Ralph managed to ruin everything.

The boys in the overhead were clamoring to get down and Elizabeth retrieved Matthew before he, too, fell over the edge. Anthony had stepped in, Dominic on his heels.

Jane asked Anthony to tell them calmly what happened. He and Dominic shouted over each other and Elizabeth caught "donkey," "trail," and "the wrong side."

Pat rapped on the door. Through the screen his face was one huge grin. A wave of disappointment washed over her. He wouldn't be grinning like that unless—

"Ralph's as comfortable as I could make him, but I think his sickroom needs a woman's touch. Liz, would you mind?"

"Yes I would mind! He's supposed to be at the bottom of the Canyon, and whether he fell there or walked there he has no business in a sick room and I'm the last person in the world to make him more comfortable."

"Pat." Jane brushed past her and was in Pat's arms. "What happened? Is he really okay?"

"He's got a badly sprained ankle, but otherwise he's fine."

"I thought he fell over the edge," Elizabeth said. "Isn't that supposed to hurt more?"

"He did his best, but sliding twenty feet along rocky dirt isn't going to kill anybody."

She knelt to clean up the cake. It was a relief to turn away, and she might be able to salvage some chocolate.

Pat was telling a more coherent story. They'd started down the zig-zagging trail to accompany Ralph a short way. Almost immediately, a group of donkeys needed to pass them. Pat guided the boys to the mountain side but Ralph stepped to the cliff side. Next thing they knew he was sliding down the embankment to where the path continued below.

"And Uncle Ralph beat the donkeys!" Dominic said.

"It was awesome! He was so tough he rolled over and let people pass him, and the donkeys too." Anthony's eyes were lit with hero-worship.

"And you made him cozy there and came back to tell us?" she asked.

"We dragged him up all by ourselves!" Dominic said.

She liked the image. "Where is he now?"

"Resting in Nellie," Pat said. "The passenger seat reclines and he's got his ankle on the dash. I drove the Vanagon back while he kept up a running commentary—he's a terrible backseat driver."

"But we were in the back," Dominic said. "Uncle Ralph was in the front."

Pat stepped past Elizabeth and opened the freezer. "Jane, can I steal these frozen peas? He needs something cold before the swelling gets worse."

"Of course. They were part of tonight's dinner, but we can spare them for Ralph."

Perfectly good peas going to waste because Ralph was a klutz and he'd ruined Plan A—avoiding him by staying here when he was there. Okay then, time to implement Plan B—if he was here, she'd simply go there.

She'd slip off to the Canyon. Not slip *off* the Canyon as he had, but return to her bench where he couldn't follow. No one would miss her; they'd be gathered around the invalid listening to tall tales.

Pat stood in the door well. "Jane, could you come out for a sec?"

"Sure, I'd like to check on Ralph myself. Lizzy, will you keep an eye on the boys?"

"Absolutely," she said. She could almost feel the bench under her, the sun warming her. Soon she'd be alone, in her happy place far from Ralph.

"Everybody in the overhead. Anthony, Dominic, take your shoes off." She hoisted Matthew up. "Should we start the movie over or do you want a new one?"

They didn't answer. Anthony had already pressed play, and she sank onto the couch, exhausted before the day had properly begun. She needed food.

She got herself a bowl of Cocoa Puffs and settled into the dinette. She ate with her eyes closed, letting the nine essential vitamins and minerals do their work while she visualized the Canyon. If she got there soon, she'd see her view at an earlier time of day than usual. The light playing on the rock would be wholly new. She couldn't wait.

The screen creaked open. She stole a peek. Just Jane. Good.

"You're the only person I know who can eat cereal with her eyes shut." Jane went to the couch and began folding Elizabeth's blanket. "One thing about RV living, there isn't too much housework. I'll miss it."

"At least we have two more days."

Jane set the blanket on the couch and patted it. She looked at Elizabeth, then shook out the blanket and began refolding it.

"What's wrong?"

Jane folded; Elizabeth waited.

"Jane, what's wrong? Is Ralph really hurt?" She'd feel bad if Jane felt bad. She hated to see her sister like this.

"Lizzy, Ralph got some bad news."

"How could he get bad news about a sprained ankle? And from whom? Did a traveling radiologist stop in and x-ray him while Pat told us what happened?" Elizabeth laughed, but stopped when she saw Jane's expression.

"Ralph got a call from Gretchen and she was really upset. He didn't tell us why, but she asked him to come back."

"And he told her he's laid up and can't? That's kind of sad, but you're too empathetic. She'll be fine."

"Ralph didn't talk to her, he got a voicemail. Apparently she called when they were on the trail, but he'd left his phone in Nellie. There it is."

"What do you mean 'There it is'? That doesn't sound like you. Is that what Pat said?"

"No, that's what Ralph said. He said, 'There it is. She wouldn't have asked me, and I shouldn't ask you, but I really need to get back.'"

"I can watch the kids while you take him to the bus station. There must be a bus station, right?" She dipped her spoon into the bowl and let droplets of chocolaty milk fall onto the table. She didn't want to hear the rest. Ten to one it wouldn't be happy.

"I'm sorry, Lizzy, but we're all going back. We leave as soon as we pack up."

There was nothing left to say. It wasn't her trip; it wasn't her RV; it wasn't her vacation, not really. She was along for the ride, and the ride was turning around with an extra passenger.

At least the bedroom in back had a door that closed. If Ralph wanted to be in there, she could stay up here. If he was up here, she could ride back there. Plan A, Plan B, either one would work. She wouldn't have to talk to him, no more than a courteous, "Oh, you're taking the back?" before she closed the door between them.

The screen creaked again.

"He's all set. Said he wants to give Liz a few pointers before we start, though."

"What, does he think I'm going to wrap his ankle? Is that my new happiness project?" She picked up her bowl and drank down the leftover milk. Pat stared at her.

"What?"

"Nellie may be old, but Ralph's got her in pristine shape. You won't be slurping milk in the Vanagon."

"Obviously not, I'd have to be in there first." She grabbed a napkin and wiped her chin. "By the way, I didn't forget your blonde date, but I'm checking it off now. Between Ralph's time with me at the Canyon and the party last night, it's taken care of."

Pat slid into the dinette seat opposite her, smiling his crocodile smile. Or was it his used car salesman smile?

"You must realize that neither of those fits the definition. A blonde date is a reasonably long interval spent alone in the company of a blonde for the purpose of getting to know each other in view of marriage."

"Marriage may be in the blonde's view, but it's not in mine."

"Leaving that aside, your time at the Canyon with him was much too brief to qualify, and last night at his birthday dinner the two of you weren't alone. But don't sweat it, I'll count your trip in the Vanagon as a date."

"Thank you." She took her bowl and spoon to the sink. "It wasn't pleasant riding back with him yesterday, but it's over, and I'm glad to know we've put the whole 'let's make Lizzy date Ralph' obsession behind us."

"I didn't get to that part," Jane said.

They were doing that thing where they gave each other meaningful looks. Jane's was worried; Pat's amused.

"What part?" What else could Pat do to her?

"I didn't mean yesterday's ride," he said. "That was a preview. Today you'll be driving."

"I can't drive this! You're joking, right? It wouldn't be safe for Jane and the boys, not to mention me, you, and Ralph."

Pat's smile grew wider still. It was the crocodile smile, no question.

"Relax. You won't be driving this monster. You'll be driving Nellie. Ralph has to get her home, but he's laid up. I'm driving the rig, I'll need Jane to take care of the boys, and that leaves you to drive the Vanagon. You were great with that stick shift you had after college. You'll be fine and I'm sure Ralph'll tell you anything special you need to know."

She gaped at him, hands on her hips, mouth open. Was he kidding?

"Don't worry about us. We'll keep movies going for the boys." He slid out of his seat and let himself out.

"Lots to do," he called through the screen. "You girls put things away inside and I'll pack up out here. Tell me when you're ready to unplug. Oh, and Lizzy, I'm glad you mentioned your paradise project. While you're on the road you ought to think about next month. This one's almost over."

Jane was in the bathroom, putting miscellaneous items in the medicine cabinet, placing them gently so as to make very little noise. That was Jane all over, considerate, serene, trying to avoid the pleading scene that might develop if she were available for comment. It was just as well, Jane couldn't save her. Pat was right, he'd need his wife to watch the boys while he drove the RV. Which left the biggest boy and his Vanagon to Elizabeth.

She relished that one blessed moment when Anthony had announced the accident. Sadly, it had been short-lived, and Ralph long-lived. He couldn't even make her happy by falling over the edge right.

CHAPTER 23

Leaving Paradise

By noon they were ready.

"I'd like to say good-bye to the Canyon," Elizabeth told Ralph.

"Sounds good. We'll be on the road longer, but if you're okay driving in the dark, a few minutes shouldn't matter."

"Oh."

One more thing he'd ruined. Now her last view would be from yesterday afternoon when she'd thought about jumping in to escape him. If she had jumped she wouldn't be in this ludicrous vehicle with his ankle propped on the dash and practically in her face.

"Don't forget to adjust the mirrors. Huge number of accidents caused by women adjusting while they drive."

She put her hand on the stick shift that stuck up from the floor between their seats.

"You'll have trouble getting in first. Once you're there, you're all set, but don't ride the clutch. Nothing worse than a woman with her foot glued to the clutch. You see where the brake is?"

She unbuckled and got out. With the door shut there was a nice solid barrier between them.

"If you need to use the bathroom again, I'm fine with that. Pat warned me, and I'm in no hurry. We'll get there when we get there."

"I do not need to use the bathroom," she said through gritted teeth. "When you said you'd sit up front to give me directions, I thought you meant navigational directions. Where to turn, which highway to take, that kind of thing."

"Exactly. We're on the same page."

"I doubt it. I don't need advice like I just got my license. I've been driving for over fifteen years."

"That long, huh?"

He was on the verge of laughing; she could tell by his smile and the dimple to the right—or was it the left?—of his mouth. She said nothing.

"I can take a hint." He extended his absurdly long arm and pushed the door open. "I'll do my best to shut up, but you need to understand, no one but me drives Nellie, not even Joe."

She got in and checked the mirrors. One foot on the clutch, the other on the brake, shift into first. Except she couldn't find first.

"Brake," he whispered. "You might want to let off the emergency brake."

"Right."

She let it off and slid the stick into first. Nothing to it. One more glance in the mirrors, she punched the gas, and the van shot backward. She slammed on the brake. This would be the longest drive of her life.

"Why don't you tell me again about shifting into first." If she found the stupid gear, at least they could leave the campground.

"My pleasure. Take it slow, you may feel a hitch. Don't force her, but stay on track or you'll put her in another gear."

The stick went into first and they were off.

"We need gas before we head out," he said.

She nodded and followed the signs to the campground exit.

"I'm famished. You want anything?"

She shook her head. For once she wasn't hungry.

He opened the glove box and she heard a grating sound like he was unscrewing something. The smell of smells flooded the camper's interior and she hit the brake. The van bucked and stalled, startling a scrub jay who screeched at them.

"What's up?" He held the jar in one hand, lid in the other.

"Put it away. Now."

He set the lid on the dash and reached into the glove box to pull out a spoon. The familiar sourness rose in the back of her throat.

Her hand shot out and she seized the jar before he could stop her. She had it almost out the window when he grabbed her wrist. He pried her fingers off, took the jar, and screwed the lid back on. He had the goods but she'd stopped him from using. A draw.

"Tell you what." He clicked the glove box shut. "How about you get me a sandwich at the gas station. Whatever you think I'd like."

"My pleasure." She started Nellie and pulled ahead twenty feet to the campground exit. At this rate they'd be home a week from Tuesday. "Which gas station?"

"Take a left here."

She turned.

"Or not. Any gas station'll be fine."

"Sorry. I'm not so good with right and left."

"It should be an interesting thirteen hours." He didn't sound like he minded.

She pulled into a Texaco. "You mean nine."

"I mean thirteen."

"It only took us nine hours to get here in the RV. Did you go the main roads?"

"Sorry I can't fill her up, but I need to keep the ankle elevated. Get the cheapest grade and when you grab my sandwich, I'm not a tuna man."

The tank filled quickly, a welcome change from Pat's rental monster. Inside the store she grabbed a ham sandwich, a Coke, and a bottled water. Perusing the candy aisle took longer.

Back in the fresh mountain air she inhaled deeply. How was it that every mini-mart in the country smelled like stale cigarette smoke and old sneakers? She popped a stick of Juicy Fruit in her mouth to get the taste out and her gaze fell on a tour bus parked alongside the restrooms. It beckoned, but she resisted. She couldn't leave Ralph and Nellie to rot in the Arizona sun; she'd left her pack in the van.

She tossed the sandwich to Ralph and got them back on the road. Easy to choose the right direction this time: ignore the sign pointing toward the Canyon. Her Canyon, where she would be right now if not for the man with the foot in her face and his sad blonde girlfriend.

"Speed limit's forty here," he said.

"Why'd you say thirteen hours?"

"Took Nellie thirteen hours, that's all."

"That's way more than all. Did you pull over and sleep on the way?"

"I forgot to ask what kind of music you like."

"Excuse me?"

"I've got some eight-tracks. America, the Beach Boys, Linda Ronstadt. Your choice."

Odd that he had good taste in music when he was otherwise such a goof.

"America, but it's nine hours."

"Not in Nellie. Which reminds me, you're sneaking up on sixty there. You don't want to do that."

"Sure I do, the speed limit's sixty-five now." This wasn't so bad. She could spend the trip correcting him.

"Nellie doesn't like to go over fifty-five."

"You don't mean fifty-five the whole way?"

"When the speed limit's fifty-five or higher. Towns you go slower."

"That's ridiculous. At least she fills up fast." Had she just referred to his van as "she"?

"Yeah, we'll have to fill her up every two hours. You might keep an eye on the gas gauge."

She could hear him chewing the ham sandwich but the mayo and mustard packs she'd provided were unopened on the dash. He was eating the sandwich dry? As long as he didn't add peanut butter, she'd mind her own business. Her cache of chocolate was in her pack behind the stick shift and she reached for it.

She felt Ralph's hand on hers and her stomach lurched. Could she slap him without losing control of the van?

"Elizabeth, you can't do that."

He was reading her mind. He was taking advantage of her because he knew she was trapped. She opened her mouth, not sure whether to scream for help or yell at him. He placed her hand on the steering wheel.

"Two hands on the wheel. Let me know what you need and I'll get it for you."

She flushed. Fabulous. His intentions were gentlemanly but now she had to ask for every little thing. Fine, he could be her slave.

"Candy bar."

"Quite a selection here. Which one?"

"Any." She wouldn't waste words on him, he wasn't worth it.

She could hear the paper ripping, but he didn't pass it over. She glanced his way—the bozo was taking the entire wrapper off her Hershey Bar. Was he planning to feed it to her, or let her make a mess?

He handed her the whole bar: all chocolate, no paper. She stuffed half in her mouth and his arm snaked behind her seat. Something fell into her lap and she glanced down. A brown paper grocery bag, or part of one. What was inside was anyone's guess.

"Sorry they're dead."

Of course. Strong he-man wrestles road kill into paper bag for fair maiden. She smelled something fermenting and focused on the taste of chocolate, sucking the life out of the bit left in her mouth.

"You know Ralph, I can't actually see what's dead now so maybe you could take the bag off my lap and show me next time we stop."

"Right." He removed the bag. "They're kind of shriveled up anyway."

She wouldn't ask. Possums? The squirrels?

"They're flowers. I thought you'd like flowers."

"I do like flowers." Something was seriously wrong with him. "But I like them alive in nature or in a vase with water."

"I had no idea they'd die so fast. I picked them right before I left home but when I saw you at the Canyon, I forgot."

She glanced at her watch. Twelve and a half more hours. If silence inspired him to pull dead things from behind her seat, she'd better talk. And if she was forced to talk, she might as well ask about something she was interested in.

"So what's wrong with Gretchen?"

"I'm glad you asked." His arm was behind her seat again, returning the flower corpses. "I was afraid you resented her needing me."

"She can need you all she wants. I don't need you, and everyone needs to be needed, so if she needs you that's fine with me."

"So you don't mind about leaving the Canyon? You seemed upset we had to go."

Was there a camera hidden in the van? If she knew the rules of this game, she might win a new car, one that liked to go the speed limit. Maybe the point of the show was not slapping him. She'd be happy winning even a bike, but she didn't know if her self-control would hold out.

"Why don't you tell me what happened to Gretchen."

"Mike left and that upset her."

Mike O'Reilly, Mark's cousin. Who was also in the race. She stared at the "How's my driving?" sticker on the semi in front of them, but she was seeing a different tableau, a vision of the avaricious O'Reillys and poor victimized Gretchen.

Fortunately Ralph was tearing the paper off a Krackel bar. With a quick motion she had it in her mouth. He could get another for himself; she needed comfort and sustenance immediately.

It was all her fault. She should have told Gretchen about the O'Reillys and the overflow but she hadn't, and now it would haunt her for the rest of her life. She'd made the same mistake as Elizabeth in *Pride and Prejudice* when she didn't reveal Wickham's evil ways. He'd continued in their circles and run off with Lydia because no one knew to protect her. Was it too late to save Gretchen?

"Can we catch them before they reach London or should we take the road to Gretna Green?"

She heard a spraying sound. He hadn't sprayed her, but if he was drinking her Coke, she'd kill him. She glanced over. Water, and he was looking at her strangely.

"Do you think we can catch who before they reach where? I just said Mike left and Gretchen's upset."

Of course. Mike had proposed to Gretchen to win his grandfather's money, and Gretchen had refused him. That would upset anyone, even an icicle.

"I know what happened," she said.

"Yeah, he finally figured out what to do about his vocation."

"I don't think you should dignify it by calling it a 'vocation.' Mark did the same thing, and it's not right."

"I didn't know Mark wanted to be a priest. I thought you and Mark broke up because you proposed to him."

She gripped the steering wheel as if her life depended on it. Which it sort of did, because if she used her hands to pummel him, they could get in a bad accident. Grip and breathe. No pummeling in a moving tin can. If she got out of this alive she could make a fortune writing self-help books or maybe a memoir.

"Ralph, I didn't quite catch that. It sounded like you said I proposed to Mark. Why don't you turn down America so I can hear you properly."

He clicked off the stereo.

"Sorry to bring it up, but I haven't told a soul, scout's honor. Mark confided to Mike, and Mike told Gretchen confidentially, and she only told me because she was so concerned. But if Mark is going to be a priest too, you shouldn't take his rejection personally."

"Were you on the phone all morning while we were packing? Is that when Gretchen told you her skewed version of my life story?"

"She told me a month ago, and she only repeated what Mike told her."

"And what did Mike tell her?"

"That you went to dinner with his family and you guys broke up in the elevator. I remember the elevator because it seemed funny their house had one and I thought you were clever to propose there."

"I didn't propose to him in the elevator. He proposed to me!"

She slapped the steering wheel. If only it were his face.

"Are you sure? That's not the impression I got from Gretchen."

"Of course I'm sure, I was there!" Breathe. Grip. Drive. She kept her eyes on the road, resisting the temptation to turn her head and level a deadly glare at him. She'd kill him with her silence instead. Except she had to know.

"What exactly did Gretchen tell you?"

"She said Mike said Mark said after you saw his family's spread you wanted to take the relationship to the next level and he wasn't surprised, he gets that all the time since they're so wealthy. I figured you proposed, but I should tell you I never thought you did it for the money."

She looked at him. He was clearly amused. She had to watch the road, she had to keep her hands on the wheel and ignore him. For now. As soon as they stopped for gas she'd trick him into getting out of the van and drive away without him.

"Why don't you tell me your side of the story?" he said.

"It's not my side of the story, it's the truth. I went to dinner at their mansion. Mark and I got in the elevator on the way to the powder room. All I wanted was to eat my chocolate protein bar, and he proposed to me. In the elevator. And not because he loved me."

"Nothing personal but I like the other version better. Yours lacks credibility. Why would he propose if he didn't love you?"

"I'll tell you but if you laugh I swear I'll pull over and kick you out of your own stupid car."

"Van. Wow, this must be good. Let me guess—he's a five-year-old trapped in a man's body dying from that Benjamin Button disease and the Make-a-Wish Foundation set this up, is that it?"

"Not even close. His grandfather is giving one hundred and seventy million dollars to the grandchild who marries first, and none of them are married yet. That's why Mark asked me to marry him, and that's why I said no."

She braced herself for his laughter, but he was silent. Finally.

"You said Gretchen's upset because Mike left her. Do you get it now?"

Still nothing.

"It's the same thing," she said. "Mike proposed so he could get the money and she said no, and she's feeling terrible like I did because she did the same dumb thing, she fell for a heart-less man and found out he was only using her. I'm glad we're going back. I don't think Gretchen wants me, but if she wants you, I'll take you to her."

She stole a glance. He was gazing out the side window.

"So what were you saying about priests?" she asked.

"Yeah. Well. I didn't know about his grandfather and the money. That's a lot of money. But I don't think Mike proposed to Gretchen. When I returned her call this morning she said he'd left for New York."

"That fits perfectly. She rejected him and he went to New York. There's loads of girls in New York who'd marry a man for money."

"But he sent an email telling her he was on the red-eye to Albany."

"Don't you get it? Albany. New York City. He'll find a girl to marry him wherever he gets off the plane."

"I don't think so. He said the monks'll be waiting for him at the airport and he gets his tonsure tonight. Hard to pick up chicks with a tonsure."

Monks. In New York. She looked over but couldn't read his expression.

"Your monks?"

"Yes ma'am."

"He's going to visit your monks?"

"If things work out he's going to be one of them."

"Will you see him on retreat next week?"

"I think I'll skip this year, what with my ankle and all. Unless Mark went with him. That might tempt me."

"I wish, but I doubt it. He's not the unworldly type and he's definitely after the money."

She could hear Ralph glugging down the water.

"He sure blew it." He tossed the empty water bottle behind him. "I don't see how he can marry someone else after you said no."

Now that was sweet. She bit her lip to keep from smiling.

"All that money to offer and he botches the proposal. Pathetic. Give it up, I say. Give your life to God."

"You're such a jerk." He was just like Pat. "But since you have all the answers, tell me this. If Mike went to the monastery, why should Gretchen be upset? She knew from the beginning he wanted to be a priest, it's not like he was leading her on."

Ralph popped in another tape, and the van reverberated with Linda's voice singing "Poor, Poor, Pitiful Me." Was that how Gretchen felt?

"Poor dumb blonde. She fell in love with him anyway, didn't she?"

"Not at all, she's happy for him."

"If Gretchen's fine, you'd better have a good reason I'm not at the Grand Canyon right now. And hurry up or next exit I'm turning around. I'll get a room at the lodge and you and Nellie can wait to be impounded."

He handed her the Coke. She hadn't asked but she needed it.

"Thanks."

"No, thank you. You're very kind to take me home and I'm sure Gretchen will appreciate it. She's low because she hasn't found her vocation, and she doesn't know what to do."

"I thought she worked at Books-a-Trillion."

"She does, but it's not the kind of soul satisfying work a person thinks of as a vocation."

"I did. I mean I wasn't giving workshops on *The Tools*, but selling children's books was fulfilling. Maybe she should switch departments."

"She's not in a department."

"She's a cashier? That could get old fast."

"She's not at the registers."

"I'm not surprised, I kind of pictured her as head of a department or something. She's always so professional looking."

She heard the telltale rip of paper. She hated to interrupt their friendly chat about Gretchen, but he ought to ask before he ate her chocolate. Could she rise above it? She would. She'd let it go, she could do that. She felt her soul blossoming with a new maturity.

"You're right," he said. "She is quite the professional. That's why she's manager."

"I knew it. So what department does she manage? I bet it's business."

"You might say that. She manages the store."

Linda was belting out "Desperado." Obviously the music was interfering with their communication.

"She manages the store," Elizabeth repeated. It sounded straightforward enough when she said it, but that couldn't be right. "Like the whole store?"

"Exactly like the whole store. They even call her store manager, that's her title I think."

Without taking her eyes off the highway she reached over and grabbed what was left of her candy bar. Good thing he had them ready when she needed them. She let the chocolate melt in her mouth and silently counted to ten. It couldn't be as bad as it sounded.

"Ralph, can I ask you a question?"

"Go for it."

She shouldn't ask. She'd only get hurt, but she couldn't stop herself.

"When did Gretchen transfer from New York?" She focused on the rusted out bumper of the farm tractor ahead of them. "Please say January."

"At your service. I can get you another candy bar or I can tell you when Gretchen moved out or I can say January. What'll you have?"

It was all coming back. Gretchen had told her she'd transferred in the fall. It hadn't sunk in because it seemed insignificant when she was just another Books-a-Trillion employee.

"Elizabeth." Ralph's voice was gentle. "I hate to tell you what to do, but you're going seventy. Nellie doesn't like to go seventy."

"Sorry." She let up on the gas and watched the needle descend. She'd pay close attention from here on out. Keep that needle on fifty-five. No need to think about Gretchen anymore, let alone talk about her. She'd forget about the woman who'd boosted Books-a-Trillion's sales, stolen their customers, and bought out their stock for a song. So what if Gretchen was the mastermind behind a hostile takeover, why should she care?

"I don't want to be a pain," he said in the same gentle voice, "but sixty-five is still a mite too fast for the old girl."

He was right. She must not be concentrating hard enough. She let up and watched the needle lose altitude. She really wasn't in a hurry. Ralph wasn't so bad. It was Gretchen she never wanted to see again.

"You're mighty quiet over there. Anything wrong?" he asked. "I mean anything besides having to leave the Grand Canyon and drive a van you don't like with a foot in your face?"

She was getting used to his foot. It wasn't a dirty foot or a smelly foot and seeing his swollen ankle helped repress her occasional desire to smack him.

"I'm fine." Of course she wasn't, but why cry over spilt venom from the fangs of a blonde snake? "But could we talk about something else?"

"Definitely. There's something bugging me about Mark."

This was his idea of a different subject? What was wrong with talking about something neutral, like politics or religion?

"From what Gretchen told me he never actually said you proposed to him, I mean not in so many words."

"Fine, he's not a liar. He's still a creep."

"But what I don't get is why he'd say that stuff about you wanting to take it to the next level. Why would he deceive Mike?"

"How should I know?" She looked at the gauge, and eased up before he could tell her to. She saw his ankle—the swelling seemed better. One quick smack shouldn't do permanent damage. "You better not be implying I made the whole thing up."

"No, I'm wondering what he had to gain. Not by proposing to you, I get that now, but giving that line to Mike."

She reached for her pack, felt his fingers touch hers, and jerked her hand away.

"Spearmint."

"One stick or two?"

"One, dork. And I have the answer. Mark knew Mike would tell Gretchen what he said, so he had to be careful. He knows his Jane Austen—he told me he's seen the movies—so he must've known Gretchen was neither Charlotte Lucas nor the future Mrs. Elton. Naturally, then, he had to keep it secret that he'd proposed to me."

"Charlotte Lucas in *Pride and Prejudice*. Mrs. Elton from *Emma*." He held the unwrapped stick of gum near her hand and she took it.

"Right. So you understand now?"

"Not at all. Say more." He'd taken a piece of gum too; she could hear his loud chewing even over Linda.

"It's simple. Very few women will say yes to a man they know has just proposed to another woman and been refused."

"I see. So if a man has just been rejected by a woman and proposes to another, the second woman won't want him either."

"Right."

"Whereas if a man has just been accepted by a woman and proposes to another, the second woman is more likely to say yes. Is that it?"

His swollen ankle was slightly below her line of vision, but she was a Good Samaritan, and Good Sams never hit their bandaged clients.

"Don't play dumb, it perpetuates the stereotype."

He laughed. "I guess I deserved that, but fill in the details for me."

"Charlotte Lucas said yes to Mr. Collins after Lizzy turned him down, and Mrs. E accepted Mr. E knowing Emma had rejected him, but Gretchen's not homely like Charlotte or desperate like Mrs. Elton, so Mark has to keep up his image."

"So he can propose to Gretchen?"

"Precisely."

"But he's way too short for her."

"He's not the type to let a few inches stand between him and his grandfather's fortune."

"But why would he propose to Gretchen when he barely knows her?"

"He'll get to know her. Now that Mike's gone, he'll move in for the kill. She's worth a lot of money to him, and she's gorgeous and Catholic besides. That's why Mark didn't tell Mike the truth, and that's why Gretchen doesn't know the truth, and that's why you should tell her."

"Tell her what?"

"The truth! Are you really this obtuse, or just obnoxious? You need to tell her Mark wants to get married so he can get rich quick, and if he acts interested that's why. You can even tell her he proposed to me in the elevator. In fact I'd appreciate it if you did."

"I don't think so."

"Why not?"

"It's not my business to tell Gretchen anything."

Her jaw clenched involuntarily. She'd send him the bill if she got that clenching jaw syndrome thing. She snapped off the stereo and the bass notes got stronger.

"Wrong knob," he said, and turned off Linda.

"Thanks." Unclench. Breathe. Speak calmly. "If Gretchen's not your business, could you please explain to me why we're going back?"

"Easy. She needs a friend."

"Do me a favor, then, and don't volunteer me for the job."

He pointed to the gas gauge. "We'd better fill her up."

"Okay, but this time you get the snacks. You can limp that far, can't you?"

"Running out of pin money for chocolate?"

She just smiled. A little camper van housework while he was gone, a quick clean out of the glove box and they'd be even. If he couldn't answer for Gretchen's heart breaking, then she wouldn't answer for his.

CHAPTER 24

How to be Happy

Elizabeth peered through the windshield at the illuminated road ahead. A furtive glance at the sleeping blonde beside her and she stealthily reached into her pack for a candy bar. She wasn't afraid of him stopping her, but she wanted to let him sleep.

He'd been a good companion. After she disposed of the peanut butter and before he found out, they'd talked about all sorts of things—her nephews and his years in Rome, his hopes for his new job and her feelings about her old one.

They shared a fondness for roast beef, and though he smothered his in horseradish, dinner at Arby's was cheap and delicious. She had an uncomfortable moment when he opened the glove box looking for dessert, but he hadn't yelled at her, just raised an eyebrow and remained silent for ten minutes.

Nellie covered the miles with a casual persistence reminiscent of Aesop's tortoise and Ralph himself. When it got dark and he who never let "even Joe" drive his precious Nellie fell asleep, she felt the compliment. He must be exhausted after injuring his ankle and fasting from his ubiquitous (though now discarded) peanut butter, but still, she took his gentle snoring as high praise.

In the light of the moon his eyelashes and eyebrows didn't glint blonde like his hair. Did he dye his hair blonde, or his eyebrows brunette? And was it even possible to dye eyelashes? She laughed aloud and he stirred.

"Mmmmph. How long have I been asleep?"

"A while. I was telling you about sixth grade when Emily and I tried out for cheerleader."

"Yeah, I missed that one." He wiped his mouth with the back of his hand. "So what happened? Did you make the squad?"

"I got it and she didn't and I should've said no. It wasn't any fun without her."

"What about Jane?"

"She was a couple grades ahead of us so we never saw her at school, but at home the three of us did everything together."

"Even college?"

"That was the beginning of the end. Jane went before we did and instead of coming home afterward she got married."

"And you gained a brother."

"For what it was worth. I often wonder why Jane couldn't have married someone normal."

"I bet you do. That's an interesting relationship you and Pat have."

"Complicated, huh?"

"Not at all. Classic older brother, younger sister."

"And you're an expert?"

"Joe and I have four younger sisters, remember?"

"I keep forgetting you're Joe's brother. I mean I forget you have the same sisters and the same parents, and all that."

"Grew up in the same house even. Mom, Dad, me and Joe and the four Marys."

"Emily told me about them and I cracked up."

"Mom and Dad aren't that funny."

"The four Marys, you idiot. Tell me their names again."

"Mary, Maria, Maureen, and Miriam, but you're stalling. Let's get back to you and Pat."

"Only if you give me a candy bar."

"You didn't eat them all while I was sleeping?"

"There's one left."

"Mind if I use my flashlight?"

"Don't shine it upward. Look for a red wrapper, it's a Krackel."

A light shone on the floor and she could hear him rummaging.

"No candy bar, but I found something better."

"Sour apple gum. I could use a piece if that's all you've got."

"Even better. It's a book."

"Which one?"

"Gretchen's."

"Gretchen wrote a book? Let me guess—a depressing Norwegian saga where all the blondes die in the end, but nobly. How did it get in my pack?"

"Gretchen Rubin."

"*The Happiness Project*? I thought I lost it." As good a reason as any for not having read it by now.

"Nope. Right here. Perfect timing, I've wanted to ask you about it for months."

They'd been having such a cozy ride, and now he'd find out she was a fraud. Time to change the subject.

"Can I have a piece of gum?"

"Sure, hold on." More rummaging and he put a stick near her hand. "So what'd you think of it?"

"I love sour apple, thanks."

"The book. Did you agree with her findings?"

Okay then, she was a big girl, she'd confess. She took a deep breath and inhaled her gum.

"Water?" she whispered.

He handed her an open bottle and she glugged. Maybe it would help her swallow more than her gum. Her pride was next.

"Thanks."

He was doing something with the flashlight.

"You're reading my book!"

"Is that a problem?"

She could hardly explain it felt wrong for him to read her copy before she did.

"I still think it's hilarious our moms gave us the same book," he said. "But I have a confession to make. I'm a bad son."

This would be so humiliating. He'd probably think she was illiterate, there was no excuse for not reading the book by now.

"Don't you want to know why?" he asked.

"Why what?" He was talking; the least she could do was listen.

"Why I'm a bad son. I'll tell you, but I'm counting on your discretion. Mum's the word when you meet my mother at Joe's wedding." He laughed. "Get it—Mum's the word?"

"What are you talking about, Ralph?"

"You'll think I'm illiterate, there's really no excuse, but I never read any of the books my mom gives me."

It was too good to be true, but he wasn't laughing now.

"You're teasing me, right? The first night we met you said it was a great book and you loved it."

"Did I? I know I wanted to impress you, but I don't think I lied. You sure I said I read it?"

"I thought you did, but it's kind of a blur. Italians yelling and Gretchen pushing away every dish. I don't remember exactly what you said."

The foot he'd faithfully kept in front of her was shaking, and he was too, silently convulsed with laughter.

"What's so funny?"

"Those Italians! They were excessively Italian, weren't they? And Gretchen—I was afraid she'd faint. She said she wouldn't eat seafood after a performance, and then everything they brought was seafood. You left before dessert, but it was decorated with a seashell."

"You're kidding. Did she eat it?"

"No, she flat out refused and I almost lost it. The Italian next to her—what was his name? Pepperoni? Zamboni? He kept taking her food. Every course she rejected he ate, and he never slowed down with his commentary on the stupid American parents, even after you left."

"I remember—Alfredo, Romano, Giuseppe!"

"That's it. What a great night." He picked up a pen and tapped it on the dashboard. "But let's get to the book. Has it given you ideas for your own happiness project? Would you recommend it? Or better yet, could you tell me about it so if my mom asks, I can sound like I've read it?"

The moment of truth, but painless now. If Ralph hadn't read it, he couldn't be shocked.

"I haven't read it," she said.

"You're kidding."

"I haven't read it either," she clarified. "But I didn't open it until Christmas Day. I bet you got yours Christmas Eve, which makes you even further behind."

"But I thought your paradise project was based on Gretchen Rubin's."

"Sort of. Except that I haven't read it. I'm terrible about reading what people recommend, and gifts are the worst. Pat says if he ever wants me to read a book he'll buy all the copies and hide them from me. He calls me a contrarian."

"That's a bit harsh."

"He can be like that. You called it classic older brother, he calls it teasing."

"Two names for the same thing. I'm an older brother myself, so I'm familiar with all the variations, and now that I know you haven't read the book, everything's clear to me."

"What's clear?"

She heard him click an eight track into the stereo and the Beach Boys broke into "Help Me, Rhonda."

"We need inspirational music and I don't have the Rocky soundtrack. Does this work for you?"

"Sure, I love the Beach Boys."

"And you want to beat Pat, right?"

"More than anything."

"And your resolution is to have a happiness project and find happiness?"

"More happiness," she corrected. "I was happy before I started."

"More happiness, then, and it's now June. Let's see what Gretchen Rubin has to say for June."

She heard him flipping pages.

"Aren't you going to start at the beginning of the book?"

"That's not the way you read a book, is it?"

"What other way is there?"

"Liz, you get to start wherever you want." He paused and tapped on the dash with the pen. "I just had a terrible thought. You read Introductions, don't you?"

"Acknowledgments, the copyright page, dedications, every word from beginning to end."

He made a noise.

"Did you say 'sheesh'?"

"Absolutely, you're way out of control. Of course you didn't read the book—you don't know how to read a book."

"As if you do! Be nice to me or I'll tell your mom. I bet you haven't read piles of books she's given you."

"You can't get anywhere if you start at the beginning. You find the good part, the interesting part, the part you want to read, and dive right in."

She gasped. It was unconscionable.

"It's not that bad, really. I'll start at the end of June and you'll see. Ready?"

"No."

"Good. I want to know what Gretchen has to say about June, and she's likely to sum up at the end of the chapter. Hang in there while I read to myself for a second."

"Don't mind me, I'll just keep driving."

"Uh huh. Here it is, I thought we'd find what we needed here. Gretchen says, 'The end of June marked the halfway point in my happiness project year, and I took some time to ponder my progress beyond my usual end-of-month assessment.' Do you have end-of-month assessments?"

"Pat does. Same difference. I wonder what else I do like the book."

"She says more but let's skip to the next paragraph."

"You can't skip, that's cheating."

"Standard grad school practice. Limit yourself to the first line of each paragraph, add in the last sentence only in cases of outrageous obfuscation. Habermas, that sort of thing."

Better not to ask. She could google it later.

"Next paragraph she says, 'Evaluating myself at the six-month milestone for my happiness project, I confirmed that yes, I was feeling happier.' Now there's an excellent question. Six month milestone. Are you happier?"

"Me?"

"You, Miss Elizabeth Benning. Think it over and be totally honest."

She didn't need to think. The last six months had been the worst half year of her life, no contest, and no thanks to him. Not that her unhappiness was entirely his fault. Gretchen—his Gretchen, not Gretchen R.—was equally responsible. Half of a half year of unhappiness was only a quarter, that was all the unhappiness she could blame him for, and if she nailed Mark with May, Ralph's portion was even less. Besides, she was happy now. He was a good driving companion and she was having fun. Didn't they say you ought to live in the moment?

"I'm happy."

"But are you happier? That's the twenty-four thousand dollar question."

She didn't have a twenty-four thousand dollar answer. She bit her lip and kept driving.

"Can I answer for you?"

"Go ahead." This could be interesting. Would he blame himself?

"I don't think you've been as happy as you could be, and I think Pat's the problem."

Genius. Who better than Pat to bear the guilt for her unhappiness? He'd never know, and if he found out he wouldn't care.

"Classic example of the big brother syndrome. You make a resolution every year and wait for his approval. He teases the heck out of you, and you always lose. Even if you didn't lose you'd lose because he's the teaser and you're the teased."

St. Albert's College wouldn't regret hiring him; he had tremendous insight.

"So how can I become the teaser? If I beat Pat at his own game I'd be much happier. I wouldn't even care whether I kept the resolution to the end."

"I was afraid of that."

"What?"

"You've fallen into the little sister trap. You'll have to change your approach."

"I will. Tell me what to do and I'll do it. How can I change things and tease Pat instead of being teased?"

"You can't. Every little sister is destined to fail when she tries to beat the big brother at his own game. The secret is not to care. You don't try to tease him—he's not scared of you and never will be. But you can stop being scared of him. You can separate yourself from the whole dynamic."

Perfect. He was telling her "the secret," and he might as well be spouting Greek. She had no idea how to separate herself from the whole dynamic. She'd been unemployed for seven months and what had she to show for it? She hadn't watched a single episode of Oprah or Dr. Phil.

"You're not saying anything."

"I don't know what a whole dynamic is. But I want to."

His laughter was like a warm blanket thrown over her shoulders; nothing like Pat's.

"I'll explain it another way. This year you're doing a happiness project. Why?"

"To beat Pat." She heard a funny noise. "Did you snort?"

"Let's try again. This year you're doing a happiness project. Why?"

"I told you. I'm doing it to beat Pat. I had to think of a New Year's resolution and I thought of the happiness project and I'm sticking with it even though it's making me miserable because I finally have a shot at beating Pat."

"So you're doing a happiness project not to become happier, but to make Pat unhappy."

"Do you have a problem with that?"

"Most people never even consider taking a year of their lives to pursue more happiness. It's a great idea, and I bet"— in her peripheral vision she could see him shaking the book like a televangelist—"that's why this book has been a bestseller. So here you are, doing this wonderful thing, pursuing more happiness, only you're not."

"I'm not what?"

"Sounds to me like you're trying to beat Pat. That's what you said."

"I am."

"So you're wasting a year of your life trying to beat Pat instead of trying to be happier."

He was merciless.

"Fine, then. I'm wasting a year of my life trying to beat Pat and thanks to my happiness project I'm beating him more than I've ever beaten him before and I've never been so unhappy. If I cry 'Uncle' will you stop the Chinese water torture?"

"Liz." His voice was gentle again. "I'm not torturing you, you're torturing yourself. Play by Pat's rules and you'll always lose, even when you seem to be winning." He turned the flashlight on and lit up the floor by his foot. "How about that. The last chocolate bar."

"Can I have some?" she asked, her voice meek, her spirit quelled.

"You can. You've been working hard and we're getting somewhere."

He gave her a chunk still in its wrapper. If he could learn, she could too.

"Tell me then, how do I escape the little sister syndrome?"

"You're in the middle of a happiness project. Focus on being happier. Forget Pat."

"But he's always in my face, and when he's not in my face, he's in my head."

"On our drive? Were you thinking about him before I brought him up?"

"No, but if I was I'd have been angry at him for trying to ruin it with the blonde date thing."

"Has he threatened to set you up with someone when you get home?"

She might as well tell him, he was turning into her therapist.

"Not a blind date, a blonde date. Last month my happiness project had to do with dating." No need to tell him she'd hunted down a man; he was only an ersatz therapist. "Pat said if I didn't have a boyfriend at the end of the month, he'd send me on a blonde date." She winced and waited, but all was quiet on the Eastern Front. "With you." A phosphorescent bug splatted on the windshield and still he said nothing. "And before we left today he said this drive would count as my blonde date because we were alone together and that kind of thing."

"And you said?"

"I argued that we spent time together at my bench yesterday and at the party last night, but he said it wasn't long enough at the Canyon or alone enough at the party to qualify as a date. So I was mad."

"And he won."

"What else could I do?"

"Do it now, it's never too late."

"You can quote book titles at me all night but what was I supposed to do?"

"I understand your being angry at Pat for trying to set you up with me, but he didn't succeed."

"But we're here. Together. Alone. For a million hours driving fifty-five."

"Thirteen. Don't you know a date's like a wedding? If someone makes you say 'I do' it doesn't count. It requires the free consent of the will. Did you enter this van on your own, or because you had to?"

"Because I had to."

"Then it doesn't count."

"Cool. Can I use your cell phone?"

"You don't need to tell Pat."

"But if I don't tweak him with it, what do I get?"

"The knowledge that he's playing a game without an opponent. The freedom to ignore him. Dare I say happiness?"

"Oh." She smiled. "Kind of like a happiness project?"

"Exactly like one."

"I get it."

"Here's the test then. July's coming. What's your plan? Not how will you beat Pat, but how will you shoot for more happiness?"

"Planning's not my gift."

"I bet it's Gretchen's." His light flashed onto the book. "End of June. Survey says . . . 'It really mattered whether I got enough sleep, got regular exercise, didn't let myself get too hungry, and kept myself warm.'" He flicked off the light. "Weird. Why would she let herself get too hungry?"

She laughed.

"That's a happier laugh than I've heard yet," he said.

"But you're funny, asking why she'd let herself get hungry. That happens to me every day of my life. I forget to eat breakfast or lunch and later I'm desperate for food."

"Odd, but I can forgive the other for being other."

"Excuse me?"

"An old Chinese saying—forgive the other for being other."

"Like I can forgive you for never forgetting to eat?"

"That's it. Though it might be better to spend July eating regularly. Or this other stuff she said. 'I got regular sleep, got regular exercise.' Do you get regular sleep?"

"Sleeping's my happiest thing. Very regular sleep."

"Regular exercise?" he asked.

"I plead the fifth."

"Good answer. Now I know what you can do for July."

"So you're a double agent working for Pat."

"This isn't about Pat anymore, don't worry about him."

"I'm not worried about Pat, I'm worried about me. I don't like to exercise. It makes me unhappy. It makes me unhappier than anything else."

"When was the last time you exercised and it made you unhappy?"

He didn't shy away from the tough questions. She readjusted her hands at ten o'clock and two o'clock.

"When I was in eighth grade and Emily and I got rollerblades and I broke my ankle the day after Christmas."

"Ouch. Sorry about that. But I mean recently."

"I told you. The last time I exercised it made me unhappy. That was in eighth grade."

He whistled. "No wonder you haven't been happy this year. How about the other years, before I knew you? Have you suffered from depression?"

"Lots of very happy people don't exercise, and for the record, depression is a serious illness which often requires medication as well as talk therapy. You can't just play basketball and be happy. I mean maybe you can, but I can't. Not that I'm on medication, but you know what I mean."

"But you're not depressed, right?"

"I wasn't even unhappy until you told me I had to exercise."

"I didn't tell you that. I'm only suggesting it."

"And then Pat will come up with his rules and make it miserable even if it would've been fun."

"We're not worrying about Pat, right?"

"You don't have to worry about him, but I do."

"What if I become your happiness project coach? Would you stop worrying about Pat if I negotiated for you?"

"What's in it for you?"

"You're giving me a ride home, holding steady at fifty-five because I asked you to, doing all the driving with my foot in your face. Let's say I owe you one."

She smiled at his ankle. "What's your plan for July, then, Hopalong?"

"Why not pick out a sport and have fun with it?"

"What if I hate what I try?"

"Then quit and try something else."

"I wouldn't have to do the same sport all month?"

"Why limit yourself? You could start with a team sport and if you don't like it you could switch to a gym, or work out at home, or swim laps."

"I'm not joining you and Pat for basketball, so you can forget that right now."

"What about joining the pro-life softball team?"

"With Emily and Joe? Are you on that team?"

"I am, and it's a blast. We started in June with a full bench, but Mike's gone and I'm injured, so we must need a new player. Can you catch?"

"In fifth grade I caught a fly ball on a Wednesday afternoon and we won the game."

"That's great. We could start you in the outfield."

"Ralph?"

"Yeah, Liz?"

She smelled citrus; he must be peeling a clementine from her pack.

"Who else is on the team? Anyone I know besides you and Em and Joe?"

"A couple people. A red-head named Andrea manages and plays second base."

The one with the microphone at speed-dating, an event she wasn't anxious to discuss with him.

He held a segment of fruit near her hand. "Would you like some?"

"Thanks." He was a good guy. She could trust him. "I'll do it. As long as I can quit if I don't like it."

"Absolutely. And then you could try something else. For fun, not for Pat."

The gas gauge pointed to E.

"Time to fill up. Think we'll get home before July?"

He laughed at her dumb joke, but something nagged at the back of her mind.

"Ralph, you didn't name the other players I might know. You, Joe, Emily, and the redhead. Is Gretchen on the team?"

"Shortstop."

"I guess shortstops don't have to be short. Anyone else I know?"

"You probably met all of them speed dating."

"Is Mark on the team?" she asked.

"Mark who?"

She could always quit the team and take up synchronized swimming.

CHAPTER 25

The Softball Game

"Hey, batter, batter, batter! Hey batter, batter, batter! Hey batter, batter, batter—Swing!"

Elizabeth ignored the chant coming from the other team's dugout. If she'd learned one thing in the last month, it was never to swing.

The softball whizzed by.

"Strike!" the umpire yelled.

He didn't fool her. If she'd swung, it still would've been a strike. Keep your eye on the ball, watch it go by, and you had a chance.

"Shake it off, Auntie Beth!"

Anthony. He played on Saturday mornings in another section of the park and she'd cheered like mad when he hit a double two hours ago.

Something white whooshed by her ear.

213

"Ball!" the ump yelled.

"Good eye, Liz, good eye!" Ralph called from the sidelines.

She'd never seen him play, but he was a very affirming coach.

She focused on the pitcher's glove, daring the ball to wing by her shoulder. She tended to panic on a full count, and it was full now. Don't panic—

"Ow!" she yelled. Whoever named this softball must never have been hit by one. Ralph had advised her not to squirm, but it was part of her form. She rubbed her shoulder.

"Ball four!"

The ump motioned her to first. She jogged over feeling her ears flame red. Emily waved from the bench and gave her a thumbs up.

"Good eye," someone said.

A sarcastic first basewoman, just what she needed. She could feel the woman willing her to go for second. The pitcher turned their direction. She gave him a thumbs up, foot glued to the base. She'd earned this walk fair and square.

Mark was at bat. She tensed up and said a prayer. If Andrea wouldn't listen to her pleas, maybe God would.

"Ball one!" the ump shouted.

Mark was waiting for his pitch, but not because he was scared to swing.

Each Saturday Andrea insisted Joe would return from his rounds at the hospital before the end of the game, and she didn't want to mess with his spot in the line-up. Week after week she stuck Elizabeth in as his replacement, and the same thing happened every time. She heard a crack and fell to the ground in self defense.

"Foul ball! Strike one!"

She dusted off her pants and glared at Mark. He gave her a stage wink and she resisted the urge to stick out her tongue.

She should be used to this by now. He had perfect control over his hitting, and the first pitch he liked, he hit directly at her. So what if it curved away before impact? A girl had to be careful.

Another crack and she left first for second. The fans were going wild, she rounded second, she saw Ralph signaling from the other side of third base as she passed him. What did that mean again, arms held up, hands pushing toward her? She was half way home when it hit her. He was signaling her to stop.

She stopped.

Apparently Mark hadn't hit the ball out of the park. Because the catcher was holding it and walking toward her. If that was his attitude, she'd sprint back to third. She pivoted, but the third baseman had a ball. Were they allowed to have two balls?

She instinctively turned to Ralph; he would save her. He was right there, he could see this infraction if the umpire couldn't, he'd tell the ump about the two balls and she'd be home free. Well, they might not give her home, but she'd take third. Gretchen was up next and sure to get a hit.

She felt someone touch her. It was the third baseman.

"Yer outa there!" the ump yelled.

Perplexed, she looked at Ralph. He led her off the field toward the dugout.

"Liz, I know what you're going to say, but they don't have two softballs in play."

"Are you sure? Because I saw the catcher with one, and then the third baseman had one."

"The catcher threw the ball to third when you turned around. That's what catchers do. And I know you never see them do it, but that's because you're so focused. Very goal oriented. That's good."

Mystified, she walked to the dugout. It wasn't really a dugout, simply a wooden bench on one side of the diamond, but she liked to think of it as a dugout like in the big leagues.

Emily scooched over and patted an empty spot on the bench. The place Joe should be sitting after gaining a run for the team, instead of an out. She sat and put her head in her hands.

"Hey, shake it off. You're always so much fun to watch, and it's about having fun, right?"

She swatted Emily's shoulder. "Fun for you, I guess."

Alex was on the other side of her. Alex her first speed date. Alex the non-stop talker.

"That was a great pratfall at first base, Lizzy, did you ever work as a clown? I had an uncle who was a clown, Uncle Benny with Ringling Brothers, no kidding. He traveled with them I don't know how many years, and Aunt Terri was one of those ladies on the horses. Those ladies on the horses are married to the clowns lots of times which you'd never expect because they're so beautiful, I mean the ladies, not the clowns. Aunt Terri's sister Sal stood on a horse too, we called her Aunt Sal but she wasn't really our Aunt, she wasn't married to my uncle's brother or anything, but she was married to a clown. I didn't have another uncle in the circus, though it's often a family business, like the families on the flying trapeze and Aunt Terri and her sister Aunt Sal were sisters, case in point, but they never went on the trapeze, that was the El Greco family and they wouldn't let anyone else on, but Uncle Andy—Uncle Benny's brother—was a mortician. Still is actually. He—"

Emily jumped up from the bench and pulled Elizabeth with her. Elizabeth cheered to drown out Alex, to be part of the team, to distract herself from the image of Uncle Andy greeting mourners in a clown suit.

She didn't know why they were cheering, but if she listened for Andrea's strident voice, she'd find out. Even from the field Andrea gave a play by play. Her dad had been a professional sportscaster before a foul ball smashed through plate glass and hit him in the larynx. Maybe that was why Andrea never chided her for ducking.

"She's done it again! She's hit a homer! O'Reilly's rounding second, she's right behind him, they're going for broke. Wait, the center fielder's coming back from the bushes. He's got the ball. O'Reilly's passing third, Gretchen's on his tail, shortstop has the ball. O'Reilly's safely home. Two outs and will she make it? It's close! She's sliding home! I think she made it!"

"Safe!" the umpire yelled.

"She made it in and what a slide! Bottom of the eighth and we're up by one!"

Elizabeth whooped with abandon. So what if she played terribly? She loved this game. The competition, the excitement, the skill of her teammates. She hugged Emily, she hugged Alex, she hugged—Gretchen? In moments of extreme emotion Gretchen accepted a high five, but some people weren't huggers and she could respect that. Ralph's Chinese wisdom was second nature now and she could forgive the other for being Gretchen. She apologized and turned to hug—

"Mark. Good job." She stuck her hand out, but he pretended not to see it and pulled her in for a hug.

"Thanks, Elizabeth. Means a lot coming from you. No hard feelings, huh?"

She pushed him away. "Sure, whatever, but no more hugs. Why don't we shake on it?"

He shook her hand, slapped her on the back, and walked over to his spot by the Ice Princess. Gretchen hadn't thawed, but he didn't seem to notice. He smiled a lot and sat near her and increased Elizabeth's anxiety that his next victim would be a tall blonde. She wanted to say something to Gretchen, something subtle like, "Don't let him near you, he's a snake!" but she didn't have the nerve and consoled herself that Gretchen was nowhere near falling in love with him anyway.

"It's a pop fly!" Andrea shouted. "Fielder's got the sun in her eyes, we may be good. Run, George, run!"

The ball descended in a perfect arc to the fielder's glove. She waited for it to fall out of the mitt, but no luck. The fielders were coming in.

"Shake a leg, team. Let's win this game and go out with a bang! Three up, three down, we call it a day!"

She grabbed her mitt from under the bench and jogged with Emily to the outfield.

"Any word from Joe?"

"He called while you were batting. Stroke victim came in, so he won't be done before we are."

"Kind of inconvenient to have a stroke on a Saturday morning, isn't it?"

"You heard Andrea, three up, three down, it's over. You won't have to bat again."

"That's what I'm counting on."

She took her place in right field, an oasis of peace amid a bustling world. On the rare occasions the ball came her way, Emily ran over from center to catch it. Which was perfectly just since the point of right field was to provide the team philosopher a place to meditate.

She kicked a tuft of grass and stretched. This was it. She'd survived a whole month of softball. Second to last day of July and the last game of the season. Next week Emily would get married, a week later Jane's baby was due. Three more outs and she'd hang up her mitt.

She squinted toward the mound and saw Mark spit. What a show off. She picked a dandelion and blew on it. Forgive the other for being other. She was an adult, able to rise above her disgust and her personal grievance. It helped that he was an excellent pitcher.

Andrea looked like a ball of energy at second; Gretchen was languid as ever, the tall shortstop. Her flaxen pony tail swung behind her as she scooped up a grounder and threw it effortlessly to first base. She might be a cold fish, but she was a cold fish with a good arm.

"Out!" the ump yelled.

One up, one down.

Andrea and Gretchen nodded to each other then took their positions facing the batter. Was Andrea's pony tail longer or Gretchen's? Hard to tell, but probably Gretchen's.

"Heads up!" Emily yelled, and then, "Mine! I got it Lizzy!"

The ball crashed into the oleanders behind them. Not good, could mean a home run and they'd be tied, but Emily crawled in after it. She came out with the ball, threw it to Gretchen who threw it to Juan at home plate, and the runner stopped at third.

"One out, runner on third, let's put these next two down and it's over," Andrea yelled from second. "Great work Emily!"

Emily pulled leaves from her hair and smiled at Elizabeth. Elizabeth smiled back.

"You're the best, Emily Lucas!" she called.

She wanted to thank her for everything but couldn't risk distracting her in case the next hit came their way. She'd thank her later; for now she let her mind wander through the last wonderful weeks.

Emily had included her in everything, from watching the Dodgers at Frank's Sports Bar with Joe and Ralph to nerf baseball in the Lucas's front yard, the rest of them laughing at Ralph as he hopped around to spare his bum ankle.

She sighed and picked a tiny yellow flower. Ralph's coaching at the team practices had been perfect. He tirelessly reminded her of the essentials of the game, and grinned as he told her to forget about Pat and enjoy herself.

She looked up to see Mark step away from the mound and walk toward second. Must be a full count. Andrea loved to heighten the tension by having Mark take a break and confer with her before he struck the batter out. She gazed at the clouds and saw a seahorse resting in a donut. She blinked and yawned.

"Yer out!" the ump yelled.

Mark was doing his part. Three up, two down. Her heart went out to the batter returning to his bench. The walk of shame; she knew it well. A chance to be a hero and he'd done nothing, poor guy. Happily, in the great mystery of baseball his suffering wouldn't be lost. Thanks to him there was only one out to go, after which she'd never have to bat again, except against a nerf ball.

"Heads up!" Emily yelled.

She waited for Emily's "I got it!"

"It's yours Lizzy! It's coming down near the fence!"

The fence was to her left. With any luck the ball would veer off into foul territory.

She moved left and scanned the sky. She saw the ball. It wasn't veering. It was heading straight for her, out of the sky and into her mitt. This was it, her chance to be a hero. The other team hadn't scored. She'd catch the ball and they'd end the season in triumph.

She opened her mitt like she'd practiced with Ralph. She could almost hear Andrea's play by play and the congratulations from her teammates. There was only one problem. The ball had disappeared.

She heard a thud and looked down. She stared at the ball, wonderingly.

Emily was yelling something. Ralph was yelling something. She could even hear Anthony yelling something. Really this was enough of a bummer without everyone yelling at her.

"Throw the ball to Gretchen!" she made out.

Oh.

She picked up the softball and threw it to Gretchen, or at least she intended to, but the ball fell short, at her feet.

"You can do it, Liz. Throw it to Gretchen!" Ralph yelled.

She picked up the ball and threw it harder. This time it reached Gretchen's glove with a satisfying smack and in half a second Gretchen had spun around and hurled it to the catcher.

"Safe!"

A new low; two errors in one play. Even Andrea was stunned into silence by her ineptness. Good, she didn't need the play by play, she could see the bases clearly. Empty. The other team had scored two, her team was losing, and she was not a hero. She held back from yelling "Aaaarghhhhh!" This wasn't a comic strip. It was her life unfortunately.

"Shake it off, Auntie Beth," Anthony yelled.

He was right. She'd shake it off like a major leaguer.

"Steeee-riiiiiike! Yer outa there!"

At last. Her legs were tired, and she was ready to sit on the bench. She jogged back with Emily, who pointed to the metal bleachers.

"Look, there's Pat and Jane!"

The boys were making a racket trooping up the steps to join Anthony in the top row. Jane sat on the bottom bench. Pat was scooping Matthew off the edge of the field.

"Pat threatened to come," Elizabeth said, "but I didn't think he'd make it."

She sat on the team bench a few feet from Jane's place in the stands.

"Just get here?" she asked her sister.

"Just now. Did we miss anything?"

Pat, holding Matthew, sat next to Jane. "Yeah, what'd we miss?"

"Not much. Emily had a hit in the first inning."

"What's the score?" he asked.

"Five to four, their lead, bottom of the ninth."

"And you're batting soon?"

Wouldn't he love that.

"No. See Jolene? She's swinging the bat to loosen up. She hits a mean triple. Then Juan's up and he's even better. He'll hit a home run and we'll win."

"That's too bad. I was hoping to see you play."

"Maybe next summer."

They watched Jolene swing and miss the ball. Elizabeth took a deep breath and willed her to hit a triple. Bingo. Jolene swung and connected. She raced around the bases and pulled up at third.

Juan was up. She'd will him to hit a home run and call it a day.

She willed, but something malfunctioned. Juan hit a single that bounced past third, and Jolene didn't go home.

Elizabeth dug her nails into the wooden bench and sucked it up. That's what you did in baseball, you took the bad with the good and looked forward to the next play. Although it was hard to look forward to the next play with Alex up. He was almost worse than she was.

He made a noble attempt and tapped the ball, knocking it forward two feet. He set the bat down carefully and was out before he left home plate, but she wouldn't panic. Andrea was at bat, and Andrea was good. A double and they could all go out for ice cream.

Elizabeth gasped and rose from the bench with the rest of the team. Andrea had hit a pop fly and they waited to see if the pitcher would catch it. He did, and swirled around like he was doing a disco move. No one tagged up, no one dared advance, it had happened too quickly and they couldn't afford a mistake. They were down by one, there were two outs, this was it.

Andrea stormed back to the bench, her face as red as her hair.

"Don't sweat it, Andrea," Elizabeth said. "Em's up next and she's been hitting like a champ. Jolene and Juan'll come home and we've won. Shake it off. " She sounded like a real ballplayer.

"Yeah, it's cool, I just can't believe I did that." A quick intake of breath and Andrea yelled, "Do it for Joe! Let's see ya knock it outa the park, Em!"

Emily swung and missed.

"Wait for your pitch," Ralph encouraged her. He turned to the bench. "Liz, on deck. You're up next."

She sauntered over and picked up the extra bat to humor him, but she wasn't up next because there was no next, only Em hitting it out of the park for Joe like Andrea said. Jolene and Juan and Emily would all score, and they'd win by two.

Emily swung again and bat met ball, sending it toward third. Emily took off like a shot. The third baseman had the ball, bobbled it, had it again. He was ready to throw to first, but Emily was there. He looked back at his own base but Jolene stood glued to the bag.

She could read Jolene's mind. *No way, I'm not gonna be the goat. Elizabeth can make the last out of the season.* At least that's what she would have thought if she were Jolene. Sadly, she wasn't Jolene, she was up.

Ralph stood beside her. "Okay, Liz. Nothing heroic, just a base hit so Jolene can make it home. Mark's up next, he'll bat Juan in and the game's ours."

Was he crazy? Who was he kidding? She wasn't capable of a base hit.

"Stay calm and a base on balls will take us where we want to be. You can do it."

Yes, she could do that. She'd wait for her pitch and if it ever came, she'd swing. Since she'd never yet seen a pitch she liked, she felt safe from seeing one now. But she'd watch and wait and wait again, and after waiting twice more she'd walk. She'd walk and Jolene could walk, or jog, or run, or even slide home if she wanted to, but Jolene would get home and then Mark would hit Juan in and be a hero, and she'd be a semi-hero. Like Robin, or Tonto.

She took her stance at home plate. She tapped the base twice with her bat, bent her knees, and waited.

The ball whizzed by.

Wasn't this supposed to be slow pitch? She waited for the ump to call it.

"Strike One!"

The man didn't know what he was talking about. There had to be a rule against pitching that fast. She tapped the plate twice, bent her knees and stared at the mound. She focused so intently on the mound she forgot to watch the pitcher and didn't know the ball was on its way until it passed her.

"Ball One!" the ump yelled.

One and one. That was good. She'd pay attention this time. She watched carefully, saw the ball leave the pitcher's mitt and stepped back as it came near her knees.

"Ball Two!"

She was doing it. She was doing her part to help the team win. Two more of those puppies sliding by and she'd be a semi-hero.

"Strike two!"

She glared at the pitcher. She hadn't even tapped home plate. He'd pitched it before she was ready. Totally unacceptable.

The pitcher smirked at her. The nerve. She knew what he was thinking. He was thinking she was an easy out. He was thinking he could put her down and end the game, just like that. Well if that's what he thought, he had another think coming. She'd wipe that smirk right off his impertinent face.

She tapped the plate twice and waited. The pitcher wound up, the ball came toward her, and in slow motion she saw something she had never seen before. She saw her pitch.

She swung the bat, felt it connect with the ball, and heard a resounding crack. Her pitch became her hit, and she watched as the ball floated toward right field, over the first baseman's head. She watched in awe as it flew through the air.

"Run, Lizzy, run!"

She couldn't make out who said it, she heard it from every direction at once. Ralph's voice blended with Anthony's and Jane's and Emily's and Pat's.

"Run, Lizzy, run!"

She ran. As she ran she listened for the umpire's voice yelling "Foul!" but she didn't wait for him. She ran as fast as she could.

"Fair ball!" the umpire cried.

She was running too fast to see, but she didn't need to see. She was the wind, she was the cheetah, she was a baseball player. All at once her vision cleared. The sarcastic first base-woman was running toward her and the base was between them.

She'd never slid before, not even in practice, but it was now or never. She closed her eyes, stretched her arms out in front of her, and dove into the dirt toward the bag. She felt the base with her right hand, she felt the first baseman's glove pound her back, and she felt something like a shoe make contact with her face.

"Safe!" the umpire yelled.

She was safe. Jolene must be home. She was a semi-hero.

She turned on her side and opened her eyes. One eye, actually. The other wanted to stay closed and she let it. There was Anthony at the top of the bleachers cheering. He was yelling something.

"You did it! You did it, Auntie Beth! You won the game!"

Juan must've made it home too, and he'd done it on her hit, not Mark's. She wasn't a semi-hero, she was Superwoman and Mark was the guy they didn't need to bat next. She should get up so her teammates could carry her on their shoulders, but it was comfortable here in the dirt and she wanted to catch her breath.

She rolled onto her back and there was Andrea leaning over her, red pony tail falling forward, shining in the sun.

"You okay, woman? That was some slide!"

Ralph stood behind Andrea, and he had a funny look on his face. His lips were pursed and he whistled.

"That'll be quite a shiner, Liz, but you won the game for us. I knew you could do it."

"What happened?"

"You finally got your pitch. You hit a beautiful soft fly just out of reach of the first baseman. The right fielder caught it on a bounce, tossed it to the first baseman, and you touched the bag in time to get her foot in your face. I've never seen anyone slide into first, but you were safe, no doubt about it."

He was grinning, and now Pat was there too.

"Did you see me Pat? Did you see my hit?"

Pat looked at her with the same odd expression Ralph had, and then he grinned too.

"I saw it all. Good job, girl. Never seen anyone slide into first. How ya feelin'?"

"I'm great, except I can't open my eye."

"Why don't you try, to make sure it still works."

Pat wasn't so bad. Considerate if you gave him a chance. She gingerly touched her eyelid and pulled it up, then let it back down. One eye was plenty for now.

"Can you see out of it?" Ralph asked.

"No problem," she said and smiled at them.

"You'll remember this day for the rest of your life," Pat said. "And if you forget, we'll have pictures to remind you."

"Did someone take pictures?" How thoughtful, they'd captured her Kodak moment. She'd blow it up and hang it under Fra Angelico, a reminder of her happiest day.

"I didn't see anyone with a camera," Pat said. "I was thinking of next Saturday when you'll be the maid of honor with the exceptionally interesting eyes."

She'd forgotten about Emily's wedding. She'd forgotten what a jerk he could be. She closed her good eye and tried to forget again. Of course Emily could find a new maid of honor. Gretchen was elegant; Andrea's hair was fantastic; Joe had four sisters who'd be here on Monday. Where was Emily, anyway?

She opened her eye and Em was right there behind Pat and Ralph.

"Don't even think about it," Emily said. "I've been counting on you since we were little girls, and you're not backing out now."

She closed her eye and thought about her brilliant slide to first. She'd rather not think of next Saturday just yet.

CHAPTER 26

The Big Day

Despite everyone's fears they wouldn't get any rest, Elizabeth and Emily were determined to have one last sleepover the night before Emily's wedding. The Lucas' house overflowed with Joe's sisters, so the two best friends stayed in Elizabeth's cottage.

Emily fell asleep as soon as her head hit the pillow. Elizabeth, who never had trouble sleeping, propped herself up for a long vigil. Emily was getting married tomorrow and one of them had to stay awake to mentally prepare.

She gazed at the bride-to-be and felt the onset of tears, but the last thing she needed was more swelling around her eye. *Never Too Late* waited patiently on her bedside table where it had rested unopened since New Year's. She picked it up and read the Introduction, then Chapter 1, "A Week of Music."

She'd begun Chapter 2, "Early Musical Memories," when the words began to blur and she drifted off.

Light was streaming through her open window, she was drooling on the book, and Emily was awake, her smile more luminous than the sunshine.

"It's morning, isn't it?" She wiped her mouth with the back of her hand, and the motion brought back the image of Ralph waking in the Vanagon. "How'd you sleep?"

"Soundly. Not one anxiety dream about the wedding."

"You didn't have the one I had? Where I hid in the bathroom and refused to walk down the aisle?"

"You promised to stop worrying about your eye. It's not a big deal."

"I promised because you made me, so it doesn't count. Besides, I can't control my dreams."

"As long as it wasn't a prophecy. Let me look at you."

Elizabeth sat up in the double bed and waited for Emily's verdict.

"You know, I just thought of something."

"You'd rather have one of the Marys as your maid of honor?"

"No, you're perfect."

"It's gone?" The miracle she'd prayed for. The palette of colors surrounding her left eye couldn't have disappeared overnight except by divine intervention.

"No, you look terrible. I was thinking how fabulous I'll look by comparison."

She threw her pillow at Emily and retreated to the rocking chair.

"You don't need a black-eyed maid of honor to set you off. You're glowing."

"Glowing or not, I won't marry Joe unless you're my witness."

"I'll be there. I'll be by your side at the church and at the reception, and when we sing 'Let Me Call You Sweetheart' I'll be the last one to kiss you good-bye."

Emily looked away.

"I don't have to be the very last one. You can kiss your mom and dad good-bye last." She rocked comfortably in the chair.

"It isn't that," Emily said. "It's about the reception."

"Not enough waiters and you want me to serve? I can do that too."

"Lizzy, please don't get mad. You know how you were going to sit next to me at the head table? It was going to be me and Joe in the center and you on my right, and Ralph on Joe's left?"

"If you want me to sit next to Joe, I will. Strange, but it's your wedding."

"There's not going to be a head table."

"Seriously?" She stopped rocking. "We don't have to sit in front, and 'Whose the girl with the crazy eye?' won't be the question on everyone's lips? That's fantastic. Why?"

As soon as she asked, she knew.

"You could still have a head table and I could sit somewhere else. I'd be totally fine with that."

"It's not about you. Yesterday Joe and I talked it over and found out we both hate being the center of attention."

"You're the bride and groom! What's your plan? To sit behind a bank of potted plants?"

"You promised to help me through this day, and if you're not supportive I'll tell Pat."

"You're only half my August. When Jane has her baby I'm taking the boys, and that's the part of my Mother Teresa month Pat cares about."

"I thought your mom was taking them."

"Technically, but I'll stay at the big house to help and have them sleep here some nights. We'll have the boys for two weeks, so your special day isn't even half my month of service. Not even a quarter."

"But it's the happiest part, isn't it?"

"We'll see. I'm fine with no head table, but if you seat me with our eighth grade class, I can't promise I'll stay to the bitter end."

Emily hid behind a pillow.

"You're making me nervous," Elizabeth said. "What aren't you telling me?"

Down went the pillow. "We had a couple late RSVPs and last night I was moving us from the head table and the whole thing was a muddle when Joe's sister Mary came in and said I was supposed to be having a good gossip with my maid of honor. Maria took away my clipboard and when I said I didn't even know where we were sitting, Maureen said they'd take care of it and Miriam pushed me out the door. They're incredibly sweet and they sent me over here without a thought as to how late they'd be up working on the seating chart."

"I bet they didn't stay up at all. They wrote the extra names in anywhere, and if I'm sitting with one of our grade school teachers, I'll kill you."

"If you kill me, Joe will kill you, then Ralph will kill Joe, and my wedding day will end like a Shakespearean tragedy, so please don't."

Elizabeth rocked with an air of innocence, but she could feel her smile giving her away.

"You're not denying Ralph would kill Joe for killing you," Emily said. "Is it too late for a double wedding?"

"More like too early."

"I knew it! Haven't I been good as gold? I've wanted to ask you for weeks, and I haven't said a word."

"You're so obvious it's pitiful. Every time the four of us are together I can see you restraining yourself."

"I knew you'd love Ralph once you gave him a chance. Was it softball that changed your mind?"

She put her hand to her eye. "Not exactly. It started before that."

"In the elevator when Mark proposed?"

"No." Elizabeth stopped rocking. "It was the Grand Canyon."

"And I told him not to go! I didn't think chasing you to Arizona would help his cause."

"At first it was awful, but when we were trapped in the Vanagon, somewhere around Needles he changed. He made me talk about Pat and said I shouldn't try to beat him anymore. If I was doing a happiness project it should be about me finding more happiness. He made a lot of sense."

"You must have taken his advice. You seem happy now."

"But nervous. I'm wondering if it's time to say something, make sure he knows I like him." She scanned Emily's face. "Unless you think that's too much."

"Doesn't he already know how you feel?"

"Look at Jane Bennet. She took it for granted Bingley knew and what a mess that was."

"But you're Elizabeth."

"That's the problem. I was pretty rough on him in April and not much nicer when he showed up at the Canyon. After all the hints to leave me alone, I'd hate to have him actually go away now that I'm interested." She twisted a strand of hair.

"I've told you he's liked you since he met you. What else can I say?"

"I want you to tell me what to do."

"My pleasure. Put your robe over your sweats so we can go to my house. Consider that your first job as my lady in waiting."

Elizabeth left the rocking chair for the bathroom.

"Let me brush my teeth and I'll be ready."

She saw her reflection in the mirror and groaned.

"Emily, it's just as bad."

"I told Dad we'd be over at nine for breakfast and Minnie's pointing at five after. Mom said she'd lay out our dresses and the four Marys have elaborate plans for my hair and your make-up."

"Have them concentrate on your hair and we'll put a paper bag over my head."

Emily's reflection appeared beside hers.

"We'll talk about that later. Right now you're coming with me so you don't miss breakfast. I know how you get without food."

"Have you been talking to Ralph, or reading Gretchen Rubin?"

"Wait till you see how much food my dad bought. Mom was furious, you know how he can't cook a hot dog without setting the toaster oven on fire, and she didn't want to cook today. So guess who came to the rescue?"

"One of Joe's sisters?"

"All of them."

"I hope they can cook. Party planning, cosmetology, catering." Elizabeth put on her robe and tied the belt. "And you can't get a single Mary to take my place at the wedding?"

"Not on your life, but you'll enjoy breakfast." Emily stood at the door. "They're preparing the eggs how you like them."

"Over easy?" Elizabeth slipped her feet into sandals.

"Without peanut butter."

CHAPTER 27

The Wedding

The Collins sisters could cook. Mary and Miriam even cleaned the kitchen afterward, saying Maria and Maureen were the hair and make-up artists. With Mrs. Lucas' help the women dressed and curled and coiffed and buttoned and zipped and worked on Elizabeth's eye until Mr. Lucas loaded them into the store van, "Adventures in Reading" still blazoned on its side.

They arrived at the church in plenty of time. While the bridesmaids giggled in anticipation, Emily and Elizabeth found a private corner and said a prayer together. Outfitted in a small tux and complete with satin ring-bearing pillow, Dominic brought the message that Father Denny was ready. The guests were seated, the bridegroom and his groomsmen waited near the altar, and Emily was about to get married.

The organist played Handel's Water Music. Elizabeth spread the bride's train and gave her one last kiss. Mr. Lucas crooked his arm and beamed at his daughter.

It was simply the most beautiful wedding ever, and if anyone disagreed, they could meet her outside the church after the recessional. As Joe and Emily said their vows, Elizabeth caught Ralph's eye. He looked as moved by the ceremony as she was. His brother and her best friend: a perfect match.

When they processed out and gathered for pictures she was quiet, savoring the day and Emily's joy. Could life get any better?

Whether or not it could get better, she soon discovered it could definitely get worse.

Thanks to Emily and the Marys she'd eaten a substantial breakfast, but she hadn't consumed a morsel of food since. The wedding party reached the reception hall at quarter after five, and she broke her seven hour fast with a guzzled flute of Korbel. Waiters circulated with appetizers, but whenever she reached for food she came up with more champagne. Her best bet was to find her place and untie the bags of candy coated almonds she and Emily had spent the week tying after Emily rejected chocolate mints as too messy. Candy covered was better than nothing.

Her place card stood alphabetically amid the ranks of names on a table near the door. Elizabeth Benning, Table 12, written in an unfamiliar hand that must belong to one of the Marys. She smiled at Emily's misgivings regarding Table 1. The room looked perfect with no dais and no long head table, a democratic gathering of identical round tables covered in white linen. Table 12 was over to one side, the large black 12 dominating a white placard stuck into the blue and peach hydrangea centerpiece.

The table was slightly screened by plants but wonderfully close to the dance floor, an ideal location. She didn't feel entirely steady on her high heels at the moment, but she'd regain her equilibrium once she ate, and she could always dance without her shoes.

She made her tottery way to the potted plants. The table hadn't attracted anyone yet, an unexpected boon. She could eat the almonds from the eight netted bags and drink a glass of water. Emily was big on hydrating and had promised two pitchers of ice water at each table.

Elizabeth sat in a plastic folding chair like the ones they used at St. Albert's College. Either the country club wasn't so fancy, or the college was upscale. She laughed softly and whispered, "What's good enough for the college is good enough for the country club."

As if summoned by her incantation, a portly form heaved into the chair beside her.

"We meet again! My, my, isn't this a delight. Mabel, look who's here."

Dr. O'Reilly turned slightly in his chair toward the little woman hiding behind him. "Providential I'd call it. We're seated next to Miss Benning, the icon girl. Haven't seen her since the night Vivian made that delicious chicken. Now we'll catch up on old times."

There must be some mistake. Several mistakes in fact. She wasn't the icon girl. The chicken could not have been delicious. And she wouldn't spend the reception catching up with the O'Reillys if she could help it.

Mabel's aged eyes shone like a girl's, her dry wizened lips pecked Elizabeth's cheek, and she alit on the chair beside her victim. As if a single thought possessed all comers to Table 12, Dr. O'Reilly with his bear paws on one side of her and Mabel with her bird claws on the other began tugging on the blue satin ribbon that held the candy coated almonds captive in peach netting. She wouldn't tell them the knots defied untying; better that they kept focused on their impossible task.

Wherever Emily was, she was in for it. She'd said the O'Reillys would be here, guests of her parents, and Elizabeth had teased that the Lucases knew everyone in town and had invited them all. Emily assured her she wouldn't have to talk to the O'Reillys. In all fairness, she'd never said Elizabeth could escape being talked to.

The four Marys—this was their fault. Emily never would have seated her at Table 12. With any luck, a couple of the Marys would sit at the table too. Then she could pull the placard-holding-stake out of the hydrangeas and stab one of them with it.

She recoiled from the image of Miriam bleeding, a number 12 sticking out of her empire waisted bridesmaid's dress. She owed it to Emily not to attack anyone tonight. If she wanted action, she should actively get up and find another place to sit.

To her dismay guests were filling the tables rapidly, though no one had joined the intimate party at Table 12. Mabel on her right and Dr. O'Reilly on her left continued to work at the ribbons. She felt trapped, but the five empty chairs encouraged her. If the proper guests claimed them, anything could happen.

She said a quick prayer that her parents would join her, but even as she prayed she glimpsed her mother across the room, seated with her father and the Moores. Jane looked extremely pregnant but not like she'd go into labor in the next five minutes, unfortunately.

Where in the world was Ralph? Wasn't he supposed to be with her? If his sisters had separated the maid of honor and the best man, they deserved a fate worse than she'd yet pictured.

"This is our table, Gretchen," said a voice she'd come to hate. It wasn't Ralph's.

Emily had warned her Gretchen was bringing Mark, but had promised her asylum at the non-existent head table. She pinched her arm, a dual purpose pinch to wake herself up from her second anxiety dream or, if worse came to worse and she were already awake, to punish herself for not escaping the table when she had the chance. Never too late, wasn't that the perennial wisdom? She'd go to her family's table and sit with a nephew on her lap. She rose, but before she could free herself from the chair, Dr. O'Reilly's massive hand pulled her back into it.

"Don't rise. She's a fine girl, but the man's the one to stand when a lady joins the company." He doffed an imaginary hat as he got to his feet. "Welcome to our humble table, Miss Gretchen."

Mark sat beside his grandfather with Gretchen to his left. The newcomers made a stunning pair. He wore a tuxedo that fit like it was made for him. Which it probably was. She wore a gold dress straight out of Jackie O's wardrobe. Okay, not really from Jackie's wardrobe, but if Gretchen stuck to her escort, she'd soon have the funds to buy the original.

Elizabeth's calculations on how much a Jackie O dress would cost broke off as suddenly as a circus lady falling from her white horse's back. What were Alex and Andrea doing here?

As they approached the table, Alex kept up a steady stream of words, presumably directed at Andrea, but when he pulled out a chair for her he re-routed the flow.

"Hey Grandpa, Grandma Mabel! Isn't this awesome? I can't tell you how many times I called Emily to let her know

I hadn't got my invitation, but yesterday she said not to worry about it, they wouldn't be checking a list at the door. Isn't she hilarious? And a beautiful bride. Andrea and I sat in the back at church because I was late picking her up. Hard to believe I made a red-head wait, but I had a good excuse, I thought Mark was picking me up and we'd all come together but one of the plugs wasn't sparking, metaphorically I mean. Hey Mark! Glad you made it buddy, I was worried your car broke down."

Dr. O'Reilly his grandfather and Mabel his grandmother? Mark must be his cousin, then, though Andrea's identity remained a mystery. Another O'Reilly? If not, then what—his date? If Alex's unceasing chatter didn't reveal all, she'd ask. This was too good to miss.

He sat next to Mabel and kissed her cheek just as Mabel had kissed Elizabeth's. The kiss interrupted his running commentary and Andrea, sitting beside him, seized the day.

"Hello Dr. O'Reilly, Mrs. O'Reilly, nice to see you again. Mark. Gretchen. See you're showing off your badge of courage there, Liz, and why not, you earned it. That was some slide."

She'd forgotten her black eye. Hopefully they'd be spared the play by play.

Mabel leaned closer. "Don't you mind it dear. I'm sure you'll find a fella."

Dr. O'Reilly guffawed. She hadn't known people actually did that.

"Hated to say anything. Thought it was the latest fashion. Never know what you girls are doing with face paint these days. Mabel never painted her face. Never needed to, did you beautiful?"

If she traded seats with him she could put him on her right where he wouldn't see her made-up eye, and he'd be closer to his little love bird. On the other hand, she'd be sitting next to Mark. Bad idea. She could switch with Mabel, but then Alex would have her ear. She'd better stay put. She willed Ralph to appear and before the willing was half done, he was there, scraping back the empty chair between Andrea and Gretchen.

"Glad you saved my place," he said, his glance taking them all in. "Had to go over my toast one more time."

He was handsome in his rented tux, his tone amused. Grateful though she was to see his kind face directly across from her, she was still surrounded by O'Reillys and he seemed too far away. Even if he received her telepathic messages, he'd be hard pressed to do much from way over there. She sighed.

He responded immediately.

"Great wedding, wasn't it, Liz?"

From the way he said it she knew he would have sat next to her if he could. The others faded away. What were O'Reillys, dozens of them even, when he looked at her like that?

"It was a lovely wedding," Mabel chirped, repopulating the table. "I would say it was the loveliest wedding I've had the privilege to witness, but that doesn't mean I might not decide that the next wedding I attend is even more special." She smiled meaningfully at Mark and Gretchen, then turned to Elizabeth. "Sorry things didn't work out for you, dear. I was rooting for you, but Mark can't stand the forward girls."

Her little bird claw patted at Elizabeth's hand. Elizabeth smiled back weakly and put her hands in her lap. It would be wrong to slap an old woman, and besides, she liked Mabel.

"Mrs. O'Reilly," Andrea said, "I sincerely hope you will enjoy the next wedding you go to." She put her hand on Alex's sleeve and smiled at Mabel more meaningfully than Mabel had smiled at Mark.

Alex prepared for his next speech with a deep breath. If he started on his own, who knew if he'd answer her questions. Elizabeth dove in first.

"Alex, I didn't realize the O'Reillys were your grandparents. I thought your last name was Decker."

"Mom's an O'Reilly but she married Dad who's a Decker and she took his name, you know like everyone used to do, I mean the ladies did, you know when they married men with different last names. I've heard of cases where women didn't need to change their names because they married men with the same names. Not like Terri and Terry but last names like—"

"That's what I wanted to ask you. Last week you told me about your Aunt Terri and your uncle the clown. Are they O'Reillys too?"

Mark rapped the table with a silver fork.

"Alex's father—Mr. Decker—has an interesting family. They're not our family, however."

Andrea pointed a steak knife at him. "What's good enough for Alex is good enough for me and his last name doesn't make him any less O'Reilly than you are."

Dr. O'Reilly pounded the table with his fist, and the netted almonds jumped.

"I like that, Andrea. Don't let Mark dismiss Alex. Your beau has just as much chance at the overflow as Mark here." He slapped Mark on the back and reached across the table to shake hands with Alex. "May the best man win."

"I'm sorry sir," Ralph said with a straight face, "but I think I'm excluded. No O'Reilly blood, not a drop I'm afraid."

Dr. O'Reilly laughed and his enormous face turned pink, then red. He'd laughed like this in the library, the night she'd been Mark's date and here was Gretchen, silent as ice, Mark's date tonight. Did it mean anything? She'd better beware, with Alex and Andrea giving him a run for the money he was bound to propose soon.

"Table 12, if you'll please follow me."

A waiter stood at attention, ready to lead them across the room to the buffet. She'd given up hope of ever eating again; their table might have been a desert island for all the sustenance she'd found on it. Now the waiter was smiling upon them and their three-hour cruise hadn't ended in disaster yet.

They fell in line behind the waiter, Ralph beside her at last.

"Exciting, isn't it?"

"You always find food exciting," he said, smiling.

"I mean the race for the overflow. I didn't know Alex was an O'Reilly, and I had no idea he and Andrea were dating. Do you think they'll beat Mark and Gretchen to the altar?"

"You're kidding, aren't you?" His voice had lost all trace of amusement.

"I don't know. It's funny, isn't it? Sitting with all those O'Reillys, and Mabel talking about weddings and everything."

"I'd marry Gretchen before I'd let her marry Mark."

His tone was serious. She took a plate from the stack, hoping he was teasing. She looked up but she'd never seen him so grave.

The servers held up their tongs expectantly and she nodded blindly at each chafing dish before her. What did he mean? Did he want to marry Gretchen, or was he saying he'd be forced to if she threatened to marry Mark? Or was it merely an expression, like if she and Mark were friends, she might say she'd marry him before she'd let him marry Gretchen. Which almost made sense.

She followed Dr. O'Reilly's bulk back to their table. He'd been in front of her at the buffet, and now she used his size as a lodestar. Her unwieldy heels and loaded plate prefaced disaster, but she kept her eyes on her feet and walked slowly, dependent on Dr. O'Reilly to lead her home.

He sat in a plastic chair and she raised her eyes. She stood before a crowded table, crowded mostly with the Collins family. She didn't see Dr. O'Reilly—she'd been following some random Uncle Collins. This was not Table 12.

Maureen looked up from her prime rib.

"Lizzy, how nice of you to stop by. I was just telling Maria how right I was. She wanted to seat you near Joe and Emily, but I insisted you and Ralph would have more fun at the O'Reilly table. Mr. Lucas told us how Dr. O'Reilly lent him the money to open the bookstore in seventy-five, and I knew you'd love to sit with your benefactors, if that's the right word."

Maria shook her silver fork. "I wasn't sure she was right. It's terribly sad the bookstore closed, and I didn't want you to think about that tonight. But then Mary reminded me Gretchen was at that table."

Sitting with Gretchen would console her for the loss of the bookstore? Maria must be the slow one.

"Of course you and Ralph had to sit together," Maureen said, "but Ralph's always had a thing for Gretchen, we wanted the two of you where she could see how dapper he looks in a tux."

"Ever since we heard he and Gretchen were near each other again we've been hoping." Maria lowered her voice conspiratorially. "Last April when we heard you turned him down, well we took it as a sign from God."

Elizabeth concentrated on keeping her plate level and her mouth closed.

"Ralph'll make a terrific husband," Maureen went on, "and Gretchen's been waiting for him so long. Mom was sure they'd get married years ago in New York, but God's timing's always best. Nothing more romantic than a wedding. Maybe you can distract Mark so Ralph can tell Gretchen how he feels."

Now Maria had a broccoli floret on her fork, and as she shook it Elizabeth watched, fascinated, to see if the little green tree would fly off.

"Fringe benefits for you." The broccoli held on. "That Mark sure is handsome. You two would make quite a couple, I was telling Maureen. Both of you as dark haired as Ralph and Gretchen are fair. There's love in the air tonight, I can feel it." Maria popped the broccoli in her mouth and speared a baby carrot with finality.

She was dismissed.

CHAPTER 28

A Painful Reception

Dr. O'Reilly pulled out her empty chair, and once she was seated, shoved her in. She thanked him and pushed out a tad. Gretchen's seat looked closer to Ralph's than it had been. Whichever sister had said it, she was right. The blondes were well matched.

"So when Mabel wanted to start an animal shelter, I said to her, 'Mabel,' I said, 'I've been reading about the animal shelter Mr. Wodehouse and his Missus started up in New York. If you think we should start an animal shelter, we need to go to New York and learn from a gentleman how it's done.' Ever since he'd answered my thank you note for *The Butler Did It* in fifty-seven, I knew Wodehouse was human, you see, not one of your fly-by-night celebrity types. So off we went to New York. We met Plum and his Ethel—salt of the earth, those two—and modeled our St. Francis Home for the Animals in Glendale precisely on theirs."

"Except for the name," Mabel corrected. "Theirs was the P.G. Wodehouse Shelter, but we named ours after the poor man of Assisi."

"Mabel's a marvel. Always knows which saint to put together with each of our causes. That's my girl." He set down his fork, reached across Elizabeth's untouched plate, and covered Mabel's petite hand with his super-sized one.

They were a dear couple, even if they made her feel like a third wheel, and they'd been responsible for her bookstore's erstwhile existence. She'd be grateful retroactively.

"What a wonderful story," she said. "I love P.G. Wodehouse."

Ralph was looking at her, cheerful again, enjoying this too.

"Sir, my brother Joe and I are huge Wodehouse fans, must've read all those orange Penguin paperbacks of his three or four times when we were teenagers. To this day I keep one by my bed for reading myself to sleep, only it usually keeps me awake. He sure could write."

Dr. O'Reilly nodded vehemently. "Absolutely, son. Glad to hear his works are still appreciated. You have a favorite?"

Gretchen had taken only salad and was eating the leaves singly. Mark was mopping up his plate with a roll. Andrea toyed with her cell phone and Alex was doing something to his. Were they texting each other? Ralph was squinting, obviously thinking hard.

"Well, sir, I hate to pick just one, but if I had to, I'd say *Leave it to Psmith*."

Dr. O'Reilly had finished his meal and picked up the bag of almonds.

"I'm not surprised at what you say, son, but I prefer the book I thanked him for. It's my opinion he never surpassed *The Butler Did It.*" He addressed Elizabeth. "What do you think, young lady? Choose a side."

"I don't know that I've read yours, or if I have, I'm afraid I've forgotten it. What's it about?"

"Tell her, Mark. Tell Elizabeth about my favorite book."

Dr. O'Reilly punched his grandson in the arm. She didn't want to hear it from Mark, but he grimaced at the blow and she smiled.

"I never read it myself," Mark said, "but I've heard the story from Grandpa countless times. A set of Wall Street tycoons each put fifty thousand bucks into a pot and agree to give it all to whichever of their sons is the last to marry."

"Maybe I have read it," she said. "That sounds familiar."

"A butler overhears their plan and keeps a look out over the next decades. The story picks up when the last two unmarried sons are both in love, and the butler tries to swing it so he can get a piece of the action."

Dr. O'Reilly's chair rocked dangerously. He shook and quaked. Was he choking on an almond? He pulled his large handkerchief from a vest pocket and she relaxed. He was laughing, silently this time except for a trace of asthmatic wheezing. Tears streamed down his mottled cheeks, and he used the handkerchief to wipe them away. He was speechless but Mabel spoke for him.

"Mark, you'd better stop, your Grandfather can't even read that book anymore for fear of laughing himself into an early grave."

She'd never figured out precisely how old he was, but certainly too old for an early grave. By the look on his face Ralph must be thinking it too. He covered his smile with a hand and pretended to cough.

With his grandfather speechless, Alex set his phone on the table, ready to step into the breach. Andrea followed suit, dropping her phone into her mini backpack, near proof they had been texting each other. Masterful. She'd found a way to cork Alex's verbal flow, at least temporarily.

"I'll tell the rest," he said, reserving the opening. He took his preparatory breath. "My grandfather and grandmother belong to a Wodehouse for Catholics book group, and you know how book groups are, always talking and discussing and reading books? Well their group is something special because they only read Wodehouse and then talk about how a Catholic might change some of the plots. He must've written a boatload of books because they've been reading him for years and years, and Grandma says the only time they ever agreed—I mean Grandma and Grandpa, not the whole group because the whole group never agrees from what Grandma says—but the one time she and Grandpa agreed, course they agree on lots of things all the time, but I mean in the book group the only time they agreed was when they talked about that very book, *The Butler Did It*. Grandma said they both laughed a lot when they read it but then they agreed it was the wrong sort of story for modern times. Grandma's very pro-life."

Alex paused and turned to Andrea as if to make sure that she, mainstay of the pro-life singles group, appreciated his grandmother.

"But what does that have to do with the book?" Andrea asked.

"She thought the tycoons should offer the pot to the first of their sons to get married, rather than the last. She always says today's young people put off marriage too long."

Mabel stopped fluffing her gray hair. "I never meant to speak against those youngsters who haven't found their kindred spirit yet. No one can be blamed for that, especially when they're trying."

She blinked and smiled at each of them in turn. First Ralph, then Gretchen, then Mark, then she swiveled her head and smiled at Andrea and Alex.

"Don't give up, sweetie," she said to Elizabeth. "There's a man out there for you somewhere, and someday you'll find him. Why look at Gretchen, she's got two beaus."

Elizabeth picked up a baby carrot like the one Maria had speared after Maureen informed her Ralph had always loved Gretchen. It was cold, the butter on it congealed. She took one bite and then another. There, she'd eaten something.

Silence prevailed, her humiliation bare for everyone to see, but no one was interested in her, thankfully. Alex had lost the thread of his story and was texting again, Andrea reading her screen as his words became visual. Having ripped open the netting, she ate coated almonds without attending to them.

Dr. O'Reilly wheezed slightly but his face had returned to a normal color.

Gretchen was whispering to Ralph, and Mark was . . . Was he admiring his reflection in the water pitcher? Elizabeth laughed.

"Miss Benning," Mabel's eyes twinkled, "you're waiting to hear the rest of what I was thinking about that book and I won't keep you on tenterhooks."

She'd forgotten about Mabel but she'd rather walk on hot coals in high heels than check if Ralph was whispering back to Gretchen.

"Don't mistake us for puritans," Mabel said. "We laughed at that story until we cried, you saw my husband, but then I had to ask myself, shouldn't we be encouraging marriage rather than laughing at it? Couldn't we come up with a better plan than this? And that was the beginning. Dr. O'Reilly and

I agreed that if we ever had the chance, we'd offer a pot of gold to someone who married at the first opportunity, rather than putting it off."

No wonder the story sounded familiar: it was the opposite of the O'Reillys' race. Mabel's head nodded and bobbed and weaved as she looked around the table. Mark continued to gaze at his reflection; Gretchen listened to something Ralph said.

She felt a sharp pain in her side and then another. She moved her hand to her ribcage and intercepted Mabel's elbow-wing as it jabbed her a third time.

"Too bad the best man's not an O'Reilly or I think he would win!" Mabel tittered.

After the opening flutes of champagne, alcohol had lost its appeal, but being poked in the ribs by a bird who echoed her thoughts was too much. She felt uncomfortably warm and thirsty. She hated to take the water pitcher from Narcissus, but her wineglass was full. Room temperature Chardonnay, it looked like. She raised the glass to her lips and drank it to the dregs. Not that there were dregs, but it sounded biblical, like the wedding feast at Cana.

Dr. O'Reilly refilled her glass.

"Thought you must be thirsty. Marvelous occasion, but damn warm in here, if you'll excuse my French."

She smiled at his French and took a sip. It tasted better this time. That was like in the Bible too.

She tried not to look across the table. She wanted to mind her own business, and Ralph had said in the Vanagon that Gretchen wasn't her business. Actually he'd said Gretchen wasn't his business, but apparently he'd changed his mind. Which was fine. Free country and she was fine over here with Mabel and Dr. O'Reilly, but she would like a glass of water and the pitcher was somewhere over there near Gretchen.

She located it in time to see, behind it, Gretchen speak to Ralph, and Ralph look at his watch.

He stood, wine glass in his right hand. He was the image of the April Dr. Collins, the new professor revealing his secret identity. The stance didn't become him, in her opinion. The only thing left for him to announce was his engagement.

"I'm afraid I'm up," he said.

Of course he was up, he was standing there and he could hardly be down if he was standing. She sipped her wine and frowned at him. He smiled back.

"Time for my toast, if you'll excuse me."

"You're excused," she said, then realized he wasn't actually asking her permission.

So Gretchen had told him it was time for his toast? Since when was Gretchen the maid of honor? Wasn't it the maid of honor's job to tell the best man when to give the toast? She wasn't sure if that was right, but it was too late. Ralph had disappeared.

"Where'd he go?" she asked Mabel.

Mabel pointed to a table featuring the bride and groom. Beside Joe stood Ralph, cordless microphone in hand.

Guests shushed each other, someone clinked a wine glass, and others took up the cue until Joe kissed Emily. The room broke out in cheers. Ralph cleared his throat and everyone quieted.

"Good looking fellow," Dr. O'Reilly said in his booming voice. "Better watch out, Mark, or he'll steal your girl for himself."

"If he hasn't done it already," Mabel sang into the silence.

Elizabeth closed her eyes to shut out Gretchen's impassive face.

Her hand clenched the stem of her wine glass. The make-up on her shiner must have worn off by now but she was past caring. She'd stay like this until the reception was over and someone brought her, eyes still closed, to her cottage.

Ralph's voice interrupted her thoughts, but she didn't open her eyes. She might have to listen, but she'd seen too much already.

CHAPTER 29

The Toast and the Toasted

"As many of you know, I'm Joe's younger brother Ralph. Our other siblings are sisters, so I've had a long time to think about what I'd say when my brother Joe got married."

A few people clapped, and someone called out, "Speech, speech!"

"I've known Joe thirty-three years, and ever since I can remember, he's been my best friend and my hero. We used to read P.G. Wodehouse together and laugh at Gussie Fink-Nottle, and Bertie with his accidental engagements, and Bingo Little who took so long to find his Rosie M. Banks."

Someone clinked a glass, and the clinking went on for a moment. Even with her eyes closed she knew when Joe and Emily kissed by the way the room quieted.

"Emily, I don't need to tell you that Joe is no Bingo Little. He's not a man who fell in love every spring. We used to talk about our ideals, and Joe always had a clear idea of the girl he was looking for, but he didn't find her until last summer when he wandered into a children's bookstore. That day he found the girl he'd told me about many times, and Emily, that girl—the only one for Joe—was you."

The clinking started up. Elizabeth opened her eyes and saw Ralph standing behind Joe and Emily, impressive in his tuxedo, very tall, very blonde, very much in command of the situation. He reminded her of the Ralph she'd met eight months ago, the night of the concert.

She closed her eyes, as if that could block out the image of January's piano Ralph and February's icon Ralph. She didn't want to think about Father Barkley's best friend Ralph from March, or Ralph the new professor she'd met in April, either. Grand Canyon Ralph was a pain in the neck, but Vanagon Ralph had been different; he'd changed. Ralph the coach was better yet, kind and patient and fun to be with.

Dr. O'Reilly coughed beside her.

Was Ralph an O'Reilly type, destined for greatness, tuxes, and Gretchen? Or was he the common man he'd been with her in the Vanagon and at the sports bar and playing nerf baseball?

Best man Ralph continued his toast.

"I would be remiss, having brought up literary couples, if I failed to mention another famous fictional pair. Joe's a touch sensitive about this comparison, but I think we ought to bring it out into the open, for the sake of contrast. Today a certain Miss Lucas was attended to the church by her best friend Miss Elizabeth B. in order to marry a man named Collins."

She opened her eyes and looked for her father. He was holding her mother's hand, smiling and nodding at the familiar joke.

"Lest there be any confusion, I want to clarify that our former Miss Lucas has not married a Mr. Collins but a Dr. Collins, and our story features no Lady Catherine, though I'm sure the four Marys will be glad to help the little woman organize the closets of her new home."

Ralph raised his glass.

"So here's to Dr. and Mrs. Collins, whose title page was inscribed this day at church, but whose book has yet to be written. May the Author of Life fill their chapters with much happiness and many little Collins, and may they show us all how to live happily ever after."

Dr. O'Reilly gripped his wine glass in his fat fist and bellowed, too close to Elizabeth's ear, "Ad multos annos!"

Not the customary response, but she appreciated the sentiment. She clinked with him and took a sip from her glass. Ralph approached his chair but before he sat, he lifted his glass to her, a questioning expression on his face. She raised her glass in return and smiled at him. It had been a perfect toast.

Dr. O'Reilly leaned his heavy frame into her shoulder and whispered loud enough for the entire table to hear, "You'll have to fight the taller girls for the bouquet, Miss Elizabeth B. I'd watch out for that one especially," he gestured with his glass toward Gretchen. "Quite the toast"—he gestured toward Ralph—"but I suppose he had to be careful since his brother might soon return the favor." He pulled out his handkerchief and blotted his forehead. "How I remember those days. My brother Melville should never have been so ribald, eh Mabel?" He looked over Elizabeth to his bride.

"It wasn't tasteful," Mabel said, "and to this day I thank my lucky stars that when you toasted him six weeks later you had more sense than to return in kind, though I did laugh when you twitted him about his weight."

"My brother Melville was rather a large man," Dr. O'Reilly explained.

Mark, who'd been playing with his silverware, admiring his reflection, and generally being a taciturn bore, now stood and stretched. Except that he wasn't stretching, he was reaching his arm across the hydrangeas toward Ralph.

Ralph stood and shook his hand.

"Wanted to congratulate you," Mark said. "You got up from the table before I could say it, but no hard feelings. She's a fine woman. I thought I could win her, but while man proposes, God disposes, eh?"

Mark had proposed to her in the elevator, but he'd long since moved on. Had he proposed to Gretchen, too? Or had Ralph? Or was this a face-saving maneuver because he didn't have a chance against Alex and Andrea, the love texters?

"Man proposes, God disposes, that's good, son. I like that," Dr. O'Reilly said. "And she's a fine woman indeed, which makes your gallantry all the more impressive."

The uncertainty of the pronouns and the ambiguity of the antecedents threatened to overwhelm her, but she wouldn't go down without a fight. Her hands, hidden in her lap by the linen tablecloth, clenched into fists, but a glimpse of Andrea matter of factly texting brought her back to reality.

She unclenched. The least a bride expected from her maid of honor was no brawling, and besides, who would she hit? Andrea and Alex hadn't done anything, Gretchen was too beautiful, Mark was too beautiful, and Ralph was too far away. She took another slug of wine. She didn't want to hit Ralph. Was it his fault he was fated to marry the Ice Princess?

The band struck up "I Can't Give You Anything But Love," Joe and Emily's first dance. There they were, just beyond Andrea, Emily looking happier than she'd ever seen her. Despite its many faults, Table 12 provided an excellent view of the dance floor.

Ralph came behind her and rested his hands on her shoulders. She tensed. Before she could think of a suitably polite yet insulting way to send him back to Gretchen, he spoke.

"You know Emily and Joe expect us to join them at the end of their song. Joe reminded me after the toast."

So Joe and Emily had sent him. Of course. She and Emily used to talk about their first dances. They'd linked pinkies one afternoon in high school after an especially awful gym class paired them with the two clumsiest dancers in the ninth grade. They'd promised that the first to marry would choose a good dancer for a husband, and an equally good dancer as best man for the maid of honor.

"So the best man has his choice of the women folk."

Dr. O'Reilly chuckled and his massive hand moved behind her to slap Ralph's back. She felt Ralph's grip tighten on her shoulders as he struggled to keep his balance. Great. Now she was the rock of ages.

"You two go out there and dance. Mabel and I used to cut up a rug in our day, didn't we Mabel?"

She missed Mabel's response; she was following Ralph. She'd fulfill every one of Emily's dreams, even if it meant dancing with Gretchen's boyfriend or fiancé or whatever he was.

"Can you dance in those shoes?" he asked. "You seem a lot taller tonight."

"I think so," she said to the chest in the tuxedo, regretting the wine.

He was facing her, holding her hand in his, his free arm around her waist. He stood very straight and reminded her of Anthony Andrews in *Brideshead*, except he looked sober; she was the slightly tipsy one. She didn't mind being this close to him as long as he held her up, but why weren't they dancing?

"Is anything wrong?" she said.

"You know," he leaned down and whispered, "I hate to ruin a picturesque moment, but I haven't danced in years, and I have no idea what to do."

The smooth Ralph had vanished, leaving Ralph the goof in his place. She wouldn't lead, but she could advise him, and she'd tell Gretchen to teach him to dance before their wedding.

"Simple two-step," she said. "Look confident and I'll count."

They danced.

She wouldn't think about Gretchen. This was almost fun, though even with her heels he towered above her. Could he even hear from that distance? What a solitary life he must lead up there among the trees.

The dance floor was filling, lending them a cloak of anonymity. The band segued into "Isn't it a Lovely Day to get Caught in the Rain?" and she and Ralph were no longer the maid of honor and best man on display for the guests to watch. They were Ginger and Fred dancing in a lonely gazebo for the sheer joy of it.

Fred stepped on her foot, but she ignored it. They bumped into another couple, and she laughed. Wine or no wine, she was definitely Elizabeth Benning dancing with Ralph Collins.

"Do you think that's enough?" she asked.

"I think that may have been too much," he said.

He led her back to their table and deposited her in her seat. He gave his little bow, and she nodded graciously, remembering his bow on the night they met, and when he introduced himself as the second Dr. Collins.

He took his rightful place beside Gretchen, who whispered to him and pointed to Mark's empty chair. He came back around the table to her.

"Do you mind if I give Gretchen a ride home? Mark's gone, and she's got a headache."

"Of course you can take her. I'll go home with my parents later."

What else could she say? And why shouldn't he? His duties to her were over. He hadn't thanked her, but he'd made a nice bow. That was something.

He went to Gretchen.

Sandwiched between Dr. O'Reilly and Mabel, she repeated to herself the words he'd said as they left the dance floor, no longer Fred and Ginger, just plain Elizabeth and Gretchen's Ralph.

"I think that may have been too much," he'd said.

She hadn't thought it was enough, but there was nothing she could do to change that now.

CHAPTER 30

Picking up the Pieces

Sunday was as calm as Saturday had been crazy. Elizabeth didn't see anyone familiar at the ten-thirty Mass. Joe and Emily were on their way to Hawaii for a month, Gretchen always went to the six-thirty, and Ralph had likely knelt in the pew beside his beloved. Her parents were going to the noon with the Moores, so she was on her own. She had so much to think about that solitude was a relief, though she didn't pay much attention at Mass.

Back in the privacy of her cottage, she crawled into bed and stared up at Fra. She ought to wrap him carefully and send him to Ralph, care of St. Albert's College since she didn't know his home address. Except it was Sunday and the post office was closed, which spared her the trouble of getting out of bed again.

Her eye looked better today, but otherwise she was a mess. Had it really been only yesterday she and Emily woke up in this bed smiling? Emily would wake up smiling every day for the rest of her life, God willing, but as for herself, she was giving up on happiness.

Yesterday she'd told Em she liked Ralph, and Em had said he liked her too. Or had she misunderstood? No, Emily had claimed all along that Ralph liked her, and she'd proudly take credit for Elizabeth and Ralph like Emma did with Miss Taylor and Mr. Weston. Except that with her and Ralph, there was nothing to take credit for.

She reached under her bed for the large heart shaped box. She didn't often raid her emergency supply of imported chocolates, but if there was a remedy for heartbreak it was in this box. She opened it and chose a mini Toblerone.

She bit off a triangle and tried to sort out the jumble of images left over from the reception. Ralph and Gretchen whispering . . . Mark admiring himself, then giving up on his reflection to congratulate Ralph . . . Two of the Marys confiding their brother had always liked Gretchen and if only Elizabeth would get out of the way . . . Ralph, solemn as death, saying he'd marry Gretchen to save her from Mark.

One memory edged the others out, neither the comfort of bed nor the rich taste of chocolate distracting her from its finality. As if Ralph stood before her, she could see him telling her he wanted to take Gretchen home. Not a word of concern for her; what he'd left unsaid had said it all. Sure she told him her family would take her home, but he hadn't even asked. His heart belonged to Gretchen. Hadn't she known that from the beginning?

When she met them in January, she'd seen immediately they were a matched set. Their appearance together at February's art show confirmed her first impression. In March they'd picked up Father Barkley, two of his favorites and he'd be the priest to marry them, no doubt. They sat next to each other at her parents' dining table in April when Ralph revealed his true colors, and later he curled up at Gretchen's feet as she sat stiff as a frozen ice-pop on the piano bench.

He'd caved to pressure that night and asked Elizabeth out, but what could he do with everyone expecting it? So he'd asked, and he'd taken her refusal in stride, and his sisters had cleared up any wishful thinking that his was a lasting passion for her. He was Gretchen's, and she was his. End of story.

If only she could delete July's chapter. It was beyond humiliating. She'd been cheering for the Dodgers, hopping on one foot in the Lucas' yard to make the nerf game fair, putting her face into a first baseman's shoe, and she'd thought she was doing it for herself, but really she'd been doing it for Ralph. Forget true love. Was even friendship worth it?

She could see now what had happened. In the Vanagon they'd become friends. She'd played softball on his advice, and he was flattered. But as soon as Mark was out of the way and Gretchen softened toward him . . .

The image of Gretchen softening was too much to swallow on its own. She reached for a Belgian chocolate. The point was, as soon as Mark bowed out, Ralph had no use for her. Sure they'd become friends, but look where it got her. A glorious sunny afternoon and she was hiding indoors, raiding her emergency import stash, wearing church clothes in bed, a recluse well before she was forty.

She wanted to think it was all a mix-up: Gretchen was his friend, his true love a short brunette, but the facts marched in battle array against her. Even if she had the power to banish the facts, what of the oppressive feeling that hung over her? She had women's intuition as well as the next girl, and it sat on her chest like an unsavory Southern antagonist, its unbearable weight pinning her down, its hot sour breath poisoning her happiness, its raucous voice yelling as if she were deaf, "Fool! Of course they belong together! You're nothing!"

With heroic strength she threw the covers off, stuffed the box under her bed, and flew to the rocking chair. Enough brooding. When Flannery O'Conner characters tyrannized her, the time had come for action. Fine, so Ralph liked Gretchen. What else was new? That Gretchen liked Ralph? She could still see Gretchen's hand on Ralph's sleeve at the dinner after the concert in January. Why should she let a relationship she'd acknowledged from the beginning hurt her at this late date?

The answer came to her like a still small voice.

Because then she hadn't known Ralph, she'd merely despised him like she despised his female sidekick. Now she knew him. She knew he was a great guy, and she'd gladly marry him to save him from the Ice Princess.

And if she was honest and admitted she wanted to marry him not merely to save him but because more than anything she wanted to be his wife, it was only fair to let his motives be similarly selfish. He'd marry Gretchen not simply to save her from Mark, but because he loved the statuesque enigmatic blonde and wanted to be her husband.

Which meant he wouldn't thank her for saving him. He was where he wanted to be, with whom he wanted to be. And she was in her cottage with only a gilded statue to show for her year of happiness. Was it enough?

Soon she'd have the happiness of helping Jane. Her nephews would be a welcome diversion from her aching heart, and by the time she returned them she'd be ready to . . .

To what? What was left? If she wanted to pick up the pieces of her happiness project, what pieces would she pick up? She scanned the floor of the room, then the dresser and tables, as if literally picking up something would help. *The Happiness Project* rested on the reading table beside her; she traced the title with her finger.

Ralph had ruined everything with all that hooey about focusing on happiness. He'd taken away her zeal for beating Pat. He'd talked her out of her competition and left her with nothing but a black eye.

She picked up the book. What if she read it? Not his stupid grad school way, no skimming for her. She was sick of his useless advice. She could read the book cover to cover and take Gretchen Rubin's advice for a change. As long as Gretchen R. didn't recommend love. Or friendship. There must be more to happiness than love and friendship.

Who was she kidding? She wasn't going to read a gift book from beginning to end, but she could learn to dip in because she wanted to, regardless of Ralph's opinions. She opened the book. The Twelve Commandments. Ten worked for her, but she'd keep an open mind. Start at the top, then.

1. Be Gretchen.

She barely restrained herself from hurling the book across the room.

"Be Gretchen"? That was all this blasted book had to offer her after she'd been carting it around for eight months and basing her life on its title? She'd rather be anyone than Gretchen. She'd even consider being Ralph.

She stared hard at the cover and the truth burst upon her.

Gretchen Rubin was telling herself to be Gretchen. And even if she was telling Elizabeth to be Gretchen too—who knew? Maybe the rest of the book was a blueprint she could follow to become Gretchen Rubin who was happy. Whatever it meant, one thing was certain. This had nothing to do with Ralph's Gretchen.

So who did she want to be?

She didn't want to be Gretchen—any Gretchen. She wanted to be Elizabeth, and she wanted to beat Pat. Here she was in August, for heaven's sake, resolution miraculously intact, and after helping with the boys she'd land on both feet in September.

Could she come up with another plan? Her first half year had been a series of failed attempts at self-fulfillment, and now she was helping others. That didn't leave much left for the ninth month.

Never Too Late seemed to mock her from the bedside table. She kept up an even rhythm in the rocking chair and stuck her chin in the air.

It wasn't too late, and she wouldn't quit. Besides, John Holt was a gentle soul, full of wise sayings, not mockery. What was that expression of his? Jane had told her a dozen times, but she couldn't remember.

Jane. Jane would have the new baby soon; her work was cut out for her. Jane was happy. And Emily was happy. She'd found her life's work as Joe's wife, and maybe she'd be a mother too by this time next year.

Elizabeth needed work of her own to do, something to make her life worth living.

That was it. "Life worth living and work worth doing," that's what John Holt used to say. Of course. She needed a job.

She stepped over to the fridge and looked inside. She'd have a glass of chocolate milk and go for a walk. A long walk, out in the sunshine, and she'd take her cell phone in case Jane had the baby today. And after she helped Jane with the baby, she'd get a job.

She'd been playing around for eight months, and it had been great. Or maybe fine. Or different, anyway. Not quite as happy as the previous years of her life, but all that would change as soon as she got a job.

By the time Pat held his Fra Angelico Career Day in late September, she'd have experience in her new field, and she could give a talk on interior decorating or mobile pet grooming. If by some strange mischance she didn't have a job by then, she'd go to the event with eyes wide open and wow some recruiter with her marketable skills.

Not that she'd wait. She'd start looking as soon as her stint helping Jane was over so she could have a job by September third or fourth. She'd find work worth doing and a life worth living and she'd beat Pat and be too happy to mind when Gretchen and Ralph announced their wedding. She had the perfect excuse for not attending. Obviously, she'd be working that day.

CHAPTER 33

Career Day

Elizabeth disagreed with the hypothesis, usually advanced by Northeastern transplants, that southern California had no seasons. She felt the transitions acutely, particularly the onset of autumn. The end of September meant crisper mornings and the light in the evening faded earlier. This year there was an added something in the air, an "I've been looking for a job all month and if nothing turns up I'm a dead duck" kind of feeling.

On September thirtieth, Career Day at the college, she wasted the chilly morning hours in another unsuccessful interview. The pro could have saved precious time by telling her over the phone he required caddies to be familiar with the game of golf, but she set him straight on her way out of the clubhouse, warning him he wouldn't scare up a new employee anytime soon if he couldn't learn to control his inappropriate laughter. She shook the dust from her feet and moved on; she made it a policy to forgive and forget these interviews as quickly as possible.

Pat had instructed her to meet him in the school cafeteria at noon. Fill her tray and find him at the lunch tables, he'd said. A student jostled her in line and she readjusted her backpack, acutely conscious of the precious notes tucked within. Pat was depending on her; she was his expert for "Careers in Bookselling," and she'd need her bullet points to keep from blurting out first thing that she hadn't sold a book for nine and a half months.

She exited the food service line with her blue tray weighing more than lunch should weigh. At the shore of the sea of tables she spied Pat half a league onward and plunged in. The black pumps that had screamed "professional" from the floor of her closet now whispered "watch your step on the industrial carpet." She kept her eyes down and walked in Pat's direction, an uncomfortable sensation overtaking her— hadn't this been the way she ended up at the Collins' table at Emily's reception? Next year she'd resolve to wear flats. That couldn't be too challenging.

He should be about here. She balanced her tray on the edge of a table. Sure enough, it was his.

Except it wasn't only his, and he wasn't surrounded by students. Nor anonymous Career Day businessmen who'd jump at the chance to hire her when she whipped out her resumé. For some obnoxious Pat-like reason, he was sitting with the O'Reilly's.

"Glad you found us, Liz. You know Dr. and Mrs. O'Reilly, of course."

"Of course," she said blankly.

She hadn't seen them since the wedding reception, and if they didn't bring it up, she wouldn't. On the bright side, the good doctor might know of an opening in the picnic supply industry. She'd be happy to work her way up from janitor if the position was available.

"A pleasure to meet again, Miss Benning."

Dr. O'Reilly gave her a gentle smack between the shoulder blades. She gripped the back of the chair in front of her and barely kept afloat. Forget the job; if she survived lunch she'd count herself lucky.

"I know what you're thinking," Dr. O'Reilly boomed, shaking a hunk of French bread at her. "But I told Pat and I'll tell you too. White bread never killed anyone! This whole grain nonsense is nothing more than a low-down gimmick to separate a man from his wallet." He dipped the quarter loaf into his clam chowder.

"And a woman from her coin purse," Mabel added, a triangle of white toast en route to her mouth.

The mountain and the mole hill. She closed her eyes and blessed herself. They'd think she was saying grace and she'd get to that, but first she had other prayers bursting from her heart. That she'd give a good talk and get a job. That she'd open her eyes to see Emily and Joe at her table instead of the O'Reillys. Couldn't faith move mountains?

"She's a very devout girl," Mabel said. "We should have Mark call her again."

"Encourage him," Pat said. "Do her good to get out a little."

Time to finish praying and share her food. If her clam chowder was hot, she'd start by dumping it in Pat's lap.

She scanned her full tray. Clam chowder, green salad, egg salad, French bread, milk, brownie, water, coffee, grilled cheese, bagel with cream cheese, English muffin with honey. The problem with cafeteria meals was everything looked so good, she took it all. She scooped up a spoonful of clam chowder. Lukewarm, desirable neither for nourishment nor scalding purposes.

"Emily said Joe's talk would be after lunch. Have you seen them?" She picked up the brownie and bit in. Chewy, not dry. A good choice.

"The happy couple," Mabel chirped. "Will they talk about careers in marriage?"

"Dr. Collins will speak on careers in medicine," Pat said, "and I don't expect them till much later, but the other Dr. Collins is here. Don't let us keep you, Liz. Go and say hello."

She ignored him and drank her milk.

"Two doctors in the family, that's a mighty fine achievement." Dr. O'Reilly stood and surveyed the tables, hand at his brow like a mariner in search of a lost sailor.

"That direction, sir."

Pat pointed. There he was, two tables away, studying while he ate a sandwich. Peanut butter. Not that she could smell it from here, but he was predictable. Beside him sat Gretchen, a salad and paperwork before her. Also predictable.

"I see him!" Mabel said, hands aflutter. "He's with Mark's girlfriend. Except she's not Mark's girlfriend anymore." Her skinny arm flew across her husband to pat Elizabeth's hand. "Not your fault you couldn't keep him, dear. These young men are so fickle."

Was she being patted for Mark or Ralph?

"But the best man did win, like my husband prophesied at the wedding. Wasn't that clever of him, Pat? Ralph was the best man, and he sat with us, but he wasn't paying attention to anyone but his heart's desire. A prophecy, that's what it was."

"She gives me too much credit," Dr. O'Reilly said, now beckoning to Ralph. "Couldn't help but see the obvious."

"We sat with those handsome blondes and Miss Elizabeth and the other youngsters," Mabel told Pat. "What a romantic evening that was, and now it's like a dream come true."

More like a nightmare come true: Ralph and Gretchen were on their way over. She couldn't bear to watch. She'd feign interest in her food.

"Ralph, Gretchen, join us," Pat said.

"Hey Liz, long time no see," Ralph said. She kept her eyes on her tray. She was here to give a talk, not help with wedding plans. "How's our goddaughter, Pat?"

Even five weeks later it stung. She didn't expect to be godmother of all their children—they'd spoiled her with Anthony and Matthew—but Pat must have other Catholic friends besides Ralph and Gretchen. Or at least Jane must. Francesca Veronica Joan Marie hadn't objected to her godparents so far, but she was only six weeks old. What did she know?

"She's more beautiful every day," Pat said. "You know the O'Reillys?"

"Of course. Nice to see you again. You remember Gretchen?"

She toyed with her grilled cheese sandwich. Cold and greasy with the cheese congealed, but the important thing was not to look up. She had enough food here to keep her eyes averted for days.

"How could we forget that lovely girl?" Mabel said. "Just yesterday I told my husband she's a dead ringer for the Hollywood stars. Kind of a cross between Joan Crawford and Katherine Hepburn with a blonde rinse. And wearing that Vera Wang suit, what a pretty sight. I never could wear olive, but it suits you, dear."

"Now, now, Mabel, none of that. No one holds a candle to you, wear what color you like," Dr. O'Reilly said. "No slight intended to the young ladies, of course."

Elizabeth smiled to show no hard feelings; he was such a dear. Ralph was sitting at the table now, but she avoided his gaze and focused on Mabel's tiny hand, patting and fluttering about her husband's thick arm, like one of those little birds that hang about hippopotami.

"Delightful to see you again, Miss Gretchen," the hippo said. "Won't you sit down?"

"Thank you, but if you'll excuse me, I'd like to go over my notes." She stood behind Ralph and gripped her red purse protectively. "Elizabeth and I have a panel presentation on careers in bookselling, and we're slated to begin in less than twenty minutes."

Elizabeth's water glass slipped from her hand into her soup. Pat had said nothing to her about a panel with Gretchen. Who actually did sell books.

"We know all about your panel presentation," Dr. O'Reilly said. "Mabel and I keep a finger on the pulse of Catholic events and when I heard the Fra Angelico series was hosting a Career Day, I knew what I had to do."

"What was that?" Ralph asked, apparently unconscious of the negative energy pouring from his beloved. With that degree of insensitivity, he'd be perfect for her.

"I called Pat and offered my services posthaste. That's when he invited me to be on the girls' panel, help them out if they lose their place or don't know an answer." He held up his hand like he was stopping traffic. "No need to thank me. My pleasure to be of assistance."

Was he making this up, or had Pat lost his mind?

Pat smiled his used car salesman smile. He might be insane, but he looked the same.

"Dr. O'Reilly was eager to share his knowledge with the students. Insistent, you might say. When he offered to give a presentation, I told him every slot was filled but he wouldn't take no for an answer. The minute he heard bookselling was on the docket—"

"I lit up like a Christmas tree, didn't I Mabel?"

"What a moment that was. You were almost too happy, knowing you'd be able to share the wealth of your experience. Seems to me that's what you live for."

Dr. O'Reilly was most likely deaf, which would explain his booming voice and this little mix-up. She'd clarify things in a jiffy by speaking slowly and distinctly.

"Excuse me, Dr. O'Reilly," she said loudly. "Our talk is on selling books." She enunciated the last two words with special care. "Wasn't your career in picnic supplies?"

"Priceless! Did Mark tell you that? Boy's stuck on the picnic supply story, isn't he Mabel? I've told him a thousand times. Picnic supplies will make your first ten million—"

"But if you don't diversify, you'll never get anywhere." The tip of Mabel's steepled fingers touched her chin and she blinked gravely.

They were so absurd, Elizabeth giggled. Pat's smile had changed to one of genuine amusement, and Ralph grinned. Gretchen alone remained unmoved.

"What excellent advice," Ralph said. "And what, if I may be so bold, did you diversify into?"

Dr. O'Reilly and Mabel exchanged a mischievous glance.

"Tell them, dear," she said.

"Ever heard of amazon.com?" Dr. O'Reilly's fat fist pounded the table. "I was in on the ground floor."

"And you're helping us give the presentation?" Gretchen's voice was somewhere between frigid and forty below.

"Absolutely. Amazon.com has taught me a thing or two about the future of the book business, and I'm not one to hide my light under a bushel basket. Glad to tell your audience everything I know."

Gretchen's face was distorted only for a moment, but in that moment she looked more like Lon Chaney than Joan Crawford or Katherine Hepburn. Good thing Mabel's eyes were on her coleslaw.

Gretchen whispered to Ralph, who nodded.

"Pat, if you'll excuse me?" she said.

"Certainly."

Gretchen left them and exited the cafeteria by the door nearest the chapel. Going to say a prayer before the presentation, maybe. A great idea.

Elizabeth grabbed her backpack and made her apologies, following in Gretchen's wake. Loathe as she was to accost the blonde, they needed to talk about their presentation. A couple rosaries first wouldn't hurt either.

She pulled open the huge bronze door and entered the chapel. Gretchen knelt in the last pew, absorbed in prayer from the looks of it.

Elizabeth dipped her fingers in the holy water font and blessed herself. This was her chance to pray, but she couldn't string three words together. "Help, please," was all that came to mind.

Should she get her notes out and review them? Probably obsolete now. She looked at the stained glass windows, admired the shiny marble floor, devoutly wished she could pray.

She hated to interrupt Gretchen, but they had a panel to go to. She tiptoed forward and tapped an olive shoulder.

"We'd better go," she whispered. "To prepare for the panel."

No answer. It was like ringing a doorbell and no one came. How soon was too soon to knock? Was the doorbell even working?

Her finger poised to tap again, Gretchen rose, made a perfect genuflection, and walked past her to the door. Elizabeth followed.

Outside she blinked in the sunshine, and Gretchen finally spoke.

"Elizabeth, I asked Ralph to apologize to Pat on my behalf. I can't do the presentation."

"Can't do it?"

"That's correct."

"Are you ill?"

"No."

"Couldn't you just stay for a little while then?"

"No."

"Did Dr. O'Reilly offend you somehow?"

Gretchen turned and strode toward the parking lot.

"I don't want to be a pain," Elizabeth called after her, "but I'm not really the expert here. If you're gonna bail on me I'd like to know why, and I don't want to ask Ralph."

Gretchen kept walking.

"I don't know how the panel's supposed to work," she shouted. "I wasn't prepared for this, but you could tell them about your job."

Gretchen turned. "I'm sure Dr. O'Reilly will have plenty to say. You don't need me."

Elizabeth jogged to her side. "Please, Gretchen. It's half an hour, that's only ten minutes each. Or we could talk for five minutes each and open it up for questions. Please?"

The woman's face was impassive, as usual.

They were wrapped in silence, but for a rustle high in the trees. Which was odd, because above Gretchen she didn't see any trees, only blue sky.

She heard the rustle again.

Incredible.

Gretchen had sighed.

Twice.

She knew from experience the variations one could achieve with a simple exhalation of breath. The wind-in-the-trees sigh was a sigh of great promise. It suggested a thaw had set in, and she couldn't leave the Ice Princess alone in the sun. She'd seen Frosty; she didn't want that on her conscience.

Pat could handle the presentation. All he had to do was unleash Dr. O'Reilly. Bookselling, picnic supplies, visits with Plum—what wouldn't he talk about? As to her need for a job, she'd apply at Tastee Freeze on the way home. She wouldn't balk at the neon uniform this time; she'd fill out the application and keep her mouth shut.

They stood at the top of the concrete stairs that led to the parking lot. Hardly knowing how she dared, she tugged on the little tag hanging from Gretchen's red purse. Coach, it said. Gretchen's eyes said more. Something like "I'll sit down but keep your hands off."

She let go. Gretchen lowered herself with perfect elegance to the top step and stretched out her long legs, crossing them neatly at the ankle. Elizabeth dropped down and stretched out her legs too. The blonde's shoes (Prada? she'd have to watch that movie again) rested on the fourth step down, while her own cheap pumps reached the second.

Where to begin? The giantess had expressed emotion, but needed help with what must be a new experience. Time to be a little vulnerable, show her how it was done.

"You know, Gretchen, I've never told you how I felt when Adventures in Reading closed. It made me sad and angry, and I blamed Books-a-Trillion. When I found out you were the one who bought our stock, I was furious. But the more I thought about it the more I thought you probably weren't trying to hurt the bookstore, and maybe what happened was for the best after all."

Gretchen said nothing.

"I'm telling you this because I want to be honest with you so you can be honest with me. Would you like to tell me what's got you so upset today?"

"Elizabeth, this is hard for me to talk about, especially with you. I didn't want to be on the panel today, but I did it for Ralph. He said Pat needed help, and I owe Ralph so much that I agreed. But I know you don't like me, and I understand why. You see me as the enemy, which I can assure you I'm not."

Really? So she and Ralph weren't an item?

"I'm not the enemy, and chain bookstores aren't either."

Right. They were talking bookselling. She stifled a sigh of her own and focused on Gretchen's perfectly manicured hands, motionless in her lap.

"Who's the enemy, then? Dr. O'Reilly?"

"In a manner of speaking. I'm surprised you don't see it, you're not entirely stupid. The enemy is Amazon." Gretchen twisted her elegant neck and glanced behind them, as if to make sure she wouldn't be overheard. "Please don't repeat this, but the reality is they're practically shutting us down."

"I've known of similar situations," Elizabeth said, but Gretchen didn't catch her sarcasm. Probably best. This was about Gretchen's complaints, not hers.

"I'm working twelve hours a day to prevent our closing, but I'm not sure it's enough. If the brainless customers keep buying their books online, they'll wake one morning to find that's the only place they can buy books and it will be their own fault."

Gretchen clearly needed reminding that the customer was always right and under no circumstances to be called brainless, but at least she was finally passionate about something. Elizabeth laughed, and Gretchen's hands jerked convulsively.

"I'm sorry. I'm not laughing at what you said. It's just that you care a lot more about bookselling than I gave you credit for. If we rush to the hall, we can still make it. I'd love to hear you talk to the students about the future of the industry."

"You might love it, but Dr. O'Reilly wouldn't."

"You got me there." She took a deep breath. She had to say it, crazy as it sounded. "I'm sorry about what's happening to your store. I had no idea."

Gretchen sighed again. At this rate she'd be human by the end of the day.

"Elizabeth, I intend to ask you something, but I would prefer you to think about it before you answer."

The woman took formality to new heights. Like the way she kept saying "Elizabeth" before she spoke, and now she "intended" to ask her, and she "would prefer" her to think about it. What could she possibly ask that required such careful consideration? It must be about something serious, like—No. She couldn't ask that, it wouldn't be fair. Were they even officially engaged yet? She looked more closely at Gretchen's hands. An exquisitely cut emerald on the third finger of her—she looked at her own hands. Small scar on the left. Back at Gretchen's. The emerald was on her right. Not an engagement ring.

"I'm ready," she said. "Ask away."

"I've been considering this for a long time, but I couldn't decide. Ralph advised me to simply ask you, and I think he's right. You can always say no."

Dang it. Well she would say no. They could ask the four Marys to be in the wedding if Gretchen didn't have any friends or sisters of her own.

"Go for it. I'll feel free to say no."

"But I don't want you to answer immediately. Think it over."

As if thinking would make it less painful. She braced herself.

"Elizabeth, I'd like you to consider taking a job in the children's department at Books-a-Trillion."

She pressed her palms onto the warm stone and looked up into the sun. They said looking straight into the sun could blind you, but how could she be more blind? Gretchen wasn't talking to her about Ralph and their wedding plans; that was none of her business. But Gretchen's business, her job kind of business, that was different, and unappealing though the subject was, it was better than talking bridesmaids.

Books-a-Trillion? It was only a bookstore, not peanut butter, and once she got over her gag reflex it would be fine.

A bookstore. Gretchen had just offered her a job in the children's department of a bookstore. Her ideal job. On the very day she most badly needed a job, the day she was planning to sell her soul to Tastee Freeze for an orange uniform and the chance to beat Pat.

"If you feel about Books-a-Trillion the way I feel about amazon.com, you might think I'm asking you to work for the enemy, but I've explained that we're not the enemy, Elizabeth."

Right. Was this what they meant by a Catch-22, or was it more like a rock and a hard place? She needed a job before tomorrow, but who was offering it to her? The devil wears Prada. How could she have missed that?

"I know that's how you feel, which is why I delayed asking until now, but I'm running out of time. The manager of our children's section is having a baby in December, and I'd like to bring you in as soon as possible to train with her. You'd start in sales, then move up to manager of the department when she leaves. Given your experience I'm confident you could handle the position if you're willing to put in the hours. That's why I don't want you to answer me now. It's a serious commitment."

She had to beat Pat. It was a pathetic *raison d'être*, as Ralph had kindly pointed out to her in the Vanagon, but she'd tried exercise and she'd tried romance, and those doors had slammed in her face. What she needed, immediately, was a job, and here was a job, ten to one without the orange uniform.

She knew what God was doing. The old "I'll answer your prayer but you'll be sorry you asked" maneuver. If she accepted this job she'd be working for the store that had put hers out of business, and she'd be working for Gretchen, the human ice sculpture. Three sighs did not a summer make, and it would be winter in that store, she could feel it already.

Did she even have a choice? She had to beat Pat. That was all.

"Yes," she said.

"I thought I made it clear I don't want you to answer me today. Think it over. You can talk to your family. It's no secret Marcella's leaving to be a stay-at-home mom, and if you don't want the job, I'll have to advertise. The only thing I ask you not to repeat is what I told you in confidence about the difficulties we're having."

Gretchen rose, flaxen hair lit by the sun, a Scandinavian goddess.

She couldn't let the goddess get away without accepting her sacrifice.

"I don't need time to think it over, I want the job. Can I start Monday?"

"If you're completely sure. I don't want you making an impulsive decision now only to fail me later."

Not the most gracious acceptance speech in history, but then goddesses didn't need tact.

"I'm sure. What time would you like me there?"

"Five-thirty. And be punctual."

"Adventures in Reading closed at six, so we never started shifts that late, but I'm not complaining. I've never been a morning person, more of a night owl really, and five-thirty suits me fine."

Gretchen was halfway down the steps.

"Five-thirty A.M., Elizabeth. See you Monday."

She waited for the goddess to unlock her car and get in. If she moved now, she'd scream. Her self-immolation had been painless until Gretchen's last tiny clarification twisted the knife. How could she have failed to ask for hours before committing herself?

She slung her backpack over her shoulder. Pat wasn't a weasel, he was a snake. She'd tell him about her new job and he'd admit he was behind it, he'd set up the whole tortuous arrangement.

Then again, even he wasn't that low.

CHAPTER 32

And the Winner Is

Elizabeth drove straight home, changed into her comfy sweats and climbed into bed. She only had a weekend before life as she knew and loved it would be over, and there was just one thing she wanted to do until then. If she hibernated now, perhaps she could store up sleep for the long wakeful winter ahead.

Too soon, her phone woke her from a deep and blissfully dreamless sleep. Jane was apologetic but slightly worried. Was she okay? Had she forgotten?

Blast. They'd agreed on the last Friday of September for the Moore's first date night since Francesca's arrival. She couldn't disappoint Jane, however gladly she'd skewer Pat's plans.

When she got to their house, Jane let her in and hugged her, but over Jane's shoulder Pat gloated.

"So good to see you," he said. "We missed you at the bookselling presentation. Couldn't think what might have become of you."

"You didn't make it? Pat, you didn't tell me Lizzy wasn't there."

Jane had her hands on her hips, an ally.

"I didn't want to upset you, dear, but it looks like your sister's happiness project finally bit the dust. Liz agreed to speak for me today, you know that, but after I treated her to a lavish lunch, she disappeared. Didn't say a word about bookselling to the students, though the hall was full."

"And Dr. O'Reilly lost his voice?" Elizabeth asked. For once she wasn't afraid. He had nothing on her. "Jane, do you remember when I agreed to speak for Pat's Career Day?"

"I do, and I talked to mom this morning. She said you were well prepared."

"I was, and quite surprised when I discovered at lunch that Pat had given away my slot. He invited Dr. O'Reilly and Gretchen to speak at the same time, in the same place. Gretchen and I decided we'd let Dr. O'Reilly have the half hour to himself. He's a man with plenty to say and we didn't want to cramp his style."

"Fair enough," Jane said. "I think you fulfilled your part of the bargain by showing up. Nothing you could do when the organizer replaced you."

"The talk did go well," Pat said, "so in light of Dr. O'Reilly's success, I'll give you a pass on the speech."

"How kind. Relief to know I'm still in the running."

"Or would be if you'd gotten a job."

So that was his angle. She smiled her simple as a dove smile.

"And if I didn't?"

"Sorry, Liz, but you gave it the old college try. Nearly made it through September, that's a record and something to be proud of, but all good things come to an end. Better luck next year."

"And if I did get a job?"

"Did you, Lizzy?" Jane asked.

"I did."

She was now smiling her wise as Pat the serpent smile, she could feel it.

"But you didn't," Pat said.

"I most certainly did."

"Wha'd you do, Auntie Beth?"

Dominic was at her side, stick in hand.

"You put that stick right outside, young man. You know the rules," Jane said.

"I got a job, Dominic, and your dad is extra happy for me, aren't you, Pat?"

"Never mind about me, it's your happiness we're concerned with," he said.

"Will you make us brownies?"

"Obey your mom and go outside with the stick, and yes, I'll make brownies. We have to celebrate."

Dominic disappeared and the back door slammed.

"So what happened? Did you get the job at the golf course?" Jane asked.

"I'll be selling books again."

She read disbelief in both their faces.

"But there isn't another independent bookstore within sixty miles of here," Jane said. "You're not moving, are you?"

She shook her head. This was the part she dreaded. Naming the megastore would instantly transform her glory to infamy. Pat had the memory of an elephant as well as an elephant's finesse and he'd never let her forget the many things she'd said over the years about Books-a-Trillion. Not very flattering things.

"Encyclopedias door to door? Cold calls on the phone selling weight loss books? Come on, Liz, out with it, we won't laugh," Pat promised.

"Gretchen hired me to work in children's at Books-a-Trillion and take over for the department manager when Marcella leaves to be a stay-at-home-mom in December," she said all in one breath.

Forget his promise, forget the elephant, he was a laughing skunk.

"Who's Marcella?" Jane asked.

"The manager of children's. Any other questions?"

"Are you serious?" Pat said, wiping his eyes.

"I start Monday morning at five-thirty."

"Oh Lizzy, I'm so sorry," Jane said. "I know how you feel about that store. We shouldn't have let it come to this. Pat, you can't make her do it."

"I'm not making her do anything. But don't worry, she won't bear the stigma long. Five-thirty? Books-a-Trillion? She won't last through the week."

"Of course I will! I'm not thrilled about working there, but selling children's books is a noble profession, and besides, Gretchen said she's not the enemy."

"Two weeks max. How much you wanna bet?"

"Stop it, Pat. Lizzy has a job and we should be congratulating her, not harassing her."

"You're right. She'll be in enough pain without us reminding her how much she hates it."

"I won't hate it. I'm a bookseller and selling books again will make me happy. You're sore because I did what I set out to do, and now you're afraid you won't win."

"Okay, then," Pat said. "If you think it'll make you happy, it's your next happiness project. Stick it out for a month at McBookstore—I believe that was your pet name for the place—and I'll eat my words."

"Happiest October of my life coming up."

"Shake on it?" he said, extending his hand.

"Not on it being the happiest," Jane said. "You can't measure that anyhow. Just that she stays one month. Is that okay, Lizzy?"

"Of course it is. Gretchen wants to make me department manager in December, and that means I'll be there a lot longer than a month."

"To October, then," Pat said.

His hand was still out and she took it. She was always surprised it wasn't slimy, not even scaly.

"As for your help with the Fra Angelico events, after today's letdown I don't know if I can trust you."

"Pat!" Jane gave him the look reserved for extremely naughty boys.

"Alright, maybe that's an exaggeration. The truth is I don't need you for the series next month. I'm giving money to the student life committee for an All Saints' party on the thirty-first and they'll take care of the rest. I'm free."

"Except you'll have to chaperone," Jane said. She pointed beyond the sofa, and Elizabeth noticed Francesca asleep in her car seat. "Pat won't need you, but I will. Can you help me take the boys trick-or-treating? Halloween is on a Monday, and I could give you the next Friday off."

"You don't have to make a deal with me. I'd love to take them, and if anyone's giving out chocolate, it would boost my happiness considerably."

"Thanks, Liz. I couldn't enjoy the party if Jane had to juggle the baby and the boys on her own. She can stay with Franny and give out candy while you go door to door."

As if. Jane at home alone with the baby, trying to answer the doorbell every other minute to give out candy? Meanwhile she'd be wandering through the dark streets trying to keep five boys from going in five directions. Pat would enjoy the party, she could easily picture that much.

"Maybe Emily and Joe could help too. Would you guys be okay with that?"

Jane and Pat exchanged one of their "Which of us should tell Lizzy?" looks.

"Did they say no? You thought of this already, but they couldn't come, huh?"

Jane wouldn't meet her gaze and fussed over the sleeping baby.

"Don't wake her, it can't be that bad. Maybe Mom and Dad would come."

"Jane, we should go while the baby's asleep."

Pat lifted the carrier and headed for the door.

"We ordered pizza for you and the kids," he said. "It'll be here soon, money's on the dining table. And the boys want you to wear a costume."

"Tonight?"

"I think he means on Halloween," Jane said.

"Dress the boys as dogs and I'll struggle door to door with them on leashes. I'll be their dog walker, and we'll call it part of our deal."

Jane and Pat were in the doorway.

"Cute, but no cigar," Pat said. "This year's theme is Star Wars. The boys were unanimous."

"Can I be Princess Leia? Maybe Dad could be Darth Vader, wouldn't that be fun?"

Pat nudged Jane out the door. "Darth Vader and Leia are taken and the boys want you to be an ewok."

They were gone and the dead bolt shot home. What a nut. Keeping the castle secure from marauders, but his sons were still outside and the pizza man had yet to come. She went to the back door.

"Ten minute warning," she yelled. "Anthony, could you come here?"

She took the milk out of the fridge, turned around and he was there.

"Can I go back now? I'm the dragon."

"I had a question for you. What's an ewok again?"

"I'll show you, just a sec."

He ran toward the bedrooms, and before she'd finished pouring the milk he was back.

"These guys," he said, pointing at a trio of cartoonish teddy-bears on a pair of pajama pants. "These are Luke's, aren't they cool?"

"They're awesome. So an ewok's like a teddy bear. Wouldn't you rather I dressed up as Princess Leia? We could have Grandpa come as Darth Vader."

"Uncle Ralph's being Darth Vader and Miss Gretchen's Princess Leia. They already have costumes but Grandpa could be the Emperor if he wants. Can I go now?"

She kissed the top of his head and shoved him out the door, then gazed after him, seeing nothing. She hadn't even started working and her boss was ruining her life. At least Ralph wasn't coming as Han Solo.

She returned to the living room and looked out the front window. No sign of the pizza man. If she hurried, she could hunt up a handful of poisonous mushrooms in the yard. The boys liked plain cheese, but Pat was a mushroom man. The least she could do was save him a slice the way he liked it.

CHAPTER 33

Playing Dress Up

When Elizabeth told Emily about her new job, Em took it in stride. When she complained she had to be an ewok for Halloween while Ralph and Gretchen were the cool romantic characters, Em said ewoks were romantic too. When she laughed and said the honeymoon obviously wasn't over yet, Emily smiled and said someday, hopefully soon, Elizabeth would understand.

When Em explained that Ralph hadn't been in touch because he was busy at work, Elizabeth said more likely he was busy with Gretchen. When Em asked whether Ralph ever showed up at the bookstore to see his supposed girlfriend, Elizabeth admitted no, not in the few weeks since she'd been working there. When Em asked why Elizabeth hadn't called for two weeks, she apologized and said new jobs were like that.

Exactly, Em said, and Ralph's new job was like that too, even she and Joe hadn't seen him since their return from Hawaii. How many times, Em asked, did she have to repeat herself? The blondes were just friends, but at least one of them thought very highly of Elizabeth. To which Elizabeth replied, "Whatever." If Em hadn't seen Ralph and Gretchen since the wedding, of course she wasn't aware of their new status. Which status, Elizabeth added, meant nothing to her. She was a modern woman, wholly occupied with her career.

That her career occupied her was true, anyhow. Waking in the middle of the night to get to work at dawn was a full time job, and then there was the full time job. It was like having two careers, one of which she enjoyed. For though she worked for the enemy, the enemy paid her well to do exactly what she loved best: mess about with books.

Not that her time in the bookstore was all roses. Gretchen worked there too. And while Elizabeth gained some measure of happiness by burying herself in work and trying to forget about Ralph, Gretchen seemed unhappier than ever, despite having both work and Ralph. Seeing her boss hiding behind that mask of an unsmiling face day after day, Elizabeth wanted to shake those angular well dressed shoulders. If only she could reach them.

Whether Ralph and Gretchen would show up for Halloween she didn't know. The unhappiest thing she could think of was wearing an unstuffed teddy bear's head with the Ice Princess Leia watching. Ever hopeful, she prepared for an alternative scenario in which Gretchen and Ralph didn't show, no one dressed as an ewok, and she got to be Leia.

She didn't work on Halloween, so she slept till early afternoon. When she woke she went straight to her little kitchen and microwaved a pair of danishes, threaded elastic through them, and fitted them over her ears. Perfect. She donned brown sweats and a brown sweater, ready for ewok hell if the fates so decreed, but tossed the petrified danishes and a long white dress from the thrift store into her pack. Pollyanna had nothing on her.

Ten minutes later she pulled in behind the Moore's mini-van. No sign of Pat's ancient Toyota. Good. No sign of Gretchen and Ralph. Even better.

Two uniformed storm troopers and three over-excited jawas in brown robes answered her knock.

"Auntie Beth, guess what? Guess what, Auntie Beth!"

They were dancing around her, speaking in various degrees of mufflement. The storm troopers wore masks, the jawas' faces were barely visible behind black tights. How they'd maneuver the streets and dodge other trick-or-treaters she couldn't imagine.

"What is it, storm troopers?"

"We're clone troopers!" the two biggest boys objected.

"Clone troopers, tell me your news."

The littlest jawa jumped, and landed on her foot. "Uncle Ralph's gonna be Darth Vader!"

She was just inside the house. Could she make a run for it?

Jane sat on the couch nursing Francesca. She couldn't abandon Jane. More importantly, her bouncing nephews had worked their way behind her and now blocked the exit.

"You did a great job with the boys' costumes," she said.

"Mommy did a better costume for you," said the middle jawa. He danced toward the dining table.

The ewok head.

The biggest jawa grabbed her arm and pumped it up and down.

"Gretchen's dressing up! You gotta dress up, Auntie Beth, or you'll look funny. Mommy can't—she has Franny—but you don't have a baby and we need an ewok."

It was pointless to resist. She pulled the brown fuzzy jacket off a dining chair and tried it on. Slightly snug, quite warm in fact, but ewok-ish. The head stared up at her, its empty eye holes like something out of a horror movie.

"Try on the head!" a clone trooper commanded.

She picked up the hideous furry thing.

"I did wash it after I took the stuffing out," Jane said.

She pulled on the head. Instant transformation.

"You're an ewok!" the boys yelled. She heard Jane's gentle laugh.

"Mommy, her eyes don't look right." She recognized the voice, it was Dominic. Could he even see her eyes? They didn't quite match up with the eye holes.

"Anthony," Jane said, "please get the glasses for Auntie Beth."

A trooper brought her a pair of sunglasses.

"Don't open them yet," Jane said. "Slip them in through an eye hole, then put them on under the bear head so your eyes look shiny. Isn't that clever? Pat thought of it."

Obeying ewok sunglass protocol, she got them on. Of course Pat thought of it. The little visibility she'd had was now reduced by eighty percent. She took a step and her knee struck the sharp corner of the piano bench.

A knock at the door drowned out her cry of pain.

"The first trick-or-treaters. Lizzy, could you get the candy from the top of the piano?"

She felt around and grasped a huge plastic bowl. Stumbling over a jawa, she landed at the door and opened it.

The bright porch light illuminated a white costume and a black one. She must be staring at the waists of the neighborhood basketball stars; these were tall kids. It always surprised her when teenagers dressed up to get candy, but at least these two weren't sporting fake blood.

Her eyes traveled up, up, up to a Darth Vader mask. Next to Darth stood Princess Leia.

Gretchen's glossy fair hair wound in perfect Leia fashion about her ears. The porch light added a warm halo to the exotic hairstyle and, combined with her natural beauty, elevated Gretchen from attractive to stunning.

That must be Ralph, then, behind the Vader mask, regal and imposing in a black turtleneck, a long black robe fastened over his shoulders with a heavy chain.

"Wow! You guys are amazing. Gretchen, you look fantastic!"

Gretchen smiled a small knowing smile. Darth inhaled and exhaled in trademark Vader fashion and raised one black gloved hand.

"Luke, I am your father. But you've changed, my son. You need a haircut. You resemble an ewok."

The boys erupted.

"Mom, you gotta see them!"

"Darth Vader doesn't say that!"

"Isn't Princess Leia beautiful? Isn't this the best night ever?"

For a moment she'd been Elizabeth answering the door, appreciating the handsome couple who'd win any costume contest hands down. Now she was a woman wearing sunglasses under a teddy bear's head. The confinement of her costume had become suffocating, and the mortification of being a stuffed animal while Gretchen and Ralph were celebrities didn't help.

She needed chocolate.

Fortunately she held the stash. The Moores always got Hershey's miniatures and pixie sticks, and she could distinguish the Krackels by their bumpy side.

Jane invited the guests in and the door closed behind them, shutting out the porch light. Her world dimmed. She couldn't see who was where, but did it matter? She had a Krackel bar in hand and could smell it through the little holes Jane had cut into her snout. She smiled in anticipation as she brought the candy to her mouth.

Except she had no mouth.

Jane, ever considerate, ever prepared, hadn't thought of this eventuality. A minor inconvenience, but she wasn't stymied. The head had other apertures and her best bet would be to slip the Krackel through an eye hole.

Bar poised for entry, she heard Gretchen's voice. She lowered her fuzzy arm. Wasn't it bad enough being a figment of George Lucas' imagination? Must she sink to eye-stuffing Halloween candy? No, she mustn't. She couldn't help looking ridiculous, but she could retain a small shred of dignity.

Jane was getting something from the kitchen—or was it Gretchen, or Ralph? She tried to visualize whether Jane had been wearing slippers or sandals. Did Gretchen have on heels or ballet flats? And Ralph—tennis shoes, dress shoes, cleats? What a revelation this was, the problem of erratic footwear habits and the crucial difference consistent shodding could make for the blind. If she ever ran for Miss America, she knew what her platform would be.

Her ewok eyes were adjusting. There was Gretchen on the couch near Jane, and Ralph on a dining chair. Or was that Vader on the couch and Leia at the dining table?

She was still standing near the door, while everyone else was sitting. Back straight, she lowered herself to the floor in a single fluid motion, a sort of ewok plié. The bowl partially spilled, but putting the candy back gave her something to do with her hands. At least Pat hadn't made her wear furry gloves.

Blindness was supposed to sharpen hearing, but that must be urban legend. She'd been blind practically forever now, a conversation was underway in this very room, and yet the voices came to her as if from a great distance. She raised a hand to cup her ear and felt fur. The teddy bear ears were covering her own. Fabulous, she was Helen the ewok Keller.

By keeping her body still and straining with all her might, she made out Gretchen's next words.

"I wasn't going to do it, but Ralph insisted and he's counting on Pat to make Elizabeth help out."

Ralph's voice came through now, deeper and louder than Gretchen's.

"It should be fun, and I know it'll help Gretchen at work. She's been taking things far too seriously. Don't worry Liz, we'll let you wear the ewok suit."

"What do you think of Ralph and Gretchen's wonderful project for November?" Jane asked.

It couldn't be any worse. She wasn't stupid, she knew what they were talking about, but they were wrong. Pat could certainly not make her help out. She'd seen the guy dressed up like the Statue of Liberty in front of the tax place, and just because Gretchen needed to boost sales and Ralph wanted to put her on the street in an ewok costume didn't mean they could make her. Even Pat couldn't force her. Whose happiness project was this, anyway?

"How's it sound, Liz? Do you have anything happy lined up for November, or will you join us?"

All innocence as though he would wear his Darth Vader costume and Gretchen her Leia. As if that would help. They were tall and good looking and everyone would rave over them while she was the laughing stock in her fat teddy bear head.

Her Krackel bar had melted. She wiped her hand on her sweats, all brown, all good, she was beyond caring. She took another bar from the bowl, peeled off the wrapper, and— were they watching? She couldn't tell.

"Do I smell something burning?"

She wasn't lying, just asking a question. When she heard movement toward the kitchen, she shoved the bar down her left eye hole. She thought she heard someone laugh, it sounded like Ralph but she couldn't sort that out now, she had a problem. The candy bar had gone AWOL. It had made it in all right, but it hadn't reached her mouth. The neck of the ewok head was tucked into her sweater and the bar had to be somewhere in her costume, the question was where. Had it gone past her mouth? She sniffed, snorted really, in an attempt to locate it. She couldn't smell anything but Jane's dryer sheet fragrance. The bar must be down her shirt.

"I don't know what you smelled, Lizzy, but everything's fine in the kitchen," Jane said.

"So what do you think of our plan?" Ralph asked.

The man was pushy. Fine, she'd push back.

"I don't have my November happiness project lined up precisely, but I won't wear the ewok suit to work, even if Pat thinks it's a good idea."

Utter silence. Not the silence of situational ewok deafness, but the eloquent quiet that usually followed her most inane remarks.

"I was joking about the ewok costume," Ralph said at last. "I'm helping Pat organize a trip for the students on Thanksgiving. We'll be working in a soup kitchen, and I thought you might like to come along."

The teddy bear head wasn't so bad, really. Kindly, protective, isolating in the best sense of the word. Now, for instance, they couldn't possibly see through it to the humiliation written all over her beet red face.

"If you're worried about Mom and Dad," Jane said, "they've got plans already. They're going with Mr. and Mrs. Lucas to Emily and Joe's for Thanksgiving dinner, so you won't be abandoning them if you head to L.A."

"I missed something. Isn't there a soup kitchen about ten minutes from here at St. Paschal's?" She sounded like a wet blanket, but if they helped in town she could hit Em's place after ladling turkey soup. "Why go all the way to Los Angeles?"

"Gretchen's doing," Ralph said. "She knows the Missionaries of Charity there and Father Barkley emailed he's going down for Thanksgiving. When I mentioned it to Pat he had a stroke of genius for his next Fra Angelico event."

She'd rather he simply had a stroke, but nothing Pat did was simple. He'd victimize her again, send her to the inner city when she should be at Emily's for Thanksgiving. There had to be a way out.

"Gretchen, are you sure the Missionaries won't mind having a college descend on them? Wouldn't we be in the way?"

"Father Barkley requested we bring students, and Pat offered the Fra Angelico money to cover transportation and incidental expenses. Ralph says most of the students will have other plans, but some will be grateful for the opportunity to work alongside the Missionaries."

"You don't have to decide now," Ralph said. "Pat will fill you in on the details later."

She nodded and the motion caused something inside her shirt to move. She shivered in reaction and it crawled further. She slapped at her stomach and felt the unmistakable stickiness of chocolate adhering to her skin.

"I hate to break up the party," Jane said, "but if we don't get the boys out soon, we won't have any candy left for our customers."

Giggles rose from around the bowl. Elizabeth reached forward and caught a small hand full of pixie sticks.

"Okay guys," she said, "put it back in the bowl. Let's go."

She pushed herself off the floor.

"I think I'll take the boys by myself," she said. "Luke and Jude on the buddy system, Dominic can hold my hand, and if Anthony doesn't let go of Matthew, we'll be fine." She stepped toward the door and the earth quaked.

"Auntie Beth!" several voices cried.

"You're standing in the candy bowl," Ralph said. "Hold on, let me help you."

She didn't want help. One damsel in distress per Sith Lord, and Gretchen was his fair lady. She felt his grip on her ankle, then he let go. Her feet were flat on the floor.

"I'll head out with Liz if you two ladies can spare me," Ralph said. "Gretch, why don't you stay and help Jane with the baby and the door."

'Gretch'? A man didn't call a woman Gretch unless he was awfully serious about the relationship, even Emily would have to admit that.

Gretchen's voice reached her.

"If Jane doesn't mind. Perhaps she wants solitude."

Jane laughed pleasantly. "This isn't a night for solitude, Gretchen. I'd love to have your company, as well as your help with the door."

"Okay then, boys," Ralph said. "Let's leave our masks here so everyone can see."

"Even Auntie Beth?"

Bless the child, she'd give him a dollar if she could figure out who he was.

"No, your Auntie Beth's an ewok. That's different from wearing a mask, she'll be fine. Jude and Luke hold hands. Anthony don't let go of Matthew. Dominic, you can lead your Auntie Ewok by the paw."

He was in league with Pat, no question. And repeating her plan as if he'd thought of it. "What exactly will you do?" she asked.

"I'll watch for cars and keep you from stepping into bowls when the kids are getting candy."

He opened the door and a flood of light poured in.

"We'll be back in about an hour," he said.

She stepped into the cool night air and inhaled deeply through her tiny snout holes. Someone grasped her hand and for a split second she thought it was Ralph. Fingernails dug into her palm—Dominic, her guide.

"Thank you honey, but that's a little tight. Let's hold hands gently. You won't lose me, I promise."

They walked together until Dominic let go and ran to the first house. She took a step without him, tripped over a crack in the sidewalk and fell with an "Oof" at the feet of a passing trick-or-treater. The child ran away, but something brushed against her cheek.

Ralph's cloak. He was helping her up, and though she couldn't see him, she could feel his suppressed laughter, a disturbance in the force.

"You okay?" he asked.

"More or less."

"I have something for you from the candy bowl."

He untucked the ewok head from her neck and stuck a piece of chocolate into her mouth, a Krackel.

"But I won't be your supplier. That's all you get from me, and don't tell Pat."

She tucked the teddy bear neck into her sweater and Dominic was back, grabbing her hand.

Hidden behind the ewok's face, her mouth curved into a smile. Ralph wasn't the only one who'd pilfered chocolate, and with practice she'd perfect her hand-eye-mouth coordination long before they returned to Jane's.

CHAPTER 34

The Eve of All Saints

By the time Darth and the boys shepherded Elizabeth home, it was a few minutes past nine. The porch light restored her sight momentarily, but coming inside was like entering a cave. No matter, in a flash she'd be back to her old self.

Delicious aromas wafted from the kitchen, pumpkin with an undertone of spiced apples and a strong bass note of chocolate. She tugged on the bear's head and called out blindly, "Jane, you're the best." As soon as she got this thing off she'd insert some form of chocolate directly into her mouth. The labyrinthine ways of her stolen Krackels had been diverting, but enough was enough.

She tugged harder, but nothing happened. She had become the ewok. Forty years from now she'd still be stumbling about, frightening small children, a misfit in human society but too tall to mingle inconspicuously with other ewoks, her fur turning gray as she aged.

She felt a pair of strong hands on her head and all at once she could see again.

Ralph stood beside her. He'd come to her aid like Captain Wentworth rescuing Anne Eliot from an awkward moment. Except in her case, Ralph had removed not only the ewok's head, but the sunglasses too. The sunglasses which were entangled in her hair. Before she could stop him, he walked away, dragging her along. She yelped in pain.

"Sorry!" he said, stopping.

He couldn't be that sorry, he was laughing.

Jane stepped forward and released her from the sunglasses, the bear's head, and Ralph.

"Glad to have you back, Lizzy," she said, and laughed too. Most unlike kind Jane.

Ralph was a bad influence on her sister, that was the only explanation, and now Jane was initiating some new torture. She pointed at Elizabeth's face and motioned for Ralph to look, then pulled a tissue from her pocket, spit on it and reached forward. Elizabeth backed away just in time.

"Jane, I'm not one of the kids! Please don't wipe my nose."

"You might want to wash your face," Ralph said. His mouth had stopped laughing, but his eyes hadn't.

She didn't know where Jane had hidden Gretchen, but she fled to the bathroom before the blonde could materialize and join the mocking crowd. She needed a moment alone to regroup.

Alone, but not alone. A madwoman she didn't recognize stared out at her from the mirror, hair disheveled, face disfigured with brown tracks and pockmarks. She looked like an escapee from a chocolate war. Elizabeth had seen ads for no-run mascara, but apparently candy makers hadn't picked up on the trend. Certainly the chocolate she'd been stuffing through her eye holes didn't have the same no-smear properties: it had run, melted, smeared, and stuck. Thank heaven Gretchen hadn't seen her; bad enough that Ralph had.

She scrubbed her cheeks clean and patted her hair into place. This never would have happened if she'd worn her danishes.

On the couch Jane held Francesca and chatted with Ralph, who sat at the dining table where the boys were sorting their loot. The night might be salvageable after all—someone had given out full-sized candy bars.

"Franny was sweet," Jane said, "but every time I tried to lay her down she woke, so Gretchen made the mulled cider and hot chocolate. She even melted chocolate chips so Lizzy could have her favorite sauce for the pumpkin pie."

Gretchen came from the kitchen with a laden tray. Instantly Ralph was on his feet, assisting her. He set the tray on the table.

"Pie for everyone?" he asked Jane.

"You know the rules, boys. Pie or candy, your choice."

The boys shoveled candy back into pillow cases.

Gretchen and Ralph had the pie distribution under control. The kitchen was a few steps away, she was there. She cut a large slice of pie for herself and ladled the melted chocolate over it.

The smell of the semi-sweet sauce blending with cinnamon, the velvety brown of the chocolate against the orange of the pumpkin, the feel of air on her face—it was paradise. In the dining room a nearly empty can of whipped cream spluttered. Tomorrow launched November, and she'd seriously consider a month devoted to hedonism.

The hot chocolate burnt her tongue, but an ice cube remedied the damage. She leaned against the counter to eat her pie. No rush, just one bite after another moving directly from hand to mouth. Heavenly. No need to join the others before she'd savored it down to the crust. They'd used up the whipped cream anyhow.

When she returned to the living room, Gretchen and Ralph sat alone. Alone together.

"Jane put the boys to bed, and took Francesca into her room," Ralph said.

"We should go home and leave her a quiet house." Gretchen scowled. Probably hadn't eaten any pie.

Ralph smiled at his love as if she'd uttered a witticism, then turned to Elizabeth.

"She asked us to wait for Pat if we could. He wants to nail down Thanksgiving plans."

She moved the ewok head from a dining chair and sat opposite the two blondes.

"Gretchen, can you tell me more about what we'd do? I need facts before Pat comes home and talks me into something. If you could explain who came up with the idea that might help too."

"Father Barkley invited me to spend Thanksgiving with the Missionaries of Charity. I can't leave the store for more than a day, and I won't drive to Los Angeles alone, so I told him no. When Ralph found out, he suggested going with a group. He said we shouldn't miss a chance to see Father Barkley since he's our spiritual director."

Of course. They could schedule their marriage prep, too.

"So where does Pat come in?"

Ralph fiddled with the purple top from the whipped cream. "When Gretchen told Father she might bring a group, he said the more the merrier. I asked Pat who to approach at the school to arrange transportation, and he took over."

"I knew it! That weasel co-opted your trip, didn't he?"
Gretchen's eyebrows went up.

"He needed an event for November," Ralph said, "and generously offered to bring our plans under the Fra Angelico umbrella."

"One big happy family," Elizabeth said.

Ralph tossed her a stray Milk Dud, and a Skittle to Gretchen. She had the Milk Dud in her mouth almost before it hit the table. Gretchen held the Skittle like a dead fly and walked to the kitchen.

"So what'll it be?" Ralph said. "Ready to cast in your lot with us or still questioning?"

She could hear Gretchen running water in the sink, drowning the Skittle-fly.

"I feel silly asking, but I've never been to something of this sort. What's it like?"

"Sublime." Gretchen rejoined them, folding her hands primly on the table.

So much for the nitty gritty details.

"She's right," Ralph said. "I did stuff like this with Gretchen in New York, and it's amazing. Kind of hard to describe."

"Can you tell me anything more specific?"

"Vans leave the college at eight in the morning Thanksgiving Day, arrive nine-thirty or ten," Ralph said. "We help cook and start serving at noon. Three o'clock we break for prayer and clean up, five o'clock Father Barkley leads the Missionaries and all helpers in a holy hour. At six we head home, stopping for burgers on the way out of L.A. We should be back around eight."

Too specific. "I guess that rules out Thanksgiving dinner at Emily and Joe's."

"I wish we could do both," he said. "I was looking forward to Joe and Emily's, but Gretchen needed my help and what can I say? It's about time I thought of someone besides myself. We'd love to have you come with us, Liz."

Gretchen's expression didn't reveal joyful anticipation, but Ralph's smile was genuine. He wanted her to go. Maybe he thought she'd make a good Missionary of Charity. He and Gretchen would get married, and she could be a nun. It was almost attractive; she didn't have any other plans.

"I'll go," she said.

"Go where?" Pat asked from the doorway.

What was with him? Always sneaking up, walking into his house without as much as a knock.

"Elizabeth's coming with us on Thanksgiving. Nice wings, man. St. Michael?"

"Absolutely, Darth. Did you wear a mask, or were you Vader in his last scene?"

"Mask's on the piano but don't keep me in suspense—what are those drooping wings made of?"

"Industrial sized coffee filters from the school. Gretchen, you make a lovely Leia. But Liz, before I forget, I'm curious about the ewok costume. Didn't fit?"

"I wore it trick-or-treating, sunglasses and all."

Pat laid his sword on the couch and sat beside it.

"October's behind you then. And you plan to go to L.A. for Thanksgiving?"

"I guess so."

"Your enthusiasm warms my heart, but there's a change in the game plan. I'll need you to stay here."

God was good, and Pat wasn't so bad. She could go to Emily's.

"You need all of us here, or just me?"

"Just you, cooking Thanksgiving dinner on campus to serve the others when they get back."

"Elizabeth, I didn't know you were a chef." Gretchen looked interested for once. "Frankly I'm relieved. I don't eat hamburgers, but if you had a green salad waiting for us, perhaps a liter of Perrier, I can assure you it would be highly appreciated."

Salad and carbonated water, a meal fit for a supermodel.

"Liz wanted to come with us," Ralph said. "Isn't it a bit harsh to make her stay and do all the work here?"

"Here, there, it's all service. I'm helping her flesh out Thanksgiving to cover the month. A paradise project is not a light undertaking, and spending an hour or two at a soup kitchen isn't likely to produce a full month's worth of happiness. With my new plan we can kill two birds with one stone, two turkeys with a single arrow, if you will. Liz can spend the month looking up recipes, preparing for the feast, being a foodie."

"But I hate food. At least I hate cooking."

Brilliant. Open mouth and, sans ewok head, insert foot directly in.

"If you have another project lined up, don't let me stop you," Pat said. "What would you rather do for November? You know, starting tomorrow."

She had nothing and he knew it. "How many people would I cook for?"

"Not many. Ralph and Gretchen and a few students."

"What about you and Jane and the kids?"

"I'll be there. I wouldn't miss your first Thanksgiving for the world, but Jane and the boys will be at Emily and Joe's."

"Good-night, Elizabeth. I'll see you tomorrow morning," Gretchen said.

She'd been so focused on Pat she hadn't noticed the Princess standing, Sith Lord at her side.

"Sorry you can't come with us Liz, but if I don't see you before Thanksgiving, good luck with the food. Don't forget the peanut butter."

He wasn't Joe's brother, he was Pat's. Same impoverished sense of humor.

Her pack was near the door, might as well grab it and leave before she was stuck here with St. Michael.

The archangel stood guard by the porch light, giving a last salute to Ralph and Gretchen. Slip past him and the evening would be over.

"Are we set for November?" he asked.

Sword in hand he blocked her escape route. A yes would unbar paradise, and what did she have to lose? In less than two hours she'd need a new project and she'd run out of ideas.

"You want me to cook Thanksgiving dinner for a few people and you won't pull any stunts, right?"

He gave her an angelic look.

"I'm serious, Pat. How many people am I cooking for, tops?"

"I don't have an exact number, but we can cap it at forty if that makes you feel better."

Skipping Thanksgiving altogether would make her feel better, but that wasn't on his list of options.

She muttered a resentful "Okay," and they shook on it.

"If you need to borrow any cookbooks, let Jane know." He kissed the top of her head and let her pass.

She returned his affection by not sucker punching him. "No mac and cheese, then?"

"Thanksgiving dinner with all the trimmings, nothing more, nothing less."

The nothing more she was comfortable with; nothing less might take a little work.

CHAPTER 35

A Charlie Brown Thanksgiving

Elizabeth in the kitchen was Elizabeth overwhelmed, though it hadn't always been this way. Last Friday she'd made Kraft macaroni and cheese for her nephews with an excess of confidence. An excess of salt, too, but they hadn't minded. It was the recipients of one's hospitality that made the difference. And possibly the menu change had unhinged her.

She knew she couldn't make mac and cheese for forty people, Pat had said she couldn't, so she'd watched Food Network with her parents and browsed the cookbook section at work. She'd talked menus with Emily and even printed off recipes from cooking blogs.

All along, however, she'd known these were ruses, attempts to placate Pat and they'd succeeded on that front, but provide her with know-how, interest, a meal and menu plan for forty, they hadn't. Going from boxed mac and cheese

to maple glazed turkey with capers, cranberries and cous-
cous stuffing wasn't bringing her more happiness, nor was it,
now that the day was here, even happening.

It didn't help that she'd spent November intensively training for the management position she now realized she didn't
want. Nor was the pressure alleviated by knowing her boss
would be her guest at the dinner Pat had foisted on her. Famil-
iarity with Gretchen hadn't revealed any endearing flaws.
She was as perfect as ever, and Elizabeth had more than one
anxiety dream in which she served buttered toast, popcorn,
and jelly beans to the woman for whom maple glazed turkey
would be barely acceptable. That Gretchen wouldn't eat more
than a helping of Caesar salad didn't ease the pain. Ten to
one the blonde would notice if the Thanksgiving board was
missing a turkey, whether she intended to partake or not.

Elizabeth's Wednesday-before-Thanksgiving shift ended
at five, and by five-fifteen she was at Costco rubbing shoulders with several hundred kindred spirits, fellow procrasti-
nators from the tri-county area. No more stalling, they were
all in the same leaky boat and it was sink or swim, cook or
be cooked.

She loaded her cart according to two simple criteria. Each
food item needed a picture on the front that looked like a
Martha Stewart Thanksgiving, and it had to be microwave-
able. Her plan was to celebrate the wonders of modern food
science and technology by hosting an insta-feast. Huge serving portions and no prep time: what could be more American? She wondered at her earlier panic; this was a breeze.

In twenty-four hours, the breeze had mounted to a
tsunami.

The winds of change blew in when she picked up *Persuasion* before bed. She should have known better. Caught
up in the story, needing to stay with Anne until Captain

Wentworth stealthily wrote his love letter, then unable to stop so near the end, Elizabeth didn't put the book down till early morning. She slept soundly until late afternoon. The minute she woke and saw the time, she threw on a pair of jeans and a clean top and headed straight into the storm.

Now, standing in the college's kitchen surrounded by massive amounts of unheated Costco pre-fab Thanksgiving and three large boxes of china, crystal, and table linens, she was on the verge of tears. Why hadn't anyone told her the kitchen staff relied on industrial sized ovens, not microwaves? Her guests would return to campus before she'd unwrapped the food, let alone cooked it practically from scratch. And the tables were still unset. Six o'clock and all was far from well.

"It's a ghost town around here."

She dropped the sheet of paper she held and stared at the specter of Ralph. If he was a ghost, her troubles were over. Too bad the vans had crashed and Ralph and Gretchen and their entourage were dead, but heaven would welcome them and she wouldn't have to.

A repulsive smell reached her sensitive nose.

"Tell me that's not a vat of peanut butter."

"I cannot tell a lie, Miss Benning, and I'm not sure there's enough for both of us."

Ghosts didn't carry vats of peanut butter, though if they did, no doubt Ralph would. Tragically, the ghost theory was vaporizing, and a much worse scenario opened before her.

"You're back? Where are the others? In the coffee shop already?"

She retrieved her schedule and began shredding it, the pieces drifting like snowflakes to the ground.

"I didn't go."

She stopped shredding. They hadn't gone? How long had they been waiting for their dinner? It was all over. Pat had won.

She sat on the floor amidst the remains of her useless schedule and mindlessly collected the bits. Ralph and his peanut butter sat next to her.

"Anything wrong?" he asked.

"If you want to help, why don't you take your peanut butter to the coffee shop and tell Pat I quit."

When he left, she'd sneak out the back door. If she kept walking south, eventually she'd reach Mexico and they weren't so strict about passports on the way in. Reverse illegal immigration. She couldn't be any unhappier there and she loved Mexican food.

"This is awesome," he said.

"Thanks for the sympathy."

"I came up for a snack, thought I'd check on your progress, and I find you ready to throw in the towel. Perfect timing, isn't it?"

"I guess you're rooting for Pat, then."

"You misjudge me. I'm in time to save the day, but I can't help until you tell me what's wrong."

"Isn't it obvious? You're so hungry you're ruining your dinner with peanut butter, and you might as well since there isn't going to be a dinner. The others must be starving too, and I can't give them frozen turkey."

He rose and surveyed the unopened packages on the metal counter. He turned over a large rectangular box of scalloped potatoes.

"Microwave directions, recommended method, remove tray from package and remove film. Heat on high for eight minutes. Revolve tray one quarter turn and heat an additional six minutes until bubbly around edges. Let stand one minute before serving. Microwave ovens vary, adjust cooking times as needed."

He set the box down. "Don't worry about the oranges if we don't have any. That was a serving suggestion, and you don't have to make it exactly like the picture."

"We have plenty of oranges. This is southern California."

"So what's the problem? They won't be back till at least seven. Plenty of time. A mere fourteen minutes and our potatoes will be bubbly around the edges, garnished with orange slices."

He picked up a large bag.

"Place unopened bag standing up on microwavable plate to evenly cook. Microwave on high twenty-two to twenty-six minutes. Wow."

"What?"

"You're awesome. Where'd you find a microwave turkey?"

"It doesn't matter. There's no microwave in here."

"I have one in my trailer. It's heavy, but I can load it into Nellie and drive around. We'll have a feast fit for the Jetsons by the time they get back."

"But I don't understand. How can you be here if they're not?"

"Grading. Realized I couldn't serve the poorest of the poor if it meant losing my job. Kind of counterproductive. My sophomores handed in thirty-five papers about six weeks ago, and this is the first chance I've had to look at them."

"So why aren't you home grading?"

"This is home. I'm living in one of the trailers. Came up for a peanut butter sandwich and you know the rest." He motioned to a box of linens. "Why don't you start on the tables while I get the microwave."

He was gone, the only sign he'd been here a vat of peanut butter at her feet. She walked around it. He could put it away when he returned.

With a load of tablecloths over her arm, she stepped through the swinging door into the coffee shop. She spread the first cloth, smoothed it, and stood back to admire. It looked like a photo on a blog.

So he hadn't gone with Gretchen. Would she ever understand them? He seemed cheerful with or without his colder half; she seemed equally unhappy with or without him. Stranger yet, she'd never seen any display of affection between them, unless she counted Gretchen's sleeve touching, and even that had cooled lately. Granted Ralph was a gentleman and Gretchen a human icicle, but could a nearly engaged couple be that platonic?

They'd known each other so long they'd become like those couples whose faces match, like brother and sister, or the dogs and their owners in the opening scene of *A Hundred and One Dalmatians*. The afghan and the artist; Ralph the faithful shaggy blonde dog, Gretchen the abstracted tall skinny prototype.

"So what can I help you with?"

She jumped and pirouetted to face him.

"I didn't mean to scare you," Ralph said, lowering a box to the floor.

"No one ever does. Did you get the microwave?"

"Turkeys are in the oven. Potatoes too."

He was setting china on the tablecloth she'd spread. She put her hand on his sleeve, then remembered Gretchen and stepped back.

"Yes?" He went to the box for more plates.

"You're ruining my turkeys—you can't put them all in at once."

He gestured to the silverware on the coffee bar.

"Start on the forks and I'll explain." He continued setting places. "You want to have this room set up first, so when they come in appetizers are waiting."

She grabbed a handful of forks and knives.

"You think we can pull it off?"

The "we" was out of her mouth and there was no taking it back. He didn't seem to notice, he was getting out the crystal. They were like a couple preparing for their first dinner party. Weird.

"Of course we can, but we needed more than one microwave so I raided the dorms. Turned up three students along with the ovens, they're in the kitchen now."

"I thought all the students were off campus for dinner. Isn't that how we got the kitchen?"

"Yeah, the kids with families nearby take their friends home for break and faculty pick up the stragglers for today's big meal, but these three slipped through the cracks."

"How sad."

"Not at all. They were playing a war game and microwaving popcorn for dinner when I requisitioned their oven, so I suggested they work for food. Now everyone's happy. They're making trays of cheese and crackers and dumping the corn into pans. Corn's okay on the stove, right? No need to microwave everything?"

She whipped him with a linen napkin.

"I have the ovens on pre-heat," he said. "To keep the food warm when it's out of the microwaves. Rolls and butter we can set out on each table, and the cranberry relish in cut glass bowls for a splash of color. How's that sound?"

"Did you work in catering?"

"Grew up in a large family, piece of cake. Speaking of which, we might as well have the boys cut and plate the pies now so you don't have to struggle to stay ahead of your guests during dinner. You can sit and eat with us."

"I don't think so. I'll have too much left to do."

"No way. We're almost finished."

He was laying out the spoons.

"The tables are lovely," she said.

He looked at his watch. "I'll tell the boys to switch out the food in the microwaves. Green bean casseroles in next, then they can set up the coffee makers and cut the pies. Why don't you sit down and have a glass of wine?"

"Shouldn't I bring in the rolls and butter?"

"I'll get those. If you open the wine now, we can pour a glass for Pat when he walks in. Mellow him straight off."

He was in the kitchen before she could reply. A bottle of red. Pat would drink it right down; the perfect beginning to his heat-and-serve dinner.

For herself she opened a bottle of Martinelli's.

"Not a big drinker, are you?" Ralph wheeled in a two tiered cart. Baskets of rolls, bowls of cranberry sauce, the cheese trays: he had it all.

"Can I get you a glass of wine?" she asked.

He set the first basket and bowl on a table. "I'll have some sparkling cider if you don't mind sharing."

"We've got plenty. I'm serving it to the students who aren't twenty-one."

She handed him the glass and tilted her head, evaluating his work. "You were right. The red of the cranberry adds a nice touch of color."

"Have a seat then, and I'll finish setting these out."

"Shouldn't I help?"

"You've done plenty. Your dinner's cooking and it smells great. My mom always said the hostess should relax for ten minutes before her company arrives. That way she's ready to meet and greet with an authentic smile."

"Like this?" She smiled, then laughed.

"You're a natural. Gretchen just called and they're about fifteen minutes away, so we have plenty of time."

She popped out of her chair. She couldn't relax with only fifteen minutes to go.

He put his hands on her shoulders and gently pushed her back into the chair.

"Trust me, it's under control, I promise."

He did seem to have everything under control, and if he didn't, was there anything she could do to fix it in fifteen minutes? She pulled out another chair and put her feet up.

"Talking to Gretchen reminded me of something I've wanted to ask you." He moved about the room, distributing rolls and butter. "How do you like your new job? She told me the other day you'll be a fine manager for the children's department."

The apple juice fermented in her mouth.

"Gretchen's not one to give compliments," he said, "so I thought I'd pass along how highly she spoke of you. In case she didn't tell you herself, afraid you'd get a big head."

"No danger there."

"That she'd praise you or that you'd get a big head?"

"Both."

Could he hear the bitterness? She needed to talk to someone, but Ralph could hardly be the one.

"So tell me about it," he said. "Do you like the bookstore?"

"I love the children's department, especially when parents come in and ask me to find books for children who don't like reading yet. I ask about the children's interests, and then I find the books I know will carry them away. It's the best feeling in the world."

"Will you do more of that when you're head of the department? Pat told me the promotion's your December happiness project."

He set the last cranberry relish in the center of the table, and sat across from her. The red really was pretty. She could lose herself in the translucent color.

"I bet you'll love being in charge. More happiness through more power and better pay—what a sweet deal. And by the end of December you'll have beaten Pat. Wasn't that your goal?"

"You told me it shouldn't be but that's not my biggest problem right now."

He looked around the room.

"You can't be worried about this. November's in the bag, so what's wrong?"

She couldn't confide in him. He wasn't just someone, he was Gretchen's someone. She went to the coffee bar and poured him a glass of wine. If it would mellow Pat, it could mellow him too. A mellow confidant, that's what she needed. Not that she'd ever seen Ralph anything but mellow. Still, she hated to drink alone. She opened the white and poured herself a glass.

"Thanks," he said, accepting his red. "Now tell me, what's your biggest problem?"

"It's like I said. I love what I do."

"I call that a first world problem."

"You don't get it. If I could keep my job like it is, I'd be fine. But when I'm head of the department, I won't be doing the things I love. I'll have to leave the floor and do ordering and inventory and go to meetings." She swirled the wine in her glass. "I hate meetings. I'll be sucked up toward corporate, and then I won't be working for the enemy, I'll be the enemy."

"We have met the enemy, and he is us."

"Excuse me?"

"Marsupial folk wisdom. Have you told Gretchen how you feel?"

Gretchen and "feel" in the same sentence. Love was blind, there was no other explanation.

"I can't. She hired me intending to give me this promotion and Marcella's spent the last month training me. Gretchen's been stressed about keeping sales numbers up, and I don't think she needs another problem."

"You're kind-hearted, Liz, but you shouldn't accept the promotion just because Gretchen wants you to. You don't need to worry about her."

"I'm not saying I'll accept, but I don't know how to tell Gretchen. If you want the truth, I've been losing sleep over it. She's going to kill me."

"I've known her a long time and she's never killed anyone yet."

"Cold comfort. There's always a first time."

"Tell you the truth, what you choose won't affect her much. I happen to know every day's bringing her closer to happiness. More than happiness. Her heart's deepest desire, you might say."

There it was. He probably had the ring in his pocket now. Good for him, but someone had to look out for Gretchen.

"What about corporate? She has to answer to them, and if I flake, she could be in trouble."

"Liz, you need to do what makes you happy. I can't tell you the details, but I'm sure you don't need to worry about Gretchen."

She didn't want the details. Where he'd propose, what he'd say, how romantic it would be. She could imagine, and she'd rather not.

"Anyway, this isn't really about Gretchen, it's about you," he said. "And if you don't want the promotion, you shouldn't take it."

"You make it sound easy, but what if I lose my job? She's a stickler for the corporate handbook, and there must be a rule about employees hired under false pretenses. If she fires me, I'm sunk. No more children's books. No more happiness."

"She won't fire you." He was actually smiling at her; he wasn't taking her seriously at all.

"Even if she doesn't, I'm done for with Pat. You said it yourself, he thinks the promotion's my December happiness project. You know how I feel?"

"Hungry?"

"It's not funny. I feel like the guy in *The Telltale Heart*, like I've committed a crime and any second I'll be found out. Whenever I see Gretchen I know I ought to tell her I don't want the promotion, but I keep putting it off and now it's too late. I've totally messed up her protocol or whatever."

She was making even less sense than usual, she could tell by the look on his face. He was no longer smiling, not quite, but not quite frowning either. Consternation? No, he wasn't consterned, exactly. It was more a quizzical look, somewhere between questioning and amused. Bemused, that's what he was.

"It's never too late," he said, "and Gretchen will be fine. Her happiness is a done deal, and you need to find yours."

"How?" If he had all the answers, she might as well ask the big questions.

"By doing what you want to do, not what you think she wants you to do."

"Then you think I should tell her I don't want the promotion?"

"Why not? Why not tell her tonight? Get it off your troubled conscience so you can sleep again."

"I'll think about it."

Marcella wasn't leaving till mid-December; she had a couple of weeks yet. Never put off until tomorrow what you can put off for fourteen days.

He was smiling, but not at her. She turned, and there was Pat coming through the glass door like he owned the place.

"Ralph, how's the grading?"

"You caught me. I'm having a drink with the hired help, but it went well, thanks. How was L.A.?"

"We missed you, but otherwise the day was perfect. Gretchen and Father Barkley took the students to the chapel for a prayer of thanks. Everyone's tired but ready to party."

Elizabeth handed him a glass of red.

"Looks like you've got things under control, Liz. Good job."

"Piece of cake. I think I'll head to the kitchen now and check on the turkey."

No need to fraternize with the guests, regardless of Ralph's invitation. He'd been an angel in her time of need. Their dinner was heated and she'd gladly serve it, but feasting alongside the happy couple tonight was beyond her powers, and neither an angel nor Ralph would convince her otherwise.

CHAPTER 36

Silent Counsel

She tried to stare him down, though she knew she'd fail. She always blinked first. He never accepted any blame, never looked guilty, never admitted so much as a whisper of responsibility for her unhappiness.

She alternated accusations with "I" statements, pouring out her heart after giving him a piece of her mind. Nothing moved him. What was he? Made of ice? No. Gretchen might be frozen, but he wasn't. And he didn't have a heart of stone. More like a heart of wood if he had a heart at all. But she needed someone to talk to, and he was the best of the lot.

She couldn't talk to Emily; they'd been over and around the subject endlessly and got nowhere. Em didn't know anything about Ralph's imminent proposal to Gretchen (Ralph hadn't confided in Joe), only that Ralph and Elizabeth were perfect for each other. Which was sweet of her to say, and

Elizabeth agreed, but if he didn't see it, they could hardly talk him into it.

As to the promotion and whether she should accept it, Emily broke into laughter every time the subject arose. The irony of her "taking over" Books-a-Trillion, as Emily put it, threatened their friendship, not because Em was angry, but because she found it so funny.

She couldn't talk about the promotion any more with Ralph; he was too close to Gretchen.

Jane was too close to Pat.

Pat was, well, Pat.

Which left her with a counselor whose lips never uttered a word in response. On the plus side, he certainly had the knack of listening for as long as she talked, his eyes wide open and full of compassion, a trait few men in her experience possessed.

Her new motto, "Eat, drink, and be merry, for in two weeks you shall hit a brick wall," had reached its brick wall. Tomorrow they'd take Marcella out for a good-bye lunch and baby shower. She wouldn't spoil Marcella's luncheon by declining the promotion then. That left today.

Today she'd march straight into Gretchen's office and say . . .

"Are you sure this is the right decision?"

He didn't blink, didn't move, but his painted eyes spoke volumes.

She went to the shelf. She needed a closer view of the statue's face. She couldn't risk missing some critical nuance, some subtle "Go ahead and take the promotion" coming from his expressively painted mouth.

Nothing.

Or nothing new, anyway. He always radiated the same sensitive understanding. He must have made a lot of decisions in his day—the real Fra, not the statue. How to best serve God with his talents, how to be happy in this life while waiting for heaven, whether to use a lighter shade of green to edge Gabriel's wing. Maybe he'd even respectfully declined a promotion to some higher office in the monastery. He'd have given his superior the same look he gave her now, an apologetic but unwavering, "With all due respect, that's a terrible idea."

An answer of sorts, but in her current dilemma they were all terrible ideas.

If she took the promotion she'd finish off the year successfully, for the first time ever. And take on a job she'd hate, ending one year of unhappiness by committing to another.

If she declined, she would lose to Pat. Again.

Last week she'd completed her commitment to Pat's Fra Anglelico series by helping with his St. Nicholas Day party. At its conclusion he rubbed his red-robed pillow-padded belly and thanked her. Unusual. Then he told her he would accept her promotion as a final passionate lunge at happiness, and if she took it, he'd concede. Unheard of.

Either being the father of a baby girl had undone him entirely, or he'd spiked the eggnog and had one too many. Whatever prompted his jolly good sportsmanship, it didn't help. She'd spent a year unhappily, her servitude was nearly at an end, and he urged her to escape through Door Number One, the door that led to more unhappiness. Thanks, but no thanks. There had to be another way out. After all these years, beating Pat didn't seem worth it.

Door Number Two would be the obvious choice, since she didn't see a Door Number Three. And behind Door Number Two? No trip to Bermuda, unless her parents paid or Books-a-Trillion had an amazing severance package for employees of less than four months duration.

No, when she walked through Gretchen's door, she'd risk it all—she'd fling down her refusal like a gauntlet and take the consequences: losing to Pat, possibly losing her job. Stated so baldly her choice didn't thrill her, but under the steady gaze of Fra she couldn't hide from the truth.

Ralph had been right. The point of a paradise project was paradise, not beating Pat. Her first choice for paradise was unavailable, so she'd have to take her happiness as she found it. Right now she loved her job. She might lose it when she refused to give it up, but that was better than purposely stepping away from it, climbing the corporate ladder Gretchen held steady. Better to take her chances on the ground and stay true to the dreams of her youth, such as they were.

So that was it. Today she'd beard the lioness in her den, croak out a polite refusal, and hop away as quickly as possible. Pat would gloat but she was used to that by now, if not wholly immune. Gretchen might fire her, but she wouldn't be any worse off than she'd been a year ago. Except for the part about the broken heart, but accepting or rejecting the promotion wouldn't heal that.

She consulted Minnie. Time to go.

One last glance at Fra to make sure he hadn't changed his mind. His wordless compassion washed over her. He approved. She picked up her purse and headed for the door.

CHAPTER 37

Like Water from a Rock

"Come in."

Gretchen waited in her den, but it was a polar bear's den; the thermostat by the door read sixty-two. No wonder the manager kept her door closed. Wouldn't want to lose that arctic edge.

Elizabeth climbed into the faux leather affair across from her, immediately at a loss. She never knew how to adjust these castered office chairs; her feet didn't touch the floor, and she felt the chair rolling as she tried to get comfortable. She gripped the edge of Gretchen's desk and pulled herself in. She'd be at a disadvantage without the use of her hands, but let go and she'd roll away, and if the chair spun, she'd be saying no to the wall on the other side of the room.

The desk was high, the chair fit under it like a bar stool, and she wanted to order a gin and tonic, but Gretchen's bottom drawer no doubt held a flask of Perrier.

"Can we begin?"

"Certainly," she said. It came out in a whisper and she cleared her throat.

"I understand you're here to discuss the impending changes," Gretchen said. "Obviously your position will shift when Marcella leaves tomorrow. I'm well aware of the experience you bring to the department, and given your month long training, I'm confident your promotion will make the new manager's transition a smooth one."

Elizabeth let go of the desk and immediately began rolling. She shot out an arm, grabbed her anchor, and steadied herself.

"I don't understand. Will there be two managers for the children's department?" It didn't matter, she wouldn't be either of them. Under her breath she practiced, "No. No. No."

"Of course not. I'm saying that with you managing children's, the transition will be easier for the new store manager. He arrives next week, and I'll train him before I leave."

"No," Elizabeth said, one of her practice "no's" escaping aloud. "I mean oh."

New store manager. Was corporate firing Gretchen? They could go on unemployment together.

"I haven't publicized my decision. In fact, you're the first in store to know I'm leaving. Corporate knows, of course, but I judged it best to wait for your official promotion today before releasing the memo announcing both of our decisions."

Gretchen had made a decision. She was leaving because she and Ralph would be married.

Elizabeth smiled a Gretchen smile. She didn't need to see her reflection in the polished glass covering Gretchen's desk to know the smile didn't reach her eyes, but it was the best she could come up with on short notice.

"Congratulations. I mean best wishes. Have you chosen a date?"

There, she was being civil. So why was Gretchen looking at her like that?

"How did you find out? Did Ralph tell you?"

"Not directly, I just knew. Women's intuition I guess." The Flannery O'Connor character was back in the room, poisoning the cold, cold air with her sour breath. "So do you have a date picked out?"

"My last day here is December twenty-fourth. Following that is the trip to see my family. Arrival in India is set for the first of January, Feast of Mary the Mother of God."

"India?"

The fat southern woman melted away like butter and the air turned sweet. In all her nightmares, Gretchen and Ralph got married at St. Paschal's and had the reception in the hall where she and Gretchen had gone speed dating.

"I know it's unusual," Gretchen said, "but India's felt like home to me since I was there when Mother passed."

"Your mother died in India?"

"Blessed Mother Teresa. I was with her the summer before she died, and I've wanted to return ever since."

Gretchen opened a desk drawer and brought out her Franklin Planner.

"I was intending to ask you next week, but now that you've brought it up, I have a favor."

Elizabeth tightened her grip on the edge of the desk. She didn't want to go to India and be in Gretchen's wedding. She didn't want to witness the demise of her happiness, and Gretchen couldn't make her. Losing her job, keeping her job, these were nothing compared to the agony it would be to watch them take their vows. She'd just say no.

Gretchen's pen was poised over the planner. "Would you be willing to make an airport run on December twenty-seventh? Ralph said the Vanagon will be in the shop, and with all the luggage, my car is too small. He suggested we borrow the Moore's mini-van, but I'd feel uncomfortable doing that unless you drive."

So now she was a courier service driving the man she loved and the woman he loved into their blissful Bollywood future. She could try out another no, but she didn't want to run out of them. Her no to the promotion was the only one that counted.

"Sure," she said.

Gretchen made a notation and closed the planner.

"And now I believe that's enough discussion of my personal affairs. You're here to find out the details of your promotion, and I won't keep you in suspense. You must have received the contract with your new salary and benefits package. Return it to me signed before you leave today. Next week you have meetings in Palo Alto at corporate, and you'll travel to Detroit for the Children's Book Festival in January."

This was it: the moment of her great No. She might spend the rest of her life alone, but she'd be a lonely bookseller, not a lonely department manager. A surge of adrenaline prepared her to restore some small measure of justice in an unjust world. Gretchen was marrying Ralph and consigning her to Detroit in January. She couldn't do anything to stop the wedding, but she could certainly say no to Detroit.

"Gretchen, I'm sorry if this causes you any inconvenience, but I won't be taking the promotion. I'm happy as a salesclerk in children's, and I don't want to be department manager."

There, she'd said it. No groveling, just a minimal apology and the facts.

Gretchen was staring at her, saying nothing.

"I appreciate your confidence in me, I mean that you think I'd be a good manager for the department, but I want to keep things as they are."

If only her feet touched the floor. A girl gripping a desk was at an extreme disadvantage, especially when facing an angry anorexic polar bear.

"Elizabeth, may I ask how long you've been planning to decline the position? Is this a sudden change in your intentions?"

"I wasn't sure what I'd decide when I started working here, but after a little while I realized I don't belong in management."

"In that case, can you explain to me why you allowed Marcella to train you for a position you weren't intending to accept?"

They said honesty was the best policy. She'd give it a shot and if they were wrong, she'd audition for *MythBusters*.

"I didn't want to tell you something that might make you unhappy?"

Gretchen didn't look convinced, and Elizabeth wasn't surprised. The blonde had never seemed particularly interested in happiness. She was the one with the happiness project. Gretchen was the one with Ralph.

"Elizabeth, I wish you'd told me earlier. Training Ashley will take time, and I don't have extra time at my disposal right now."

Of course Gretchen was busy, her time at a premium, but whose fault was that? No one was making her get married in three weeks, and in India of all places. Besides, she was so absurdly capable she could train Ashley in her sleep or long distance—

Gretchen's words sunk in.

"You're going to train Ashley? I don't know how I missed that. She's perfect. Why didn't Marcella train her instead of me in the first place?"

Gretchen's eyes narrowed and a crease that didn't bode well marred her alabaster brow.

"I asked Marcella to train you because I thought you wanted the position. Now that you inform me you are declining it, my job is to train the second most likely candidate before I leave. I have plenty to do in the next couple of weeks, and I would have preferred not to add this to my schedule. I'm already working double shifts."

"Could I help?"

"I appreciate your offer, but I don't see how you can train Ashley while you're selling on the floor."

Gretchen had re-opened the Franklin Planner and was examining it minutely, as if by implacable determination she'd scare extra hours out of the days.

"Why couldn't I work double shifts too? I could train her when I'm not supposed to be working. I could do that for you Gretchen, if it would help."

She was the virtuous woman. This was the way to live. Selflessly.

"That would help, and considering you've caused this problem, I appreciate your contributing to its solution."

Gretchen's perfect eyebrows were slightly raised, and she was almost smiling. Elizabeth basked in the relative warmth.

"I could do more, if you want."

Why not go the extra mile? Not to India, of course, but she could show goodwill. After all, it sounded like Gretchen wasn't firing her. Why not return the favor, so to speak?

"I can make the favors for you. I did that for Emily."

"Pardon me?" Gretchen's eyebrows went up in earnest.

"They don't have to be candy almonds in netting, but I could make the favors if you tell me what you want and how many you need. Will it be a large or small wedding?"

Gretchen's small almost-smile disappeared. Maybe they'd argued over the number of guests.

"The clothing ceremony won't be fancy," she said.

"Is that an Indian custom?"

"A Catholic custom."

"Will Ralph be part of that ceremony too? I've seen the turban wrapping in Bollywood movies, but I never know how much of that is made up. I don't suppose you'll sing, though that would be lovely."

She almost regretted she wasn't going. An Indian wedding would be gorgeous.

"Ralph won't be there. He's not coming with me to India."

The clothing ceremony must come first, just for the bride. A shame Ralph couldn't fly over with his fiancée, but the Indians had stricter standards, like never kissing on screen.

"Will he be flying to India with your parents, then?"

"Ralph's not coming to India."

"Never?"

Gretchen must be getting her wedding clothes in India, then coming back to marry him, like in *Persuasion* when the Musgroves went to Bath for Henrietta's and Louisa's clothes.

"I suppose he might come for my final vows, but that's years away."

The Church frowned upon long engagements, Gretchen must be aware of that. A long separation would be so challenging.

"Are you staying there until the vows, then?" she asked. "I guess it's not hard to have a long distance relationship these days. You and Ralph can email and Skype."

"Elizabeth, what are you talking about? The Missionaries of Charity don't have computers, and Ralph isn't expecting to hear from me. He knows I'm doing God's will, and we'll pray for each other."

"But praying for each other isn't enough, not if you'll be separated for years. When exactly are you and Ralph getting married?"

Gretchen's face did the Lon Chaney thing for a fraction of a second.

"Never! I'm going to India to become a Missionary of Charity. I thought you said you knew."

Elizabeth stared at Gretchen who wasn't marrying Ralph. Gretchen, whose face was finally alive, no longer a mask but full of remarkable changes. After the Lon look came impatience, complete with shaking of the head and what sounded like tsking. Then understanding lit up Gretchen's eyes, and amusement, then a ravishing smile that was pure joy to behold. Elizabeth wanted to keep staring, to appreciate the beautiful light that suffused Gretchen's face, but she felt a blush creeping up her neck at her mistake.

Gretchen wasn't marrying Ralph.

She looked at her hands. She was clutching the edge of the desk so hard her knuckles had turned white. Perhaps she should let go, push off, and roll out of the office before she burst into song. Except if her hands left the desk they'd clap, and that might startle the exquisite smile off Gretchen's adorable face.

For once she knew what to do. She climbed down from the chair, reached across the desk, and grasped Gretchen's right hand in both of hers. A compromise. More touch than

Gretchen was used to, but nothing like the hug Elizabeth longed to give.

She ought to say congratulations. She hoped it wouldn't come out set to music.

"Congratulations, Gretchen." Not bad. Her voice was high and squeaky, but she'd said it. "I'm really happy for you."

"Thank you, Elizabeth."

Gretchen inclined her head in a moment of gracious acknowledgment, then pulled her hand away and returned to business.

"Your double shifts will start Monday. I'll need you in at six each morning, I'll give you an hour for lunch, a short break in the afternoon, and an hour for dinner. If you train Ashley by Christmas, you can take the next week off in compensation and start back with a normal schedule on January second. At least that's what I'll recommend to your new manager."

She nodded, humbly accepting her commission.

"That's all for now." Gretchen reached for the phone.

She made it out of the office without clapping. If she could get through the next six hours without becoming hysterical, it would be a miracle.

She took the escalator to children's and went to the Beverly Cleary shelf. Beverly always calmed her. She could think for a few minutes, here with Ramona and Beezus and Henry Huggins and Ribsy. And there, tucked between *Ellen Tebbits* and *Otis Spofford*, there was Ralph S. Mouse with his motorcycle. Just like her Ralph and his Vanagon. She smiled.

She'd pictured Ralph so often as Gretchen's groom, it would take time to expunge the image. But he couldn't marry her, Gretchen was going to India, and he wouldn't be going with her because Gretchen was going to be a nun in a blue and white sari. The very thought of Gretchen in a sari made her dizzy with relief.

She lowered herself to the floor of the children's department, which was thankfully empty but for Ashley setting up a display on the opposite side of the room.

She was like Elinor Dashwood in *Sense and Sensibility*, when Elinor discovered Edward was free to marry her. And yet as Elizabeth bowed her head and burst into tears of joy, which at first she thought would never cease, it was a sign of the depth of her feeling that for once she stopped thinking of great moments in Jane Austen, and thought instead simply of herself, and Ralph, and the happiness she hoped was waiting for them.

CHAPTER 38

Twenty Questions

In her initial reaction to Gretchen's news, Elizabeth felt only happiness at Ralph's freedom. Later, when the shock wore off and she was home again with Fra, she had time to consider the masculine viewpoint. Naturally, Gretchen's departure would be painful for Ralph. Like Edmond Bertram in *Mansfield Park* when he parted from Mary Crawford and Fanny waited in the wings, Ralph might need a period of adjustment before he realized Elizabeth was the woman for him.

She was so far from the meek and patient Fanny, and Gretchen so unlike the high spirited Mary Crawford, that the comparison wouldn't stick. More fitting for her situation were the last scenes of *Persuasion* when Anne, still separated by circumstances from Wentworth, comforted herself that if there be constant attachment on each side, hearts must understand each other ere long. Like Anne and Wentworth, she and Ralph were not girl and boy, captiously irritable, misled by every moment's inadvertence, and wantonly playing with their own happiness.

Or so she hoped. "Constant attachment on both sides" wasn't the first description she'd apply to the vicissitudes of her relationship with Ralph. She'd spent the first half of their acquaintance in a state of constant irritation and dislike of him. He'd spent the second half in attendance on Gretchen and apparent disinterest in herself.

As to how things stood between her and Ralph now—that remained a mystery not even Jane Austen could solve.

It was the twenty-seventh of December and she was driving the Moore's mini-van to the airport, Ralph riding shotgun, Gretchen sitting in the back, the Louis Vuitton luggage in the way back. Gretchen would fly out of LAX to Idaho and her parents, and on the thirty-first Father Barkley would meet her at JFK and accompany her to Calcutta.

Elizabeth hadn't seen Ralph since Thanksgiving. Then he'd spoken blithely of Gretchen's achieving the desire of her heart, but how deeply he felt the separation now she couldn't tell. Was it tension or sadness or impatience that predominated in the van? Her own feelings were hard enough to decipher, let alone Ralph's and Gretchen's.

The ride to the airport was stressful. Shortly after merging onto the interstate, traffic slowed to a crawl. She hated driving into L.A. but Gretchen insisted it was her relatives' van, and only she should drive it. And so the three of them made their way into the future at ten miles an hour: a stressed chauffeur, two silent blondes, and an endless Bach fugue playing on the stereo, per the future Missionary's request. She was ready to ask for a final smoke if neither of the others did.

Gretchen's flight left at four in the afternoon, she preferred to be there by two, and thanks to her insistence they leave hours earlier than Elizabeth thought they should, the van pulled into Departures at two o'clock on the nose.

Gretchen said no to parking, even in short term, and Elizabeth respected her desire to say good-bye to Ralph alone. Security wouldn't let the van loiter curbside, so Ralph suggested she drive around the airport loop until he reappeared. He and Gretchen unloaded her luggage, and into the terminal they went with the six designer bags, Gretchen's black leather valise, and her red Coach purse. Elizabeth drove off and tried to imagine their last poignant good-bye. Her imagination wasn't that vivid. She'd never understood their friendship, their romance, their relationship whatever it had been, and she was certainly at a loss now to visualize how they would part.

She circled twice and wondered. What would become of the Louis Vuitton luggage: would Gretchen bring the bags to Calcutta or leave them in Idaho? Come January first, who would be wearing her Coach purse: would she sell it in Idaho and give the money to the poor, or simply leave it with her mother or a sister? Did Gretchen have a sister? She'd known the woman for almost a year but she knew very little about her. She couldn't see Gretchen's future any more clearly than she'd seen her past.

Ralph at the curb looked fine, and when he got in the van she saw no signs of moisture about his eyes. They were alone together for the first time in four weeks and five days. She'd start the ball rolling; a kind word was never out of place.

"Are you feeling okay?"

"Hungry," he said. "Can we go through In 'n Out before we get back on the freeway?"

Not the kind of feeling she meant, but she could use a chocolate shake.

She drove while he directed, and before long they were on the road again equipped with burgers, fries, and milkshakes.

"You know what I've been thinking this whole time?" Ralph said.

She was merging onto the freeway with a cheeseburger in her lap, her mouth full of French fries.

"Mmmph?" she said.

"Ever since you picked me up in this van, I've been wondering why I'm not driving. You don't seem to be enjoying yourself."

She swallowed. "Gretchen thought the insurance wouldn't cover you and it was easier to drive than to argue. I guess you could have driven us home."

"I'm comfortable. It's like old times. I can put my foot on the dash if it'll calm you."

"No, I'm good."

"I enjoyed that drive."

"Me too."

That was when she'd changed her mind about him. She put down her cheeseburger without taking a bite.

"I've been thinking a lot about something since then, something about you," he said.

Good instinct to hold off on the cheeseburger. He sounded serious.

"Shall I tell you what I'm thinking?" he asked.

"You can tell me anything."

"You won't think I'm being forward?"

"Not at all."

"If you're sure then—you're ready to hear the question I've wanted to ask you since the end of last month?"

Her cheeseburger felt cold on her lap, but what was food when Ralph was about to—propose? She hadn't expected it quite so soon, but they weren't kids and she'd known for longer than a month what she'd answer if he ever asked.

"I'm ready."

He was silent. He must be nervous. She wanted to give him an encouraging look, but traffic was heavy and she couldn't risk it.

"Okay then, I'll just ask."

She held her breath.

"What are you doing for your December happiness project?"

She picked up her cheeseburger. No reason not to eat and she didn't trust herself to speak.

Of course she was an idiot; silly to expect him to move on from Gretchen that quickly. She was reading into his words, setting herself up for disappointment. Still, couldn't he have asked something else? Anything else, really.

"Lately Pat reminds me of the cat who swallowed the canary. He has a sleek well-fed look that makes me think of you."

She put her burger down and tried not to look sleek and well fed.

"I'm sorry, that came out wrong. I mean he's looking devilishly contented, and he hasn't told me about your latest pursuit, so I had a feeling you might be in trouble."

"Very kind of you to think of me."

She felt the beginning of tears. This was pathetic. Was she going to cry now, as if Pat mattered?

"So what's the latest, has he given you some outrageous final task? Because I'm still of the same mind. Don't wait for his approval. Go for happiness. That shouldn't be too hard. Aristotle and St. Thomas say you can't help it."

"If they think it's easy, they've never read Gretchen Rubin. Thanks for your concern but it's over. I shot myself in the foot."

He was silent.

"Pat said I could take the promotion as my final project and I didn't."

"Sure, but he couldn't prevent your choosing something else."

"He didn't need to do anything. I've been so busy training Ashley and buying Christmas presents and taking Gretchen to the airport—"

She wouldn't cry about this, it was too stupid.

"You didn't think of doing something else, did you?" Ralph asked softly.

She brushed a tear from her cheek.

"And you think that means you lost?" he asked, still quietly.

She nodded and brushed away another tear.

"Elizabeth," he said, "you haven't lost. December's not over. You have five days left, and we can think of something to make you happier. You don't need to cry, okay?"

She wiped her nose with her sleeve. Gretchen would never do that. Maybe she ought to start wearing a WWGD bracelet. Gretchen, the giraffe in the living room.

"I have a question, if you don't mind my asking. It's about Gretchen."

"Go for it," he said. "If I know the answer, it's yours."

"I thought the Missionaries of Charity had to smile a lot to make the poor feel loved. Won't that be a problem for her?"

He laughed.

"I'm serious." She took another bite of her burger. Thinking of Gretchen in India made her feel better.

"She might not stay with the regular Missionaries," he said. "She's thinking of joining their contemplative branch. In which case her smiles will be between her and God, I suppose."

She took a long swallow of chocolate shake.

"Plus she's been unhappy a long time," he said, "resisting this vocation. Now that she's feeling peaceful, I'm sure she'll smile more."

"I guess so." She sounded grudging, but he was right; Gretchen had smiled radiantly that day in the office. "That makes sense."

"Okay, then, back to your happiness project. Five days, one more chance at paradise. What will you do?"

"Quit?"

"Can't. You owe it to Jane to knock Pat down a peg."

"I'd love to, but I'm out of ideas and actually, I've decided happiness is over-rated."

"Stick to fundamentals. What one thing do you want to do more than anything?"

More than anything she wanted to marry him, but that didn't seem like the right answer. Fanny would never say it, Anne wouldn't, Marianne Dashwood probably had, but she knew better than to follow her example. She put a few cold fries in her mouth. They tasted awful, but there they were.

"I mean besides French fries, what do you want more than anything?"

She could hear the smile in his voice; at least one of them was having fun.

"You're chewing. Would you rather I answer for you?"

She nodded.

"I've been watching you, and I think I know what you want. You're embarrassed to tell me, but I know because I've been feeling the same way."

She stopped chewing so she could hear better.

"You don't need to be embarrassed. Lots of girls feel that way."

He'd always been self-assured, but that was a bit rich.

"You don't need to hold back. It's okay to feel the way you do."

She swallowed. She didn't want French fries in her mouth when he finally said—

"Skydiving isn't just for men anymore."

"Skydiving?"

If this was a metaphor, she wasn't getting it.

"My sister Maureen felt the same way and none of us knew what was wrong with her. Finally she told us what she wanted and we signed her up for a class, and ever since then I've wanted to do it too. We can skydive together, I mean you and me, and it can be your final happiness project."

"Are you kidding? That's the last thing I want to do, except for maybe bungee jumping off a bridge."

"Huh. So you won't go with me?"

"No, but I'd happily push you out of a plane."

"Pat wouldn't go for that. We'll have to think of something else."

She changed lanes to pass a Vanagon.

"I thought this wasn't about Pat."

"If you won't tell me your heart's deepest desire I don't have much to go on, but obviously beating Pat is still important to you, and I like to root for the underdog."

Had he ever compared Gretchen to a dog? Doubtful.

"Let's review what you've done," he said. "No point my suggesting things that have made you happy already."

"Not much chance of that."

"Then we can score you."

"What is this, the Olympics?"

"Not at all. We're going to score your happiness. Ready?"

Of course she wasn't ready. Was anyone ever ready to flunk?

"Do you want to play a CD or something? I think Jane's got *Beethoven Lives Upstairs.*"

"Don't try to change the subject."

"Fine then, you know everything I did," she said. "Why don't you score it?"

"My pleasure. January you met me and Gretchen at the dinner. Most definitely a happy event."

She smiled.

"February you won the statue, another bright moment."

Experience had taught her not to argue with him about the statue.

"March you resisted the pressure to don a habit at Vocations Day. And since happiness includes knowing what won't make you happy, you're three for three."

"And April I got to read tons of poetry. That was happy." Until he'd revealed he was Joe's brother and asked her out and she rejected him, but she was willing to leave that out if he was.

"In May you got to tour the O'Reilly mansion, and you didn't even have to pay the entrance fee. Five for five."

His summary was bare, but adequate for their purposes; she'd rather not revisit May.

"June was the Grand Canyon. You loved it there until I came, don't deny it, but then I let you drive Nellie home, and that more than made up for my ruining the family vacation. Six for six, and July was your glorious softball career."

"That was a great slide, wasn't it?" She touched the corner of her eye.

"You were awesome. And in August you helped Emily and took the boys for Jane, which brings you to eight for

351

eight. September you got your job, October you sold children's books, and November—what can I say? Points directly to your December project."

"I'm afraid to ask."

"Cooking with Costco, what else? Call the Food Network tomorrow and pitch it, you'll be their next big star."

"They might take this week off, you know, between Christmas and New Year's," she said. "Not to mention I never would have gotten dinner to the table, or even set the tables, without your help."

"There you go again, selling yourself short. I didn't do the shopping, all I did was show up with a couple microwaves in your hour of need." He slurped the last of his milkshake. "And the final tally: eleven for eleven. I hardly see how you can pack more happiness into this year."

"I guess that's it then, we're almost home."

"That's the spirit, never say die." He stretched in his seat. "Though you have a point. We should resolve this before we pick up the boys."

"I don't know where you're taking them, but after I return the Moore's van I'm going home for a long nap."

"That would be your third mistake."

"Wasn't I eleven for eleven?"

"Your first mistake was wasting half of December not turning down the promotion. Your second mistake was working double shifts and celebrating Christmas and forgetting to make one more conscious and artificial attempt at happiness. You were good till then, but now you have two strikes. As your coach, I advise against the third."

"But I'm tired."

"You can sleep in January. Tonight I have a foolproof plan to keep you awake. I promised Pat and Jane we'd pick up the boys to show them Christmas lights at the country club."

"I love Christmas lights!"

"I thought so, especially when Jane told me you did. I'm not a big light man myself, but I'm looking forward to seeing the O'Reilly spread."

"Don't even think about it. Christmas lights at the country club means driving by the fancy houses, not going in."

"That's what I mean. I'll get a good look at their place as we drive by."

"As long as we don't slow down."

"We'll see. Meanwhile I've come up with your December project. You loved your trip to the Grand Canyon, and what was that about?"

She ate the last cold fry thoughtfully.

"Nature?"

"Recreational vehicles. Buy a motorhome tomorrow. Pat was so into the rental, you know he'd go for it."

"Two miles to the next exit, then five minutes to the Moore's. That leaves seven minutes, and no, I won't buy a motorhome. If you don't have a good idea, just say so."

"What about Jane Austen?"

"I've read her books every year since I was fifteen, that's nothing new."

"But you could do something related to her. Sew a period costume, or join a Jane Austen fan club and write a paper to present at their international convention. Cash in on your Janeite genes."

"That's an idea," she said. "But I have a confession to make."

"Now it comes out. You don't really like her novels, do you? You've read them out of duty, but secretly you're a Brontë girl, is that it?"

"That isn't it. Her books are what I love most, but the truth is I've never gone in for all the Jane Austen accessorizing. I see the movies when they come out, but then I want to read the books again, not go country dancing."

"I suppose not every girl could whip up a period costume in three days, but it was impressive when Gretchen did it in New York."

"I'm sure she did a fabulous job, but this isn't about Gretchen, it's about me. And not only me. You told me not to cry, you said you'd help, and all you've come up with is sky-diving in an empire waistline. That doesn't help, so let's hear it, Einstein. You must have something better lined up for my final happiness project. What will it be?"

She turned right at a traffic signal.

"Three minute warning. We're almost there and I'm getting a headache. Any big ideas before I turn in my resignation to Pat?"

She glanced down. The greasy hamburger paper was spread across her lap. No wonder he was thinking about Gretchen; she never even ate burgers, let alone wore them.

"Cheer up," he said. "We've got time left and I've got plenty of ideas. Homeopathic medicine, tap dancing, African violets, knitting. geo-caching, parasailing, astronomy, cosmetology, ham radio."

"You have a fertile imagination. I'm sorry I doubted you."

"So which will it be?"

"None of them, they're all absurd."

"Thousands of devotees disagree with you, but let's not argue. Society for Creative Anachronism? Open a cupcake business? No, don't settle, you could get into the *Guinness Book of World Records*."

"Dare I ask?"

"Undo the curse of the ewok by stuffing a thousand teddy bears at the Stuff-a-Bear store in the mall."

She turned into the Moore's driveway.

"I'm willing to forget this entire conversation if you are."

"You don't like *any* of my ideas? How about this—when you were a kid did you read *How to Eat Fried Worms*?"

"That's okay. I can do this alone, like I've been doing it alone for the past eleven months."

"Harsh. What about softball? Whose idea was that?"

"Fine, you had one good idea six months ago, but otherwise you're a bust."

"If you give me a little more time I could fix everything, but I understand, you're in a hurry. Don't say I didn't offer."

"It's not my fault December has only thirty-one days." She got out of the van and headed for the house. "Time's running out, and I can't wait for you anymore."

Before she could knock, Jane opened the door and five boyish forms flashed past.

"Wow. I guess they're ready to see the lights."

"They've been waiting almost since you left. I warned Pat not to tell them, but he didn't listen, and they've been dying for you to get back."

"Is it even dark enough yet?"

"It will be soon, but they're so eager they wouldn't mind if it was daylight."

"We're ready, Auntie Beth," Ralph called from the van.

He was in the driver's seat, Anthony behind him where the Ice Princess had reigned. This would be a different drive. She gave Jane a kiss and walked across the lawn.

CHAPTER 39

Detour

The consensus was that if Luke had gone to the bathroom before he left home, Elizabeth wouldn't have found her happiness that night. But he hadn't, and ten minutes into their country club light viewing extravaganza, he announced he had to go to the bathroom now and couldn't hold it any longer. Elizabeth blamed Ralph for Luke's desperate moment occurring as they were passing the O'Reilly mansion. Ralph smiled and claimed some things were out of his control.

"I'll pull into the driveway," he said

"You can't pull into the driveway. They might see us."

"We want them to see us, Liz. I'm not suggesting we send Luke into the bushes. Although what's good enough for the common people . . ."

"Not funny."

He parked a good distance away from the seven car garage. "Don't want to block anyone in."

"Why not? You can invite them to come with us to see the lights."

"That's good, I'm glad you're loosening up."

She glared at him. "So what's next?"

"You're on speaking terms with the butler, aren't you? Mention Luke's quandary and then wait while he uses the bathroom. Simple enough."

"It's not simple and I'm not going in, Mark might be there. Dr. O'Reilly and Mabel might be there. Or I might get lost and never be seen again. I'd spend the rest of my life wandering hallways and looking for the powder room."

"That sounds creepy," Anthony said from the back seat.

"It is creepy, Anthony." What was she saying? She shouldn't be scaring her nephews. "I mean it's fine, but I don't want to go in again, that's all."

Ralph sighed loudly and put his hand to his forehead.

"Okay, I'll go with you."

"Give me a break, that's what you've been angling for since you pulled in. How will that even help?"

"I can drop breadcrumbs on our way to the bathroom. When Luke is done, we'll follow them out, unless the maid's swept them up."

"That's like Hansel and Gretel!" yelled Luke.

"Shhh!" Elizabeth said. "If Matthew wakes up and starts fussing we'll never get out of here."

Ralph turned to Anthony. "Can you handle Matthew if he wakes, or should you guys all come in?"

Elizabeth moaned.

"Liz, it'll be okay. I'll give Anthony my phone and he can call us on yours if Matthew wakes up. We'll leave Dominic and Jude, too, if that makes you feel better."

She didn't answer; she was thinking. If she drove home now and Luke had an accident on the way, she could clean him and the van up at Jane's.

"If you'd rather all the boys come in, though, Anthony could watch them in the foyer," he said. "Did you guys bring a basketball?"

One kid, in and out, Ralph and the breadcrumbs, that was his best offer.

"Anthony, are you okay watching your brothers in the van?" she asked.

"If Uncle Ralph gives us his phone, we can play games till you come back."

Anthony looked competent, Jude and Dominic were nodding, Matthew was still asleep. Luke—well, the sooner they got that kid to a bathroom, the better. He was jiggling his legs and holding his breath.

"Let's go," she said, grabbing her backpack. "Ralph, make sure your phone is set to call mine."

"I know how to use it," Anthony said. "Don't worry Auntie Beth."

"Okay then." Ralph got out of the van. "Let's go, Luke."

They crunched along the gravel walk and Ralph smiled down at her. Clearly he thought her anxiety was cute, but his admiration meant nothing. He was winning, that was all. He'd get to see inside, and if they ran into Mark, no skin off his teeth, or however that stupid expression went.

They reached the front door far too soon for her peace of mind. Luke hopped while she quizzed Ralph.

"What do I say? Where do we go? What do I do?"

"You say Luke needs to use the bathroom, and we follow the butler to the designated room. Then you go in with Luke and leave me on guard to fight off would-be suitors and marriageable O'Reillys."

She reached up to ring the bell, and it sounded exactly like her cell phone. Must be some high-tech sensor bell that felt the warmth of her hand before she touched it. The sound came again.

"You better answer, Liz, it could be Anthony," Ralph said.

"Hello?" She looked back to the van, parked in a shadow of the drive. "Yes, Anthony, you can unstrap him. We'll wait here for you—can you see us at the front door?" She nodded. "Uh-huh . . . I understand . . . No, honey, I'm not mad. I'll send Uncle Ralph to help you."

She snapped her phone shut. Luke was still hopping and there were plenty of bushes nearby. Why hadn't Ralph thought of that to begin with?

"The boys were fighting over the phone," she said. "Dominic elbowed Jude in the face, and now Jude's got a bloody nose. Matthew woke, he's crying, and Anthony needs reinforcements."

The door opened and before them stood the butler. She was fairly certain she hadn't pressed the bell, but perhaps he'd sensed something amiss. Maybe he was another Jeeves and would take everything in hand.

She shouldn't get her hopes up. Given her luck he was more likely Mark's cousin and would propose.

"May I assist you?" the butler said.

"We're friends of the O'Reillys and we don't want to bother them but my nephew Luke needs to use the facilities and so we hoped you could direct us to the nearest one and we won't stay and certainly we won't bother the O'Reillys and if they're out you can tell them later that Miss Benning and Dr. Collins came by but if they're in please don't interrupt them since they're probably having their chicken and all we need is to use the bathroom but not for me just for Luke but

I should go with him and then we'll be going and we won't disturb anyone if that's okay is that okay?"

"Of course Miss Benning. The O'Reillys are out, but if you'll follow me." The butler kept his white gloved hand on the door, waiting for her to enter. Luke was already inside, hopping on marble.

"If you're okay with Luke, I'd better go help Anthony," Ralph said.

She ought to appreciate his heroic sacrifice, he was missing his free tour, but he was also abandoning her. She had to go in again, alone. Luke hardly counted.

"You're not answering," Ralph said. "Do you want to help Anthony and I'll go with Luke? I can give you my handkerchief to staunch the flow of blood."

Blood. Right. Her decision was made.

"You help the boys, Ralph. I'm going in." She sounded like someone from a war movie, about to launch a dangerous reconnaissance mission. No matter; that's how she felt.

Ralph was jogging to the van. She followed the butler. She wished she knew his name.

"What's your name?"

Nothing like a nephew to break the ice with the household staff.

"Smith, at your service, young sir."

If the 'P' was silent and he merely chose not to advertise the fact, he could actually be a relative of Psmith. She shook her head, she was losing her mind. Or maybe she needed to eat. They passed a doorway and the repulsive memory of peanut butter sauced chicken flooded her imagination. She concentrated on Psmith's black shiny shoes to keep from gagging.

His shoes walked on and on. She had hoped for a half bath near the front door, and here she was, miles in again.

Mark had told her all the bathrooms had different names, but Psmith should have known it didn't matter, they were dealing with a little boy. She'd asked for "the facilities." For all she knew she'd asked for Mabel's fourth floor private bath. Down the hallways they went. Up stairways, around bends, everything was familiarly unfamiliar.

The butler stopped in front of what looked like an ordinary bathroom. He turned to depart.

"Wait!" Elizabeth shouted. She lowered her voice. "I'm not sure we know our way back."

Psmith motioned to the wall beside him. She recognized the tapestry door.

"Simply press this button and the elevator will be at your service."

"Great. Gotcha. Okey dokey." Why let tomorrow's troubles intrude on today? She'd deal with it later.

Luke had disappeared into the bathroom and she followed. A golden toilet seat wouldn't impress him, but she didn't want him climbing into the chandelier if there was one.

The room had a separate stall for the toilet. A bit over the top in a residential bathroom, but convenient for the poor kid's privacy. A gargantuan expanse of mirror covered the length of the wall above the three sinks. She looked ashen. The taps were golden, if not gold, and she ran cold water to splash on her face. Invigorating, that's what this water was. Maybe they imported it from the fountain of youth.

Luke was taking his time, so she reapplied her bronze lipstick, pinched her cheeks, and ate half the chocolate protein bar she found in her backpack. It must have been some latent survival instinct that inspired her to schlep the whole pack into the house. Her brain fog evaporated and she saved the rest of the bar for later. If only she'd brought a compass, she might make it back to the front door and Ralph.

Luke was feeling better too, calm and smiling as he washed his hands, and when they exited the bathroom he asked if he could push the elevator button.

"Of course, honey. Then we'll get in the van and see more lights." Good. Be positive. Think happy thoughts and soon they'd be safe in the van. Everything was fine, everything was going to be fine, things couldn't be finer. This was the best of all possible worlds, as long as she didn't run into any O'Reillys.

The elevator door opened and there, beneath God and Adam, stood Mark.

CHAPTER 40

Re-enactment

"Liz, what a s'prise. You look wonderful."

She couldn't return the compliment. Mark's lips and teeth were purplish, and a red stain colored the white shirt-front under his sport coat. Blood? Maybe he'd been eating strawberries.

"Lift down?" he asked. "Plenty a room."

She could grab Luke's hand and make a run for it, but she had no idea where they were and the butler was long gone. Or they could get in the elevator with Mark, and God willing they'd soon attain the first floor, the front door, and Ralph. She ought to be safe from any return of Mark's unwanted attentions. What man would propose again after the thwacking she'd given him?

The answer was obvious. A man who stands to gain a lot of money by re-proposing. Piles of the green stuff. Mansions full and then some. She dismissed the thought. A quick ride down and they'd say good-bye forever.

Inside the elevator, Luke asked what the funny smell was and wanted to know which button he could press. She smelled something too, but couldn't identify it. She pointed to the button with the big "G" and Luke pressed it with all his might. This wasn't like her prior elevator experience; they wouldn't spend twenty minutes up here at a standstill.

"Liz, we don't have much time," Mark said.

Hadn't he said that before? Not a promising start. She pulled Luke in front of her.

"Alex and Andrea get married New Year's Day."

"That's great," she said.

"Not for me, but now you're here it'll be fine. I returned unexpectedly. Doesn't that remind you of something?"

"My worst nightmare?" she said.

"Pemberley. You came to my estate when you thought I was gone."

"Your grandfather's estate," she corrected him.

"But I returned unexpectedly," he repeated, "and I found you here." He waved his hand at Luke. "He's like Mrs. Gard'ner, and you're my own dear Lizzy, and I'm your Darcy who proposed to you once and hold on a sec, I've been ready in case this ever happened—"

He was searching his pockets, and she identified the smell in the elevator. It was red wine, and the smell was emanating from Mark. No wonder his teeth and lips were that funny color. No wonder he was talking nonsense about being Darcy.

Swaying slightly, he pulled a crumpled slip of paper from the inner pocket of his sport coat. The elevator came to rest and the door opened, but he was so intent on his paper he didn't look up.

Luke jumped out and grabbed Ralph's hand. For there, to her relief, was Ralph, and her nephews too, standing outside the elevator, waiting for her.

Ralph, looking so handsome, so tall and blonde, so clean and sober. He was everything Mark wasn't, and she wished she could hold his other hand, but Matthew was gripping it already.

Meanwhile, in the elevator next to her, unaware of his audience, eyes fixed on his paper, Mark was reading aloud, and when she realized the source of his quotation, she regretted the absence of her black sequined purse. Her pack was much too heavy, not for him but for her.

"You are too generous to trifle with me," he read woodenly. "If your feelings are what they were last, um, last, um—Lizzy, when did I propose to you last?"

Without thinking, she answered him.

"May."

"If your feelings are what they were last May—"

"Yes," she said.

"Yes?" he said.

"Yes?" Ralph said.

"Yes, my feelings are what they were last May, only more so if possible."

"Oh," Mark said. "So you don't mean yes you'll marry me?" He leaned against the wall of the elevator.

"Of course not."

She turned to Ralph. "I think we're ready to go. Unless someone else needs to use the nearest toilet."

She wasn't usually so direct. There were many fine euphemisms for 'toilet,' but she wouldn't risk being sent back into the depths of the castle.

"I'm fine," Ralph said. "How about you guys?"

The boys were fine, too.

She stepped toward Ralph, but Mark detained her, his hand on her arm.

"Lizbeth, I know Gretchen's gone. She said she'd be a nun, but don't catch him on the rebound. He can't give you anything but love, like that song. I can give you lots more. Alex isn't getting married till next week and—"

Ralph stepped into the elevator, Matthew and Luke still clinging to him, and Mark stopped rambling. The box was surprisingly roomy. It had seemed so much smaller when only she and Mark occupied it. Anthony and Jude and Dominic ventured in, and still it felt spacious.

"Just wanted to see a couple things before we left," Ralph explained. "Guys, look up at the ceiling. That's cool, isn't it?"

The boys tipped their heads back and stared, mouths open, at the fresco.

"And while we're here, I was curious if this is a magic elevator."

"Like in *Charlie and the Chocolate Factory*?" Dominic asked him.

"Kind of, but not exactly. It seems like it makes people ask your Auntie Beth to marry them."

"Does it, Uncle Ralph?" Jude asked.

"Let's see. Everyone shut your eyes, put your hands over your ears, and count to fifty, slowly and loudly."

All the boys, including Mark, obeyed. Elizabeth kept her eyes open and watched Ralph.

He bent down on one knee and took Elizabeth's hand in his. Then scooping up the scrap of paper Mark had dropped, he held it out to her. She took it and read silently.

"You are too generous to trifle with me. If your feelings are still what they were last April, tell me so at once. *My* affections and wishes are unchanged, but one word from you will silence me on this subject for ever."

Darcy's speech was redeemed. With laughter on her lips, she looked down at Ralph.

His left hand was open, and on his palm rested a golden band with a solitaire. The diamond wasn't as big as a Ritz, but it sparkled under the track lighting. She felt sparkly too, and if anyone asked her, she'd say this was surely a magic elevator.

She knew her part by heart. She must force herself to speak and immediately, if not very fluently, give him to understand that her sentiments had undergone so material a change since the period to which he alluded as to make her receive with gratitude and pleasure his present assurances, and the ring he offered.

Jude, the fastest counter, was approaching the number fifty, and she hadn't much time.

"Yes," she said, looking into Ralph's eyes.

Her lack of fluency combined with her excess of gratitude and love limited her to this one simple word, but she repeated it. Everyone in the now silent elevator heard her say it the second time. Jude and Ralph had heard her say it twice. Mark was the first to speak.

"So you mean 'No' to him too?"

Ralph took over. She was in good hands; this was his proposal scene now.

"Everyone shut your eyes again, cover your ears, and count slowly and loudly, but this time to one hundred. The last person to reach one hundred gets a dollar."

Mark seemed as interested in the dollar as her nephews. He and the boys obediently shut, covered, and counted again, only this time more slowly.

Ralph and Elizabeth were, in a sense, alone, although he had to speak quite loudly to be heard over the counting.

"So let's get this straight. Your response is, if I remember the scene rightly, supposed to produce such happiness in me as I've probably never felt before."

"Is it working?" she asked.

"Of course. I take your 'Yes' as affirming that your feelings have changed since you refused to go out with me in April, and I understand that you do now receive my present assurances with gratitude and pleasure. Yes?"

She nodded.

"And did I actually remember to give my present assurances?"

"I'm not sure," she said above the cacophony of the counting.

He rose from the elevator floor, slipped the ring on her finger, and under cover of the noisy, blind, and deaf counters, he whispered in her ear. No doubt he expressed himself on the occasion as sensibly and as warmly as a man violently in love can be supposed to do, and he had the advantage over Darcy of a well-developed sense of humor to aid his delivery.

Elizabeth, for her part, had an advantage over her namesake, for she was able—likely due to her modern sensibilities—to encounter Ralph's eyes, and thus she saw how well the expression of heart-felt delight, diffused over his face, became him. Her happiness seemed, at long last, nearly complete.

It would have been more complete if the counting had gone on forever, but alas, even the slowest counter will finally reach an end if he's only counting to one hundred. Ralph let go of Elizabeth's hand to get a dollar from his wallet for the winner, and when he took her hand in his again, they were no longer alone.

"Uncle Ralph, is the elevator magic?" Jude asked.

"No," he answered sadly.

It had felt magical to her, but maybe she hadn't understood.

"I wondered if it made people ask Auntie Beth to marry them," he said, "and it does, but I thought maybe it made her always say 'No' to them, too."

"So did you ask her to marry you, Uncle Ralph, but she said 'Yes'?" Anthony was looking at their hands, still joined.

"Exactly. So you can see it's not a magic elevator after all. And now I'll have to pay for my mistake and marry her."

Ralph winked at her, his smile so genuine it restored her confidence in the elevator's magic.

They stepped out of the elevator and back into the real world, and she counted heads to make sure she had all the boys. She was only missing one. Mark was still in the elevator, leaning against the wall.

"Ready, Liz?" Ralph asked.

"Wanted to congratulate you, man," Mark said. "She's a fine woman."

He'd said the same thing at the wedding, and she'd thought he meant Gretchen.

She laughed and noticed Dominic, hand clenched into a fist gripping the dollar he'd won. By the looks of it, he wasn't taking any chances on Uncle Ralph needing it back to pay for his mistake.

CHAPTER 41

How to Keep a Secret

Blessed indeed the newly engaged couple who, having reached an understanding, find leisure for the conversations that bring them to yet further understanding. Such happy couples were Elizabeth Bennet and Mr. Darcy; Anne Elliot and Captain Wentworth; Emma Woodhouse and Mr. Knightley.

Elizabeth Benning regretfully concluded that she and her Darcy (or Wentworth or Knightley, for Ralph's true likeness had yet to be named) would not be among their number. She pictured their near future progressing along the lines, rather, of Elinor Dashwood and Edward Ferrars', or Catherine Morland and her Tilney's, deprived as they were of the solitude which crowns the beatitude of the recently engaged.

In short, their understanding had an audience. Nearly half a dozen nephews had witnessed their engagement, and with Emily and Joe's wedding such a recent highlight of the boys' young lives, they were likely to spill the beans within minutes of their return home.

The van inched forward at a snail's pace through the country club lanes, and Elizabeth consoled herself that at least for now the boys were uninterested in her news, distracted by the blazing light displays.

Ralph yielded to the boys' pleading and pulled over beside a light show she guessed was a three dimensional ad for Lego. She wasn't far off, Ralph told her. He'd read in the paper that a retired Danish master builder had recently bought the home. By all appearances he was a master electrician as well.

The boys' admiration found relief in an extended discussion of which Lego sets they'd save up to buy. Elizabeth thanked heaven for brightly colored plastic bricks. With an occasional "Uh-huh" thrown back to the boys, she and Ralph were free to talk.

"I guess Jane and Pat will be the first to know," she began.

Ralph took her hand. "Are you really going to marry me?"

"It's too late for either of us to escape." She looked behind her. "They know, and they're counting on another wedding. Heedless adults, chocolate cake, an unlimited supply of fruit punch. You're stuck."

"I have no objections, but I'm worried about you."

"Don't I look happy?"

"Someday when we're reminiscing in front of the hearth, entertaining our great grandchildren with the story of this night, you may regret mine wasn't a romantic proposal complete with champagne and a privation of nephews."

"It was a perfect proposal, but I'm worried about you."

"I assure you I'm fine."

"What if you get to know me and I'm not who you think I am? You may regret marrying me before we even dated."

"If it makes you feel better, think of this whole year as our courtship. Consider the last few months: we've had our first wedding together, our first Halloween, our first Thanksgiving. And think of all the roles I've seen you play. Artist, athlete, ewok. I doubt you have any secrets left."

"But what about Mark's comment? Gretchen just left. What if I'm catching you on the rebound?"

He squeezed her hand. "I'm resigned to telling you daily for the rest of our lives that Gretchen and I have always been friends, and only friends. Not to mention I've been waiting to ask you to marry me for months."

"But if you were waiting all that time, why didn't you propose sooner?"

"Every man waits for the right moment, so I waited. When I saw that elevator tonight and Mark's slip of paper and you so glad to see me, I knew it was time."

"About time, more like."

He laughed. "So that's your attitude. You think Pat and Jane will be as blasé? I bet they're surprised when they see your ring."

She looked down. It was a beautiful ring. She sighed.

The boys' jabbering continued, but even with their excited voices filling the van, her sigh was audible.

"I knew it," Ralph said. "The diamond's too small, isn't it? Mark might still be in the elevator. I hate to think of you regretting those lost millions."

"The ring is perfect, it isn't that. It's Pat and Jane finding out tonight."

"I knew it. You're afraid your family won't accept me. They'll discover I'm only a poor professor, and Pat, forgetting he's a poor professor himself, will cast me off, or talk you out of it like in one of your novels. He'll be Lady Russell and we'll have to wait another ten years, is that it?"

"It's not like a Jane Austen novel at all and that's the problem."

"Handsome leading man, beautiful and beguiling ingénue, she's made him the happiest of men, and so on. Other than the period costumes—and I'm not suggesting those again—what's missing?"

"That part in *Pride and Prejudice* after Elizabeth and Darcy finally get together, and Anne and Captain Wentworth in *Persuasion*, and Emma and Knightley too, though Emma's not my very favorite. You know, the part where the two lovers review their history and revel in their present happiness. I've always thought those pages were the best."

"I'm all for reviewing and reveling. Count me in."

"That's just it. We won't have that because in less than an hour we'll bring the boys home and they'll tell about the elevator. Pat will know we're engaged and he's no Bingley. He won't quietly congratulate us and then focus on his Jane. He'll tease me to death, and you and I won't have a chance to secretly gloat. I know it's a silly reason to feel unhappy when I'm happier than I've ever been, but my favorite part won't happen for us."

A tear slid down her cheek.

"Oh, I hate crying! Now my nose will get stuffy and I'll have to blow it, and then you won't want to marry me."

Ralph let go of her hand to wipe away the tear, and turned to the boys in the back.

"Quiet down, guys. I've got a question, and you need to answer carefully."

He'd listened to her, but he hadn't said anything in response, and now he was talking to her nephews. A wonderful man, but he had a lot to learn about women.

"How would you each like a new Lego set on New Year's?"

Bedlam.

"Quiet down, guys, you have to earn it."

Silence.

"You guys were with us in the elevator, and even though it wasn't a magic elevator, I get to marry Auntie Beth, right?"

"Yes!" came their unanimous consent.

"Good. So here's your job. Auntie Beth wants to play a little joke on your dad and keep it a secret that she's going to marry me, and if you help her, you get a reward. If we don't tell your dad, then on New Year's at your grandma's party she'll surprise him and we'll all laugh. If you can keep the secret for five whole days all the way to New Year's, then when you go to the playroom at your grandma's party, you'll find something under the bean bag chairs."

"I know what the something is!" Dominic shouted. "It's Legos!"

"Honey, you're right," Elizabeth whispered. "But let's start our secret now and not wake up Matthew, okay?"

He closed his lips tightly and nodded.

"Do we have a deal, boys?" Ralph asked.

"Deal!" they yelled.

Matthew let out a squall. Elizabeth put her hand over her eyes and Ralph started the van.

"Sorry Auntie Beth," Anthony said.

"Don't worry," Ralph responded, pulling onto the road. "If you keep her secret, Auntie Beth will forgive you lots of things."

You're right," she said to Ralph. "If your Lego bribery works, I'll forgive all of you."

"No time to lose then, especially if you want those best pages. I'll come tomorrow morning and walk with you, and as we revel we can decide on your December happiness project."

"Don't you think finding true love counts?"

"I didn't say anything about my happiness project. I'm good, but if we're talking about yours, Pat's on the verge of winning and true love won't move him. Doesn't he have to approve your project each month?"

"He approves of you."

"But we don't want him to approve of me yet. We'll think of a more mundane project so you can get his approval before December's over."

"And if he thinks I'm busy with something else, that'll throw him off the scent and we can surprise him on New Year's with my real happiness."

A smile broke across her face. She'd have to get used to smiling hugely.

"I was afraid of that. Your true heart's desire is now revealed," he said. "Clearly, it's beating Pat."

She didn't correct him. Time enough later for him to understand her heart completely.

"I should be ready by eleven," she said. "Wouldn't want you to see me before I get my beauty sleep."

"You don't need to get any more beautiful. I'll be there at ten."

Her smile became a laugh.

"Smooth, but I'll be grumpy at ten."

"You're the girl who requested reveling, and reveling officially starts at ten, so I don't want to hear any complaints."

She couldn't stop looking at her ring.

"I don't know what you're talking about," she said. "I'll never complain again."

Chapter 42

The Best Part

According to Minnie Mouse it was precisely ten o'clock when Elizabeth woke to the sound of barking. Or rather, the sound of barking woke her. Had she known this baritone bark would wake her every morning for the next several years, she might have reacted differently.

With robe securely tied and slippers on her feet, she opened the cottage door to see a black standard poodle on her stoop, standing on its hind legs to reach the dog biscuit Ralph held high over his head. The poodle barked and Ralph, seeing his affianced in the doorway, dropped the biscuit to the dog.

"Ralph, I'm barely awake."

"And what a joy to discover you look this adorable when the mists of sleep are still about you."

"Ralph, I want to go back to bed."

"Poor love. I should have waited till eleven, but I did warn you I'd be here at ten."

She closed her eyes. "I know, but I've got to go back to bed, and I can't do that with you here. Couldn't we meet at noon?"

"The dog seems ready for our walk now."

She opened her eyes. "He's gorgeous."

She did love standard poodles, though why Ralph had one on her stoop was a mystery. Unless—

"Is he it?"

"I didn't think you were a cat person."

She gave a squeal and reached forward to hug Ralph, but the red plaid of her robe sleeve reminded her she wasn't quite ready for the day.

"Back in a sec," she said and shut the door in their faces.

When she opened the door fifteen minutes later, the man and the poodle were seated. At her appearance they both stood.

"Well, aren't you beautiful," Ralph said.

Elizabeth let the dog sniff her fingers.

"After you proposed, I couldn't think of anything that would make me happier. How did you know?"

"I still maintain that a happiness project should actually be about being happy, and I thought this fit the bill. You've always wanted a poodle."

"You're right, but I never told you that, did I?"

"Not that I recall, but I've always wanted a poodle, so I figured you must too. And then to be sure, I asked Emily."

The dog, after his polite greeting, was again seated on the stoop. Elizabeth rubbed his furry head and took the leash from Ralph.

"I'm ready now," she said.

They walked past the big house to the road, and at long last Elizabeth began her version of the pages she'd so often read, only with the addition of a big black dog walking between the lovers.

"He's absolutely perfect," she said, "but how did you find him between last night and ten this morning?"

"Three weeks ago I went to a poodle rescue ranch. When I saw Duke, I knew he was yours. He's been living with me in the trailer, but I couldn't introduce you till today."

"I wish you hadn't waited. I've always wanted a puppy for Christmas."

"You don't mind that he's full grown?"

"Puppy, dog, he's perfect, but why did you wait so long?"

"I had to propose first. If I'd let you meet him before you said yes, how could I be sure you weren't marrying me for my dog?"

"Our dog," she corrected. "And while we're on the subject of your proposal, I'm ready for you to recount the history of your love for me. I believe that comes next."

"Fair enough, if you don't think I'll bore you."

She assured him he wouldn't, and far from boring her, so eloquent was he, so vivid his recounting, so true and yet amusing his portrayal of the year (and his love) in review, that he and Elizabeth, like Darcy and another Elizabeth before them, walked on without knowing in what direction. There was too much to be thought, and felt, and said, for attention to any other objects.

To her surprise, Elizabeth learned they owed their present happiness to—certainly not to a wealthy aunt, for as Ralph had explained in his wedding toast, there was no Lady Catherine in the case, but rather to the Ice Princess herself.

"She said you had the wrong impression, something about my marrying her under the Indian sun, but your reaction when she straightened that out, well it gave her the idea you might be receptive to my proposal yourself."

"She told you that?"

"She did, and she also wanted me to wish you joy in the event that you accepted."

"But would you have proposed if she hadn't suggested it?"

Ralph's expression left her in no doubt, but he was obliging enough to explain at length what she could have read in his eyes.

Eventually they found themselves standing again before the big house.

"I hate to interrupt our walk, but I'm hungry," she said.

"Faint with love, I bet. Let's get you some raisin cakes and apples."

"Cheese and crackers will do."

He'd never been inside the cottage, so while Elizabeth ate in the kitchen and Duke rested near the door, Ralph gave himself a self-guided tour. Completing his circuit, he stood before her dresser and looked to the shelf above it.

"Isn't he amazing?" Elizabeth asked from the kitchen. "I didn't want to admit it, but you were wonderful to let me bring him home."

Ralph took down the gilded statue, handling it gently.

"I don't think I saw him closely enough. That must be why I let him go." He replaced the statue and joined Elizabeth at the table.

"For me he was a moral dilemma," she said. "You wouldn't take him, I couldn't let Pat take him, and keeping him felt like theft."

"And it took you till last night to find the solution? You could've proposed to me in February and saved a lot of time and heartache," he said. He placed his hand on hers. "But I guess if none of Jane Austen's heroines popped the question, I should've known not to wait for you."

"And it took you till last night to realize you had to do the asking?"

"The elevator tipped me off. You have a habit of being proposed to there, not proposing, if I'm to believe your side of the story. But I'm having trouble with something."

He didn't look like a troubled man.

"Now that we're living out your perfect Jane Austen romance, which of her heroines are you?"

"Elizabeth Bennet, of course. Don't worry about being Mr. Collins—your brother's the one who married Miss Lucas. And you didn't merely propose to me. I said yes, so that makes you Darcy."

"But that's exactly what's bothering me. I've never been stern and earnest enough to play a convincing Darcy."

He wiggled his ears and she laughed.

"You see what I mean, then, but I have another idea."

"If you say Edmund Bertram or Edward Ferrars because you were thinking of the ministry, we're in trouble. I'm not patient enough to be Fanny and I'm not serene and virtuous like Elinor."

"I'd never agree you lack any heroine's graces, but since I'm neither of the Eddies, you're safe. Besides, I know who you are. Is your Jane Austen at hand?" Ralph pushed his chair back.

"Don't you dare make me Catherine Morland so you can be Henry Tilney and tell me I was in love with you first."

He checked the books on Elizabeth's nightstand, then went to the reading table beside the rocking chair.

"Here we are. Now if I can find the right volume." He ran his finger down the pile of books and selected one. "Got it."

He lowered himself into the rocker and paged through the book.

"So you think you know who I am?" she asked.

"I have my theory," he said, rocking, "and I've found the compelling passage. Tell me if this reminds you of someone. Kind of a Jane Austen happiness project, a passion a month, none carrying over, but you can tell there's going to be a solution—something she'll grow into, someone who's been waiting until she's ready for his love."

Elizabeth put her elbows on the table and rested her chin in her hands.

Ralph began to read.

"She had always wanted to do everything, and had made more progress both in drawing and music than many might have done with so little labour as she would ever submit to. She played and sang;—and drew in almost every style; but steadiness had always been wanting; and in nothing had she approached the degree of excellence which she would have been glad to command, and ought not to have failed of. She was not much deceived as to her own skill either as an artist or a musician, but she was not unwilling to have others deceived, or sorry to know her reputation for accomplishment often higher than it deserved."

He looked at Fra Angelico on the shelf above her dresser, then at her.

He was reading her life; the words applied to her as much as to Emma. She'd always avoided practice and lacked steadiness; her happiness project was a prime example. Pat had told her she could stick with something for more than a month if it engaged her, but she had no resources. Nothing had engaged her until Ralph.

She felt the sting of tears, but a sudden thought caused her to raise her chin and point her finger at him.

"You want to be Knightley! He's obviously the best of her heroes, and you get to be him if I'm Emma!"

Ralph stopped rocking and grinned. "Do you deny I was reading about you?"

"I'm not saying your passage didn't resonate. I suppose I am Emma, but if that's the way you'll have it, then you must tell me—are you planning on marrying me and moving into my father's house? Because he's not exactly an invalid, and my mother is alive and well. You can't argue he needs us like Mr. Woodhouse needed Emma, and I won't live in a trailer."

Ralph rocked in the chair, but more quickly. A less sanguine motion, if she knew her rocking.

"So I've uncovered your pitiful scheme. You moved into the trailer on campus when Joe got married. Pat told me it didn't make sense for you to stay in Joe's old place when he was selling it and new professors can live on campus until they find another residence. It's been six months and you're still in the trailer. Don't think for a minute you'll carry me over that threshold. "

Ralph laughed, prompting Duke to bark. Elizabeth went to the dog and rubbed his head. Someone loved her, anyhow.

"I hate to throw cold water on your dreams, but I have no dastardly plans to move in with your parents or install you in a trailer. I don't know if this will work for you—I can't afford to buy, so we'd just be renting, and it's not as big as Joe and Emily's place, but I was hoping to marry you in the spring when school gets out, then take you on a honeymoon, then set you up in the house across the street from your best friend."

"Really?"

"Scout's honor. I hope you'll be very happy there."

"I will. I had no idea." She gave him her broadest smile. "But I have one more request."

"What is it, my Emma? What else does your heart desire?"

"I'm hungry." She stepped to the dresser for the leash. "My snack hit the spot, but if you take me out to lunch, my happiness will be complete."

"I don't think your happiness is anywhere near complete. You've still got Pat to humble, me to marry, and hopefully a baby Collins or two in your future. But I'll buy you lunch first. I wouldn't want you to starve when you're so close to achieving your goal."

"And you still think beating Pat is my goal?"

Ralph opened the door and the winter sunshine streamed in.

"I meant marrying me," he said.

CODA

New Year's Day

They were gathered in the family room, the See's candy and champagne opened, the toasts about to begin. From her place on the floor next to the love seat, Elizabeth watched Pat, clueless, fill his glass. The boys had been faithful conspirators and were now in the playroom with their Lego sets, their excited voices carrying down the hall, confirming she and Ralph had chosen well.

Her parents sat in their usual places, side by side in the wingback chairs.

Emily and Joe were behind her in the love seat, and she knew without looking that Emily glowed with maternal joy. They wouldn't announce her pregnancy tonight, but the Bennings and the Moores must have guessed when Emily, giggling, refused champagne. She'd have to teach Em how to keep a secret.

Duke lay next to her on the floor, his manners all they should be. She was glad to have his black curly hair to bury her hand in, and she'd told Emily and Joe all about him as they waited for the toasts. He was a safe topic to keep her from talking about wedding plans.

Ralph had settled on the floor near the sofa Jane and Pat occupied. He was watching his goddaughter as she slept on the couch beside her mother.

Elizabeth took an anticipatory sip of champagne, and a shiver ran through her. She'd finally kept a New Year's resolution, but even better, she and Ralph had fooled Pat. He was the only one of them who didn't know, and she couldn't regret a single moment of the unhappiness that had brought her here, to paradise.

They'd told Emily and Joe first and sworn them to secrecy; Jane, next, promised to keep mum; her parents were doing their level best not to look upon Ralph too frequently or too fondly. Her father had teased her like Mr. Bennet teased Lizzy, his remarks quite unlike anything Mr. Woodhouse had said to Emma on a similar occasion.

After the toasts, she'd resolve to be a calm bride come May. If Pat hit his head on the coffee table when he fell off the sofa in surprise, what could she do? She'd try not to laugh.

He lifted his champagne flute and cleared his throat. He always did a great job with the formal toast, she had to give him that.

"I raise my glass to the New Year, to the joys and sufferings that await us. May we embrace whatever the good Lord sends, support one another in friendship, and together offer our resolutions for the greater glory of God."

He clinked glasses with Jane, took a swallow of champagne, then raised his glass again.

"I'd like to propose a special second toast to Gretchen. Today she arrives at her new home in Calcutta. May her Beloved shower her with every blessing."

More clinking and they all drank to the missing blonde.

Pat held the box of See's toward Elizabeth, and she smiled her thanks, taking a chocolate in honor of her former boss. Reassuring to know Gretchen wouldn't miss chocolate if she never had it again—she'd never indulged to begin with.

"I wanted to make sure Liz had first pick from the See's. I think before we make any resolutions, I owe a word to my sister-in-law."

He raised his glass a third time.

"To Lizzy, who after countless years—at least I'm too lazy to count them—has surprised me at last."

He wasn't supposed to know yet. Had Jane slipped?

"Our Lizzy has succeeded in fulfilling her New Year's Resolution, proving that a happiness project is a family affair. I know I appreciated her help with my events, from the concert she missed in January to St. Nicholas Day last month. She showed us it's never too late for happiness, and I congratulate her from the bottom of my heart. Here's to Lizzy. And if one can raise a glass to a dog, here's to Duke as well, who arrived in time to carry her resolution safely into the New Year. Cheers!"

Glasses clinked and she let out the breath she'd been holding. He hadn't guessed.

"And now," Pat said, "I'd like to offer the first resolution of the year. I'll get mine out of the way, so you can all relax and tease me if I don't carry it through. With Lizzy on a winning streak, this might be the year I fail."

He paused to refill his glass. Every year he resolved to be a good husband and father, and Jane never accused him of failing, but this sounded different. Would he finally give her a chance to catch him out? That would frost the chocolate cake of her happiness.

With a thoughtful expression, Pat lifted his glass yet again.

"I, Patrick Joseph Finbar Moore, hereby resolve to be an excellent brother-in-law to the newest professor."

Something was wrong. She passed the champagne flute from her right hand to her left and waited for him to continue.

"And I resolve not to drink too much at Lizzy's wedding, nor to cry excessively, nor to let my children eat the cake before she has a slice." He'd never looked so full of himself. "And I'd like to complete my resolution with a final toast. Here's to Ralph and Lizzy, the future Dr. and Mrs. Collins— it's about time!"

She didn't know the proper response to such a toast, but she did what came naturally. She tipped her glass in dismay and spilled champagne on her dog. Mrs. Benning's champagne was of the finest quality. Duke didn't flinch and as the alcohol soaked into the nape of his neck, she noticed no horrible wet dog smell. Of course she wasn't in much of a state to smell anything. She could only gape at Pat.

Her Knightley, however, knew exactly what to do. He stood and reached across Jane to Pat.

"I'm sorry you won't be the best man," Ralph said as they shook hands, "but I owe that to Joe. As for your resolution, I'll hold you to it."

He ousted Duke and sat on the floor beside Elizabeth.

Very quietly, he whispered in her ear. "You heard Pat, you get the first slice of our wedding cake. That means chocolate."

Everyone was looking at her.

Pat smiled at her, but it wasn't his crocodile smile or his used car salesman smile. His eyes looked different. Almost like—was that respect she saw gleaming out?

"I think I'm up next." She held out her flute. "But I'm afraid my glass is empty."

Pat poured, and the bubbles rose to the top.

"Best wishes, Liz. I'd say your cup is full now."

She sat back and raised her glass.

"Here's to the New Year. I'm grateful for the year that's past, for my family and my friends," she looked around the room, "and especially for my dog."

Ralph nudged her.

"And most of all," she continued with a smile, "I'm grateful for Mr. Right, who's going to resolve never to play my sonata again, always to keep Fra Angelico in a place of honor, and to love and cherish me as long as we both shall live." She nudged him back. "As for me, I resolve—"

"To be the best bride since Emily, to love and cherish your husband, and to live happily ever after, isn't that it?" Ralph said.

"Well, yeah. That about sums it up."

She looked at the man beside her. She looked at Pat, smug on the couch next to Jane, and at Emily on the loveseat next to Joe. She and Jane and Emily, the three girls who'd sat in this room from childhood to the dear present—they all had their Princes Charming now. Not that she thought Pat was charming, but she was ready to forgive him for being other. Her own private New Year's Resolution.

She laughed and Duke barked.

John Holt had been right—it was never too late. She reached for the See's. With any luck, she'd find a dark chocolate waiting for her in the box. Her happiness project might be over, but her happiness was just beginning.

The End